RULE
NUMBER
ONE

RULE NUMBER ONE

A Harrison Pius Mystery

ANDY NOTTENKAMPER

iUniverse, Inc.

New York Lincoln Shanghai

Rule Number One
A Harrison Pius Mystery

iUniverse books may be ordered through booksellers or by contacting:

iUniverse
2021 Pine Lake Road, Suite 100
Lincoln, NE 68512
www.iuniverse.com
1-800-Authors (1-800-288-4677)

ISBN-13: 978-0-595-39386-2 (pbk)
ISBN-13: 978-0-595-83785-4 (ebk)
ISBN-10: 0-595-39386-1 (pbk)
ISBN-10: 0-595-83785-9 (ebk)

Printed in the United States of America

For
Mark, Matt, Drew
and
Margo

A prince should strive to demonstrate in his actions grandeur, courage, sobriety and strength. When settling disputes, he should ensure that his judgment is irrevocable; and he should be so regarded that no one ever dreams of trying to deceive or trick him.

—*Niccolo Machiavelli*
1469–1527
Italy

If a body could just find out the exact proper proportion and quantity that ought to be drunk everyday, and keep to that, I verily vow that he might live forever without dying at all, and that doctors and graveyards would go out of fashion.

—*James Hogg*
1770–1830
Scotland

Prologue

I live my life trying to follow a few simple rules. My rules may not be perfect and they certainly aren't for everyone, but they work for me. There are only five rules, and if I use my head and don't screw up, holding fast to these five rules keeps me out of trouble.

Now, you would think with just five of the silly things it would be easy for me to stay on the straight and narrow. But it's tough for me because I'm weak when in pursuit of life's magical moments, those special times when we have the chance to really enjoy living. Of course, it always helps if we can see the magic and make the best of the moment. I figure we only come to this party one time so we may as well drink the first drink and dance the last dance with a pretty girl.

But back to the point, each rule requires some restraint. For example, Rule Number One:

NEVER GO TO BED WITH SOMEONE WHO HAS MORE TROUBLES THAN YOU.

Sounds easy enough. But I've always been a sucker for a woman in trouble, especially if she has a great body. So Rule Number One is the rule I break most often.

Most of the really fine women I've known have been troubled. The more trouble they have, the more appealing I find them. And, if they have a mountain of trouble they're inevitably great between the sheets. I wonder why that is.

I've got a psychiatrist lady friend who says I'm an enabler. She and I have had three relationships with each other, spread out over twenty years. We saw each other between her first and second marriage, her fourth and fifth, and recently, while she was engaged to her sixth husband. She says an enabler is someone that allows other people to feel better about their fuck-ups. Anyway I've decided it's best to stick with Rule Number One, at least when it comes to her.

I'm really a simple guy and I've got a good heart. I live a quiet life, mostly alone. I'm reasonably intelligent, except when it comes to women. I can be dumb as a fence post when a beautiful woman is involved. On the other hand I'm very smart when it comes to money. Some years I make a lot of money, and some years I don't make any at all. On balance, however, you could say I'm well off. I can hang out in Scotland for six months playing golf, yet the bills still get paid. But I only go to Scotland every two or three years. Most of my regular vacations are spent playing golf in Ireland, which I do a couple of times a year. The rest of the time I'm a business consultant—but not one of those who borrows your watch and then tells you what time it is. I'm the expert you hire when your doughnut shop is making twice as many doughnuts this year as it made last year but sales are down and you want to know why. I conduct a supply chain analysis supported by a time and motion spread sheet, which in turn is tied to an industry margin and growth rate projection that will point out that your new sales clerk has gained sixty-two pounds since you hired him and maybe the two of you should have a chat. I have a nose for smelling out a thief and I get involved in some tricky industrial thefts for which I charge outrageous fees—once I catch the bad guy. I have a good track record and turn down more jobs than I take because I don't like for work to interfere with my golf or my drinking. Also, I'm not happy when my work gets in the way of rescuing a pretty lady in serious trouble. There's something else. I play cards for money in high stakes poker games. That's how I make the really big bucks.

My name is Harrison Pius and you can call me Mr. Pius, Harrison or just Harry. But don't call me the Pope. You don't know me well enough...at least not yet.

1

Junkie Bill laughed.

He wasn't laughing at me and he wasn't laughing at himself. It was more a case of laughing at the situation. Five years ago he came out of the caddy shack at Pacific Heights Country Club to a life he had never even dreamed about. He left the guard house hovel he lived in at the back of an auto parts junkyard and moved to Hillsborough with the widow O'Reilly. She had his teeth fixed, had him shower daily, and dressed him in Polo, Gucci and Armani. Then she put him behind the wheel of a red Carrera and married him. Now she was dead, and he had twenty million dollars.

"You know I never thought I really loved her," he said. "I liked her as much as any woman I've ever known—and now that she's gone I miss her."

We were sitting in the sunroom of the mansion he had lived in for five years, but would soon vacate. "I can't stay in this house. She left it to me, but I'm gonna give it to her boys. Hell, she left them fifty million apiece, which they don't need. They don't want to live here, either. But they're both great young guys who like me as much as I like them, and I love their kids. So I'll give them the house and they can do with it whatever they want. Besides, the guest house has three thousand square feet, I think I'll just move in there for the time being."

I started wondering why I was having coffee with an old guy who I'd always known as a drunk and a bum, who had occasionally caddied for me at my Club. I knew Maggie O'Reilly had seen something in him no one else had seen, and with some work, she had turned him into a respectable citizen. He was still a crusty old dude, but it was hard not to like him.

"Junkie, what do you want?" I asked. "The message you left was confusing. It's good to see you again, but you said you needed my help. What's going on?"

"That's the point," he said. "There's nothin' goin' on. The cops don't give a shit and nobody's doin' a goddam' thing."

For the first time that morning I got a fleeting glimpse of his pain. His eyes gave him away. "Junkie, it was ruled a suicide. A bottle of gin and fifty Valium will usually kill you and it killed her."

"Bullshit!" he exploded. "She didn't drink gin—didn't like the taste. I've had a love affair with gin for fifty years, but she wouldn't touch the stuff. She didn't take Valium, either. I never saw her drink anything but white wine and the only pill she ever took was a vitamin. It's total bullshit—she didn't kill herself, Harry."

It was then I realized why Junkie had called me, and I was starting to get a bad feeling in my gut. "Okay, the cops think it was a suicide, the medical examiner thinks it was a suicide, but you don't. So why tell me?" I asked.

He lifted his chin and his eyes widened. "Cause of what I just told you. She didn't take pills. I think somebody killed her and I want you to find out who and why."

There it was. I had to admit I saw it coming. I picked up my coffee cup and took a long, slow sip. It was cold and so was I. "Junkie, you've got it all wrong. That's not what I do. I'm not a private eye. I've never investigated a murder—hell, I've never even met a murderer. You need a pro, not a guy that pokes his nose into corporate theft."

Junkie put his cup down and scowled at me. "Harry, you're a smart guy—everybody knows you're good at cutting through the crap to get to the real crap. That's what I need. Maggie didn't kill herself and if anyone can figure out what the hell happened I think you can."

He paused, took a deep breath and continued with the part of his speech that was the toughest for him to get out. "Look, Harry, I've got a shitload of money—more than I'll ever need. I don't care how much it costs. I don't care what your fee is—I know you soak your clients. I don't care. Just find out what happened."

He was dangerously close to insulting me. I don't like to talk about money, but he didn't know that. Money and religion are what we go to war over. All the bad shit in the world, since the beginning of time, has been because of religion and money. That's why I don't like to talk about either one. I earn money by discovering the clever ways that corporate wise guys cheat and I've found they all have a common thread that binds them…they love to talk about money and how hard they worked to earn it. It's only after they steal it—by cooking the books or diverting inventory assets—then, they talk about values and their corporate family.

Sitting with Junkie Bill that cold, foggy morning drinking coffee and discussing a fee was not how I wanted to start my day. I knew that Maggie O'Reilly had been rich. I had played golf for years with her first husband, Dermot. He was a wild redheaded Irishman right out of the movies and County Sligo, Ireland. If you ever saw "The Quiet Man" with John Wayne and Maureen O'Hara—Dermot O'Reilly was Victor McLaughlin in a bigger package. He played hard, drank harder and whored around in such a way that just thinking about it made most men tired. And all the while he built a construction business that, when he died in a whorehouse in Chinatown, had a book value of 200 million dollars. After he died Maggie and her two sons took over the business and began to make serious money. Dermot's legacy that Maggie and her sons kept faith with was they never cheated or lied to their customers or business friends. Dermot would have been shocked at how much Maggie knew about his business and how easy it was for her to slip into his chair when he died. She showed all of his old managers the door with nice retirement packages. Then put the two boys in charge of day-to-day operations and she became the toughest bid analyst in the history of Northern California Bridge and Highway construction.

"How do you expect me to find out what happened?" I asked. "As I said before the Medical Examiner ruled suicide, the cops think she killed herself. You're out on a limb by yourself on this."

"They didn't know her the way I did." He shook his head and leaned in closer. "She quit goin' to church years ago. All those years she was raisin' the boys and bein' a good wife she thought the good Lord had abandoned her because Dermot was such a snake. But, the last couple of years she's been sneakin' off to Mass and when I was goin' through her stuff I found a rosary in her purse. She couldn't kill herself—she was still an Irish Catholic girl at heart—and good Irish Catholic girls don't kill themselves."

"Okay, let's say, for the sake of the argument, you're right." I put my coffee cup down and leaned back in the chair. "Who do you think killed her and why?"

Junkie Bill leaned back and without hesitation declared, "I haven't got the slightest idea. She didn't have an enemy in the world."

His response came out so quick I thought I might have misunderstood, but once again, his eyes sent a signal. He meant it. He didn't have a clue. But, I knew he was stuck. He didn't believe Maggie O'Reilly had gone to her great reward willingly. "Junkie, I don't know what to say or where to begin."

He scowled at me and moved his chair closer. "You know about business…start with the business. Look at the books."

"What about her sons?" I asked. "Will they go along with me snooping around?"

"Yeah, they think I'm barkin' up the wrong tree. But, they've got a problem with all this, too."

"What's their problem, other than the death of their mother?"

Junkie Bill smiled for the first time since I had arrived. It wasn't a happy smile, but a smile nonetheless. He looked like a guy that just discovered a four-letter word for disingenuous. "They can't believe that anyone would want to harm a wonderful woman like their mom and they can't imagine anything in her life that would make her want to commit suicide." He sighed, "They're as stuck on this thing as I am."

I closed my eyes and put my head back. I didn't need this. I didn't want this. I was slightly pissed off for even sitting with Junkie talking about his problems. But, I was struggling with who to be pissed off at...him or me. "Junkie, I don't want to have anything to do with this, but you're not letting me off the hook. You think my curiosity will get the best of me and I'll jump into this mess with both feet and you're partially right and that's pissing me off."

At that, Junkie not only smiled he even came up with a slight chuckle. "Harry you're a good man. I knew you'd come through."

"I'm not saying I'll do it."

"Well, what are you saying?" he asked.

"I'm going to think about it." But, a part of me had been thinking about Maggie O'Reilly all along. The little guy that sits on my shoulder and regulates my bullshit meter was suddenly sitting at attention and whispering in my ear. I looked Junkie in the eye and said, "I'll get back to you."

I didn't tell Junkie Bill when I would get back to him, but I called him later that evening and agreed to "look into the problem." He informed me that my operating budget was a million bucks. He laughed when he said it, but I knew he was serious. I thought at the time that Junkie might be one of those types that only come alive with the thrill of spending someone else's money.

2

The man walked along the beach with the Slieve Donard Hotel rising majestically on his left. He was a small man wearing a green windbreaker with a Nike swoosh on the chest. He had faded corduroys, scuffed sneakers and a bright orange skullcap pulled tight around his ears. A sleek, brown Doberman ran in front of him and would quickly run to the water's edge and look back as if asking permission to go further. The man seemed to ignore the dog, but would routinely give a soft whistle and the dog would rapidly retreat from the pounding surf and return to his side.

He walked closer to the water's edge and turned to look back at the fourth floor turrets of the hotel. His eyes seemed to roam the entire front of the structure in an easy surveillance, and then he continued his walk along the beach.

Dundrum Bay on his right was beginning its evening rush to the shore. As the tide poured across the flat sandy waste the wind quickened and the temperature began to drop. The dog sensed the change and moved closer to the man, abandoning its rush to explore the approaching waves. The man passed other walkers. Several recognized him. Women noticed him, but they averted their eyes and quickened their step.

It began to rain. The man slowed his pace. His breath was slow and rhythmic as he turned once again and looked to his left. The brown and green fairways of the Royal County Down Golf Links flowed before him. He crossed the beach and entered the golf course grounds through a narrow break in the gorse. He continued at a slow walk and began to look from side to side. He was out of the wind and he felt suddenly warm. He began to perspire. The dog remained at his side, but its ears were alert.

It had first rained at noon and now five hours later it was still wet along the path through the gorse as the rain began again. At that moment a second man stepped from the shadows into the path, blocking the way.

"You're early," the second man growled. "The others aren't here."

"I'm early for a reason. I don't want to see the others."

"They won't like it," he declared and continued to block the way.

The man with the dog abruptly turned and looked back at the other man. "You can walk along the beach with me, or not. It's up to you. If you choose not to speak with me alone, that's okay…for now. But, remember I'm the guy with the money."

Referring to himself as "the guy" gave him away. He wasn't part of Ireland anymore—if he was, he would have called himself a bloke. The second man followed at a distance.

Impatient, the man with the dog was growing tired of the game. "Tell the others that we're ready, but they have to do their part." He took a quick look around as if expecting someone to be listening. In fact, they were alone with the waves, the wind and the dog. "We can't continue until we know her itinerary. I won't make a move until we're certain she's coming to San Francisco. We have to have more information," he demanded.

The other man remained silent.

"You don't get it," the man knelt in the sand and began to rub his dog behind the ears. "You and the others are stupid. You think this is going to be another roadside bombing with a couple of Her Majesty's Finest getting their asses blown off…and nobody gives a shit about it anyway." He was challenging the other man to prove him wrong—or at least provide some new information. The other man knelt beside the dog and got a menacing growl in return.

"My dog doesn't like you and I don't like you either, but I'm stuck with you and the others," he continued. "This needs to be done, but it has to be done right. I'm not sure you and the rest of your buddies can pull it off."

"Wait just a minute," the other man growled.

"No, you wait a minute" the man with the dog stood and shouted. "We've come too far for a bunch of misfits to fuck up the plan. We've got everything and everybody in place, but we need good information." His cold eyes remained steady. "Hell, at this point we'll settle for any information we can get. You and your team haven't given us jack—shit and we're out on a limb as it is. The woman had to be taken care of—we had no choice. We have to be more careful than ever and now there are others involved and that increases the risk." His voice quickened as he turned and gazed at the incoming tide. "You and your bunch have no risk. All you've got to do is come up with accurate information about if she's coming, and when, and then you're out of it."

"We're doing the best that we can," the other man explained. "If you'll just wait a few more minutes the others will be here and you can hear it from them."

"I'm not waiting any longer. Anyway, I don't want to be seen with you." He whistled to his dog and began to walk away.

"How will we reach you?" the other man shouted.

"You won't. You'll hear from me again, and next time I won't be so nice."

3

I'm not sure why I thought I could help Junkie with his problem, but I did. Too often I get caught up in building a castle out of a rock pile and this was one of those times, but I had slept on it and the thought of poking around the death of Maggie O'Reilly had me intrigued. I never thought of myself as a private eye, but who knows, maybe I could be the new Phillip Marlowe. I knew one thing for sure, though. If I was going to be a dick for hire, I wasn't going to take up smoking or wear a trench coat.

After I left Junkie's mansion I drove to the club for lunch with the idea that I might hook up with a money game later in the afternoon with the owners. The owners gathered after lunch for the high stakes golf matches for which Pacific Heights Golf Club is famous. They really aren't the owners of the club; they're just called that because they act like they own the joint. Although I'm a regular member of the group, I'm never referred to as "one of the owners" by the other more sedate members. I'm considered too nice a guy to be lumped in with the group that gambles too much, drinks too much and gives the club an undeserved reputation for boorish behavior.

Pacific Heights is an old San Francisco golf club—old in that it's been at its current location for about 80 years. Before the turn of the century it was a downtown athletic club where businessmen could work out, shoot pool, play cards and drink. In the early 1920's a group of members who wanted a place to play golf—to go along with their card playing and drinking—bought three hundred and fifty acres of worthless land south of the city, and formed the Pacific Heights Golf Club. The land wasn't very close to the Pacific and the highest spot in the three hundred and fifty acres was, maybe, fifty feet above sea level, but the founding members thought the name Pacific Heights had a nice ring to it.

They almost went broke twice. First, during construction when it was discovered that three hundred of the acres were practically solid rock, and second, during the late 1930's, when most of the members either went broke, shot themselves or jumped out of their stockbroker's window. Construction of the golf course took three years and the design of the clubhouse was so elaborate that, upon completion, it was the most expensive single story structure in the San Francisco Bay area.

Technically the location of the club is South San Francisco, but most of the members don't like the reference to anything that connects the club to "South City" or "that Club near the airport." Today, the worthless three hundred and fifty acres of the past is worth at least three hundred million dollars because of its proximity to San Francisco International Airport. And after waiting five or six years to get into the club, if you're lucky enough to make it through the screening process, the initiation fee will set you back a cool three hundred thousand. Groucho Marx once said he would never belong to a club that would be dumb enough to have him as a member—we have a lot of Grouchos in the club. The nearby airport can be a distraction, especially if you have a four-foot putt on the 18th hole, with five hundred dollars riding on the outcome, and a 747 jumbo jet comes roaring over you at a thousand feet on its way to London. If the putt goes in the hole you don't hear the noise, but if you miss the putt it's not your fault and "we need some kind of noise abatement program in this goddam' city." Even with the distraction of the airport, Pacific Heights golf course is considered by the experts to be one of the top fifty in the country.

It was exactly 12:00 noon when I turned my car over to the attendant at the club and made my way to the men's grill. As I walked past the men's locker room I remembered my watch was still in my locker.

I had forgotten it the day before. There was a sticky note stuck to my locker with a message. "I want your ass today for as much money as your choke point can stand. I'm at the window in the corner of the grill and I'm going to sign your name to my lunch tag if you don't show up." There was no signature on the note, but it didn't need one.

Gerry Murphy was one of my golfing cronies. I wouldn't call him a friend exactly—more a guy that I played golf with, drank with and occasionally we had dinner together. But, I had never been to his home or met his family. I knew he was big-time rich, kept his wife at home, and that he liked to fool around with young girls—really young girls—as in teenage girls. I considered him one of the dark people.

I found him in the far corner of the men's grill with his back to the window. "Ah, it's the Pope," he said. I was friendly enough with Gerry to let him get away with calling me "the Pope."

"So you think you're gonna' get in my pocket today," I replied.

"We've got Sweeper and Jack, too." Gerry went on, "Jack and me are taking you and Sweeper straight up for fun tickets four ways."

That was Gerry's way of saying he and Dr. Jack Swift were going to play me and Jim Broome, also known as "Sweeper," in a golf match for four hundred dollars. In Gerry's world hundred dollar bills were known as "fun tickets" and he threw them around like they were quarters.

I looked surprised. In fact I was shocked. On the best day Gerry and Jack ever had, they couldn't beat the Sweeper and me. Something was going on and he was feeling he had an edge. He threw money around as if it meant nothing, but Gerry hated to lose on the golf course.

He saw my surprise and began to laugh. "Sweeper's playing so bad he can't break 80. You haven't played with our group for a couple of weeks or you'd know he's gone in the tank. You guys took us for four hundred last month and we're going to get it all back today."

With that said we made our way to the buffet. I loaded up on salad and fruit while Gerry dove into the roast beef and mashed potatoes—he liked his groceries piled high. Seated at our table again, I reminded him that I could fix Sweeper's swing problems in five minutes on the practice range and it would be a good idea for him to make sure he had four hundred dollars in his pocket because he was going to lose.

"Gerry, it's a done deal—you're going to lose," I said.

He paused and swallowed about a half pound of mashed potatoes. "Harrison, my boy, I've probably got four thousand in my pocket," he replied. "But, just beating the best player in the club once in a while is good enough for me."

"I'm not the best player in the club, anymore," I stated matter-of-factly. "All of the new young guys that have joined the last couple of years are kicking my ass."

"Ah Po-pee, you're still the best money player around," he smiled. "But, not today—today you're mine in a basket."

Suddenly he changed the subject and went where he knew I didn't want to go; he had information about me that no one else knew and he loved to needle me. "You still fuckin' that black chick? You know her boyfriend is going to have one of his boys shoot your lily white ass one of these days. If you want to live that dangerous I've got a little cheerleader at State I'll be glad to share with you."

"Gerry, you know about Vanessa because of my dumb bad luck. No one has ever seen the two of us together except you and that was an accident on my part." I was pissed and he knew he had pushed my hot button. He went on.

"Ah, come on Pope don't be so thin-skinned. I'm not going to give up your big secret. But I've got to tell you, man, dipping the pink panatela in that cop's main squeeze is the kind of trouble you don't need."

"Gerry, if dipping the sausage where it doesn't belong was life threatening you'd have been dead thirty years ago," I said.

"Yeah, but her boyfriend is a mean bastard and he's got hundreds of cops reporting to him. They'll kick your ass just to stay in shape."

"I don't think so," I said.

"You don't think so. You don't think so!" he exclaimed. "Shit, Pope, this guy is bad news and you know it. He could put you in the Bay and never miss a beat." He frowned, chewed on some roast beef and uttered what he considered a profound, gospel truth. "No matter how great you think the pussy is, there's always some out there that's better. And if she tells you that you're the greatest fuck she's ever had—guess what—she's lying. If her hot-shot boyfriend finds out about you—well, your ass is grass."

I wasn't going to admit it, but Gerry was probably right. Vanessa and I had no future and no plans past tomorrow night—for her it was just sex. "Gerry, if all this chatter about my sex life is meant to throw me off my game this afternoon—it isn't working." I had finished my lunch and was ready to go. "Let's put the balls in the air and play some golf."

We were on the first tee when Gerry looked at his partner Jack Swift and gave his typical pre-round pronouncement. "Let us bless this moment, have faith in ourselves and expect the very best."

With that he hit his opening tee shot deep into the woods to the right of the first fairway and began, what was for he and Jack, a long and expensive afternoon. Four and a half hours later, in the Men's Grill over drinks, he and Jack each peeled off eight fun tickets and handed them over to Sweeper and me. It totaled sixteen hundred dollars—eight hundred each—because Gerry insisted on throwing good money after bad and doubled the bet on the last hole—which they lost. Before we left the grill Gerry and Jack were going to do their best to drink up part of our winnings.

Gerry took a long, slow drag off a foul smelling cigar. "The only good thing about losing to you, Po-pee, is you don't complain when I drink fifteen-dollar-a-shot single malt on your tab."

"Anything for you, Gerry."

"Anything?"

"Name it."

"Okay. You can take me to dinner at Bertolucci's." He finished his fifth single malt scotch with a flourish. I signed the tab and we left for our favorite Italian restaurant.

4

The next morning my first cup of coffee to start off the day had never tasted better. Too many Lagavulen single malts and way too much Ferrari Carrano merlot had caused me to awaken with a severe case of the vapors. Plus, the state of my body and my general disposition gave Juanita her usual opportunity to criticize me, harass me, berate me and worst of all, laugh at me. Juanita is my next-door neighbor, my housekeeper, my cook and sometimes my conscience. But, most important, she is my best friend and the best woman I have ever known.

She had been banging around the house since 7:00 a.m. and finally, in desperation, had come up the stairs with a cup of coffee about 8:30, demanding that I get up and come down for breakfast. I came downstairs quickly because I could smell the eggs and chorizo cooking and when Juanita cooks breakfast, lunch or dinner the world should come to attention. In addition, it's not a good idea to argue with a sixty-five year old Mexican woman that successfully raised three sons and put up with an alcoholic husband for over forty years—and, at two hundred pounds, she can quickly get your attention.

I won't try to record her speech patterns on paper because you wouldn't understand and neither would I, so I'll try to keep it simple and write the word "you" instead of "chew."

She started in on me. "What time did you get home last night? Where did you eat dinner? Don't tell me you had dinner with her…I don't want to hear it. I had enchiladas, rice and beans for you and you didn't show up. Why didn't you call?" She paused and went on. "Did you play golf? Did you win any money? There's no grocery money in the bread box and I spent forty-five dollars on Girl Scout cookies—don't eat them all at once—there's fifteen boxes." She saw the look on my face. "I know, I know, I'm a sucker for little girls. I spent practically my whole life with four men in my house, not counting you, you'd think God would have given me one little girl, someone that would treat me good."

I held out my hand. "Stop!" I exclaimed. "Enough—besides I took you to Mexico last year for a month. Doesn't that count for something?"

"I worry when I think you're coming home for dinner and then you don't show up." She took a very deep breath. "Yeah, you took me to Mexico and you played golf 12 times while we were there. If it weren't for swimming pools, room service and margaritas I wouldn't have had anything to do. Besides, it turned out I don't like Mexico—it's too hot and there's too many Mexicans. If I want Mexicans I can ride the J car to the Mission district for 65 cents. Next time we're going to Hawaii."

"If you'll stop bitching at me," I said, "I'll take you to Hawaii for Christmas."

Juanita spooned more eggs and chorizo on my plate and smiled. "I think I'll like Hawaii, but I'll have to learn how to drink Penny Coolado's."

"I don't think you'll have any trouble," I said

"And don't complain about me bitching at you," she smiled knowingly. "You're the one who told me, a long time ago, that there's only two kinds of women in the world—women that bitch and women that don't."

"And we all know which camp you fall into," I said.

"It's my nature. Latino women have to bitch otherwise nothin' ever gets done." She put a hand on her hip and assumed the all-knowing pose that I loved. "I've got a paid-for house, in one of the best neighborhoods in the City, because I bitched Carlos to work everyday of his tequila drinkin' life. The only thing I couldn't bitch him out of was his tequila, and it killed him."

"I'm going up on the roof and finish my coffee."

"Are you gonna' be here for dinner?" Juanita asked. "I'm going to fix chicken and rice and leave it in the oven. The fruit salad will be in the fridge. But, I don't want to go to the trouble if you're not gonna' be here."

"Make enough for two," I replied, as I made my way to the stairs leading to the roof of my house.

Before I could get to the stairs the rubber spatula bounced off the banister, just missing me, and she screeched, "I hate to cook for that woman and you know it. I was going to stay and have dinner with you tonight, but not now. No, no, I'll fix the food, but I'm not eatin' with her. I'll go to the movies instead."

When I got to the third floor landing, which led to the roof, I could still hear her mumbling and swearing to herself.

Another person, I thought, who doesn't like my choice of girl-friend.

My house was built, or you could say re-built after the earthquake. In the last one hundred years there have been over five thousand measured earthquakes in San Francisco, but there's only been one that people talk about as THE earthquake and that's the one in 1906. Not even the quake that knocked out the World Series in 1989 gets talked about or written about the way the one that happened in 1906 does. Like most of the houses in my neighborhood, mine didn't burn down. It mostly fell down. But, it didn't burn thanks to a fire hydrant two blocks down on Church Street that, in the days after the catastrophe, was the only working fire hydrant in the entire city. Every year, on the anniversary of the quake, the San Francisco Fire Department gives the old hydrant a fresh coat of gold paint to commemorate the day.

The previous owner of my house rebuilt it in 1907 and it stayed pretty much the same until I bought it twenty-five years ago. I gutted it and then furnished it with hardwood floors, marble bathrooms and a kitchen even Wolfgang Puck would like.

I'm not any good in the kitchen, but Juanita likes it. I bought it before the real estate prices in the City got completely out of hand the way they are now, but I got carried away with the remodel and spent a small fortune. Of course I didn't care; I was twenty-three years old and I was spending "found money." It wasn't money I felt like I had earned. Before the dealers and management at the casinos in Reno and Las Vegas figured out what this baby faced kid was doing at the blackjack tables I clipped them for about eight hundred and fifty large—as in thousand. What I did was perfectly legal, and I didn't adhere to the identity of a casino gambler, which is "born loser." I tried to keep my winnings under ten thousand at each casino I visited, so I was getting paid off in cash. I was trying not to arouse suspicion and it worked until I lost my cool at the old Desert Inn in Vegas. I was jumping in and out of cabs and going from casino to casino all over the town. Every time I got ten thousand ahead I put the cash in a Fed-Ex box and sent it off to my brother in Salinas.

I was flying high and getting ready to quit anyway when I encountered a smart ass dealer at the Desert Inn and my ego got the best of me. I was about five thousand up and this guy makes a crack about the way I was dressed. He didn't like the color of my tee shirt—at least I wasn't wearing a baseball cap backward. Then he called me "Scooter." It's not a good idea to call me "the Pope," but to call me Scooter and embarrass me in front of some high-class Vegas types wearing spiffy polyester sport coats was more than I could handle. Before the dealer could continue to put the wet-nosed kid in his place, I quickly rang his register up to about forty large. It was then that a guy about eight feet tall with a twenty-eight-inch neck, in a tuxedo no less, asked if he could have a word with me in the floor manager's office. In a very loud voice I refused to go anywhere with him, so he summoned his three bigger brothers and they put me on the sidewalk in front of the casino and gave me a piece of advice that I accepted graciously.

"Leave Nevada and don't ever come back!"

I left and I've never gone back. Juanita has tried to get me to take her to Reno or Las Vegas for years and I always refuse. I tell her, "I don't like the odds."

Thanks to my old friends in Nevada I own—as in paid for—a beautiful old house in the City which has a small deck under the eaves of the third story gable where I can sit and think or just watch all the crazy commuters as they struggle to get on the Bay Bridge to go where Gertrude Stein once said, "there's no 'there' there."

My coffee cup felt warm in my hand as I sat and watched the fog move in and out like smoke in the wind through streets that stretched below me all the way to the Mission District. My thoughts went back to the night before and dinner with Gerry Murphy.

The waiter at Bertolucci's had finished tossing our Caesar salad and put the ice-cold plates in front of us.

"So, you said you saw Junkie Bill today. What's that lucky old bastard doing, besides counting his money? It's a good thing Maggie's kids like him or he'd be back living in the junkyard." While we were on the golf course I had mentioned to Gerry that I spent the morning with Junkie.

"Well, it was damned interesting and we talked about something that's hard to believe. Keep this under your hat, but Junkie doesn't think Maggie killed herself."

Gerry practically came out of his chair. "You have got to be fuckin' kidding me. Has he lost his goddam mind? I knew that crazy bastard was nuts."

"Hang on. First of all, he's dead serious and second, he makes a damn good point…"

"Point," Gerry interrupted. "The only point he's got is on top of his head."

I held out my hand to finish. "Gerry calm down. This has nothing to do with you, so don't get excited, but Junkie does have a very good argument against the notion of suicide."

"He's a fool," he said dismissively. "If she didn't kill herself, what the hell does he think happened?"

"This is the part that's tough to deal with," I said, between bites of salad. "He says somebody killed her."

"I don't believe it."

I paused and suddenly felt foolish. "He says it's a Catholic thing. A good Irish Catholic woman wouldn't kill herself."

"Maggie was a good woman and she was definitely Irish. I don't know about the Catholic part."

"How well did you know her? I asked.

Gerry looked at me slowly and said, "I hardly knew her. But, I knew Dermot from the old days when he was getting started in his business. He and I played golf together in the days when he was a good player and we did some serious drinking from time to time. Plus, we chased some 'poon' together and even shared a few of them." Gerry continued matter-of-factly, "I can tell you one thing for sure—Maggie O'Reilly was a patient, forgiving woman."

"Why do you say that?"

"She knew all about Dermot and his running around and she looked the other way."

"She sounds like a strong-willed woman or else she was very dumb," I said.

"Oh, I know for sure she was strong-willed and I think, in her own way, she loved Dermot. But, she knew what he was like and early in the marriage probably decided to look the other way," he replied.

"Probably for the sake of their kids," I said.

"No, I think it was more than that," Gerry said. "Like I told you, I didn't know her all that well, but listening to Dermot talk about her I got the impression she knew from the beginning she was hooked up with a wild Irishman and was prepared for a wild ride. And from some other things he told me about her she sure as hell wasn't dumb."

I nodded in agreement. "On the surface it would appear she was very smart. I hear that after he died she came out of the kitchen—so to speak—and took over the business with her two boys and made millions."

Gerry was making quick work of his Dover sole but talked between bites. "You got that right! She took a very successful construction business and turned it into a giant cash cow. She had a way of taking the worst jobs, jobs nobody wanted at a fixed price, and turning them into winners. Remember the bridge that collapsed south of Big Sur?" he asked.

I nodded in agreement again. "You mean the rain…"

Gerry interrupted, "Yeah, yeah that one. She negotiated an early finish bonus on the deal and the state ended up paying her an extra 10 million because the job finished two months ahead of schedule." This remark caused Gerry to laugh so hard he had to stop and take a big gulp of merlot. "Those assholes with the State Highway Commission shit a brick over that one. But, I hear Maggie could make chicken salad out of chicken shit every time she and the boys took on a tough job. Yeah, she was dumb like a fox."

"All right," I said. "She puts up with Dermot for twenty-five years, he dies and leaves her a wealthy woman. Not satisfied with laying on a beach somewhere, counting coupons, she takes over the business and makes bigger bucks." I continued. "She takes Junkie on as a reclamation project and, maybe, for the first time in her life she's got a man she can control. Plus, she's got two great sons, grandkids and, if you can believe Junkie, she was in perfect health for a woman sixty years old. Why kill herself?"

"Why does anyone do the big casino?" he asked. "She had something going on. You know how women are…I've known hundreds of women. Old ones, young ones, fat and skinny, smart and dumb, gorgeous and butt ugly and one thing I know for sure: I never *really* knew any of them. The way a woman thinks is beyond me. Just when you think you've got it all figured out they'll do something that'll turn you inside out and you wonder what the hell that was all about."

I started to speak, but Gerry pointed his fork at me and continued. "I know, I know. I've got no right to talk about anybody."

"Oh really," I said sarcastically.

He pointed his fork at me again. The effects of six or seven single malt scotches and half a bottle of merlot were starting to kick in. "You don't have to remind me about what a shithead I am, but I'm honest about it. I admit it. I was never the guy that you would want to take home and introduce to mom. I've been down so many dark alleys I quit looking back years ago." His eyes fixed on mine and he was smiling.

"You're just a lovable old scoundrel with honesty in your heart," I said. "It's just too bad your dick is such a prick. But, it's late and we've both had an elegant sufficiency of food and drink, so let's get out of here."

I paid the check, we said good night to Gina Bertolucci, retrieved our cars and I drove ever so cautiously home.

5

"The only thing we can't figure out is the five hundred thousand dollar transfer." Peter O'Reilly shifted in his chair and continued. "The money is still in the account she set up, but we don't know why she set the account up in the first place."

Before I left my house that morning I called O'Reilly Construction and scheduled an appointment with Peter O'Reilly, Maggie's oldest son. Woody Allen says if you want to be a success, "tell the truth and be on time." My appointment was for one o'clock—I didn't get there until one-fifteen. Sean, his younger brother, was in Wyoming checking on a repair job they were doing on twenty-five miles of Highway 40.

Peter was in his early forties and looked younger. In a gray polo shirt and jeans it seemed he'd be more at home in a college setting than heading up a major construction conglomerate. His dark hair, slim build and piercing blue eyes contributed to his youthful appearance, but in conversation he was all business and a very serious individual. I knew he had a wife, a daughter and was considered a stand-up guy.

He continued. "My mother didn't have secrets—she was an open book. What you saw was what you got. Bill doesn't know anything about the transfer of money either."

I noticed that he called his mother's husband Bill and not Junkie. "Go on," I said.

"We didn't discover the money transfer until after she died and even then we didn't think it all that unusual."

"Had she ever transferred that much money before?" I asked.

"Never, but it didn't seem strange because the money had been in the account for a couple of months and never been touched. She had it in an interest bearing account, so it had earned a few hundred bucks, but that was all there was to it."

"What about the bank? What did they make of it?" Before he could answer I had a different thought. "Am I missing something here? Was this a company account or her personal account?"

"Oh, I should have been clearer," Peter said. "It was her personal account. She couldn't move money around like that using company funds—none of us can. After Dad died she set it up so that none of the family could make any financial decisions without the approval of each member, plus our CFO Stuart Zelinka has to sign off on it as well. She called it the 'Bluebell' policy."

I was confused and must have looked it. "The 'Bluebell' what?"

"About twenty years ago Dad decided to get in the horse racing business. He didn't bet on the ponies, but he figured he could make a fast buck if he bought and sold racehorses. Of course, he didn't know anything about horses and with the help of a shady character named Cotton Tackitt he plunged headfirst into the world of buying and selling breeder stock." Peter paused and leaned forward in his chair. "When Dad finally woke up and smelled the coffee he was upside down about six hundred and fifty thousand dollars of company money and his new buddy, Cotton Tackitt, had skipped town."

"Okay, but why 'Bluebell'?"

"Dad set up a dummy account in the company called Bluebell Development, named after the first horse he bought. The whole thing was a disaster and we laugh about it now, but it wasn't funny then. Mom didn't know anything about it at the time, because Dad didn't involve her in the business, but after he died we found all the records and realized how close he came to sinking the company. But, we discovered a lot of things that he did that were bad for business and some things that hurt Mom deeply."

"Hurt her in what way?"

"Well, for one thing, there are at least twenty women, that we know of, who received their college education courtesy of Dad's largesse."

"You're kidding," I said.

"No I'm not kidding," he said, with what I detected as a slight case of mischievous envy. "Good ole Dad set up another company account for deserving college students, which on the surface, was a nice gesture on his part. There was just one catch…"

"Let me guess," I interrupted. "All the money went to young, good looking girls who were more than willing to make themselves available to service their sugar daddy."

"Mr. Pius you're very astute," he said and the mischievous smile appeared again. "Hell, I can even give you most of the names of the young ladies he helped—some of them have turned out quite well here in the area. But, I don't think a list of my father's young muffins will help you find out what really happened with my mother."

"I'm not sure if I'm astute enough to figure out what happened with your mother, anyway." I waited for a reaction, got none and continued. "I'm not sure how you and your brother feel about me snooping around the details of your mother's death."

Peter O'Reilly said nothing for a moment, so I turned and looked out the window. His office was in a portable building at the rear of a four or five acre construction yard in South City. There were three small buildings clustered together each with a nameplate that said Peter, Sean and Margaret on their respective front doors—simple surroundings, for such a thriving construction company.

Finally he said, "I phoned my brother this morning, after you called me, and we're both struggling with all of this."

"I'm sure you have conflicting emotions," I added.

"Not what you might think. First of all, we think very highly of the man you refer to as Junkie Bill. We value his opinion which probably surprises you," he said. "I see by the look on your face that you're shocked to hear me say that."

"Yeah, I must admit, I'm surprised that you feel that way."

"Oh, make no mistake, we didn't feel that way in the beginning. When she brought him home, like a stray, mangy dog, I thought she had lost her mind. But, all that changed."

"What changed your mind?"

"We discovered what she saw in him and we liked what we found out about him," Peter smiled fondly as he said it.

I looked at him and asked, "So what's the story with the guy you call Bill and the guy we all know as Junkie?"

"Well, as I said, first of all we think highly of him because he was so kind to mom, and second we found out very quickly he didn't want anything in return except to hang out with her."

"What do you mean 'hang out'?"

He shook his head. "Not hang out the way teenagers hang out. That's not what I mean," he explained. "He cooked her breakfast in the morning—she never had a man cook a meal for her in her life—and he talked to her while she ate. He asked her what she thought about the world. He was interested in her world and her life. Dad never asked her opinion about anything the entire time the two of them were married. She and Bill went to the movies together and went on picnics and he made her laugh. Mom loved to play golf, but Dad would never play with her; she and Bill played golf together all the time—they went to Ireland several times and traveled around playing all the famous old courses. And, then we discovered something about Bill that she had known from the very beginning."

I leaned forward in my chair, my curiosity aroused. "What was that?"

Peter smiled, obviously enjoying the moment and said, "The guy you know as Junkie Bill, the man who carried golf bags around for a living and lived in a shack at the back of a junkyard, is the most intelligent man I've ever known. He's probably a genius."

I sat straight up and my eyes widened in disbelief. "You must be kidding…and why in the world would you believe something like that?"

"He's one of the smartest guys I've ever known," he said. "I'll tell you one quick story to illustrate my point. My oldest daughter was about seventeen and she was in the honors program at Sacred Heart High School—she's going to Cal-Berkeley now. Well, one night about four years ago Mom and Bill are over for dinner at our house—this is after she's cleaned him up and got his teeth fixed—and my daughter Kate is stomping around the house in an absolute fit because she's stumped over her Physics assignment. Physics is way beyond my wife and I and Kate is driving us nuts. Bill, who we think is a nice old guy, but is a few bricks short of a load, says to Kate, 'maybe I can give you a hand'."

"Don't tell me he—"

"You got it," Peter answered. "Good old Junkie Bill helped her weave her way through her Physics assignment that night. From that point on he became her mentor and she aced the course. A few weeks later she asked Bill, again at dinner, if he had ever read Hamlet. Her advanced literature course had decided to spend the balance of the semester studying Hamlet and she wanted to get an A."

"Don't tell me Junkie Bill is an authority on Shakespeare," I said.

"Mr. Pius, Bill had the entire family enthralled for over an hour as he gave us his opinion on Shakespeare's most famous play."

"His opinion?" I asked.

"Yeah, Bill put forth the notion that the play, and the tragedies that followed, were the result of the death of Shakespeare's young son. The son's name, interestingly enough, was Hamnet. Then Bill went off on the fact that support for his opinion could be found in the novel *Ulysses* by James Joyce and with that he got way over everybody's head, but my daughter Kate loved it. And Mom just beamed with pride."

Then Peter O'Reilly admonished me, "Mr. Pius, there's a lot of stuff you don't know about the guy you call Junkie Bill."

I started to ask Peter to tell me more of what I didn't know when he glanced at his watch, pushed back his chair and sent a signal that my time was up. "I don't mean to be rude, but I've got a two-thirty with a prospective client and I've got to go." He paused and saw the questioning look on my face. "When my brother gets back, we'll get together and talk some more. I can't believe anyone would harm my mother, but I just can't believe she would take her own life, either."

"Please call me when your brother gets back," I said. "I've got a lot more questions."

As I squeezed into the Boxster I realized I was hungry. I went west on Grand Avenue and picked up the Bayshore toward The City while thinking of a sardine sandwich at Crazy Mary's washed down by a bottle of Anchor Steam. San Francisco is known for many fine things: sourdough bread, cable cars, the Golden Gate Bridge—but its finest creation might just be Anchor Steam beer.

After a sandwich of lettuce, tomato, mustard and Norway sardines on sourdough bread and two bottles of Anchor Steam I was certain of one thing for sure. I needed to talk with Junkie again, and soon.

6

From Crazy Mary's I headed up Army Street toward home thinking how pleasant it would be if Juanita had prepared a nice dinner to be heated later. But, most important, it would be great if she had fixed everything and gone home and wasn't around to bitch at me about my relationship with Vanessa.

Her real name is Ethel Mae...Ethel Mae Johnson. Sometime around her first year of law school Vanessa decided that Ethel Mae wouldn't look good on a business card or a brass nameplate on a full partner's door, so she changed her name to Vanessa Burke Johnson. After only three years as an associate in San Francisco's most prestigious law firm, she hasn't made partner yet, but she's getting close. The combination of brains, stunning good looks, and a twelve-hour-a-day work habit has propelled her career dramatically. She is aloof, ruthless and unwavering in her devotion to what she wants to accomplish; to be the first female African-American governor of the state by the time she's forty. I wouldn't bet against it. She's only got two problems. First is her boyfriend William Crawford Dean—Willie to his friends. Second is her biggest problem, and that would be me.

Willie is a problem because he has political ambitions of his own and is just as ruthless. Beyond his current role as the first black Chief of Detectives of the SFPD, he aspires to be the City's second black mayor named Willie. The first Mayor Willie had style, class and a genuine regard for all people; plus, he was charming. Vanessa's Willie has none of these characteristics and he is a stone cold racist at heart. I'm a problem because I have to be her best-kept secret. Vanessa and I have never been out to dinner, seen a movie or gone for a walk.

We sat on a bench one night and watched the sun go down and *of all the benches, in all the towns, in all the world,* Gerry Murphy walked by ours. Other than that slip-up no one has ever seen us together. Vanessa swears she has never spoken to anyone about our affair. The only person aware of our romance in my world is Juanita, and while Juanita doesn't approve, she would never betray a confidence of mine. Our relationship exists only within the walls of my house, which suits me perfectly. Gerry is correct. If William Crawford Dean ever found out about me I could kiss my ass good-bye.

It was after ten p.m. Juanita's dinner was superb and the sex with Ethel Mae even better. I was kissing her toes and she was kissing mine. Her head was nestled in the pillows, her long slender legs were parted and I was enjoying the view.

"You're the only man that's ever kissed my feet."

"Your choice or theirs?"

"Mine."

"For a girl who likes oral sex as much as you, what's so special about your feet?" I asked.

"My feet are special to me because they've always been ignored by the men in my life so, I keep them to myself. You can't be involved with a man and keep your tits, your pussy or your ass to yourself. I keep my feet for myself. They're my last holdout…until you." Vanessa sighed, "Harrison, what you don't know about women would fill a book."

"You're right, what I don't know about *you* would fill a very big book," I replied. "But, I think I've got part of you figured out—I just don't know the real you. I've never been able to able to get past the surface."

"Oh, I think you've done a pretty good job of gettin' inside of little ol' Ethel Mae."

I laughed, "That's the only part I have figured out." I sat up and kissed her stomach. "I know you're in this for the sex, but where do we go from here?"

"Why do we have to go anywhere? Why not just let it happen and enjoy ourselves." She pushed my head lower and began to wiggle her hips playfully.

"Come on, I'm serious," I replied. I sat up cross-legged and took her hand in mine. "Look, this is great. You're number two on my scorecard of great sex partners and no one can touch us when we're in my house—it's snug and cozy and neither one of us has to pretend or fake anything we don't feel. But…"

She interrupted, "Harrison, I've spent a lifetime faking it. On the rare occasions when I don't enjoy it with you—I still enjoy it. And if you've got me figured out you know what I mean when I say that."

"I know, I know, but you've got Willie—"

"Don't go there," she commanded. "Willie is a completely different animal and I mean animal. He thinks his cock is a shrine to be worshipped and it's never dawned on him that it's not his precious dick I'm interested in. He's important to me for the long haul and if I have to let him give me a fast fuck once or twice a week it's no big deal. He's got all the right moves, but he's like Chinese food. One hour later and you're always hungry again."

"If Willie knew you thought he was Chinese food I don't think he would be amused," I said.

"Willie is like most men and a lot of women. He thinks that because I give him a wild ride now and then I must like him. Think of all the women you've known who think just because some guy wants to fuck them then the guy must like them." Vanessa sat up and brushed her other hand across my chest. "Honey, you're sweet, but no wonder you got your heart handed to you on a platter."

"You don't know what you're talking about." I suddenly felt cold and for the first time in our relationship I wanted her to leave my house. She knew too much, but she didn't know anything about what happened three years ago because I had never told her anything. "You don't know anything about my past."

"You're right. I don't even know the name of your last girlfriend. You might have a steady girlfriend, even now, that I don't know about. I seriously doubt it, but in a lot of ways I wish you did." She paused and her eyes seemed to look through me causing me to blink and try to cover my naked body. "Harrison, you're such a little boy. I've offended you and now you want me to leave, but I'm not going to go—not just yet. I want you inside me again and I don't want you to move…just lie with me."

I started to protest, "Vanessa, I…"

"Shush, don't say anything. I want you to fall asleep inside me." She turned on her side and put her sweet, lovely ass in just the right position. "Someday I want the Pope to tell me about the girl that broke his heart."

I awakened about an hour later and she was gone.

7

"Junkie, I need to talk to you." There was a long pause on the end of the line. "Yes, this morning—I can be there in an hour. See you then." I hung up the phone and as I took my hand away it rang, startling me. Caller ID gave her away and I answered quickly.

"Good morning Ethel Mae."

"That was quick, were you sitting on the phone?"

"You know me…just like a rabbit."

"Yeah, and I love the way you hop Mr. Rabbit…especially on and off."

"Why are you intruding on my morning?"

"Who *is* number one on your sex score card?"

"I haven't met her, yet."

"Oh, I think you've met her and now you're in denial."

"Denial?"

"Yeah, you can't admit that I'm the best thing that ever happened to you."

"You had your way with me last night and now you're teasing me."

"I had a lovely time."

"So did I."

"Tell Juanita that next time she should put a touch more paprika on the chicken."

"Not a chance." I smiled and hung up the phone.

On my way to meet with Junkie I couldn't help but think I was in over my head. I couldn't see what my next step should be. I had a lot of questions for everybody—Junkie, Peter, Sean and the company accountant Stuart Zelinka. I wanted to get together with Gerry Murphy and try to get a handle on the secret life of Dermot O'Reilly, as well. But, my questions were the result of my curiosity not my inductive or deductive detecting skills. I knew eventually I would need to talk to the police, but I was putting it off because I didn't want to make a fool of myself—"Hi there, I'm Harrison Pius and I'm a private eye, just like in the movies. Now tell me everything about this caper and I'll solve the mystery." Yeah, right. I once spent two months trying to find twelve hundred cartons of duplicator paper for a client that specialized in office products sales. The paper was only worth about twenty thousand bucks, but the client figured it was the tip of the iceberg, so to speak. He was right. He had a warehouse supervisor who developed a creative inventory management process that enabled him, along with a delivery driver, to set up their own warehouse and shuffle inventory assets. Because the warehouse supervisor was a "dedicated" employee he took on the hard work of maintaining the inventory control entries himself and was able to show stock levels on the books that didn't exist. A portion of the inventory was diverted to his private warehouse and sold out the back door. The order replenishment cycle kept him and his partner four weeks ahead of the system at all times, regardless of legitimate sales. It took me two months to figure out their scheme.

What made it amusing was their illegal warehouse was only four blocks away from the main company warehouse. When the client paid my fee he couldn't help but ask why I hadn't simply "taken a walk around the block" in the first place. A good detective would have done that, but a high priced consultant, like me, has to interview everybody in the company, write a twenty-five page report every week and submit a bill for seventy thousand dollars for two months' work. As it turned out the client got his money's worth, but I considered my fee as an example, once more, of "found money." Hey, at least I didn't hire a focus group.

There was a sticky note stuck to the front door with the words "meet me out back" printed in neat, block letters. I made my way around the front of the house and was, once again, struck by its size. Measured against my forty-two hundred square feet, this place had to be ten thousand. I stepped back and surveyed the roof. I counted eight chimneys—what a waste. The used brick patio was at the rear and Junkie was stretched out on a lounge chair with his eyes closed obviously expecting the morning sun to burn its way through the thick fog. I pulled a heavy wrought iron chair over next to him and sat down.

"Hey it's you—good morning." He turned over to face me and sat up. "You want some coffee—juice—a beer—you had breakfast?"

"I'm not here to eat," I said.

"You sound pissed."

"I'm not pissed. I'm confused," I informed him. "I've got a built-in bullshit meter and it's on full alert right now—you haven't leveled with me."

"You talked to Peter," he said.

"Yeah, I talked to Peter and either you're the all-time con artist or you're somebody I don't know. Who the hell are you?"

There was a long pause. Then he said, "Pope, it's a long story and it really doesn't have anything to do with Maggie, but let me explain."

He began speaking. "My real name is William Morrison and I was born in a little town in Oklahoma sixty-five years ago. Yeah, I know I look older—I'm a couple years younger than Maggie. I didn't take very good care of myself for about fifteen years and I damn near died a couple of times. Then I met Maggie and she brought me back to life. Until I was forty I lived in Boca Raton, Florida with my wife and son, and I taught in the English Literature department at Florida Atlantic University. My specialty was the contemporary American novel. Actually if you want me to be completely accurate, I'm William Morrison, PhD., but you don't have to call me Dr. Morrison." He smiled and continued. "My IQ is somewhere in the neighborhood of 160 and I can play the piano. I've published a book of poetry, which nobody bought, and I am a very good caddy and a lousy night watchman."

I didn't say anything, but the look on my face must have said I didn't believe it. As if reading my mind he continued.

"I realize this is hard for you to believe, but it's all true—and very painful. But I owe you the truth." He took a deep breath, closed his eyes for a moment and continued. "I graduated from the University of Oklahoma when I was nineteen years old, earned a Masters degree at twenty and a PhD by age twenty-two. I had a young, beautiful wife, and an infant son."

"The future couldn't have been brighter. I taught for a year at Oklahoma and then we moved to Florida when I was accepted in the English department at FAU in 1963. We lived on the Intercoastal and we were enjoying the American dream. I was a world away from the dirt-poor farm in Oklahoma and I could do all the things I loved. And I was loved. As the years went on my wife grew more beautiful and she loved me dearly. She was a warm, devoted mother to our son and she created an environment where I could write my poems and spend time on my boat."

Junkie fell silent and I could see he was having trouble breathing and tears were beginning to form in his eyes. I'm not good in these situations. This was when I should have reached out and squeezed Bill on the shoulder or given him a pat on the back, but I remained frozen. He seemed to gather himself and went on.

"It was a typical Florida summer day; hot and humid. We went sailing. The horizon to the east was a broken series of thunderheads and by late afternoon they would gather together. We expected the daily South Florida rain showers. But, we didn't get an afternoon rain shower that day. What we got was a major thunderstorm, and because of my stupidity we got caught in it." He paused and turned his head to the side, shielding his face from me. His hands began to shake. "Pope, I can't give you all the details because I won't get through it."

"Bill—"

"No, No! I'm okay. In a crazy kind of way it's good for me to do this. Maggie sent me to a shrink and it did help, because I had never been able to talk about it before."

More deep breathing and he continued. "We had started back when the storm hit and I didn't have the skill as a sailor to do the right thing. We capsized and I washed up on the beach an hour later, without a life preserver, clinging to a sofa cushion. I had a concussion and a broken leg, but I was alive. My wife and son were both wearing life preservers and they were never seen again."

"I can't imagine what that must have been like," I said.

"In the abstract neither can I. It's too painful even if it had happened to someone else instead of me," he replied. "The conventional wisdom dictates that you must move on—you can't live in the past. But, the problem is in your convoluted wisdom, you run the risk of trivializing the heartache. I re-visited that day everyday for twenty years because if I didn't it must have meant I didn't care as much as I should have. Intellectually I didn't want to get over it. Emotionally it drove me insane. Does that make sense?"

"It makes perfect sense, especially to me," I said and immediately regretted it. Now was not the time to bring my heartache into the conversation. In my fucked-up past no one had died.

Bill smiled for the first time in an hour. "We've all got our demons, I guess. I was too weak to deal with mine."

"Don't be too hard on yourself," I replied.

"Well, the rest of the story is the typical 'down the tubes' scenario. Too much booze, some drugs, lost the job, lost the house, the cars, and what little money we had saved, I squandered. I ended up as a night watchman in a junkyard and a part-time caddy in South San Francisco. Then I met Maggie and now I've lost her, too."

"Bill, I'm glad you told me about some of your past—it makes it easier for me to take you seriously, but I need to know more about you and Maggie. How did you meet her?"

He tilted his head back and smiled broadly. "It was late in the afternoon about five years ago. I had caddied for Mr. Arnstein and he had paid me sixty bucks for the loop, so I was flush and ready for a bottle of muscatel. Jimmy, the caddy master, grabbed me just as I was leaving and told me Mrs. O'Reilly wanted to play a fast nine holes and I had to caddy for her. I was really pissed, but I had no choice—all the other caddies had gone home, so I was stuck. It was colder than a whore's heart and the fog was blowing in but away we went."

"Had you ever caddied for her before?"

He shook his head. "No, I had seen her around. I knew she was a widow and had more money than God, but that was about it. She was good lookin' for her age, and even the younger guys talked about getting her behind the caddy shed for a 'show me yours and I'll show you mine,' but I didn't pay much attention. Of course, I didn't pay much attention to anything or anybody in those days."

"So what happened?"

"Nothing really, except I showed off a little."

"You showed off how?" I wondered aloud.

"Well, it was damned cold and I made a comment along the lines of what Mark Twain had said."

"You mean about the coldest winter?"

"Yeah, when he said the coldest winter he ever experienced was a summer he spent in San Francisco, and that's what I said to Maggie."

"And that comment surprised her," I said.

"It seemed to blow her away. She didn't expect a broken down old caddy to even know who Mark Twain was, much less quote him," Bill replied.

"How was that showing off?" I asked.

"Oh, the conversation just took off from there, and between her hitting golf shots and me walking along carrying her bag, I gave her a history lesson on Samuel Clemons and how he came to call himself Mark Twain. We walked in after six holes and then we sat on the bench by the starters shed and I explained to her why Huckleberry Finn might be the greatest American novel ever written and anyone who thinks it is racist is an idiot. She agreed with me." Junkie paused and stated matter-of-factly. "By the way, Maggie O'Reilly was a very smart woman."

"Because she agreed with you?" I asked.

"Yeah, that was part of it," he said. "But something clicked between us while we walked along the course. I liked her and felt comfortable, and I knew she liked me."

"And that was the beginning?"

"Yeah. She offered to give me a ride, so I had her drop me off at my favorite gin mill." Now Bill laughed out loud. "It was funny. We got so engrossed in conversation she forgot to pay me."

"And—?"

"The next day she dropped by the club—I was already out on a loop—and explained to Jimmy that she had forgotten to pay me. She gave Jimmy an envelope with some money in it. When I opened the envelope there was forty bucks with a note asking me to meet her for a drink at the Bunker at six o'clock. She said in the note she was reading Atlas Shrugged by Ayn Rand and wanted my opinion on Objectivism. Nobody had asked my opinion on anything for a long time, so my ego and my curiosity got the best of me and I met her for a drink. I told her that I thought Ayn Rand was the greatest thinker of the twentieth century. She disagreed with me. Most other people, especially college professors and dumb-ass critics disagree with me on that one too. Then, I told her my life story and we went from there."

"Bill, let's jump ahead." I couldn't bring myself to call him "Junkie" anymore. "What's the deal with the five hundred thousand dollars?"

He frowned, "I really don't know. She had a lot of money—I mean a lot—big bucks! But, she didn't throw it around in a flashy kind of way. Most of it was already in trust accounts for Sean and Peter and she was generous to several charities. And, of course, she spoiled her grandkids, but in a good way."

"Do you think she was planning on using the money for something she didn't want anyone to know about?" I asked.

"If she did," he said, "she never told me about it, or the boys for that matter." He gave a long slow nod of his head. "I remember last year she was involved with Gerry Murphy on some Irish charity event or something like that—no wait a minute, it was a fund raiser for a

Catholic charity, I think. She made out a check one day and joked about spending some of my inheritance. I kidded her back and said she would out-live me by twenty years. I was sure wrong about that."

I could see the wheels turning in his head. "Bill, do you think there is a connection to the five hundred thousand and this charity event?" I asked.

"I don't know," he answered. "Maybe Gerry can shed some light on that."

"Were he and Maggie that close?"

"I don't think they were close at all," he responded. "As a matter of fact I don't think Maggie liked Gerry—she blamed him for a lot of Dermot's craziness when the two of them ran around together chasin' pussy." Bill stood up and announced, "I'm gonna' have a gin bloody. You want one?"

"No, I'm fine." There's something about drinking a Bloody Mary for breakfast that offends my taste buds. I once had a lady friend that drank warm cokes in the morning—not my idea of a good way to start the day.

When he returned with his drink he continued, "I told Maggie that maybe Gerry's wife, in turn, blamed Dermot for all of his bimbo babes down through the years. Maggie thought I was probably right."

I watched him drink his Bloody Mary. I said, "I guess I should talk to Gerry about the charity, but it's probably a dead end. I can't imagine Gerry Murphy supporting a Catholic charity event, unless maybe it involved a golf tournament. I'll give him a call."

On the drive down the peninsula to Junkie's house I realized I had been postponing the inevitable; at some point I needed to know what happened the day Maggie died. The morning sun warmed the patio as it broke through the fog and I thought about how best to broach the subject of Maggie's last day.

We were both quiet for a minute, lost in our thoughts. As if he had been reading my mind again, Junkie broke the silence. "You haven't asked me anything about the day she died," he said.

"I know," I replied. "You think there's something sinister going on, so I thought I'd get the story from the cops first. That way it would be straight up and 'just the facts'. But, as long as I'm here go ahead and tell me what happened that day."

Junkie breathed in sharply. His dark brown eyes averted mine and he stared over my shoulder as if looking for someone to suddenly appear around the corner and help him out. "I'm not trying to duck the question...it's like I don't know where to begin."

"How about when you got up that morning," I said.

He smiled warmly as he thought back. "Maggie was a morning girl in every way. As she innocently put it, she loved to frolic in the morning. She was well over sixty but she had the sexual energy of a twenty-five year old. I was only the second man in her life and Dermot had been a dud in the sack. What turned old Dermot on was a raunchy screamer and that was not the way Maggie was or wanted to be. That morning we had a long, slow 'eye-opener' and then I fixed her some coffee and a bagel and served her in bed. As I was getting in my shower I heard the phone ring, but it only rang once, so I'm sure she picked it up. Guille doesn't come in until around ten every day and she doesn't answer the phone any way."

"Guille is your housekeeper?"

"Yeah, she's been with the family since the boys were little guys," he replied. "She's been in this country for forty years and she can barely speak English, but Maggie and the boys love her. She's been so upset since Maggie died that she comes in everyday and just sits in the kitchen and cries—I don't know what I'm going to do with her."

"Maybe you could send her on a vacation—does she have a family?"

"She doesn't have anyone—she was never married—and, Hellsbells, she can go anywhere she wants on her own. Maggie left her an annuity that'll pay her about fifty grand a year for the rest of her life. Plus her salary for taking care of me is five hundred a week."

"Did Guille see or talk to Maggie that morning?" I asked.

"Yes she talked to her!" Bill answered quickly.

The mid-morning sun had broken through the fog and it had warmed up considerably on the patio so I moved my chair into the shade. Bill's reaction to my question confused me. "Did that surprise you? You say it as if it surprised you."

"No! No! Not the fact they talked—it's what Maggie said to Guille." He saw the puzzled look on my face. "Maggie asked Guille to stick around at the end of the day and have dinner with us—we'd have bar-b-qued steaks and fruit salad with chocolate sundaes for dessert. That's Guille's favorite meal." He clasped his hands together and looked in my eyes. "Pope, why would Maggie do that if she knew she was going to kill herself?"

"Maybe something happened that day to send Maggie over the edge," I said softly.

"Okay, okay," he conceded. "Let's say something happened during the day to make a healthy woman in the prime of her life kill herself." Bill paused as if to emphasize his next point, "Where did she get fifty Valium tablets without a prescription?"

"Any high school kid can probably tell you were to get a thousand Valium if you wanted them," I answered.

"Yeah, but Maggie wasn't the type of woman that would know how to do that."

"That's a good point, Bill. But, let's save the 'did she or didn't she' argument for later and tell me what happened the rest of the day—if you know?"

"We don't know much," he replied. "She came back upstairs, after visiting with Guille, kissed me on the cheek as I was shaving and reminded me she was playing nine holes with Alice Adkins later that afternoon. She left the house around ten-thirty and was at the office by eleven. The boys were in a meeting with Stuart Zelinka and said 'hi' when she stopped by the conference room in building 4. She went over to her building, went through the mail and was out the door by noon. None of us ever saw her alive again."

He almost lost it with that statement—took a large gulp of air and continued. "We know she stopped at Nordstrom and bought a sweater, a dress and picked out a couple of tennis outfits for her grand-daughter Kate—the kid that goes to Cal-Berkeley—her birthday was coming up. Some birthday…the kid hasn't been back to school since Maggie died. I think she's going to drop out the rest of this semester and pick it up again in the fall."

"Go on."

"She was driving her big Lexus. She loved that car…the boys bought it for her last Christmas." He had to gulp for air again. On the surface he seemed to be handling her death reasonably well. But, now and then the emotion would pour over him and I got the feeling he was like a man that was drowning. "I should get rid of that car—she died in it."

"Where was the car found?"

"About six o'clock some guys pulled in the parking lot down Skyline Boulevard just below the entrance to the Olympic Club." He frowned, trying to think of something. "What do you call it? You know…when they jump off the cliffs there next to the ocean and fly around?"

"You mean hang gliders?"

"Yeah, that's it," he said dismissively. "Anyway…they were getting their gear together and noticed a woman sitting in her car with no other cars parked anywhere near her and she was just sitting there not doing any thing. It didn't seem all that unusual to them at first, but about fifteen minutes after they started doing their flying thing one of them came back to his pick-up truck to get a jacket and noticed the woman was still there. He got suspicious, so he went over to take a look."

Junkie had pressed his fingertips to his eyes and was shaking his head back and forth.

He continued, "It wasn't pretty. She had thrown up all over the front of her dress and her face was the color of chalk. One of the guys had a cell phone and he called 911 and the paramedics were there in about five minutes, but she was already dead and there was nothing they could do."

"Did you request an autopsy?" I asked.

Junkie smiled. "Pope you're not much of a private eye."

"Why do you say that?"

"If you were a real 'gumshoe' you'd know that when someone dies the way Maggie did, the law requires an autopsy be performed."

"I didn't know."

"That's okay, neither did I," he said.

"What was the result of the autopsy?" I asked.

"She died of acute respiratory failure brought on by cardiac arrest...end of story."

"But not for you," I stated.

"The cops found an empty bottle of gin in the front seat next to her, along with her purse. Nothing was missing and she had all her credit cards, drivers license, pictures of the grand kids and normal junk she always had with her. Plus, there was about three hundred dollars in cash in her pocket book."

There was a long pause. I didn't say anything because I sensed he was going to tell me something that he thought was very important. He didn't disappoint me.

"Pope, when you meet with the cop that investigated the case, ask him why they didn't find a pill bottle in the car." He reacted to the surprise on my face. "Yeah, my friend, she was wearing a cotton dress with no pockets—what happened to the bottle or container for the fifty Valium? They searched every trash container in the parking lot—if you're wondering about that—and they didn't find a damn thing that looked like something you would carry pills around in. Unless she brought them in a Starbucks coffee cup or an empty Pepsi bottle, because that's all they found."

"I think it's time for me to bite the bullet and talk to the cops," I said.

"I've got the name of the cop that came to the house to ask me about Maggie, if you want it," he said.

I nodded my head. "Yeah, I've got to talk to him sooner or later."

"Hey, he's a nice guy—you'll like him. He thinks the boys and I are in denial and he's got a mountain of statistics to back up the suicide theory."

I got up from the chair and reached out to shake his hand and said, "Bill, take some time and think some more about what you're asking me to do. Maybe Maggie had demons you didn't know about. She was almost seventy years old. She had lived sixty-five years before she ever met you and a lot of things can happen to a person in sixty-five years. Some of the best people you'll ever know have dark alleys they've walked down and can't forget."

"I've looked at it from every angle," he said. "It still doesn't make sense." He handed me a business card with the gold seal of the South San Francisco Police Department embossed on the upper right hand corner and began walking with me to the front door. "And one more thing, Pope. You don't have to stop calling me 'Junkie' just because you know my name is Dr. Morrison. I've had nicknames my entire life—some day I'll tell you why everyone called me 'Snaffy' when I was a kid back on the farm in Oklahoma."

"Save it for later," I said. "I've had enough surprises for today."

8

In 1916 the small town of Everett, Washington was the scene of an armed confrontation that became known as the Everett Massacre. The conflict was between the IWW union and the local sheriff. Seven of the combatants were killed and today nobody in the town, except for a few old timers, knows what it was all about. Nothing much exciting happened in Everett for the next fifty years until June 1966 when the Boeing Commercial Aircraft Company purchased seven hundred and eighty acres on the outskirts of town. Shortly after the purchase of the land the Boeing Company risked one billion dollars on the notion that the world was ready for a jet aircraft that would carry four hundred passengers in comfort and safety around the world. They would call the jumbo jet a Boeing 747 and it would become the largest passenger airliner in the world and remain so for forty years. It would be built to fly at subsonic speeds—565 mph—and have a range of 8000 miles.

Pan American Airlines immediately ordered twenty-five of the planes and five other airlines followed quickly bringing the total sales to $1.8 billion in only four months. There was only one problem with the opening orders; $1.8 billion in total sales was only 80 planes. Boeing needed to sell 400 planes for the venture to be considered a success. There was another small problem to reckon with. Boeing didn't have a factory large enough to assemble the jumbo jet and that's where the little town of Everett and the seven hundred and eighty acres entered the picture. Pan Am expected the first of their planes to be delivered in four years so the Boeing Company had to build an all-new assembly building on their newly acquired property. Everett lost its claim to fame as the site of the Everett Massacre and became known as the site of the largest building ever built in the world.

The Boeing Company had gambled their future and came close to bankruptcy in the early 1970s. However, the gamble was a success and Boeing has enjoyed a monopoly on jumbo jets that has lasted thirty-five years. In October 1975 the worldwide 747 fleet carried its 100 millionth passenger. And on June 5th 1986 the United States Air Force ordered two specially equipped 747s to transport the President of the United States.

The newest model is the 747-400. It has an all-new glass cockpit, winglets for increased fuel efficiency, an all-new interior and tail fuel tanks. It is capable of carrying 568 passengers and every day British Airways flies a 747-400 from San Francisco to London in less than ten hours.

There have been seventeen specific disasters involving the 747. Very few have been the result of design flaws: most have been because of faulty maintenance or pilot error. Pan Am flight 103 in 1988 over Lockerbie, Scotland is the most notable exception.

9

The next morning I called Detective Bert Brogger of the South San Francisco Police Department and made an appointment for later in the day. He was investigating a homicide involving some juvenile gang members in downtown South City so I suggested Bertolucci's for lunch. He accepted but, "only if you pay for lunch," he said he "couldn't afford Bertolucci's."

Earlier that morning I had gone for a long walk and surfaced at one of my favorite neighborhood hangouts. Church Street runs for five miles from north to south in the City. It starts at Market Street and ends at the end. I don't know the name of the street at the end because I've never been there—but I know, for a fact, that it dead-ends because Juanita told me it does. Four blocks from my house, located at the corner of Church and 24th, is the Happy Donut. They make terrible donuts. But, the old lady that works from midnight until eight a.m. makes the best egg salad sandwich available anywhere in the world. I am an expert on sardine, liverwurst and egg salad sandwiches—not mixed together, of course—and an egg salad sandwich at 5:00 in the morning with the J Street Car shaking the building as it lumbers down Church Street is heaven. Juanita is good for two sleep-ins a week, so that's my excuse to step out for breakfast at the Happy Donut. With my sandwich in front of me I was trying to read our daily rag, the *Chronicle*, but it gave me such a pain in the ass I gave up. I spend about two weeks a year down on the Monterey Peninsula and even the *Monterey County Herald* has a better sports page than the *Chronicle*. Every television station and every newspaper needs at least one curmudgeon, and when Herb Caen died the *Chronicle* and the

City lost their last hope for balance. Political correctness is the new world order and San Francisco is leading the way. Only in this town is a receptionist called a *Director of First Impressions.* Hell, I even remember when the word gay was an adjective meaning a happy, lively mood. Maybe I'm a curmudgeon.

I folded my paper napkin in a neat square and dropped it in the trash container at the entrance to Happy Donut, but not before paying my compliments to the chef with a five dollar bill in the tip jar. I walked the four blocks back to my house and jumped in the shower. As the warm water eased the morning chill out of my body I was grinning like a fool and felt self-conscious even though I was alone. Funny how a simple thing like leaving a five-dollar tip for a four-dollar sandwich can put a dumb-ass grin on your face and set the stage for a pleasant day.

Heading to South City to meet with Detective Brogger, I could only wonder where I was going with my investigation. I didn't know very much and I wasn't sure what the right questions were. Usually, when I'm stumped I follow the Cardinal Rule of cutting through the bullshit to get to the real bullshit: follow the money. But, there wasn't any money; at least there wasn't any money that was missing and there wasn't any money that somebody else wanted. All the players—Junkie Bill, Peter and Sean—had all the money they could ever want when Maggie was alive. Her death didn't give them anything they didn't already have or would have inherited someday anyway. I guess I could look at the two wives, but that might get tricky. And my gut told me this wasn't a messy family problem.

Finding a good spot to park at Bertoluuci's could be a problem unless you got there early and the valet guys still had room in the lot. I didn't want to put the Boxster on the street so I got there early.

As I surrendered the car to the Jeff Gordon-wannabe valet I remembered I had promised Vanessa I would call her and confirm our date for the evening. I reached for my cell phone and was surprised to discover I had forgotten to turn it on. I pushed the button and the message light blinked back at me.

"I just missed you at your house—your housekeeper is a piece of work—anyway, call me when you get this. I've got a name for you." Junkie's voice was pitched about two octaves higher than normal and he delivered the message so fast I had to re-play it twice to make sure I had it right. I punched in his number and listened to it ring. No answer and no answering machine. I tried Vanessa on her cell phone and got her voice mail—I left her a message saying I would be home all evening and would fix her dinner.

I went through the back entrance to the restaurant, past the service bar, and Gina put me in the banquette near the only window in the place. It was early, but a couple of guys at a table in the center of the room were getting a jump-start on their three-martini lunch. The fat one in the yellow power tie was describing the great round he shot on Saturday at his club—hole by hole, shot by shot—all ninety-two strokes! There is nothing worse, except going to the dentist, than being forced to listen to an autopsy of a bad round of golf.

"So, mister big time private eye, have you solved Northern California's biggest mystery yet?" He was smiling as he said it and slipped into the booth extending his hand in a firm handshake.

Bert Brogger was built like me, slim and medium height, but much younger—too young to be a detective grade already. If what Vanessa told me about police detectives was true, he was either well connected or had pictures of his Captain with his shorts around his knees. His voice was deep and my first thought was he should be delivering the evening news on television. "I didn't know the death of a wealthy matron from Atherton qualified as Northern California's biggest mystery," I replied.

"Ah, I'm not talkin' about that," he said. "Inquiring minds want to know…is Bonds on steroids?"

"Of course he is," I declared. "Look at his head. You can work out and exercise twelve hours a day—it won't make your head bigger. If he's not on steroids he's certainly on human growth hormones." This was a nice touch on the Detective's part, an introductory conversation on *his* terms, not mine. He was well trained. "Okay, Detective…"

"Call me Bert."

"Okay, Bert. Are you really interested in my thoughts about the state of professional athletics or is this a way to break the ice and humor an amateur sleuth?"

He smiled again. "Both, but there's more."

"What else?"

"I'm going to have a Grey Goose on the rocks—only one, because I'm on the clock—a Caesar salad and lobster ravioli. I want you to pay for lunch, so I'm being nice and engaging."

Now I was smiling. "Once we've gotten to know each other better we can debate the pros and cons of steroid use in professional sports," I said.

"Fair enough," he replied.

Someone once said that artists should remain anonymous. I think that applies to most professional athletes, as well. The ability to hit a baseball traveling at ninety-five miles an hour is remarkable and only a small group of individuals in the world can do it. There are more good poets than there are hitters; the same can be said about other professional athletes, even professional golfers who are the most educated of athletes. There are roughly ten million golfers in the world and about ten percent of them can shoot a score of less than a 100 for 18 holes. Of that ten percent there are about three hundred that play the game at its highest level. There are more exceptional brain surgeons than exceptional golfers. With few exceptions, professional athletes, in particular baseball players, share a common characteristic; outside of their chosen profession they are as dumb as infield dirt. Which is why they should remain anonymous and keep their mouths shut. I said, "I think we probably both agree that if Barry Bonds couldn't hit a baseball he'd be selling programs at the front gate." Detective Brogger nodded in agreement and I continued. "Now that we've got the preliminaries out of the way why don't you be nice and engaging and tell me what you can about the death of Maggie O'Reilly."

"You want the short version or the long one?"

"Sister Mary Robert told me when I was in the third grade that I had a short attention span, so I better get the short one." I answered.

Anthony, our waiter, appeared and inquired about drinks, and then recited a list of eight specials while giving us way too much information about the preparation of each dish. I didn't need to know what part of the bay the scallops came from or where in the San Joaquin Valley the asparagus was grown. We ordered and Detective Brogger was true to his word except it was a double Grey Goose on the rocks. I wondered…what if he wasn't "on the clock."

"The short version is not only short, it's simple. A very healthy, fit woman just a couple of months shy of her seventieth birthday swallowed approximately fifty 10 milligram tablets of Diazepam—they're the blue ones—commonly known as Valium, and washed them all down with a fifth of gin. It probably took twenty to thirty minutes for the first jolt to hit her, she drooled down the front of her dress and tried to wipe it off—she had a mixture of saliva and gin on her hands—and she nodded off."

"You mean she just went to sleep?" I asked.

"Yeah, at first. Then she…" Anthony serving our drinks interrupted him.

My Johnnie Walker Black clinked against his Grey Goose, we said "cheers" and he continued. "She either dozed off or was very, very drowsy when she went into cardiac arrest. That's when she threw up—she just didn't throw up enough—and suffocated on her own vomit."

I started to take a sip of scotch and stopped abruptly. "What did she throw up?"

"I can tell you want to get this part over with before our lunch is served," he smiled and went on. "She threw up her breakfast *and* her lunch."

"She had breakfast at home because Junkie fixed it and…"

"Who's Junkie?" His investigators' curiosity went on full alert. "I don't know anything about a person named Junkie," he said in a tone that reminded me once again of Sister Mary Robert.

"Hang on," I said nervously. "You know him as William Morrison, Maggie's husband. At our club we know him as Junkie Bill."

"Is he on drugs?"

"No!" I said as Anthony served Detective Brogger his lobster ravioli and me my petrale sole. Neither one of us had bit on the specials.

"Would either of you gentlemen care for another cocktail?" he asked.

I shook my head no and Detective Brogger nodded his head yes. So much for being "on the clock."

I continued. "Before Maggie and Junkie got married he lived behind Garibaldi Auto Salvage. Somebody at the club started calling him 'Junkie' and the name stuck."

"What? Is the guy a bum?"

"Not any more," I said. "He's actually very well educated…he just dropped out of society for a few years. She helped him solve some personal problems and I think they were very happy with each other." For some strange reason I didn't want the detective to think Junkie was a low-life. "He's a guy that was lost for fifteen years of his life and finally found happiness. Then one morning while he's shaving his wife tells him she's going to run a couple of errands and might play nine holes of golf with a girlfriend later that afternoon, gives him a kiss on the cheek, tells him she loves him, then goes out the door and he never sees her alive again." I took a bite of steamed broccoli and chewed slowly while waiting for a reaction. Detective Brogger was concentrating on his ravioli or lost in thought at something I said. He didn't say anything.

"You say she had lunch. Where?" I asked.

"We don't know," he answered. "She had some kind of tossed salad with sour dough bread because the M.E. identified it as part of what she 'tossed' when she threw up, but we don't know where she ate it."

"M.E.? I'm guessing that's Medical Examiner," I said.

"You learn fast for a rookie," he said sarcastically. He caught my displeasure, "Hey, relax. Don't look so pissed—I'm just bustin' your nuts a little. Good cops do that."

"I'm a little defensive about my role in this," I said. My lack of familiarity with the way a homicide detective works was making me uneasy with Detective Brogger. "I'm not pissed at you, I'm just frustrated. I think there's a lot more to this than a simple suicide."

Detective Brogger turned and signaled the busboy standing at the entrance to the kitchen. The detective made a "clear our plates" motion with his hands and said, "Young man if you see Anthony tell him to have the goose fly by me…one more time."

I thought to myself that if Detective Brogger stays "on the clock" after three double vodkas, I wouldn't want to be the next guy he runs into. "Don't you think it's strange that a woman with everything going for her would suddenly kill herself?" I asked.

"Harry, if the strange behavior of human beings bothered me, I'd have to find a different line of work." He paused and accepted his latest "goose" from Anthony. "I'll tell you something…call it advice…poke around in this for a while. Play at being Sherlock Holmes…whatever. Let the family grieve and get used to the fact that this woman, like all of us, had some problems that finally got to her. One day down the road…and trust me it'll happen sooner than later, they'll come to accept that she killed herself." He saw the look on my face and held up his hand. "Listen to me Harry. I said they'll learn to accept this, but believe me, they'll never understand why…and that'll be the hard part."

"I know, but…"

"Let me finish," he demanded. Only "finish" came out "fin-nith."

"You pokin' around in this is okay, it probably makes Mr. Morrison and her boys feel better…they don't feel so useless. But, don't get carried away and make a pest of yourself."

Suddenly he took in a breath so deep it made his eyes water. "You think I'm hammered and you're probably right. But something just occurred to me about what her plans were for the afternoon she died and I need to ask Mr. Morrison a couple more questions, so I'm gonna' bail outta' here." He swallowed the last of his cocktail with a quick flourish, slid out of the booth and said, "I'll tell him you took me to lunch, that way you can put it on your expense report." He flashed his best little boy smile at me and walked away.

Just then Anthony appeared with the lunch check and as they passed each other I couldn't help overhear Anthony say softly, "See ya' later, Bert."

10

The South City fog had yet to make an appearance as I paid the ransom to retrieve the Boxster from the valet. The sun was warm at the back of Bertolucci's so I shed my jacket and dug around for some sunglasses. I gave the kid a couple of bucks extra because I noticed he had parked my prized possession right in front of his booth out of harm's way. I got buckled in and exited the parking lot and remembered I needed to return Junkie's call. I pulled off to the side of the street just as my cell phone rang causing me to stall the five-speed in my rush to answer.

"How was lunch?" It was Junkie.

"The lunch was excellent," I said. "I'm not so sure about this guy Brogger, though. He's got a hollow leg when it comes to putting away the vodka, but he seems like an okay guy."

"I didn't know they served vodka at Burger King."

"Burger King?" I asked. "What are you talking about? We had lunch at Bertolucci's."

Junkie laughed on the other end. "I think he was fuckin' with me." He laughed so hard this time he started coughing. "He told me you took him to Burger King for lunch and to keep an eye out for a bogus entry on your expense report."

"If you or Detective Brogger knew me better, you'd know that having lunch, or anything to eat, at Burger King would be impossible." I stated. "I might be the only human being left in the world that has never eaten a bite of food at Burger King or any of the other fast food slop houses that pollute the beauty of our nation's strip malls. You called me—?"

"We've got something we can't figure out," he said.

"What have you got and what can't you figure out?"

"Sandy—that's Peter's wife—came over this morning and was sorting through some of Maggie's stuff—we're getting all of her clothes ready to donate to Goodwill," he added. "Anyway, she was going through all the pockets and found a money order receipt for five grand."

"Okay, that's what you've got," I said. "What is it you can't figure out?"

"It's the name on the receipt for the money order," Junkie answered. "We don't know who the hell the guy is that the check was made out to."

"What's the guy's..."

"Tommy Gavin," he blurted out before I could finish the question.

"Who's Tommy Gavin?"

"We don't know. I asked the boys and no one's ever heard of a Tommy Gavin."

"We should get this information to Detective Brogger," I said.

"He's already got it."

"How did he get it?" I asked.

"He called about ten minutes ago—he said he had a quick question and I told him about the money order." There was a long pause and Junkie continued, "He sounded strange over the phone, maybe it was the vodka."

"Did the name Tommy Gavin ring any bells with him?" I asked.

"He said no, but he'd check it out."

"What else did he say?"

"Well, he wanted to know about the last time I saw Maggie. You know, when I was shaving and she came back upstairs to tell me goodbye. But, he specifically asked me over and over if I was sure she said she was going to play golf that afternoon." Junkie paused, then added. "He seemed to be pissed that I can't remember what she was wearing that morning. Hell, Pope I can't remem..."

Then it hit me. I knew where Detective Brogger was going with his questions. The vodka hadn't hit him as hard as I thought. "Junkie, are you calling from home?"

"Where else would I be?" he said impatiently.

"Stay there—I need to talk to you some more and I'm coming right over," I said. "You make yourself useful and see if you can find Maggie's checkbook and all her personal bank statements for as far back as you can come up with."

"Can I ask what's goin' on?"

I made a u-turn and pointed the nose of the Boxster south toward the Bayshore Freeway. "I'll tell you when I get there," I answered.

As a day-to-day car a Porsche Boxster doesn't make much sense, which is why it spends more time parked in the garage under my house than driving on the streets of San Francisco. My respectable, consultant-type car is a black Lincoln sedan that Juanita describes as an "old fart cart." But, whenever I think I might be spending some time on a freeway and not burdened by stop and go traffic I roll out the Boxster and stretch its legs. From turnoff to turnoff, Hillsborough is only about eight miles from South City and I made it in five minutes flat. Hillsborough is south of Brisbane, but it might as well be on the moon. It's where all the rich people live. When the Silicon Valley exploded with wealth and all of the twenty-eight year old, dot-com nerds suddenly found themselves with millions in disposable income, some savvy, old time residents of Hillsborough took advantage of easy pickings. They put their old mansions up for sale at double the appraised value and the young millionaires from the start-up companies fell all over themselves to pay cash for the opportunity to live in Hillsborough. After the first wave of buyers, some of the other old time owners decided to triple what they thought their houses were worth and that became the norm. It didn't stop the new rich from their rush to snag a Hillsborough address—the prices just kept on going up until a house that was worth three million ten years ago carried a fifteen million dollar price tag today; if you can find one for sale.

As I pulled into the curving brick drive of the late Maggie O'Reilly's ten thousand square foot bungalow, I thought fifteen to twenty million was a good guess at its current value. The house, bathed in afternoon sun instead of the usual fog, looked bigger than I remembered it. I looked more closely and saw that it sat on at least a half acre surrounded by pine trees and Italian cypress with the occasional eucalyptus thrown in. I revised my estimate. Twenty million at least.

A woman who was half the size of Juanita answered the door and in barely a whisper asked, "Are you Mister Pius?" I answered her with a nod of my head and she gestured for me to follow her. Junkie was in the sunroom with a woman that should be in the movies. She was wearing baggy jeans, a faded sweatshirt and sneakers that had seen better days. Her long brown hair was going in several different directions and she was drop dead gorgeous. She looked up as I entered the room and her green eyes stopped me in my tracks.

"Pope, get your chin off your chest, it's unbecoming." Junkie was obviously enjoying the moment. "This is Sandy O'Reilly. She's got a daughter in college and a great husband named Peter and an old surrogate father-in-law that will protect her from the likes of you."

She stuck out her hand and grasped my hand firmly. "It's nice to meet you, Mr. Pius. Don't pay any attention to Bill, I think he's either going blind or having too many senior moments." Her smile made me smile. "Call me Sandy."

"Sandy, I'm not going blind and I'm not eligible for senior moments," I said. "But, of one thing I'm sure—Peter O'Reilly is a very lucky man—and please, call me Harry."

"And I'm a very lucky girl," she added. "Bill," she turned toward Junkie and asked, "shall I get the pink copy of the money order for Harry?"

"I've got it right here," he answered. "The detective took the green copy when he left, but you can still see the payee's name on this part." He handed the single 3 by 8 sheet to me.

I could easily make out the name Tommy Gavin on the copy. "What was Detective Brogger's reaction to the money order receipt?" I asked.

"He didn't seem all that interested." Junkie glanced at Sandy O'Reilly for her agreement.

She nodded her head as if to agree and added, "I thought he would make a bigger deal out of it than he did. He was much more interested in the other thing."

Before she could continue, I interrupted. "Let me guess." I paused to collect my thoughts, but I also wanted to impress them if my hunch was correct. "Detective Brogger asked you again what Maggie was wearing, the last morning you saw her—you know, when she kissed you on the cheek and left the house."

Junkie Bill and Sandy O'Reilly looked at each other quickly and Sandy exclaimed, "How did you know he would be so interested in that?"

I sat down on a wicker chair facing them. I held up a finger for emphasis, "I think he and I got to it at just about the same time," I said.

"Got to what?" Bill exclaimed.

I ignored his question for the moment. "Junkie did you tell him what Maggie was wearing when she left the house?"

"Pope, I don't remember what I was wearing that day, much less Maggie—hell, I don't remember what I had on yesterday, for that matter."

Sandy interjected. "Harry, if I had to make a guess, Maggie would have worn a sweater and slacks if she was going to play golf that afternoon."

"Pope, what are you getting at?" Junkie asked.

"Can the two of you imagine her playing golf at Pacific Heights, on a cold afternoon, in a cotton dress?" Junkie was leaning back in his chair and suddenly sat straight up, shaking his head. Now he had it and the look on Sandy's face told me she, too, was following my logic. "She left the house around ten o'clock dressed for golf, she goes to the office, then goes shopping at Nordstrom, has lunch someplace and is found dead around six o'clock. If Detective Brogger is telling it straight she was wearing a cotton dress when she was found and she had thrown up down the front of the dress."

Junkie Bill and Sandy O'Reilly sat motionless for a moment and then both started to speak at once.

I held up my hand again and said, "Before we go any further, where's the dress?"

"Oh God, I get it," Sandy said. "The detective asked me if we still had the dress and seemed upset when I told him I had put it in the trash."

I switched gears. "Did he want to know if you had the receipt for the items she bought at Nordstrom?" I asked.

"Yeah, he asked about that, too," Junkie interjected. "Sandy had that covered though."

Sandy quickly nodded her head and added, "Harry it was strange. He asked about the Nordstrom receipt and I had it right in my purse."

"Why in your purse?"

"Maggie bought my daughter a couple of tennis outfits for her birthday and when the police gave us the Nordstrom shopping bag with the stuff in it I saved the receipt—I don't know why I saved it…force of habit I guess…or maybe I wanted to save something with Maggie's signature."

"But, why were you carrying the receipt around in your purse?"

"Oh! I'm sorry…I don't mean to be so vague—the detective asked me the same question and right now I'm a little flustered." She paused took several deep breaths and continued. "It turned out that one of the outfits doesn't fit Kate properly and I've been intending to exchange it, so I was glad I had kept the receipt." She smiled and added, "But with Nordstrom you never need your receipt—they take back anything."

"And Detective Brogger has the receipt now?" I asked.

"Pope, he grabbed that receipt and practically ran out of here." Junkie said.

I leaned back and closed my eyes for a moment. Switching gears again I asked, "Junkie did you go to the morgue to identify the body?"

"Yeah, with Peter and Sean."

"What was she wearing when you viewed the body?"

Sandy and Junkie Bill heaved a collective sigh and he flinched like some one had just hit him in the stomach. "She was naked under a heavy gray sheet."

"She wasn't wearing the cotton dress," I asked.

"No."

"Did they give you her belongings?"

"I got a plastic garbage bag with her purse, her shoes, the dress and her underwear."

"What about jewelry?"

"I got a small white envelope with her earrings and wedding band…they gave me that to identify before we viewed the body."

"What about the…?"

"I almost forgot," he added. "They gave me the Nordstrom's shopping bag with the stuff she had purchased that afternoon."

Sandy chimed in, "Wait a minute! What we got was her purse, her jewelry, the clothes she was wearing when she died and…"

Junkie Bill reached across and grabbed Sandy's hand in his, opened his mouth to speak and nothing came out.

I spoke for him instead, "If she left the house that morning dressed for a golf game later that day, what happened to the golf outfit and why did she change into the cotton dress?"

Sandy started to speak just as the phone rang. "Yes…speaking," she answered. "We've been sorting through—Mr. Pius is here—all the stuff about the day my mother-in-law died. Here—you can speak with him."

She handed me the phone and the voice on the other end had lost the lighthearted banter on display at lunch. "Well, Harry we've got ourselves a shit storm developing."

"Some things don't add up," I responded.

"Yeah, it's suddenly gotten complicated…more than you know," he said. "I've got a lot of ground to cover over the next few hours, but if you've got some time let's meet for coffee in the morning. Give me your number and I'll call you around seven."

I had a dozen questions, but he stopped me and I gave him my private number at home.

"We'll cover it all in the morning," he was obviously in a rush. "And Harry, don't run all over the place looking for Tommy Gavin, we've got him."

"You've got him! How…"

"A kid on a sailboard discovered his body floating off Coyote Point yesterday afternoon. I didn't make the connection until I got back to the office and saw yesterday's log book."

"Detective Brogger…"

"Hold on! Just hold it—I'll give you what I know in the morning," and the phone went dead.

Sandy and Junkie were sitting quietly looking like two deer caught in a car's headlights. I said it quick. "Tommy Gavin's body was found yesterday floating in the water off of Coyote Point."

No sound came from either of them. "I'm meeting with Brogger in the morning…I'll know more then."

"Holy shit," Junkie muttered.

"Holy shit is right," I said. "But, I think the cops are going to get a little more interested now." I stood up to leave.

"Pope we—," Junkie started.

"No, let's let all this percolate for a little while—besides I've got to go," I said. "I'll call you in the morning after I meet with the detective and give you an update."

They both started to protest and I waved then off. "I need to sort some of this out before I see him." I started for the door and remembered, "Junkie did you find Maggie's check registers?"

"I found a box full of cancelled checks and statements, but I didn't have time to sort through it all. Detective Brogger showed up just as I started to try and make sense of it."

"That's okay, give me all of it and I'll sort through everything." Sandy was looking a little deflated and Junkie just looked confused; his genius IQ wasn't letting him see the forest for the trees or maybe he was coming to grips with the reality that his wife just might have been murdered. Junkie carried the box to the car. I put it in the front trunk and drove away.

The box with the receipts was an intrusion. Vanessa was coming at seven o'clock for our bi-weekly get together, I was meeting Detective Brogger early the next morning, and Gerry Murphy had included me in a high stakes golf game for the afternoon. That didn't leave much time to sort through the cancelled checks and statements.

Once I hit the freeway I slipped Errol Garner's *Concert By The Sea* in the disc player and cranked up the volume. Forget Basie—nobody ever did *April in Paris* like Garner.

I was twenty minutes from home and my thoughts turned to the evening ahead and Vanessa Burke Johnson.

The first time I met Vanessa she was standing on a step stool trying to dislodge a law book from the top shelf in the law library of Ehrens and Rough. She didn't know I was watching and the combination of her outstretched arm, a too short skirt and the height of the stool gave me an unobstructed view of her panty-clad ass. When she caught me staring up her skirt her reaction was cool and detached, "Pick your tongue off the floor, boy, and give me a hand here."

With not the slightest show of modesty she then put both arms in the air and tugged at the trapped book giving me an even better look.

Within the space of a few days, I would discover that modesty was not part of Vanessa's persona.

The book surrendered its spot on the shelf, she put an arm out and I supported her descent from her lofty perch. Slipping her spiked heels back on her slender feet and standing in front of me she was slightly taller than my six feet and definitely an eyeful. Coffee colored skin, small breasts, legs that went on forever and the most dazzling smile I had ever seen; she was beautiful and she knew it…and she was a wise guy.

"You must be the Pius guy that's supposed to interview me." Before I could answer she added, "Are you really pious?"

"That's me," and I stuck out my hand.

She waved my hand away, "No, you're too good looking to be pious—you're probably a scoundrel or maybe even a shitheel."

"I got it," I said. "You must think you're the first person to ever have fun with my name and I'm neither one—at least I don't think I'm a shitheel."

She shook her head, laughed, pulled a chair out from the conference table and sat. She crossed her legs and gave me another glimpse of white cotton panty. She was having a lot of fun at my expense and loving every minute of it. "You're one or the other—all men are—I hope you're not a shitheel. I much prefer scoundrels."

I was on a job. I had a contract with her law firm to investigate a company involved in a lawsuit over distribution rights for a DVD poker game. It seems their client wasn't getting the royalties they felt they deserved because the distributor was pushing product through non-traditional channels and cooking the books. Vanessa had drawn up the initial distribution contract and I had some questions about the wording of the document. She put on her professional hat and was all business for the thirty minutes or so it took for me to get what I needed.

At the beginning of the interview I had given her my card and as I stood up to leave she took it between two fingers and flipped it back across the table. She said, "So, have you made up your mind?"

"I think your client..."

"That's not what I mean," she sighed. She cocked her head to the side and gave me a grin for the ages. "Have you decided yet if you want to take me to bed?"

All the air went out of the room. I tried to think of something clever and couldn't get anything out.

She went on, "I've embarrassed you—that's so sweet." She took my card and handed it back to me. "Here Mr. Harrison Pius, write your home number on the back and I'll call you. You're not married are you? It doesn't matter if you are, but I don't want to talk to your wife on the phone."

I reached across the table, took her gold Mont Blanc in my hand and nervously scribbled my home number on the back of my business card. She called the next evening about six o'clock and asked what I was doing. I suggested a drink at the Fairmont; she said she'd rather see my house and a dry, white wine would be nice. I gave her my address and that began the ride of my life.

I like Vanessa as much as any woman I've ever known, but she's not someone I can love. She's intelligent, quick witted, funny, fiercely independent and most important for me—she's brutally honest. I discovered these things, and more, our first evening together. A City cab dropped her at my front door at precisely six o'clock and she greeted me with a kiss and a mouthful of peppermint-flavored tongue. There was no hesitation about letting me know why she had come to my house. Within fifteen minutes—the time it took to open a chilled bottle of Ferrari Carrano Fume Blanc and rush to the bedroom—her legs were wrapped around my neck and she had captured me in the most intense sexual experience of my life. She was under me, over me, beside me, biting me, licking me and sucking me, and it seemed to go on forever. She was painful, joyful, open, mysterious and never self-conscious. But, I knew from the beginning she wasn't a woman I could ever love because I learned quickly that all of her needs could only be satisfied on her terms and conditions. But, she was honest about herself and her needs, including what she told me about her boyfriend Willie.

But then, I'm not lovable either. Some very good women, in the recent past, have un-lovingly referred to me as an ice-cold bastard, and they're right on the mark. The good that came from getting my heart broken five years ago was the knowledge that I need more than great sex and fun times for love to last. It was the best and worst lesson of my life. The best part of the lesson I learned gave me the knowledge that a selfish woman, or man, can talk about love, but if they're dishonest it's all bullshit. The worst part of the lesson was admitting the mistake was mine and I had only myself to blame. I fell in love with a woman who could only see the world, including me, with an awareness based on her short-term needs. She loved me, but her love for me had room for an occasional romp with another guy. Yes, the love of my life was described best in a quote from Hamlet, *one may smile, and smile and be a villain.*" She was dishonest with me as well as herself, and that made for the worst kind of *villain.* I didn't see it until it was too late and became determined to never make that mistake again—even if it means remaining, deep down, an ice-cold bastard.

I tossed the car keys on the counter at the back door and was headed to the refrigerator when I saw the note.

> She called 3 times this afternoon. Said she'd be here by seven. Harry you're loco. Meatloaf's in the fridge. Did you make any money today—a guy named Bert something called he'll meet you at the Fog something at 6:30.

Juanita you're priceless, I thought as I checked out the meatloaf she had prepared earlier in the day. "Did I make any money today?" Juanita believes in her heart there is something fundamentally wrong with a man that doesn't go to work everyday and get a paycheck every Friday. She has a vested interest in my ability to "put the beans on the stove," because it takes a lot of cash to keep two households going...hers and mine. She is in a constant fret that I'm deficit spending and we'll end up pan handling in the Mission District even though she has money of her own. Last month I located a Michael Parkes stone lithograph that set me back eight thousand, and Juanita sulked for a week. There are twelve Parkes stone lithos scattered throughout three floors of wall space in my house. There are also forty-two other pieces by various artists. She says, "At least we don't have to paint the walls, they're already covered."

Dinner would include cold meatloaf—sliced thin—along with slices of cheddar cheese, raw broccoli, melon, apple wedges and saltine crackers all served on a platter on the deck up under the overhang on the roof. Dressed warmly, Vanessa and I could relax and watch the inhabitants of my neighborhood rush to their own frenetic beat below us. A chilled Trefethen chardonnay would complement the food and, most likely, speed us along the path to bed. But first, I took the time to look through the stuff Junkie had given me and it didn't take long to catch it. I reached for the phone and dialed a number I was getting all too familiar with.

He answered on the first ring. "Junkie, it's me, Harry—I've got a quick question."

"Pope, we're all here and everybody's a mess. Peter and Sean are..."

"Junkie, tell them all to cool it," I interrupted. "I think this guy Brogger is starting to surmise Maggie's death is more than just a little suspicious, so we're making progress."

"I know but..." and his voice dropped to barely a whisper, "the boys are worried about the rest of the family—are the kids in danger—Sandy and Peter are calling Kate every fifteen minutes just to hear the sound of her voice. We're all spooked and a little bit scared."

"Junkie, tell everyone to calm down. But, I need some information."

"Okay, what do you need?"

I said, "Think back—how much cash did you and Maggie go through every week or two?"

"You mean cash, cash—as in greenbacks—or how much money we spent?"

"I mean cold hard cash."

"Very little," he said. "Maggie put everything she could on credit cards and paid everything else by check. The only time she needed cash was for valet parking and bridge tolls…and I don't need cash for much of anything."

"Maybe three or four hundred a month?" I asked.

"On second thought, more than that…I forgot about caddy fees. We spent that much on caddies, but that was probably our biggest cash outlay and I always took care of paying the caddies—and, I overpaid them. Nobody tips a caddy better than an ex-caddy."

"So, never more than, maybe, a grand a month?" I asked.

"At the most," he replied.

"That's what I need to know. I'll talk to you tomorrow," and before he could ask any more questions I hung up the phone. There was no one standing in front of me to see the puzzled look on my face as I wondered—why had Maggie O'Reilly written out checks to herself, for cash, that totaled over a hundred thousand dollars in just six months' time? More for Detective Brogger and I to talk about over coffee—if coffee was on his menu. The Fog Horn, down on the Embarcadero, made terrible coffee. But, if a gin Bloody Mary was the way to get your day started, the Fog Horn was the best place to do it.

11

"We could make love up here."

"Too tough on the knees."

"Just because I'm a sophisticated, uppity black woman doesn't mean I don't know how to be a cowgirl."

"Too tough on the back," I replied. A fat seagull sat on the railing of the deck eyeing us and darting quick glances at the last remnants of our food. A seagull is like a shark—they'll eat anything. This one had swallowed pieces of broccoli, cheese and apple—in rapid succession—as I tossed the last bits and pieces to the far edge of the deck. "I guess I could bring a mattress up here. Juanita would love that."

"Pope, don't get me started on that woman. You're blind…"

I held up my hand; signaling her to stop. "Vanessa, we've beat this to death and nothing is going to change. Juanita is, and has been for a long, long time, the only constant thing in my life. She's always there for me and she always will be. I will always be around for her, as well. I plan on taking very good care of her for the rest of her life. You don't know her like I do, so let's drop it."

"What about her kids? Why don't they take care of her?"

"It's a long story—and you know the story—why go over it again and again." I was getting impatient. "We agreed to disagree when it comes to Juanita—she has nothing to do with you and me, so let's drop it." I put my hand behind her neck and pulled her face to mine, "Did you say something about making love?"

Between the deck and the bed she had obviously decided to prove her ability at doing the cowgirl thing. I had the feeling, as she arched her back and took me deeper and deeper, that she had been thinking about this all day. "Pope, I love this. I fuckin' love it!" she screamed. She was moving faster and her hands were digging into the pillow behind my head. Soon she would start pulling at my hair. Afterward we lay on our backs with our heads propped on pillows and ate ice cream from the carton.

"Can you stay all night?"

"Yes, but promise you'll get me up early. I came straight here from the office and I need to get home in the morning and do the girl stuff so I can be in the office by eight thirty."

"If you had a normal, black woman 'doo' you could cut thirty minutes off your prep time in the morning," I said and immediately regretted it.

"There is no such thing as a normal, black woman 'doo'," she fired back. "We make a statement with our hair—and don't roll your eyes at me—we make a statement the same way you stuffed shirt 'crackers' make a statement with your yellow ties and Gucci loafers."

"I don't wear yellow ties," I interjected, "and I didn't say I don't like your hair. It's just…you always look wet."

"It's supposed to look wet you dummy," she fired back again. "It's a Jehri Curl and that's the look I want." Her eyes suddenly softened and she gave me the Ethel Mae grin, "'Course honey chile, jus' bein' roun' you makes me wet all over."

"I can't win," I whispered.

"You're no match for a superior black woman like me."

I nodded in mock surrender and asked, "Willie not checking up on you tonight?"

"He doesn't have time for me these days," she answered. "Don't get me wrong—I don't really care, but he's so wrapped up in the job he doesn't even know I exist."

"What's got him so busy?"

"I'm not sure. It's all a big hush-hush operation. He did tell me one big secret though." She paused and pretended to whisper in my ear, "The Secret Service is in town doing background checks on people all over the City." She laughed, "He wouldn't tell me why, but

Willie and his top aides have been running down every crook and jay-walker in the bay area—maybe the President is coming to town."

"If the President is coming to San Francisco, Willie will figure out a way to get his picture on the cover of Time magazine even if he has to create a crisis," I said. "But, I don't want to talk about Willie." I turned on my side, leaned down and gave her an ice cream kiss on her right nipple. My cold mouth had the desired effect.

"Oh!" she squealed, "I think somebody's happy to see you…don't be selfish, now you have to do the other one."

I did the other one and then discovered more things to do with Vanilla Swiss Almond ice cream than the people who make Hagen Dazs ever thought possible.

12

The clock blinked 5:00 just as I opened one eye and awakened. Vanessa lay next to me in her usual spread eagle position. She needed more than her share of the bed space with her legs spread and her hands tucked under the pillow behind her head—I've never seen anyone sleep that way—and she never moves. I reached under the covers and put my hand between her legs, feeling the warm wetness, and pulled her toward me.

"Don't even think about it, you pervert," she mumbled.

Only it came out "Don efin thin uh bow dit u puur furt."

"Then I have no choice but to throw your sweet ass out on the street," I said, and I pulled all the covers back and piled them at the foot of the bed. Six feet of long legs and slender torso scrunched into a tiny ball and began to yell obscenities at me.

I picked her off the bed and carried her into the master bath where I deposited her on the cold marble floor of the shower and turned on the water. At first the water was cold and she shrieked more obscenities. After a few minutes I looked in on her and she looked so delicious, all lathered in soap, I decided to join her. After she finished covering me in suds and noticing the result, it didn't take much convincing for her to play our game of "drop the soap." That's where I drop the soap in front of her and she bends over to pick it up and—well, you get the picture.

At exactly six o'clock I had her settled in the back of a City cab with a cup of black coffee, almost ready to face the day—but not before I got to pull one of my favorite stunts, the one that gets her every time. At the exact moment the cabbie looks back over his shoulder to make sure she's all buckled up, I flash a twenty-dollar bill, shove it in her hand, give her a quick kiss on the cheek and as I close the door, say in a loud voice, "Thanks for last night, baby—you were great!" Then, I sprint like hell for my front door. That morning was no exception—I got her again.

The Fog Horn is a small bar and restaurant located at the end of Bryant street almost directly under the overhead ramp to the Bay Bridge. The owner/operator is a former cop who did his twenty and bailed out. His girl friend does the cooking and it's only breakfast, but she'll cook it for you until she runs out of eggs, bacon or pancake mix. When she's out of the stuff to cook, she shuts down the grill, hits it with the sandstone and splits. Some of the time she splits by nine o'clock in the morning, other days she's there until after lunch. If you want a fried egg sandwich or a bacon and egg sandwich you'll get two eggs on a platter with toast on the side. Don't pretend to be Jack Nicholson and do the 5 Easy Pieces restaurant scene—she'll throw you out of the joint and you can't ever come back.

I parked the Lincoln in the lot next to the Fog Horn, tight up against one of the wooden railroad ties that prevent the drunks from driving into the bay. The lot was empty. No government issue Ford or Chevy that might belong to Detective Brogger was evident, but I was a few minutes early.

Nick was pulling the chairs off the tables and arranging them four-up in the room next to the bar. The Fog Horn consisted of two rooms in the front separated by the bar. One side of the bar is for eating the other side for drinking—after about two o'clock in the afternoon both sides are for drinking. Nick's girlfriend had fired up the grill and was sorting through the day's allotment of provisions.

"Hey Pope, long time no see, how you doin'?"

"I'm doing good, Nick—how's the biz'?"

Nick paused. "Ya know, I don't know—if that makes sense. The fuckers over at city hall raised my rent again, the bastards. I own an apartment house up on Diamond Court and I can't raise the rent on the units cuz' of the fuckin' rent control, but those bastards raise my rent every fuckin' year cuz' the city owns the fuckin' waterfront. I'm back to runnin' two cash registers again—one for me and one for the fuckin' government—it's the only way I can make it." He paused again, wrinkling his nose like he just smelled something bad and asked, "You eatin' or drinkin'?"

"I'm eating. Tell Janice to give me three scrambled, some well-done hash browns and bacon on a separate plate."

"Pope, you fuckin' tell her. But, it won't change nuthin', you'll get it all on one plate and the hash browns will be crisp and if you don't like it she'll tell us both to go fuck ourselves."

"Nick, with all due respect, she's got to be the greatest piece of ass in the world for you to put up with her."

Nick laughed out loud. "Nah, the only reason I keep her around is she works cheap."

"I can hear both of you assholes," a voice from the kitchen yelled back, "and Pope, if that's you talkin', why don't you go up to the Mark Hopkins, where you belong, and have eggs benedict with foo-foo sauce."

"Hey Janice, you know I love you," I yelled back at her just as Detective Bert Brogger walked through the front door.

As he walked over to greet me I saw Nick grab a mason jar from under the bar, pour four fingers of Bombay gin over a couple of ice cubes, mix in some tomato juice, celery salt, Worcestershire, a dash of Tabasco and set it on the bar next to me. "Mornin' Bert," he said. "You guys know each other?"

"Nick, what's happening?" Bert took a long pull off his Bloody Mary, shuddered and pointed to a table in the corner. "Harry let's sit at a table so we can stretch out." As he walked toward the table in the corner he turned to Nick and muttered, "Yeah, we're old buddies."

"How do you know Nick?" he asked.

"I was just about to ask you the same question," I replied.

"We used to work together when I was with the cops in the City. How about you?"

"Nick saved my ass one time when I was hustling some guys who thought they were good poker players and…"

"Wait a sec'," Bert took another big hit on the Mason jar, raised it over his head and signaled to Nick to bring another one. Continuing with me he said, "Mister outstanding citizen, Harrison Pius, a card shark hustler—I don't believe it."

"Believe it, Bert—but, that was in my youth and Nick came to my rescue and we've been friends ever since."

Nick put another bloody in front of Bert and slid my breakfast, all on one plate, in front of me. He looked at me and said, "If the potatoes aren't done enough don't say one fuckin' word."

I nodded, indicating that keeping my mouth shut was probably a good idea as Nick walked back behind the bar to take care of a couple of rowdy longshoremen who had just barged in. "Okay. Detective Brogger what's happening that gets you up so early and out of your jurisdiction?"

"For one thing, when I'm out of my jurisdiction, on my day off, my shit-bird Captain can't count the bloodies. Plus, this whole Maggie O'Reilly business is starting to have the faint aroma of monkey shit and I want you to get some information for me from the family and I told you, call me Bert."

"Okay Bert, why me? They'll cooperate with you—just ask them."

He shrugged and said, "I'm not ready to give them everything, yet. If I start asking them about some stuff I'm curious about, they may clam up." He took another hit on his Bloody Mary, settled back in his chair and shuddered. "This thing could get messy."

"Why would they clam up?" I asked. "And, yeah, you're right, except this thing is already messy—why don't you tell me what's goin' on."

"First, let me ask you a question." Bert stared off in the direction of Nick and I thought he was going to raise the Mason jar in the air again. Instead he got Nick's attention and pointed at my coffee cup. Nick got the message and brought him a hot steaming mug and me a refill. "You know anything about a drug named Rohypnol?" he asked.

"Not a clue," I replied.

"How about roofies?"

"Same answer—what are you getting at?"

"A good lookin' guy like you wouldn't know about roofies, but it's become the date rape drug of choice by assholes who can't get laid on their own."

He saw the look of confusion on my face and went on. "When Rohypnol, or a 'Roofie' as it's known on the street, is combined with booze, grass or cocaine it can produce a king size high and there's no trace and no odor. There are literally thousands of young girls walking around who have been gang banged and they never knew it. They wake up somewhere with no clothes on, in strange surroundings and realize they've been sexually assaulted, but don't know who did it or how many might have been involved."

Bert looked at me as if anticipating my question and continued. "A roofie is pretty much the same as Valium, only twenty times stronger, and once it wears off it's almost impossible to trace."

"If someone takes a roofie," I asked, "how long does it take to kick in?"

Detective Brogger reached in his jacket pocket and unfolded a single sheet of paper. "I jotted down some notes when I talked to the Medical Examiner." Glancing at the sheet of paper he continued, "The M.E. said a roofie, in twenty minutes' time, can produce loss of muscle control and all the symptoms of being drunk as a skunk—and, get this—it can cause respiratory depression, which can kill you."

My plate was almost empty and I wanted a cigarette. After breakfast is the only time I still crave a Pall Mall. After ten years you'd think the urge would go away. "You think Maggie O'Reilly died from a roofie?" I asked.

"Right now I don't know what to think," he replied. "But, some things are starting to suggest her husband may not be as far off base as we thought." He signaled Nick with the Mason jar, which meant another Bloody Mary was in his future. Then he came out of left field with a question. "You know where Newcastle is?"

"England or Ireland?" I asked with sudden irritation, and then said. "C'mon detective, you're tap dancing through the raindrops here—why don't you quit playing games and just lay it all out."

The detective watched Nick as he put another Bloody in front of him and turned his attention back to me. "Gavin—the guy we fished out of the bay—is from Newcastle, Northern Ireland." He ran his fingers through his thinning hair, made a face and asked, "Pius, why are you smiling?"

"Bert, I play golf—it's my passion in life and I'm pretty damned good at it and I love great courses," I said. "I've played golf all over the world—from Pebble Beach to Saint Andrews in Scotland—and if I only had one round of golf left to play in my life it would be at Royal County Down Links in Newcastle, Northern Ireland." I paused and added, "I've been there dozens of times."

"So, you know the area and the question is, why would Maggie O'Reilly give a guy from bum-fuck-nowhere Ireland five thousand dollars, and her family doesn't know about it and we don't..."

"Probably more," I said.

"What do you mean—more than what?"

"More than five thousand dollars. Maybe more like one hundred thousand." I looked behind me and signaled Nick for more coffee. "I went through Maggie's bank statements last night and I can tell you she wrote checks made out to cash for almost a hundred thousand bucks over the last six months and they were all in increments of five thousand."

"Did you ask her husband about the cash?" he asked and his voice took on a tone of surprise. "Holy shit! You think she was giving all that money away, too? Maybe to this Gavin guy?"

"You know Bert you're really starting to piss me off," I said angrily. "I know I'm a rookie in this whole mess, but you're fuckin' with me. Quit playing like the dumb cop."

Before he could respond I laid it out. "You lay this 'roofie' business on me and don't explain, and now we've jumped all the way over to Northern Ireland. Next thing you'll be saying 'golly gee' and slap yourself in the forehead. Why don't we put all of it out in front and look at it together. I make my living being logical and cutting through the crap, so don't bullshit me."

There was a long pause and I knew he was trying to make up his mind about how far he was going to let me in. Finally he said, "Okay, I think I can trust your judgment—here's what we know," and he held up his right hand, stretching his fingers to use as a counting guide.

"One—she leaves the house dressed in slacks and sweater and says she's going to play golf later in the day."

"Two—she stops by her office and says 'hi' to her two boys and leaves around noon."

"Three—at one forty-eight she signs a charge slip on her Nordstrom credit card for a sweater, a dress and a couple of tennis outfits; expensive stuff, the charge was over six hundred bucks."

"Four—shortly after she leaves Nordstrom she has some lunch. We don't know where she ate or if she was with somebody."

"Five—sometime around six o'clock a couple of hang glider types discover her in her car and she's deader than Canseco's nuts."

He was out of fingers and it gave me a chance to jump in. "And she was wearing the dress she had just bought at Nordstrom's."

"And mister private eye," he interrupted. "Where was the sweater and slacks she was wearing when she left the house that morning? And maybe, just maybe—somebody started her off with a roofie for lunch and when she was almost comatose they poured a fifth of gin down her, mixed with fifty Valium."

"Can you trace the roofie?"

"Only if you're looking for it. With Maggie O'Reilly there was so much Valium the forensics guys didn't go any further." He looked around as if someone might be listening and took a big gulp of his bloody. "Harry, here's where it gets messy. This guy Gavin was alive when he went in the water and he drowned." He took a sip this time and looked at his notes again. "But, the M.E. found traces of a benzodiazepine tranquilizer in his stomach that could have been a roofie."

"So, somebody slips him a roofie and drops him in the bay. Neat," I said.

"Too neat," he said. "Two people connected only by a five thousand dollar money order and they're both dead and it looks like both of them may have been drugged."

"What have you found out about Gavin?"

"Not a goddam' thing," he answered quickly. "Nada, zip, nothing! We don't have a car. We don't have an address in the states—nothing. The only reason we think he's from Ireland is he had an identification label sewn on the inside of his jacket printed with the name Tommy Gavin, and an address in Newcastle, Northern Ireland."

"Let's hope the jacket he was wearing belonged to him." I said.

He smirked at my comment and said, "You're starting to think like a detective."

I thought about that. "Yeah, but now I'm stumped—I'm not sure what to do next."

Bert shrugged and his mood darkened. He said, "For me the next move is simple—I'm going to eat that last piece of toast on your plate, if you don't mind. Then I'm going to call my ex and see what she has planned that will fuck-up my day with my son."

"You have a son?"

"Yeah, he's only three, but he's a great little guy and we have a lot of fun together when I don't have the bitch from hell beating the shit out of me." His eyes were downcast and he seemed to sink further in his chair. "I only get him two days a month and she acts like I'm going to run off to Mexico with him."

"What happened?—No, wait—I think I can guess."

I hit his hot button. The half eaten piece of toast dropped to the table and his dead eyes came alive. "Mister hot shot, you can't guess a fuckin' thing!" His voice boomed across the room and it got very quiet. I thought he was going to take a swing at me and out of the corner of my eye I saw Nick on the move.

"Bert listen to me," Nick was speaking in measured tones with his finger pressed firmly on the detective's chest. "You and I go way back and the Pope and I go way back. But, you've got problems and he doesn't—and your problems don't belong in my place, so back off. I don't baby-sit your drinks, but I guess I should—I keep thinkin' you're gonna' get over all the shit you've brought on yourself—maybe you'll never grow up."

Nick stepped back. He continued, "The last time this happened I threw you out and it cost me a fifty dollar cab ride to get you home—I don't want to go there again."

Bert put his hands in the air, in mock surrender, and nodded slowly. "Hey man, you're right—you're right." He turned and facing me said, "Sorry about that Harry—I was outta' line."

The tension drained out of my shoulders and my clenched fist relaxed. I reached across the table and patted his hand, which surprised me more than it did him. I liked Detective Bert Brogger, but I could see he was another one of the dark people about to slide into my life. "Why don't you have some eggs to go with my toast, drink a couple of cups of coffee, go for a walk down the pier and then call your ex-wife," I said.

Nick beat me to the punch. I no sooner had suggested a couple of eggs than he put a platter of eggs, bacon, potatoes and toast in front of Bert. "All of this stuff, except the booze, is on the house—it's cheaper than a cab ride. And Bert, I want you to remember somethin'." Nick pointed a beefy finger in my direction. "The Pope is a stand-up guy. If you're ever walkin' down a dark alley you want him with you." Nick waited for a response from Bert and got a flicker of a smile in return. He turned abruptly and walked back behind the bar. He must have winked at Janice because I saw her smile as he walked by.

"Bert, I've got my regular Friday afternoon golf game at the club later today, but if you hear anything more about Tommy Gavin let me know—call me on my cell phone." I walked over to the bar and threw a twenty and two fives at Nick and said, "I'm only doing my part to help with the rent."

Nick gave me a big grin and said, "Pope, you're a prince."

I circled back to Bert as he was wolfing down the last of his breakfast. "Have a good time with your little boy today." He smiled broadly and I realized the mention of "little boy" was his warm and fuzzy button.

I headed for the front and was surprised when a warm gust of air greeted me as I passed through the door. The weather in San Francisco is anybody's guess.

I pointed the old fart cart back up Bryant Street and headed for home.

13

Juanita was making bread pudding and the kitchen smelled of vanilla and nutmeg. Bread pudding is an art form that begs for simplicity. Just stale bread, cream, raisins, walnuts, and chunks of butter, vanilla, and nutmeg arranged neatly in a buttered Pyrex bowl and baked for about an hour at 375 degrees. The bowl must rest in the oven—and this is the important part—rest in a pan with an inch of water in it. Her bread pudding is one more thing that contributes to Juanita's place in my heart.

"Where you been?" She looked up from the morning *Chronicle* and before I could answer she said, "I changed your sheets." She made a face, "I don't like the way that woman smells—your bed smelled like a gypsy sleeping bag."

I made a face back. "I don't know what a gypsy sleeping bag smells like and if you're half the woman I think you are, you don't either—and Vanessa is the tidiest woman I've ever known, so let it alone for awhile."

"You and your "tidy"—your one true love was tidy and look what it got you." She saw the look on my face and quickly changed the subject. "You home for dinner? I'm making enchiladas to go with bread pudding for dessert."

"My darling, I wouldn't miss it for the world, especially if you dine with me—are you going to make a batch?"

"I've got enough fixins to make six dozen, so we'll have them in the freezer for awhile. Yeah, I'll be here."

That brought a smile back to my face. Even with a belly full of breakfast, I was getting hunger pangs. I headed for the stairs and she called after me, "A guy, said his name was 'Junie' or somethin' like that, called a little while ago and wants you to call him back."

"I'm going to change clothes—I've got a game later—then I'll call him," I said, "and his name is Junkie."

I threw on a pair of khakis, a gray polo golf shirt and a cashmere sweater that had a Ballybunion logo on the sleeve and headed back to the kitchen. The bread pudding was cooling on a rack and Juanita was intently lathering her special sauce on flour tortillas that she had filled with seasoned ground beef, grated cheese, chopped onions and olives, then rolled and crimped at both ends. Twelve aluminum trays each had six enchiladas nestled tightly together and they would be covered with tin foil and go in the freezer, except for the six she would re-heat for our dinner. I grabbed the Boxster keys off the hook at the back door and started down the stairs to the garage.

"Don't forget to call Junie," she yelled at my back.

I caught Junkie just as he was leaving his house. He answered the phone obviously out of breath. "Hey Pope, I was hoping it was you."

"You sound like you're in a hurry—want me to call back later—after I play golf?" Just as I said that the phone slipped out from between my shoulder and ear and fell at my feet. Driving a five speed sports car and talking on a cell phone is tough—probably should be against the law. I shouted back in the phone, "Junkie, you still there?"

"Yeah, but I gotta' go. We're on our way to Palo Alto to talk to a guy that may have a line on Gavin."

"Who's 'we' and what 'guy'?"

"Me, Peter and Sean. Remember Tarzan?"

"Junkie?"

"I know, I know—I'm rambling. Let me start over."

"Hold on I'm pullin' over." Thinking I should have called him from home, I nosed the Boxster into the Burger King parking lot at the foot of Army Street, killed the engine and said, "Okay, start over."

"Remember the little Mexican guy that caddied for years at the club and we called him Tarzan?" Junkie said. "We called him Tarzan because he never wore anything but a white tee shirt, no matter how cold it was, and old Tommy Larkin would tease him about who did he think he was—Tarzan?"

"Vaguely," I replied.

"Well, no matter," he said. "He and I got to be pretty good friends, hangin' out in the caddy yard, and after Maggie and I got married he used to caddy for us. Maggie liked him and would ask for him all the time when she played with her girlfriends. Well, he quit caddying a couple of years ago and he's a janitor at a grammar school over in East Palo Alto—he called me this morning."

With the top down it was warm in the sun and I got out and leaned against the side of the car. Two teen-age girls walked by and gave me big smiles. They both had shiny braces and rubber bands on their teeth and were obviously impressed—with the car, not me. I suddenly felt old.

"So what's up with Tarzan?"

"He called me this morning because he had just heard about Maggie and he wanted to tell me how sorry he was." Junkie paused and took a deep breath, "Well, after one thing and another, I mentioned that a guy named Tommy Gavin might be tied to her death and you won't believe what he said next."

"Junkie," I said impatiently. "I'm growing old while you drag this out."

"Pope," he exclaimed, "Tarzan knew the guy! He says Gavin caddied a few times at the club about two years ago and then moved back to Ireland. We're goin' over to talk to Tarzan—as soon as I get through with you, we're leaving."

"Junkie, if I was a 'for real' private eye, right about now I would be saying—this is the break we've been waiting for."

"Ya' never know," he said. "It could be nuthin', call me when you get off the golf course and I'll let you know what Tarzan had to say. Gotta' go…" and he hung up the phone.

My chip shot skidded across the smooth surface of the eighteenth green and came to rest twenty-five feet from the hole—a bad shot. From the edge of a green I can hit a shot to less than three feet nine out of ten times—that afternoon was not one of my good days. I was dangerously close to losing about six hundred dollars to my nemesis Gerry Murphy.

"Harrison, my boy, if you've got a weak heart you'd better not watch this," he yelled out. And with that he set his putter behind the ball, took his jerky little stroke and boldly jabbed a thirty-foot putt, with a left to right slope of at least four feet, solidly into the bottom of the hole. That made it seven hundred dollars.

"That," he exclaimed, "is the name of the game." And without so much as a glance back in my direction he high-fived his partner, Jack Swift, and strode briskly away.

My partner, Jim Broome, shrugged his shoulders in my direction and said, "Hey Pope we gotta' let them win once in a while or they'd never come back."

"I don't mind losing," I said. "But I hate losing to Gerry Murphy."

Our regular Friday afternoon golf date was over and I had been so preoccupied with the morning's events I scarcely remembered a shot played. My breakfast with Detective Brogger had left me unnerved and as the day wore on I had developed an uneasy awareness of the complexities of the man and his demons. I felt I should have called him immediately with the news about Junkie and his friend Tarzan, but I didn't want to intrude on his day with his little boy. Not very professional on my part, I thought, but what the hell, I'm not a professional private eye anyway. I followed Jim and the caddies up the winding brick path behind the eighteenth green that led to the back door of the men's locker room.

I thought about showering, decided against it, found my street shoes freshly shined by Gene the locker room attendant, retrieved my watch and money clip from my locker and headed for the men's grill. I went down the stairs past the showers, detoured around the indoor swimming pool and bumped into a very wet Tony Minetti as he emerged from the shallow end.

"Murphy got you again, huh?" He exclaimed, "A forty-footer on eighteen—amazing!"

I smiled—word had traveled fast, all the way to the pool. Gerry was telling everybody he had gotten in the Pope's shorts for seven fun tickets and he was livin' large. The thirty-foot putt had increased in length to forty feet in less than fifteen minutes. By tomorrow it would be fifty feet with a triple break.

"Tony," I said, "Gerry is a definite piece of work."

"Yeah," Tony agreed. "It's bad enough that he's so fuckin' rich and acts like he owns the joint, but now that he's on the Grounds Committee, he's an even bigger pain in the ass."

Tony saw the look on my face and read it right.

"Ha! You don't know do you?" Before I could answer he said, "Yeah the Grounds—he'll spend the Clubs money so fast we'll be swimming in assessments."

"I'll try and keep him under control," I said. I turned away and walked to the double-door marked MEN'S GRILL stepped through and made my way between the gin-rummy games to the large table under the bay window. Before I sat down I took my money clip from my back pocket, peeled off seven fun tickets and placed them in a neat row in front of Gerry Murphy. If he sat at the table for two hours or two days he wouldn't touch the money until he left the room—it would remain in front of him so everyone could see it. Behind me the feeble, rail-thin form of Archie appeared with a tray full of drinks and my Talisker on the rocks was the first drink he served.

Gerry snorted and his dark side suddenly emerged. "You know Archie, you've got your little pets and some of us you treat like trash—I was here ten minutes before he was and he gets served before I do. I know your game and I don't like it—you could be replaced."

It was embarrassingly silent around the table as Archie continued to place drinks in front of the group. "As you wish, Mister Murphy," he replied and winked at me as he walked away.

I sipped my first drink of the day. Talisker should be sipped and savored and no amount of bad behavior by Gerry was going to spoil it for me. "Back off, Gerry," I said. "Archie is seventy years old and he was in charge of this room when you were pounding nails on your first house in the Avenues. He'll have a place at this club until he dies or retires. You can't touch him because there are three hundred members here and two hundred and ninety nine of us love him. So shut the fuck up!"

He saw the look in my eye and changed the subject.

Gerry is only ten years my senior and looks old enough to be my father. He's got a round red face topped with a full mane of snow white hair, but his eyebrows are black and long enough to comb. He's what you would call craggy—he always looks like he just came in out of a windstorm. He eats too much, drinks too much and smokes too many cigars. Plus, his penchant for young girls costs him a small fortune and keeps him in constant hot water with the long-suffering Mrs. Murphy. Fortunately, he has a large fortune and she has spent most of her adult life forgiving Gerry's weakness for young stuff. When the water gets excessively hot, he comes up with a diamond ring, bracelet or earrings and all is peaceful for a while.

He scooped the seven bills off the table and waving a ham-sized fist in my direction said, "I'm going to take a couple of these and take you to the Oyster House for dinner."

I took a long, slow sip of Talisker. "Gerry, you're tempting me—they've had fresh abalone on the menu for three weeks running, but I can't make it tonight. Juanita's expecting me for dinner and I'm beat. Out with you tonight and I'd be worthless tomorrow and I've got a lot of people to see and I need to be sharp."

Gerry dismissed my excuses with a wave of his hand and persisted. "Call that crazy Mexican and tell her to feed it to the cat. I'm talkin' the Oyster, man!"

"No," I said firmly. "You might want to hang on to some of your winnings, because I'm getting it back, with interest, when we play on

Wednesday—we're still on for a rematch, right?" I looked around the table and Jack Swift and Jim Broome nodded their heads approvingly.

Gerry grinned and slapped the green cushioned table, then took in a bushel of air and exclaimed, "Pope, you and Mr. Broome here are dead meat."

Broome and Swift had grown tired of Gerry and got up to leave. I wanted to leave as well but Gerry grabbed my wrist and shook his head as if he had something important to say. "Archie," he bellowed, "bring Mr. Pius another scotch and bring me another 'woodie'."

"Gerry I'll have one more and then I've got to go."

"Yeah, me too. If you won't have dinner with me I'll go home and surprise the wife—maybe take her out—make her feel good."

"You're a real prince, Gerry."

He smiled and changed the subject. "What ya' got goin' on that makes you busy on a Saturday—you could get in the sweeps tomorrow morning—we might even be partners."

"No, this business with Maggie O'Reilly has taken a different turn," I said. "I'm starting to think it might be more than a simple suicide." I added, "Junkie may be right after all," and immediately regretted saying it. Gerry has a big mouth and I didn't want him shouting to everybody in the club that Maggie might have been murdered.

"Pope, why are you getting involved in this mess—you're gonna' end up lookin' like a fool." He looked at me briefly and then looked away, seemingly lost in thought for just a moment. "You can't be doin' it for the money. Hell, man, you can make a grand a day playing gin with guys you don't know—nobody in this club will play cards with you—but, you can always find some action someplace."

I finished my drink and stood up to leave. "Gerry there's a lot more going on with this situation than I can talk about and I'd appreciate if you didn't talk it up—just let it lie and someday I'll tell you all about it."

He swirled the last of the gin and ice in his glass, tilted his massive head back and swallowed deeply. "Okay, but you're still pokin' around where you don't belong."

We said our goodbyes and went for our cars. It was only about six o'clock and the parking lot was almost empty. The fog had rolled in and what had been a soft afternoon breeze had turned to a stiff, wet wind that was typical of a San Francisco Bay Area summer evening. San Francisco is the only city in the world where you use your windshield wipers more in the summer than in the winter. The kid in the parking lot brought the Boxster up the narrow drive—a little too fast—pulled under the awning, jumped out and held the door open. "Steve, I promised to loan you this car for your graduation weekend, but you're starting to worry me."

"Oh, Mr. Pius you don't have to worry about me," he said. "If I ever get this beauty out on the street I'll treat it, like, sweet."

I hit him with a five and crawled in. I was tired and the thought of enchiladas, fruit salad, cold beer and bread pudding for dessert was going to make the drive home easier. I punched the button on the radio and tuned in the Giants game. They were losing to the Reds in the seventh at Cincinnati. I switched to the A's. They were losing to the Royals. Today was turning into a loser all around. I switched to KJAZ just in time to hear Nina Simone swinging to *Love Me or Leave Me* with her own accompaniment. Too bad Nina let being constantly pissed-off get in the way of her career.

14

I was thinking a shower before bed would feel good when the phone rang the first time. Out of habit I let it ring—if my phone rings after eleven in the evening it won't get answered. I had just gotten back in the house after walking Juanita down the back stairs and through our shared gate to her back door. I had been preoccupied all evening with conflicting thoughts about Maggie, Junkie, a man named Tommy Gavin, and my concern for the problems of a detective I barely knew. I was regretting not answering the phone thinking it might have been Junkie when it rang again. I grabbed it on the first ring and said "Hello."

"Harrison, please don't hang up the phone."

The long day collapsed on top of me. I sat on the edge of the bed and tried not to answer the voice on the other end. My brain was screaming at me to run and my heart caved in—"Hello Julie," I said.

"Oh Harrison, thank you! Thank you!"

It all came out in a rush and I interrupted, "Julie, what do you want?"

"If I could only have what I want—if only—I would be with you this very minute. I would snap my fingers and all the hurt and misery I brought into our life would disappear. I would..."

"Stop it—please stop. You can't undo the past."

Her voice softened to almost a whisper. "Harrison, I can make it up to you—I know I can. Please give me a chance."

"I gave you a chance. I gave you ten chances!" I exclaimed.

"I know. I know you did and I was stupid—I was so stupid Harrison. Please, I..."

"Julie, it's late and I'm tired." I paused and realized I suddenly had a splitting headache. "We've gone over this a thousand times and the result is the same—you want me to forgive and forget and I will never, ever forget."

There was a heart stopping silence. In the past she had torn my insides out and served it all up to me on a platter. But, I knew she had hurt herself as well, in ways even she didn't understand. The difference was I "got it" and she didn't. "Julie, I'm not going to hang up on you, but I am going to end this conversation. Goodnight." I hung up the phone and headed for the basement and my cave.

The basement garage is accessible from the stairs at the rear of the kitchen or from the back at the end of the flagstone driveway that curves around the side of the house. In the corner, beyond where the cars are parked, is a small ten by twelve foot corner room where I can hide. It is a windowless enclave with walls painted in muted sienna hues with a floor of rough green slate. The floor is partially covered by an oval braided rug and dominated by a well-worn brown leather coach. Above the couch Aldo Luongo's *The Good Life* serigraph hangs next to a signed Chagall that came to me as a payoff after a three-day poker game last year in New Orleans. Along the long wall is a floor to ceiling, custom-built cabinet containing an audio-visual entertainment system and a hundred and sixteen bottles of rare single malt scotch.

I grabbed a crystal glass and a bottle of Bowmore and collapsed on the couch. The only person ever allowed in my cave, other than Juanita, was the long-lost Julie. I lost myself in the memory.

Juanita crossed her arms and shaking her head said, "You slept downstairs." She pulled a chair away from the kitchen table and gestured for me to sit. "I'll fix you some breakfast—you need it." She added, "Harry stay out of that room."

I didn't answer and reached for the cup of coffee she put in front of me. Juanita didn't like silence in the kitchen. She wanted conversation, laughter and good food—and if the Bose was cranking out her favorite Basie tunes she would dance and sing—and I loved it, but not today.

"That guy Junkie called while you were in the shower, says to call him on his cell—I wrote the number down."

"Did he say anything else?"

"Jus' call as soon as you can."

I asked, "Did he sound like it was urgent—was he upset?"

"Harry, I don't know," she said dismissively. "You want scrambled or fried?"

"Scrambled, but I'm going to call Junkie first," I replied.

She poured cream in a bowl with the eggs and began to stir the mixture quickly. "Ya' got five minutes then get back in here—I wanna' get some food in you."

I took the handset in the dayroom and called Junkie's cell phone. "Junkie, it's Harry."

"Hold on," he said, and I could hear other voices, then silence and a voice in the background say my name. "Yeah, it's him—Harry, is there any way we can get together today—I think we need to bring you up to date."

"What's goin' on?"

"We're at the South City substation with Detective Brogger." He paused and said, "Hang on, he wants to talk to you."

A voice that sounded crisp and businesslike said, "Harry, it's Bert Brogger—can you get down here, right away?"

"I can probably get there in about an hour, but what's going on?" and I added, "Who's there?"

"I've got the whole family with me. We'll go next door and grab a cup of coffee while we wait for you to get here—hurry up—remember, we're just off Grand Avenue."

I wolfed down three eggs, bacon and a mound of cottage cheese and felt much better as a result. Juanita stood over me and watched every bite, occasionally rubbing my shoulder. When she knew I had Julie on my mind she became motherly and protective. "I'll be gone most of the day, but I'll be home for dinner," I said. "I think Vanessa will be here, so you might want to see if there's a movie you want to go and see."

She made a face and nodded. "You spend the night buried in a bottle because of a bad woman and now you've got another bad one coming over tonight." She shrugged her shoulders and sighed, "I'll see if Stella wants to go see that George Clooney movie that has the Puerto Rican girl with the big butt in it."

"You mean J. Lo?" I asked.

"Yeah that's her." She laughed and continued, "I'll go to the market and get a couple of steaks and some fresh broccoli—you can cook for yourselves—course, I know she can't boil water, so you'll have to do it all without any help from her."

"You're a tough old broad, and I love you madly," I said emphatically and gave her a bear hug.

She hugged me back and seemed not to want to let go, then swatted me on the backside and said, "Get outta' here—and drive slow!"

I headed for the stairs and turned back to see her beautiful brown face smiling back at me. The sweet, beautiful smile that, over the next few weeks, would haunt me, and then propel me into a complex world of intrigue.

15

Outside the fog had burned away and, with the top down on the Boxster, the blast of cold air on a San Francisco morning, combined with Juanita's tasty breakfast, brushed away the last of my vapors. I went down Army Street and caught the 101 south. The morning rush was over and I got to the Grand Avenue exit in twenty minutes and headed west. The police station was on a corner across from a small park that was full of Saturday morning dads pushing little kids on the swings. Next to the park was a coffee shop that had an OPEN sign in the corner of the front window—if they were at the coffee shop 'next door' this was probably the one, I thought. I was right, they were all seated around a large circular table in the rear and Junkie caught my eye as I stepped through the front.

"Pope! Over here!" Junkie exclaimed. They were all there, including Bert Brogger, and everyone had plates of food in front of them. Junkie waved in the direction of two people I hadn't met, but assumed were Sean O'Reilly and his wife. "Harrison Pius, say hello to Susan and Sean," he said.

Rather than reach across the table I gave a perfunctory wave and grabbed a chair from an adjoining table and moved it closer. Sean O'Reilly was smaller than his brother. Not shorter, but smaller, all the way around. Other than that they could have been twins—the same blue eyes, dark hair and college boy good looks. Susan, on the other hand, was something else. My grandpa had an expression along the lines of "plain as a mud fence." Well I've never seen a mud fence, but Sean's Susan fit the description. She was a five-foot, hundred and twenty pound package and looked ten years younger than Sean. But, it took me only a few seconds to understand why he married her—she was captivating. At first glance you would have thought her to be a pudgy teenager. She had short brown hair—stuck to her head in tight little curls—firm white skin, a tiny waist, green eyes that sparkled in every direction and a little girl grin that seemed to say, "yes Mr. Pius I've never met you, but I know everything about you…you have no secrets from me." She was the only one in the group that stood as I approached the table and she reached around her husband's back and grasped my hand. Her hand was extraordinarily warm and she held mine an extra, awkward moment, all the while staring directly in my eyes. I had spent two hours with Peter's wife, Sandy, who had movie star looks and I never thought about her sexually. All I could think about, looking at Susan, was what she might be like in bed. Plus, she had honest to goodness dimples in her cheeks.

Detective Brogger broke into my naughty thoughts, "Harry we're almost finished here—you want coffee?"

I shook my head no and noticed that, other than Susan, the group seemed to be in a very somber mood. Maybe they were starting to come to grips with the fact that their mother might have been murdered. "I'll walk across the street and wait on the bench in front of the station—let me know when you're finished," I said.

"We'll only be a few more minutes, Harry," Detective Brogger said in a gritty, no-nonsense voice that I hadn't heard him use before.

I strolled out of the coffee shop and crossed the street to sit on the bench in the sun. Almost on cue, a skinny little guy who slid in next to me wanted to know if I had any spare change. He didn't smell bad, but he looked terrible—it looked like someone had hit him in the face with a waffle iron and he didn't have any hair. In these politically correct times he would be described as a 'non-goal-oriented member of society'…you and I would call him a bum. But, the purple bruises on his bare arms and the crusted sores around his ears and on his bare head gave it away—he was a bum with AIDS.

"Have you had anything to eat today?" I asked.

He shook his head and made a sound I didn't get.

"Come with me," I said. He reluctantly followed me back across the street and he hesitated at the entrance to the coffee shop as I held the door open. "Come on, it's okay."

Junkie, his family and the detective were settling up with the cashier as I walked by. We made our way to the back corner table through a room full of patrons at first hostile, and then frightened by this modern day leper. A three hundred pound blob of fat and muscle rushed out of the kitchen and shoved a hand in my chest.

Before I could react a voice behind me said in a quiet, but almost vicious tone, "Mick, don't even think about it."

I turned and Bert Brogger said to me, "Go ahead Harry and do whatever it is you're going to do—and Mick, you get your fat ass back in the kitchen." He turned to leave and said over his shoulder, "We'll wait for you Harry, but hurry up."

I deposited my "economically non-affluent" friend at the small table next to the entrance to the kitchen and waved for the nearest waitress. A reluctant redhead who had obviously failed charm school sashayed over and said, "What'll it be?"

I reached for my money clip and said, "Here's the drill." I handed her two twenties and continued, "Bring him all the food this twenty bucks will buy and the other one's for you."

Her mood changed at the sight of the money and she shoved both twenties in her apron pocket. "You joining him?" she asked.

"No," I answered. "I'll be across the street in a meeting with Detective Brogger, but I'll be back to look in on my friend here." Then I added, "I'll check in on you, too." I turned and walked away and didn't look back.

I retraced my route to the police station and was greeted by the uniform on duty. He thumb waved me in the direction of a narrow, windowless hallway and said, "They're waiting for you—first door on the right."

I didn't knock and as I entered the room I was greeted by six voices all talking at once. It got very quiet and Junkie got in the first word. "Harry, just in time—we were talking about you."

All eyes were on me, especially Susan's, and I felt like I was supposed to say something important. "Hey, I'm here at Detective Brogger's request and I'm curious about what we know about Tommy Gavin."

They all started in again and Brogger held up his hand and in a brusque voice commanded, "Everybody shut up!" He went on, "I'm going to make quick work of this, so I want all of you to keep quiet and listen."

We all stared at him for a few seconds, waiting for him to speak. "Harry, you're not up to speed on the information we got from this guy Tarzan—we didn't get much." He sighed and continued. "We know that Tommy Gavin first showed his face out at your country club about a year ago and his appearance coincided with the withdrawals that Mrs. O'Reilly began to make from her checking account."

Junkie interrupted, "But we don't…"

"Mr. Morrison, cool it." Brogger demanded. I could see his patience was just about gone. "We know that he went back to Ireland shortly after Mrs. O'Reilly died, stayed for about three months, and just recently returned to the states. We know that on his first trip to the States he would, from time to time, caddy for Mrs. O'Reilly and seemed to take a particular interest in her affairs."

Brogger had restored order in the room and seemed to have everyone's attention—he had mine. "Tarzan," he explained, "now that he's had time to think about it, remembers Gavin asking a lot of questions about the O'Reilly family and their money."

"Tell him about the other stuff," Peter interjected.

"I'm getting to that," Brogger shot back impatiently. My eyes drifted from Peter surveying the group and I noticed that Susan's eyes were riveted on me. The detective continued, "We have a theory we're working on—my Captain has given me the 'go-ahead'—and

I'm going to give you some information and then I want everyone in this room to butt-out of the investigation."

He looked from person to person, expecting a protest—got none and went on. "We think Tommy Gavin may have been extorting money from Mrs. O'Reilly on behalf of somebody else and that somebody killed both of them."

Peter stood up. He looked ten years older than when I saw him last. He glared at the detective and said, "That's crazy! My mother didn't have anything in her life that would enable someone to extort anything from her." Every one of the family members, including Susan, nodded their heads approvingly. He sat down and said, "Detective Brogger, we have the utmost respect for you and your job—you have to understand, we're the ones going crazy. It's beginning to look like our mother was murdered! We feel helpless…and you tell us to butt-out!"

Junkie butted in, "If my wife had been involved in a shakedown, she would have told me."

Now it was Sandy's turn to butt-in. She looked directly at me and said, "How do you feel about this Mr. Pius? After all, you've been hired by Bill to investigate this affair…where do you stand?" Before I could answer she continued, "Really it doesn't matter what Mr. Pius thinks." She gestured in Detective Brogger's direction and addressed him, "The only thing that matters is the police have finally come to their senses and are ready to admit that Maggie couldn't have killed herself." Brogger started to speak and she continued and looked back at me, "We'll pay Mr. Pius for his time and he can get back to his regular business."

I admit the thought of extricating myself from this mess had a lot of appeal. "I'm more than happy to remove myself from the fray," I responded. "And you don't owe me anything because I haven't done anything. But, I do have a couple of questions."

This time I was the one that stood up and all eyes were on me except the detective's. He seemed to be bored by the ranting of a bunch of amateurs, but out of courtesy was giving us our say. "Are the police checking out this Mr. Gavin and his connection to Newcastle, Northern Ireland?" I asked. "And what about friends or family here in the Bay Area? What about the money? Where did the money go that Maggie supposedly gave him?"

It was Detective Brogger's turn. He broke out of his reverie and said, "Harry, we're looking at everything. We're starting from scratch—we've talked to over twenty members of your golf club already about Gavin. Nobody seems to remember much about him—not even the guy in charge of caddies could tell us much." He smiled back at me, "By the way, Harry, somebody at your club has a big mouth—everyone we spoke with knows you are somehow involved in the investigation of Mrs. O'Reilly's death."

Gerry Murphy's big mouth, I surmised. "Yeah, some of my golf buddies think the idea of me as a private eye is a joke…. And they're probably correct. But I repeat, what about Ireland? Who's looking into that?"

Brogger nodded in my direction. "Harry, I was on the phone this morning at four a.m. with the local authorities in Newcastle—that's four a.m. my time by the way—and they're on it. They seemed to know about Mr. Gavin, but they're not ready to talk, just yet."

"How about if I go over to Newcastle and poke around?" I asked, and that started an uproar, with everybody talking at once. I held up my hand, "Hang on, I'm half kidding, but the member-guest at Royal County Down is coming up in ten days and I've got a standing invitation from my friend Tim Flynn to be his partner in the tournament."

Suddenly Junkie jumped in with what seemed to be an unusually strong admonition, "Harry, that's silly. We can't allow you to interfere with the police investigation—I won't allow it!" He stammered and tried to soften his command. "I mean, after all Harry, we've accomplished our objective—why don't we let the police handle it from here—and I'm going to pay you for the time you've put in, no argument!"

That started everybody jabbering again and Detective Brogger had had enough. "All right that's it," he said with finality. "I want all of you to go home and leave this investigation to the cops—we know about the bad guys and you don't. So, calm down and let us do our job." He stood and signaled the meeting was over.

I got up. "I'm outta' this, but I've got one more thing I want to do just to satisfy my curiosity." Everybody stared at me, except Brogger. He glared. I answered his glare, "Easy, easy, I'm not going to interfere with anything you're doing. I'm curious about something so I'm going to make a quick stop on my way home and ask a couple of questions that relate to golf—not murder." I smiled and added, "And, I might pop over and play in the member guest at County Down, so I can be your eyes and ears in Ireland, if needed."

Brogger's exasperation boiled over, "Harry, stay the fuck outta' this—sorry ladies—Harry, leave it alone."

"That's right Harry," Junkie said. "Your part in this is over," and he handed me a plain white envelope with my name printed on the front in neat block letters. Everyone stood, without looking at me, and began to file out of the conference room single file—everyone except Susan.

As I stood aside to let her pass in front of me she took my arm and placed my elbow firmly against her left breast and whispered, "It was a pleasure to meet you Harry and I hope we have a chance to see each other again some time under better circumstances." She pressed a card in my hand and bounced out of the room. A thought occurred to me—I had been in the company of her husband for almost two hours and he never said a word. Without looking at the card I put it with the envelope in my back pocket.

I stepped into bright sunlight at the front of the police station. Detective Brogger was waiting for me. "Harry, I don't know what you've got goin' on and I don't want to know, but you need to understand something." He turned to shield his eyes from the sun and continued, "We've got two people dead. They may not be connected, but my gut tells me they are. We're talkin' murder here and I don't want anyone else to get hurt—and that includes you. So, please, I'm asking you again, stay outta' this."

I held up both hands in mock surrender, "I got it, I got it." But, I had an idea to run by him. "There's a bar on Chestnut Street where all the caddies from Lakeside hang out and I want to ask a couple of them if Gavin ever caddied at their club. Plus, it's an Irish bar and maybe someone knows about his connection to Newcastle."

Brogger gave me another exasperated sigh. "I'm working with a homicide detective out of the Mission District—he's an old friend of mine—what's the name of this bar—I'll have him go in there."

"It's called the 'Dirty Sally'—I used to play poker in the back room until I ran out of pigeons. It's kind of a dive."

"I'll get somebody in there—you don't have to bother, understand?" It was an order, not a suggestion.

I said "Okay" to his back as he turned abruptly and walked back into the police station.

I stood with the warm afternoon sun at my back; reached in the back pocket of my slacks and extracted the envelope Junkie had given me and the card from Susan. The envelope contained a personal check from William Morrison made out to Harrison Pius in the amount of fifty thousand dollars. For roughly five days' work, that amount exceeded my normal daily rate by eight thousand a day. The card from Susan contained a message that was brief, but to the point, "I want to see you again. Please call." There was a phone number printed in bold strokes and underlined.

There was a city trash can chained to a light pole across the street, and as I crossed the street I tore the check from Junkie and the card from Susan in as many small pieces as I could manage and deposited it all in the trash. I looked in the coffee shop and the reluctant redhead caught my eye, waved me in and said, "He's gone, but not before he ate about twenty-two bucks worth of food, then went in the Men's room and made a hulluva' mess. Mick's pissed like you wouldn't believe."

I peeled off another twenty and shoved it at her, "Give this to Mick and tell him I said thanks."

As I walked to the car I had to laugh. I'd gone through fifty thousand and sixty dollars that morning. As some U.S. Senator said one time when he was debating a billion dollar appropriations bill, "Pretty soon, we'll be talking about '*real money*'."

16

Dirty Sally's is a dump, but I like it because it's a clean dump and a place that'll let you make a sandwich, for free—if you buy a beer. However, the great make-your-own deli sandwiches and overall ambience is overshadowed by the action that goes on behind the walk-in refrigerator. If you are one of owner Salvatore Ferrante's *compari* you are welcome to take an open seat at one of the two wooden tables behind the walk-in and fasten your chinstrap because you will be involved in the highest stake draw poker games this side of Vegas. Before the locals caught on to my prowess with any game that involves a deck of cards, plastic chips, and money, I was a regular at Sally's. I'm still welcome, but only to drink or have a sandwich. I can't go behind the walk-in and gamble anymore, although I still pop in from time to time and have a beer and a sandwich and watch the action.

I wasn't interested in back room action that afternoon. It was some of the caddies from the Olympic Club I was most interested in, and I wasn't disappointed. There were two Soprano types sitting at the bar that I had never seen before, but three guys, one of whom I recognized, were sitting next to the window watching the high school girls from St. Mary's Academy, in their little short skirts, go up and down the street. These guys were part of the crew that scattered quarters on the sidewalk just to watch the girls bend over to pick them up.

"Hey Billy, long time."

"Mr. Pope, where ya' been? Say hello to Frankie and Spitter."

Nods and handshakes all around and I asked "How about I buy you guys a few beers?"

There was a brief pause and Billy winked at his two companions. Pointing at them he said, "Listen up you two. Don't ever play cards with the Pope, don't play golf with him for anythin' more than a dollar and don't ever introduce him to your girlfriend." He laughed out loud. "Mr. Pope set your self down."

Billy was a few bricks short of a full load in the brain department, but he was an okay guy when he wasn't on a bender. I met him some years back at a poker game in a motel out near the zoo. Billy was in charge of security and was supposed to bang on the door to the room if anything remotely looking like a cop showed up. Instead, fortified by a bottle of muscatel, he fell asleep sitting in the warm sun outside the door and we came alarmingly close to getting busted. A first time player from Alameda got up to take a pee and caught a brief glimpse, through a crack in the drapes, of a squad car as it pulled into the parking lot. The cards and the money were out of sight when one of Angel Garcia's girl friend's answered the door and invited the two uniformed cops to make themselves at home. The other girlfriend was lying next to me on the bed clad in only her thong underpants. At Angel's signal both girls had quickly pulled off their shorts and halter-tops. The two cops were all eyes as they entered the room—Angel liked his ladies well endowed. The cops knew they had no basis for entering the room and after some perfunctory conversation, gave us the obligatory warning and left. In their mind it was all right to have a couple of very young, topless girls in a motel room with five guys, but gambling for money is the devil's workshop. We decided to break for the day and enjoyed a good laugh—everybody except Angel. He was the only loser. He was down about five large and left in a rage with his honeys in tow. He was still steaming the next day and had two of his boys take batting practice on Billy's knees with their Louisville Sluggers. It took Billy a year to recover enough so he could go back to being a caddy and walk eighteen holes. Not long after the incident at the motel, Angel got caught in a drive-by shooting in the Mission District and took one through the spine. The last time I saw him he was in a wheelchair and blubbered a lot. At least Billy can walk and talk.

Our drinks arrived and I decided the best strategy was to act like I was in the know. "Here's to absent friends," I said solemnly. "I guess the latest is Tommy Gavin."

The three caddies exchanged looks and Spitter said, "I'll drink to absent friends, but not to that prick Gavin."

Absent came out "abshent" and he sprayed the table with saliva. I grasped quickly why he was called Spitter. I switched tactics. "Well, I didn't know him—not really—just saw him around Pacific Heights once in a while—heard he washed up on the beach."

"Yeah," Billy said. "He hung around Olympic and was always gettin' into it with the other caddies and Sid, the caddy master. Sid ran him off a couple weeks ago—then, he turns up a floater."

"What do you mean 'getting into it'?" I asked.

Frankie spoke up. "He liked to pick fights with some of the older guys. Ya' know, guys that he knew he could handle. He was always goin' on about the fuckin' Brits—he had a hard-on for anything English—he even hated Bush because of the guy that runs England."

"You mean Tony Blair?"

"Yeah, that's the guy." Billy said. "Gavin was always screamin' about the Brits in Iraq and how the little kids in his country weren't safe and it was all the Brits' fault—he was a fuckin' crazy bastard."

"Did he ever mess with you guys?"

"Nah, he pretty much left us alone—I jus' didn't pay any mind to him as long as he stayed outta' my face. Course old man Churchill never had a chance." Billy paused and the other two nodded in approval. "Remember him Pope? Church had the bad arm and could only take one bag. Well, Gavin got on him one day about the fuckin' Brits and one thing led to another and Gavin popped him one. Then Sammy Belleci stepped in and stiffed Gavin and we didn't see him for about three months—we heard he was goin' back and forth from here to some town in Ireland where he had family."

"Yeah, funny thing…." Frankie emptied his glass in one gulp, paused, looked to see if I was going to spring for another round of drinks and continued, "Old man Churchill doesn't know English from buckwheat. He couldn't figure out why Gavin was always pickin' on him."

They all looked at their empty glasses and then back at me. I put my hand in the air and sent Sid, behind the bar, a signal for another round. "Was Gavin just another crazy Irishman or do you think he was some kind of IRA type?" I asked.

"You mean the guys that blow up shit in Ireland?" Frankie asked.

"Yeah, those guys," I answered. Bert Brogger had ordered me to butt-out and suddenly I had a germ of an idea about what might be going on. "Did Gavin act like he was okay for money—I mean, did he look and act like he was broke?"

"Ya' know, now that you mention it, some of us wondered why he caddied," Frankie said quickly. "He'd make a sixty dollar loop and come over here to Sally's and spend it all on some of his 'mick' buddies."

"So, he hung out here, with his buddies, on a regular basis and was a big spender…"

Spitter interrupted, "Those two guys that just went out the door were a couple of his drinkin' pals…"

I leapt from the table and rushed to the street and didn't see anything of the two that I had noticed when I first walked in. I immediately regretted not paying more attention.

I beat it back to the bar and found Sid drying glasses. "Hey Sid, who were those two 'strong arms' sittin' here?"

Sid stared at me. "You guys should get together." He saw the confused look on my face. "Pope, the skinny one asked me if you were Harrison Pius and when I said 'Yeah do you want to meet him,' he threw a twenty on the bar and they split."

"You ever see them in here before?"

"Yeah, I seen 'em, but I don't know who they are—they're not my usual clientele and they never ask to go in the back." Sid swiveled his head in the direction of the walk-in indicating they weren't card players. "They've come in a few times with one or two of the loopers from Olympic, but they're not regulars."

I said thanks and made my way back to the table by the window. Billy asked, "Hey, Pope, what's goin' on? Ya' know those thugs?"

I shook my head and returned to my seat. "I don't know them, but they seem to know me."

"They was sure watchin' you Mr. Pope," Spitter said suddenly. "I thought maybe's they was gamblin' types and ya' knew 'em from the back room."

"Pope you're actin' awful mysterious," Billy said. "Why you care about Gavin.... and now you're all excited about a couple a slicks askin' about you—maybe they jus' lookin' for some action and they heard you play cards for real money."

"Yeah, you're probably right," I said darkly. A few years ago, Julie fooled me, but I don't get fooled very often—my bullshit meter was back on full alert. Something was starting to smell and I couldn't see it. "I'm curious about Gavin because he caddied for me a few times at Pacific Heights, and if those two hard cases at the bar are looking for some action, I can always use some fresh pigeons. It all doesn't amount to a hill of beans in this crazy mixed up world, though." I smiled at the thought of Bogey and stood to leave.

Hand shakes all around, a chorus of thanks from Billy and the boys, a wave to Sid and I made my way to the street.

17

Recently I read an article in a magazine written about San Francisco and the author made the point that if all the inhabitants of the City decided to go out for dinner at precisely the same time there would be seating for everyone—there are that many restaurants in town. All you have to do is drive the length of Chestnut Street to understand the validity of that statement. There at least ten places to eat on every block. I pointed myself east on Chestnut and headed for home more tired than I had a right to be, but buoyed by the prospect of an evening with Vanessa.

I turned on to Church Street and headed south. I had only gone two blocks when I saw the flashing lights and heard the staccato burst of the paramedics' truck behind me. I found a driveway and sidled in to let them pass. Before I could pull away I had to wait as they were closely followed by a patrol car hurrying to catch up. I took a hard right and made my way up to Diamond in the direction of the towers. My thought was to avoid an accident on Church Street that would create a big mess because of the J streetcar line. As I waited to turn left on Diamond two young men in trim cut suits and bright colored power ties crossed in front of me and stopped at the corner. They were holding hands and the taller of the two pulled his partner to him and gave him a hall of fame lip lock. It was a kiss that would have done Brad Pitt proud. I gave them a beep and a wave and smiled as I pulled away.

The thought occurred to me that in the two years I had been crazy in love with Julie, I don't think I ever kissed her in public…maybe I should have. But, after thousands of hours sitting in my cave sucking on a bottle of scotch trying to figure where I went wrong, I knew there wasn't anything I should have done. I got involved with a woman that is wired in a different way than most of us and nothing I did or didn't do would have changed the outcome. When a guy meets her for the first time and treats her with respect, as I did, and doesn't try to come on to her she will quickly take on the role of a chaste, unapproachable ice princess and make the guy pursue her.

My pursuit of her was classic—right out of the movies—flowers, love letters, candlelit dinners...I even wrote a few corny poems. Once we settled into a quiet loving relationship she did everything to convince me a brief fling in her early twenties was the only thing standing in the way of her virginity—and all the wonderful things we did in bed were brand new experiences in her sex life.

However, when she was feeling lonely and went on the prowl, a man could meet up with her in a bar and treat her like a whore—and if he acted like he was not all that interested she'd take him home and fuck his eyeballs out and then see if he wanted to ask some of his friends to come over and join in the fun. One time I came home from a business trip three days early and used my key to her front door to surprise her—she was very surprised to see me—and the two guys in bed with her were surprised, as well. I'm embarrassed to admit it, but when she went into therapy I took her back. The therapy was for my benefit and after I took her back she quit therapy and resumed sport fucking. I found out the hard way, again, only the next time she was in my house with someone who is no longer a friend of mine. Juanita walked in on them and by the time she had quit swinging at them with the fireplace tongs, she had broken my ex-friends nose, put an eight inch gash in Julie's ass and practically destroyed the second floor guest room. The two lovers made it to the street with most of his clothes and none of hers. To this day I don't know how they got to their cars without causing a riot. Julie wants me back again, but I don't feel up to repeating the biggest mistake I've ever made.

I turned on to my street and was met by flashing lights, police cars, and the ambulance that had roared by me only moments before. A crowd of about fifty people was milling in front of my house and Mrs. Mulhaupt, from two doors down, was leaning against the wall at the corner of my house sobbing uncontrollably.

A uniformed patrolman stuck up his hand and yelled as I pulled to a stop in the middle of my street. "Hey, you!" he exclaimed. "Turn that thing around, this street is closed."

I got a sick wave of nausea as I leaped from the car and rushed past his outstretched arm screaming, "That's my house!" My first thought was fire, but as I got closer to the front vestibule I realized there wasn't any smoke.

She was lying on her side, at an odd angle, and her right leg was sticking out from under a canvas bag that had obviously contained some groceries. Apples, oranges, a quart of milk and sundry other items were scattered on the marble entryway. There were two young medics hovering around her and the plastic gloves on their hands were covered in blood.

I felt a strong grip on my shoulder and a different cop tried to pull me away. "This is my house and that woman is my housekeeper," I said with all the calmness I could muster while distracted by the seemingly foreign language coming from the medics.

The medic who seemed to be in charge was speaking into a small microphone clipped to his shirt. "We've got an elderly woman on our hands and, and at the least, she's got a compound fracture above the knee," he said. The other medic began to rub her knuckle vigorously across Juanita's chest causing Juanita to groan and thrash about. Juanita's dress was bunched around her bare legs and I could see bits of bone protruding through the bloody skin above her right knee. I felt helpless and wanted desperately to do something. "She's responsive to pain," the medic said. "We're going to move her, but I think she's going to need an orthopedic specialist…plus, we think she's got a dislocated hip." There was a pause and he added, "Yeah, we'll wait."

I was pulled away by the stern voice of the cop at my elbow, "We need some information from you," he stated matter-of-factly. "Let's start with your name." As I turned to face him I noticed the medic give Juanita another shot of something straight into her right hip. I asked him to pull her dress down and he looked at me as if I was crazy—her dignity and modesty was not high on his list. Just then his female partner produced a heavy wool blanket and they placed it over her and she groaned softly.

Within five minutes I gave the patrolman everything I could think of, given my agitated state. He had all the vital stuff, but I was the one with the questions and the only witness was still hanging around to talk to me. I already knew his screams, from across the street, was the reason the attacker had run away.

"Harry, he hit Juanita with a baseball bat." Mr. Miller's voice cracked and I thought he might be on the edge of hysteria. "I was getting my mail and all of a sudden I saw this guy jump out of a car and start swinging. It was like he was waiting for her. He was dressed like he was a banker, but Harry…he was carrying a baseball bat, for God's sakes!"

"Mr. Miller, if the police are through with you please go home. I know your wife must be frantic—we'll talk later. As soon as we get Juanita to the hospital I'll call you and let you know." He began to shake his head and I said sharply, "Please Mr. Miller, your wife needs you." He and Alice have been married for over fifty years and she has been in a wheelchair for thirty of those years. Mr. Miller is one of the living saints we encounter rarely in life. "Please go home," I repeated.

The traffic cop had pulled my car into my driveway and traffic was moving slowly as the medics were preparing to put Juanita on a gurney. The cop handed me my car keys and cell phone, then motioned me in the direction of my front door. There a woman in a gray pants suit with an official badge stuck in her lapel pocket was alternately barking orders at the uniformed police officers and speaking into a hand held tape recorder. I turned and was walking in her direction when I saw a taxi stop at the edge of the chaos that was swirling around me—and for a fleeting moment my spirits were lifted.

Vanessa stepped from the taxi and my joy at seeing her quickly vanished as I recognized the same panic in her eyes that I saw the afternoon Gerry Murphy had caught us walking on the beach at Sears Point. For a fleeting instant her eyes met mine and then she abruptly shifted her gaze to the police officers, television cameras and general confusion playing out before her. Our eyes met again and with a vigorous shake of her head in my direction, she re-entered the taxi and it slowly pulled away. In that moment I realized how much I knew about Vanessa—her panicked reaction didn't surprise me. While overcome with concern for Juanita I still had time to wish I had been wrong about Vanessa.

A television reporter was belligerently trying to get my attention by shoving a microphone in my face and I realized what I should have done the moment I saw Juanita's condition. I scrolled for a familiar number programmed in my cell phone. In the midst of all the confusion it had quietly occurred to me that I needed to speak with my favorite golf partner and close friend, who happens to be Dr. Jack Swift, orthopedic surgeon at Stanford Medical Center. I hit the auto dial for his home number and waited.

He answered on the first ring. "Pope, I don't blame you if you never want me for a partner again," and laughed.

I got straight to the point, "Jack I've got a big problem and I need your help."

The tone of my voice changed his demeanor immediately. "Harry what's wrong?"

I poured it all out as fast as I could. The medics were loading Juanita into the back of the ambulance van and the lady cop obviously wanted to talk to me, so I gave Jack the short version. He was quick and to the point. "Harry, let me talk to the medical technician supervisor and then you can get in the van and come with them."

I handed the phone to the medic, who seemed to be in charge, and started to climb in the back of his van. "Hold it!" yelled a voice from behind me. "I need to talk to you, mister." The gray pants suit was pushing through the crowd in my direction. The medic ignored the voice behind me, listened and then said into my cell phone, "Okay Doc we're on our way." He handed my phone back to me and said, "If you're coming with us you've gotta' get in NOW! We're going to Stanford Med Center and we need to hurry!"

The pants suit reached out to grab my arm and I gave her a dismissive brush off, "It'll have to wait," I said, and I jumped in the back of the ambulance just as the medic slammed the doors.

18

The ride to Stanford Medical Center with Juanita was agonizingly slow and painful. The ambulance driver did his best to navigate his way down the Bayshore, but it was slow going. I held tightly to Juanita's hand and tried to reassure her that it was going to be all right. She slipped in and out of consciousness and on one occasion whispered my name and started to cry. It was breaking my heart to look at her. I wanted to take her in my arms and hold her and make it all go away, yet I was afraid to touch her for fear of disturbing the immobile position the medics had placed her in on the gurney. At one point in the ride she began to shiver and her body seemed to grow rigid. Quickly the EMT gave her another shot of something and her breathing resumed a more normal rhythm while I realized I had been holding my breath.

Jack Swift was waiting at the door to Stanford Medical Center Emergency as we came to a stop. He barely acknowledged my presence as the EMT handed him a clipboard. The golfing buddy I knew from Pacific Heights Golf Club with the bad golf swing and the herky-jerky putting stroke became someone I didn't recognize. There was no wasted motion, no idle chatter and the laid back guy I hung out with was, without a doubt, the man in charge. At the back of the ambulance, as Juanita was unloaded, I watched the ballet of discipline unfold and I knew I would never look at Jack Swift the same way again. For the first time since I saw the flashing lights in front of my house I had the feeling that things might turn out okay and I began to understand why doctors can take on God-like qualities in the eyes of us mere mortals.

Ignoring me, the two EMTs, a couple of nurses and Jack Swift all pushed past me and entered the emergency area through the automatic sliding doors. Before I could follow them I felt a gentle tug on my arm. I was greeted by a grim faced, little old lady in a striped uniform who escorted me to admissions.

Three hours and what seemed like twenty diet cokes later I was slouched on a couch in a waiting room outside of Orthopedic Intensive Care. For over an hour I had been trying to get information about Juanita's condition, from anyone and everyone, without any luck. I had reached a point of almost total frustration when a nurse with a green mask hanging from her neck and a severe case of bad hair day entered the room and announced that Dr. Swift would come to see me in a few minutes.

Forty-five minutes later a weary Jack Swift slumped onto the couch next to me and smiled, "Pope, she's going to be all right."

I resisted the urge to hug him and asked, "What do you mean by 'all right'?"

"She won't be running the hundred yard dash any time soon, but she'll recover—she won't be the same, but she'll be okay."

"What do you mean, 'she won't be the same'?"

"Pope, she's got a compound fracture of her femur and a dislocated hip. She's in great shape for her age and she's tougher than a two-dollar steak, but still…she's sixty-five years old." He rubbed his eyes with both hands and sighed, "It's gonna' take some time—she'll probably walk with a limp—and she'll need therapy, lots of it, but we did a good job and we were lucky to have a sixty-five year old woman with the bone structure of someone half her age."

"Speaking of two dollars…"

"I know what you're gonna' say, so don't say it." My friend Jack Swift took my right hand and said, "Pull me up."

I pulled him to his feet. He put a muscular arm around my shoulder and said, "Pope, what Medicare doesn't cover will be on me. I can never repay you for what you once did for my family. Now, go home and get some rest, I'll see you back here about ten o'clock tomorrow morning." He turned to walk away and stopped, "No wait! Tomorrow's Sunday—make it eleven."

So as not to break the hospital rules I had the ring turned off on my cell phone and I could feel it vibrate in my pocket. I glanced at the small illuminated screen, saw it was Vanessa and turned it off. I headed for the front entrance to see if I could find a cabbie that wanted a fare into the City.

Someone had cleaned the vestibule at the front of my house. I entered the front door and flipped on the light and with the door open looked for traces of the violence that had occurred only hours before. The marble floor had been freshly scrubbed, evidenced by the faint aroma of some type of disinfectant. *Thank you Mrs. Mulhaupt*, I thought.

There was a Pyrex bowl sitting on a cooling rack in the kitchen. When I saw the bread pudding my eyes filled and I almost lost it—*'You're a tough old broad, and I love you madly.'*

I spooned a pint of vanilla ice cream on top of the bread pudding and headed for my cave. Between bites of the pudding and ice cream I called Juanita's boys and filled them in on their mom's condition. I had taken the time during surgery to break the news to them and they had been waiting for more information before driving to the City.

I had two more calls to make and I wasn't looking forward to either conversation. I knew that both calls would lead to an argument and one was certain to get heated. Whether Detective Brogger and Junkie Bill approved, or not, I was back in it. I was still confused about Junkie's quick decision to get me out of the investigation, but I put it down to his getting what he wanted. Namely, the authorities were now treating Maggie's death as a possible homicide. After the attack on Juanita I was more convinced than ever that Junkie had been closer to the truth, all along, than the cops were willing to admit. They both wanted me to step aside and I was ready to agree, but a guy with a baseball bat had changed everything. Now I was in it and I had a couple of hole cards that gave me a slight edge. My friends, my brother, Juanita and the IRS know me as a successful, self-employed businessman with substantial assets and a healthy income. What those closest to me know, and the IRS doesn't know, is the other income and the location of the safety deposit box with enough cash in it to last ten lifetimes. I still stay out of Nevada, but I spend a week, four times a year, in Atlantic City and I'm smarter than I was when I got thrown out of Nevada twenty-five years ago. Plus, when I travel with the express purpose of gambling, I have my two traveling companions Manu and Tua Tamua along for the ride.

Manu is a six foot four inch, three hundred pound Samoan devoted to my well being because I kept him out of jail. His big brother Tua has sworn himself to a lifetime of allegiance to me because that's what Samoans do for a 'brudda.' Manu got in over his head as the bodyguard for a Silicon Valley CEO who was diverting company funds to his girlfriend's account in the Bahamas. His Board of Directors hired me to find out how he was doing it and I did. Manu and his brother were involved on the periphery as couriers of the cash and when I brought the operation down I kept both of them out of it because I knew they were unwittingly being used. They swore their everlasting obligation to me and I use them for peace of mind whenever I play in a high stakes poker game. It doesn't matter whether it's somebody's garage or a casino on an Indian reservation; if I don't know the players involved I have one or both of the 'bruddas' by my side. If provoked, they are both lethal. I made a mental note to call them the following morning.

I had the cordless phone in my hand and was trying to remember Bert Brogger's phone number without success. If you deal fifty-two cards face up in front of me as fast as you can I will repeat back to you the exact order in which they were dealt—I've won bets using three decks—but, I often forget my own phone number.

The phone rang, startling me, and before I could answer I heard the front door bell ring as well. I punched the button and said hello while quickly mounting the stairs and wondering who could be calling at this hour and who the hell could be at the front door. In a mini-second I was chilled by the thought of a guy greeting me with a baseball bat as I opened the door. Instead I was chilled by a voice on the phone I didn't recognize. I didn't need to worry about the man with the baseball bat because his voice stopped me mid-stride on the stairs.

"I hit a single with the spic," the voice sounded like the Aflac duck, not someone who was adept with a bat. "Next time, it'll be you and I'll hit a home run—stay away from our business! Ya' never heard the name Gavin—got it?" The line went dead.

The front door bell continued to ring and I grabbed the old 3-iron at the top of the stairs, the one Juanita sometime uses for a cane, and wondered whether or not I should take a full back swing at the intruder. I looked through the peephole and stood motionless for what seemed an eternity.

A pleading voice said softly, "Harry, please open the door. Please."

I was aware of her image and nothing more. She was there and as much as I hated it I knew that at that moment I wanted her with me. I opened the door and without a word she slipped an arm around me and buried her face against my chest. After a moment she looked up and said, "Harry, I'm so sorry. You look so alone—I'm here—use me any way you want. Anything you want or need—just don't send me away."

Without waiting for me to respond she led the way without hesitation. She didn't ask for permission and she didn't need directions. She took me to my bathroom and I allowed her to strip the clothes from my exhausted body and place me in a steaming shower. As I emerged she was waiting with a warm towel from my warming rack and a finger of Talisker in a shot glass.

She reached to stroke my face, pushing my wet hair back from my forehead, "Finish your scotch and come with me," she said, and taking me by the hand she steered me gently to the bed. In a moment she joined me in the bed and we melted into each other in gentle desperation. She whispered into my mouth, "Sleep Harry, sleep."

Sometime in the middle of that long night, half asleep I rolled over and in a familiar motion I entered her body and she pulled me deep inside her incredible warmth. We didn't move to the usual thrusts of sex—we made love. Ours was a sharing of breath, a sharing of hands, a sharing of motion, a desire to admit the knowledge of uniqueness that only first love can experience.

"You know I hate you," I said.

Julie held me tighter and said, "I hate me too, Harry."

I slept late—late for me. It was seven a.m. and I was alone in my bed. I could hear the sounds of someone moving back and forth in the kitchen and I could smell the welcome aroma of fresh brewed coffee. I was confused for a moment and then remembered and silently berated myself. Why couldn't I be strong? *Of all the gin joints, in all the towns, in all the world, she walked into mine*—and I fold like a cheap chair.

As usual, I awoke with a numerical list in my head of the things I wanted to accomplish for the day. As I slipped on a T-shirt and shorts and started for the kitchen I knew that even though it was early on a Sunday morning I wanted to speak with Bert Brogger as soon as possible. Also, Junkie Bill and Manu were high on the list.

Julie stood at the bay window in the kitchen alcove warming herself in the morning sun. She was wearing my "Spin Stops Here" sweatshirt, which hung just above her knees. I came up behind her and slipped my hand up under the sweatshirt, cupping her left breast in my hand. She leaned into me pressing my hand tight until the pain made her shudder with pleasure. She abruptly turned and in one motion pushed me onto the bench seat under the bay window while pulling my shorts down around my ankles. She knelt in front of me and began the familiar ritual of her ultimate power trip. She was doing what she did best and what she enjoyed most. It was all about me, but it was all about her, too. She didn't say anything—she never did—there was nothing to be said. The little man on my shoulder was doing all the talking. The little man screaming in my ear, saying over and over again, *"You fool, you fool, you fool!"*

I put my head back and gave in to her fierce willfulness, embarrassed at the realization of my weakness.

19

Later that morning I spoke with Manu and arranged to pick him up on my way to the hospital. His quiet rage at the news of Juanita's attack was expected and I knew he would be available wherever and whenever necessary. I didn't have any luck with Junkie or the detective, but I left messages for both of them on their cell phones.

Julie had showered and left. We were careful not to say "call me" or "see you later," instead we reacted as if it had been a one-night stand accompanied by the usual morning-after awkwardness.

Junkie called first. Since our meeting at the police station I had been troubled by his abrupt dismissal of the need for my help. I was further surprised by his cavalier attitude when I told him about what happened to Juanita. He quickly offered to take care of all expenses related to her recovery, which immediately pissed me off. It seemed Junkie was falling into the trap that newfound wealth can bring—money solves everything. He hadn't learned that wealth just puts your problems on a grander scale. He said he would be at home all day and we agreed to meet after I checked on Juanita at the hospital. Bert Brogger called soon after and we agreed to meet at the hospital at noon. He said he might have his son with him, in which case he would prefer to meet at the park adjacent to the hospital parking lot. I told him to call when he knew about his son and I grabbed the keys to the Boxster. I got half way to the basement when I remembered the Boxster wouldn't work—Manu doesn't fit in a sports car. I retrieved the keys to the Lincoln and drove through the bustle of my neighborhood on a bright Sunday morning. The absence of fog and the warmth of the sun had everyone out for church, breakfast or a lei-surely stroll. For some it was all three.

I went down Mission Street to Market and headed east toward Chinatown. At the corner of Grant and Post I saw a moving mountain sipping a Starbucks and petting a young girl's dog. As I got closer the young girl began to look more like a young woman and as I pulled to the curb she gave Manu a kiss on the cheek and sauntered away. She couldn't have weighed more than a hundred pounds and looked to be about twenty years old. Manu is six-four and three hundred pounds—I had to laugh at the image in my mind.

"What's so funny, brudda?" he said as he slid in and hit the button to move the seat back as far as it would go. It wasn't far enough for comfort, but no automobile was ever comfortable for Manu.

"I was just thinking about you and your little friend."

"I know what you thinkin'," he said with a smirk. "But you more curious than anythin'—so jus' so's you know—she always takes the upper berth and sez' I better than the roller coaster at Great America." He smiled and changed the subject, "How's Juanita?"

"I called just before I got here and was told no calls were being put through, but we could see her at eleven-thirty when the Doctor was finished checking on her. Jack Swift's taking care of her," I added.

"He that bone crusher wit' the daughter what run off to that com-mune in Santa Cruz a couple years ago?"

"Yeah, that's the guy...of course you were the one that found her and brought her back."

Manu laughed and I felt the car shake as I merged on the Bayshore Freeway. "Man, she was more than ready to come back home when we found her. Jus' them long hair, hippie dudes wasn't through messin' wit' her, yet. She thought she was gonna' git away from mommy and daddy and live the simple life wit' nature." Manu snorted, "Hah, after that whole bunch of hippies, includin' the hippy-dykes, got through gang bangin' her every day for a month, she wuz' ready to come home. Man, it wuz' fun bustin' up all them flower chil-dren. Course Tua put six a them mother-fuckers in the hospital."

Manu gave me a grin about a foot wide. "Brudda, they ain't nothin' better than a hippy on the run."

"Well it all worked out for the best and she's back in school. Jack says she's thinking about getting an MBA after she graduates."

"Tua say MBA mean 'more business assholes,' but I don't know MBA from NBA."

It was my turn to laugh. "Tua is a very smart dude," I said. "But, Jack took good care of you guys—didn't he?"

"He paid us enough to get Mama Lani out of Makaha and she live wit' us now," he said. "Now we eat much better—she cook good, you bet."

I kept the obvious comment about Manu and Tua not missing any meals to myself and concentrated on watching for the Palo Alto turn-off that leads to the Stanford Medical Center. We were quiet in the car and I could sense Manu's uneasiness. As I pulled in to the parking lot at the south side of the main building he broke the silence. "Pope, like what you want me to do for ya'?"

"Manu, I admit this whole business has me scared." I put the Lincoln in park and turned to face him. "I just like having you around. Just knowing you're watching my back makes me feel a whole lot better."

"Okay, brudda, I be wit' you from now on—least til you say enough is enough—and when Tua git' back, he join the party. Tua, he gonna' be pissed when he find out about Juanita."

"Well, let's go find out how she's doing." We exited the Lincoln and walked to the front entrance.

We made our way to the second floor and were greeted by Detective Bert Brogger who was doing his best to conceal a raging hangover. He was standing outside Juanita's room and he didn't have his little boy with him. I made the perfunctory introduction from Manu to Brogger and they mutually extended their danger antenna between one another. I saw the need to explain. "Hey, guys, we're all on the same team here." I nodded in Bert's direction, "Manu is one of the good guys and he's my first call if I need to walk down a dark alley." I paused and put my hand on the detective's shoulder. I was close enough to smell the mouthwash and cologne he had used to unsuccessfully hide his success as a drunk. "Let's all relax—I need to find out how Juanita's doing."

Brogger didn't say anything. He walked away and bent from the waist in front of a drinking fountain embedded in the wall. He placed one hand on the wall for support and for a moment I thought he might topple backwards. He returned and smiled sheepishly, "I got a hold of some bad ice last night guys—just give me a minute and I'll be okay." He pointed a shaking finger in my direction, "Harry I need a lot of information from you. Check in on your housekeeper and then let's find a quiet place to talk."

"She's not my housekeeper, Bert. She's my best friend and the mother I never had," I said sternly. I liked him. At his core I suspected he was a good man. But, somewhere along the line he got side tracked and he was spiraling into a deep, black hole and drowning in vodka.

I started to enter Juanita's room when he stopped me. "Her boys are in there and I think the doc is getting ready to throw them out. They've been yelling and shouting at each other for about the last fifteen minutes or so."

I was afraid it would happen. I referred to them as the three stooges…Carlos, Roberto and Manny—their father's sons. Juanita had tossed them out, one by one, as they had grown to manhood, although none of them had ever achieved real manhood. She hoped they would be able to take over the restaurant when she got tired of working seven days a week. It didn't take long for her to figure out that none of the three had the talent or ambition to manage her restaurant, so she sold it, for a lot of money, to a Greek who owned the Chinese restaurant two doors down from her place. The boys never forgave her and blamed each other for her lack of trust. She didn't see much of them unless they needed to borrow money. With my guidance she had quit being a soft touch and they rightly blamed me for managing her finances to the extent that they couldn't get at her savings. I entered the room and saw Dr. Jack Swift shifting from foot to foot, ready to blow his stack.

I can't pretend to be satisfied with my ability to be diplomatic in times of stress and that morning was no exception. My patience with the Morales boys has a short fuse even when they're on their best behavior. They were all talking at once and yelling at each other in a mixture of English and Spanish, which further serves to piss me off. If you are born and raised in this country, speak the goddam' language.

Juanita was lying immobile with her eyes closed. Her breathing was steady and rhythmic. Her left leg was suspended from a cable apparatus attached to the ceiling and she had tubes running in every direction. I touched her hand and she smiled. I knew she wanted the boys out of her room and expected me to restore order. I was happy to oblige.

"Out!" I said and pointed first at the three of them and then the door. They started to protest and Jack Swift weighed in.

"I want all three of you out of this room—now," he commanded.

I marched them out the door and headed for the waiting room. They followed me and we found ourselves with the room to ourselves. I hadn't seen any of them in over two years, but there no handshakes. "Listen to me very carefully," I said. "Your mother has been seriously hurt and it's my fault."

They looked at each other and all started to speak at once. I cut them off. "I've gotten myself involved in a murder investigation and I'm afraid Juanita has been an innocent victim." They started chattering again. I held my hand up and gestured in the direction of Manu who had followed us into the waiting room. "Your mother will be protected, round the clock, starting now." I nodded at Manu. "I am taking total responsibility for her welfare which will include her protection."

Manny started to say something and I cut him off. "When her doctor says she can come home she will come to my house and I will arrange for her care and well-being." Now it was Carlos turn to object and I stopped him. "I know what she would want. I suggest you go back in her room and each of you give her a kiss on the cheek, tell her you love her and get out of here until this evening. Go to her house—you know how to find the key—and relax. The doctor has a job to do and the police need information—you're just in the way." They started to protest, but between Manu and me, we got them hustled down the hall to Juanita's room. They said their good-byes and left.

Bert Brogger and I entered Juanita's room to find Jack Swift turning dials on her monitor and adjusting the myriad of tubes hooked to her hand and arm. I took her free hand in mine; she opened her eyes and said, "Hi Harry." I remembered my last words to her as I was leaving the kitchen the day before…"*You're a tough old broad…*" How prophetic it was—and true.

"Hi sweetheart. How are you feeling?"

"I feel like somebody hit me with a baseball bat, Harry. What happened?"

"Somebody *did* hit you with a baseball bat, my darling." I said. "Your attacker used you to send me a message."

Jack left the room announcing he would "be back shortly" and Brogger moved to the other side of the bed. His face was starting to get some color back. He reached in his pocket for another breath mint, coughed and grunted his approval. "Mrs. Morales we agree with Harry—your assailant came after you to get to Harry."

Juanita's eyes seemed to be somewhere else. I couldn't tell if it was pain or anger that was driving her emotions. After a long moment she said, "Harry does this have to do with some gamblers you've made angry? Is Manu with you?"

I took my own long moment to answer. "No and yes," I said. "No it doesn't have anything to do with anybody I play cards with and yes Manu is with me." She turned her head looking for Manu. "He's out in the hallway and he and Tua are going to watch over you until you come home." She and Brogger both looked at me as if they wanted to protest. "No discussion," I said. "That's the way it's going to be. Manu and Tua will take turns outside your room, around the clock, until you're released from the hospital. Then you're coming home to my house." I paused to let it sink in and continued as Jack reentered the room. "We're going to convert the first floor guest room, next to the kitchen, into a combination hospital/therapy center—no argument!"

Jack Swift nodded approvingly and said, "Juanita, you're going to recover from this but it's going to take time and a lot of hard work on your part. Listen to the Pope and go along with what he puts together for you."

I could see Bert Brogger was anxious to talk to me. He wasn't going to get any information out of Juanita because she hadn't seen her attacker. She had her back to the street when the first blow hit her just above the knee and she didn't remember anything after that. She had a faint memory of the ambulance ride, but that was all. He moved toward the door and said, "Harry I'll see you outside."

I didn't expect Jack to give us good news, but I was surprised. "It's not as bad as it looks," he said. "And, it's not nearly as bad as I thought, when I first saw the x-rays yesterday." A broad smile crossed his face. "Juanita, you're going to need lots of rest and TLC. Between me and Harry we'll get you back to normal quicker than you think."

"When can I...?"

Jack stopped her by putting his hand to her face. "I know what you're going to ask and we can't even think about that now. You'll be here at least a week."

For the first time I saw the flash in her eyes that I loved. Next she'd start yelling at me. I wasn't disappointed. "Goddammit Harry! Get me outta here—I can't stay here a week!" she exclaimed. At that moment Jack and I turned to see a young priest stick his head through the opening in the door.

"Did I hear someone call out for my assistance?" he said with a smirk.

Jack and I beat a hasty retreat and I knew if Juanita had had something in her hand she would have thrown it at me.

20

Bert Brogger was waiting patiently for me in the shade of a Live Oak tree in the park adjacent to the parking area. There can be a thirty-degree swing in the temperature from The City to areas down the Peninsula. This was one of those days. It was only a little after noon and the temperature was already inching toward eighty—it was probably in the low fifties at my house. Bert was sitting at a picnic table with his head resting on his folded arm. I thought, at first glance, he might be sleeping. Slowly he lifted his head as I approached and said, "Well, mister private eye, you've got yourself up to your ass in alligators, don't you?"

I walked to the picnic table and sat. There was a warm breeze sifting its way through the grove of trees and the filtered sunlight was warm on my back. As I slid sideways onto the bench I felt my cell phone shift in my back pocket. I removed it and noticed I had two unanswered calls. I hit view and saw two numbers I recognized—one from Gerry Murphy and the other from Vanessa—they could both wait.

Suddenly the giant shadow of Manu loomed over us and a beefy hand placed two Styrofoam cups of coffee and a couple of poppy seed muffins in front of us. "I got these from the cafeteria," he said. "You want I should stay with Juanita, Harry?"

"Yeah, stay with her, Manu."

He turned and headed back to the hospital entrance. Bert followed him with his eyes and scowled, "You think him hangin' around is really necessary?"

I opened the bag and put the two muffins on a napkin in front of us. The coffee was too hot to drink, so I dunked a corner of a muffin in the cup and took a bite. Between bites I said, "No, I don't think Juanita needs to be protected—the message has been sent. But, having Manu around will make her feel better and that's all I care about right now."

"I told you to butt out of this mess. You don't listen very well, do you?"

"Bert, I made one stop," I said. "I went to Dirty Sally's to satisfy my curiosity. I never dreamed anything like this would happen."

Bert sat straight up on the bench, took in a bushel of air and said, "You're a bullshit artist Harry."

"What do mean by…"

"You're a bullshitter. You come off as 'mister upstanding citizen' and you pal around with the likes of that fuckin' Neanderthal Manu. Ya' know I've had you checked out and you're the man of mystery." He sipped his coffee and the scowl lessened. "Everybody we talk to says you're loaded—you live like a guy with a pile—and nobody knows exactly what you do except it's common knowledge that you are a fuckin' hall of fame poker player and you also gamble for big bucks on the golf course."

"What's that got to do with Juanita and Maggie O'Reilly—and Tommy Gavin?"

"Maybe nothing." He paused and abruptly changed the subject. "Bill Morrison was watching you when you crossed the street yesterday and went back in the coffee shop. He says you probably tore up his check and dropped it in the trash."

"He overpaid—and that bothered me." There was a long moment of silence as we sipped our coffee. Bert wasn't touching his muffin.

"Okay, so he overpaid—and I guess you don't need the money. I don't give a shit. But, I'm gonna' tell you again—I want you to stay out of our hair. We've got a full-blown murder investigation going on and we don't need amateurs getting in the way."

"Who's the *we*?" I could see confusion in his eyes. "You say *we*—is that you and the San Francisco cops?"

"Yeah, and by the way, I covered your ass with the lead detective on the case from the Mission District precinct—she was pissed."

The gray pants suit, I thought. "Was she the one at my house when I took off with the ambulance?"

"That's the one Harry." Bert sighed and emitted a belch that started somewhere around his toes. He scowled and continued, "Phyllis Bennett is her name and she's one of the good ones. I've worked with her before and she's a good cop. She wasn't happy when you took off the way you did." He took another deep breath and his hand was trembling. "You're lucky, I squared it with her. She went to Dirty Sally's last night and got nowhere. Nobody's ever seen the two 'suits' in there before."

"They must have followed me there."

"How'd they know to follow you, Harry?"

I shook my head. "I don't know. I've been thinking about it a lot, though."

"Did they pick you up as you left the coffee shop? They had to. You told the beat cop they came in to Dirty Sally's after you got there."

"That's right." *A lie.*

"And they left the bar before you did."

"Right again…." *The truth.*

"How did they know—?"

"Where I lived—and the most important point," I added. "Was I their first target or, when they got to my house before I did, and saw an old lady at my front door, did they decide she made a better target for them to make a statement?"

The park was on the west side of the parking lot and the sun was sending slanted pillars of light through the oaks. Several families were gathered at the various picnic tables and were trying to enjoy the quiet and the warm weather, under the trees. One young couple was huddled together in front of a picnic table and the man was stroking the woman's hair as they rocked back and forth. It appeared they were both sobbing. A couple with a sick child I thought. This wasn't a picnic area for happy people. Bert's attention had been drifting between the young couple and me and I could tell he was bothered.

"It's probably a good thing my ex-wife stiffed me with the little guy this morning," he said.

This was the time that most people would commiserate with each other and say something along the lines of "why would the bitch keep a guy from seeing his son on a Sunday morning?" Not my style. People deserve the truth even when it's not theirs to grasp. I nodded in agreement. "She figured out you wouldn't have been very good company this morning, Bert. At least not for a three year old."

I half expected an explosion, but he surprised me. "Yeah, you're right. I'm not good company for anybody these days, but Annie sure knows how to bust my balls."

"Did she always bust your balls?"

"Nah, we had it pretty good for a few years."

"What happened?"

He shook his head. "I don't know for sure, it just kind of crept up on us."

"Have you always been a drinker?" I asked. In an undergraduate Basic Logic class that question is classified as classic *argumentum ad ignorantium.* Kind of like, "Have you quit beating your wife?" No matter what your answer—you're a wife beater.

Bert Brogger smiled for the first time that morning. "Oh Harry, you're a clever one." He paused and let that sink in. "No, I wasn't always a drinker. I'm thirty-three years old and I spent the first thirty years of my life as a non-drinker."

"How'd you get to be so good at it?"

"One day I got pissed off and had a couple of drinks and the anger went away. I tried it again the next day and it worked again. It got real easy after that."

"What were you pissed off about?"

"Right now—I really don't remember." He paused and ran his fingers through his long brown hair. He was badly in need of a haircut. "Sometimes I think I had been pissed off for a long time and just didn't know it."

"Did your wife know how angry you were?"

"Yeah, she knows everything." He saw the look on my face. "No, No, I know what you're thinking. I don't mean it that way. Annie's the only person that really knows me. She says I'm a good person that just does bad things."

My guess was that ex-wife Annie had a pretty good head on her shoulders. "And knowing that 'Bert will be Bert' makes it all right in your mind. But, it wasn't all right for her?"

"No she didn't have any patience for a husband coming home drunk at three in the morning."

"How about other women?"

"You mean fuckin' around?"

"Yeah."

"Never!"

"Never!"

"Not one time." He leaned across the table and looked straight in my eyes. "The last time I had sex with someone, other than Annie, was two weeks before I met her—nine years ago. And I haven't been with Annie for two years."

"How about her? Anybody in her life?"

He looked like I had punched him in the stomach. "I don't think so. She lives with her mother and little Bert takes up all of her time, when she's not working."

"Bert it sounds to me like you're still carrying a torch for your ex-wife. Why don't you do something about it?" Before he could answer, I said, "If you cleaned yourself up and cut back on the booze you think you might be able to get her back?"

"I don't know if I want her back, besides, she's better off without me."

"Bullshit Bert. That's a cop-out and you know it. Next thing you'll be telling me the world is better off without you and you'll eat your gun. Bullshit! Think about that little three-year old boy. You want somebody else to be his daddy?"

That hit the hot button. The pain in his eyes gave way to tears. He brushed his eyes with the back of his hand and pulled some notes from his jacket pocket. "Enough of this. Let's finish up with this business about your housekeeper."

"She's not my housekeeper. She's my next door neighbor and my best friend." I was growing tired of explaining my relationship with Juanita to Bert.

"Okay. Let's finish with your best friend." He shook his head as if to clear his thoughts. "Look, Harry, I know you think all this is connected, but what if it isn't?"

"Bert, you're playing 'dumb cop' with me again. You've got the San Francisco cops checking me out and they've already been to Dirty Sally's to check out the two guys in the suits. How about we cut out the bullshit. You know Maggie O'Reilly and Tommy Gavin were killed because they were involved in something that she was bank-rolling—or Gavin was blackmailing her. The attack on Juanita is connected—I know that. Plus, you've got the authorities in Ireland involved, as well." It was my turn to take a deep breath. "Yet you keep dickin' around and acting like maybe there's nothing to all the stuff that points to something bigger than a couple of people dying under strange circumstances. If this isn't all connected in some mysterious way, then you're going to a lot of trouble for nothing."

A long minute passed while Detective Brogger sat motionless at the picnic table. Just then the young couple to our right disengaged themselves as the young man answered the soft chime of his cell phone. The conversation was brief. He snapped the phone shut with a flourish, threw his arms around his companion and lifted her in the air. He gave her a quick kiss and they ran toward the entrance to the hospital hand in hand. Good news.

Detective Brogger smiled broadly as he watched them skip away. "Harry, you know just about as much as we do. We can't connect the O'Reilly woman to Gavin. We know there's a connection—we know it's money and it probably has something to do with Ireland—we just don't know what."

Now it was my turn for a cell phone to ring. I gave a quick glance to the caller ID, saw it was Vanessa and let it ring. I wasn't ready to confront Vanessa.

"Bert, you've told me on numerous occasions that I'm an amateur and should butt out of your investigation. You're right—I'm an amateur. But, everything changed when the bad guys came after Juanita. I'm back in it and I'm in it for the long haul. Whoever attacked her is going to pay and pay big time. I've got resources you can't imagine..."

"Hang on Harry, you..."

"No Bert, you hang on. You've got me pegged right." He nodded his head in agreement. "Yeah, I make a few bucks as a consultant and yeah I'm a gambler. But, I'm rare in the dark world of people who deal in games that involve lots of cash. I'm honest. And because I'm honest I've got lots of friends that would otherwise not be my friends, because I win a helluva' lot more than I lose."

He started to say something. "Wait, let me finish. A lot of the guys in my other life, like Manu and his brother, are not just my friends. They also like me because I keep them out of trouble. A professional gambler's biggest enemy is not other gamblers. A real pro only has to worry about one thing—the IRS—and I know how to keep them out of trouble with those bloodsuckers. So, they owe me, and I intend to collect some of the markers I'm owed. Juanita and I are going to have 'round the clock protection until this mess is cleared up, and Bert—trust me on this—I'm back in it."

He stared at his notes, folded them and carefully placed them back in his jacket. "I'm sorry to hear that, Harry," he said. "I can't tell you what to do. But, don't get in my way—and if you piss off other cops I can't protect you."

He untangled himself from the bench and said, "Take care of yourself, Harry." He didn't shake hands, just turned and walked away.

As I watched his back I thought, what does an alcoholic cop do on a Sunday afternoon when the two people he loves most are missing from his life?

As I made my way back to the hospital to say good-bye to Juanita I wondered how things could get so fucked up in good peoples' lives.

21

The highest point on the Pacific Heights Golf Club property is just above the fourth green where there are two abandoned maintenance sheds. The run-down buildings are in a clearing surrounded by pine trees at the end of a one-lane blacktop road. When the club was first organized the buildings housed all of the maintenance equipment used for the care of the golf course. After newer, more modern maintenance buildings were constructed, closer to the main clubhouse, the old ones became the venue for stag parties, card games and anything else the members wanted to hide. With the advent of a more family-friendly membership, the "top of the hill" gang took their fun and games elsewhere. Today the buildings are mostly forgotten and virtually ignored. The trees around the buildings have been allowed to grow unchecked which is why the buildings cannot be seen from anywhere on the golf course.

The sight of anyone at this spot on the club property would be rare. That is why the man sitting on a folding chair and leaning against the side of the back building would have been cause for curiosity had there been anyone to see him. The late afternoon sun was warm on his face and he tugged his Giants cap lower on his head to shield his eyes. He lifted his clipboard and pencil from their place beside his chair as he noticed another jumbo-jet poised at the end of the south-to north runway at San Francisco International Airport. From his westerly vantage point he could see out over the golf course and across Highway 380 as it weaved its way down to the Bayshore where the two freeways merged in front of the airport. The jumbo jet at the end of the runway would bank to the west and fly directly over his head in about two minutes.

At the exact moment the plane began to move forward the man extended his left arm and pushed a button on the side of his watch. The seconds began to tick off as the plane gathered speed and sped down the runway. Two minutes and eight seconds later the British Airways 747 roared over his head. He punched the button on his watch and noted the time. "Right on the money," he thought.

He made some further notes on his clipboard, stood and stretched in the warmth of the sun. He walked around to the back of the building and approached the door to an abandoned office that was losing a battle to waist-high weeds. The dilapidated door stood in stark contrast to the gleaming master-lock securing it to a stainless steel hinge. He unlocked the door, with the only existing key, and placed the folding chair against the wall under a sheet of plastic. In the middle of the small room there was a wooden crate supported by two sawhorses. The sawhorses were new and constructed of four-by-fours instead of the usual two-by-twos. They were spaced exactly six feet apart and the wooden crate was secured to its resting place by a series of angle irons bolted to the top brace of each sawhorse. The man placed his hand on the crate and smiled. He stroked the crate as if he had just returned from a long trip and he was greeting his lover. Finished with his inspection he closed the door and snapped the lock in place. He was careful not to disturb the overgrown brush as he stepped away from the front of the door. He added to the camouflage by throwing pine boughs across the entrance. Satisfied with his work, he began the long walk back to his car where he had parked on a side street at the west end of the golf course.

22

As I approached the door to Juanita's room I could hear her voice and she didn't sound happy. "I can't eat this!" she exclaimed.

Manu was standing at the foot of Juanita's bed glaring at her. A male nurse was patiently rearranging plates of food he had placed on the rolling tray next to her bed. He had the unruffled attitude of someone who suffered the wrath of patients on a regular basis. In contrast, the look on Manu's face as I entered was one of complete relief. "Pope, this woman outta' control," he said. "She not listening to nobody and she gotta' eat."

"I don't gotta' eat this garbage, Harry. Do I?"

I looked at the tray and it didn't look good to me either. Juice, jello and chicken broth were not a lunch that was likely to excite Juanita, but I knew there was a reason for the meager provisions. I assumed the sternest manner I could adopt, without breaking into laughter, and said, "Sweetheart, you're a captive here and you may as well quit bitchin' about it. Just do what you're told and relax—there's a reason for everything that's going on, including your diet, so be a good girl and eat your lunch."

"Be a good girl, my ass!" she exclaimed. "I'm good, but I'm not a little girl so don't start treating me like one. Anyway—I'm not hungry."

I knew this was a battle that wouldn't be won on the first day. But, I knew she would eat whatever they put in front of her when she got hungry enough. Also, if she missed a couple of meals she might lose a few of the extra pounds she was always complaining about. "Drink the juice," I suggested. "I'm sure dinner will be more to your liking."

I reached for her hand and nodded in Manu's direction. "I've got to get going—I want to catch up with Bill Morrison sometime today. Manu will stay with you until I get back and then we'll make arrangements for him and Tua to take turns watching you."

"I don't need them babysittin' me."

"*I* need them watching you," I explained. "It's as much for me as it is for you. I've got a lot of things to do and I don't want to be worrying about your safety. What happened to you is my fault and you've got to let me take care of this my way." I kissed her hand, gave Manu a gentle jab to his massive shoulder and left her room.

I went back to the bench in the park where Detective Brogger and I had been sitting. I had a couple of calls to make and I didn't want to be distracted. I scanned the calls received screen and dialed Vanessa's number. She answered on the first ring. "Harry, why haven't you called me back? I saw everything on the news last night—how's Juanita? What's going on? How are you? Are you mad at me?"

I didn't know where to begin. "I've been pretty busy the last twenty-four hours, Vanessa." I suddenly realized, in matters of importance, I didn't have much to say to her.

"Well, what the hell happened, Harry?"

"Someone attacked Juanita with a baseball bat—she's got a badly broken leg."

"Who would do something like that?"

"We don't know who, but we think we know why." I said. "That business I told you about with the woman from the Club that died—well, it looks like she was murdered and somebody doesn't want me poking my nose in it. So, they sent me a message and used Juanita to make their point."

"Why haven't you called me back—are you ignoring me?"

"Since you're not asking about Juanita, I'll tell you anyway. She's doing just fine. She's in a lot of pain right now, but she's tough and she'll recover...in time."

There was a long pause. "Harry I can tell you're pissed...and I think I know why."

When I didn't say anything she continued. "I couldn't take the chance that my face would end up on the evening news—Willie thought I was out to dinner with a client. Of all people I would think you'd understand."

"Oh I understand all right...I just don't like it. And I don't like being involved with someone who always thinks of themselves first." I was on a roll. "It would have been nice if your first reaction would have been concern for a person who means the world to me."

"I couldn't take the chance."

"If I'm not worth taking a chance on then why do you care if I'm pissed off?"

"Come on Harry, don't re-define our relationship just because you suddenly think I'm not one of your 'stand up guys'...get off it."

"I don't have to *get off* anything Vanessa...and I'm tired of this conversation. Let's not say anything more that we're going to regret—."

"When can I see you?"

"I've got a lot of things going on right now." I said. "Why don't we give it a few days and then get together for dinner or something."

"Don't wait too long Harry...I need you."

I needed you yesterday, I thought, but didn't say it. "I'll call you in a couple of days. Give me some time to get things sorted out."

We said our good-byes and I got the feeling Vanessa was disappointed in my reaction. In a very short time my quiet simple life had begun to unravel around me. I was making too many mistakes and Julie was at the top of the list. Throw Vanessa in the mix along with my worries about Juanita and I had too much on my plate.

If I had been able to look over my shoulder and see the black Chevy Suburban parked in the shade of the tree next to the entrance to the park it would have added to my worries—and the two figures seated in the front seat watching me would have made it even worse.

23

Junkie Bill was seated in his favorite chair, on the deck at the back of his house. Susan was passing around a tray filled with sliced apples, cheese and crackers. The other family members, sitting in wicker chairs with drinks in hand, were engaged in animated conversation. The only one who smiled as I came into view was Susan. She headed straight for me.

"Oh, Mr. Pius, what a pleasant surprise!" With her back to the group she whispered, "Please call me when you have a chance."

No one stood to greet me and Junkie Bill was the first to speak. "Harry, we're all terribly sorry about what happened to your house-keeper."

I stood there thinking how tired I was of pointing out that Juanita wasn't my housekeeper. Apparently everyone assumed she was some-how in my employ, so I decided to let it go. I looked for an empty chair, saw there wasn't one and decided I was better off standing. It gave me the opportunity to address the entire group. I had something to say and I wanted them to hear it all together, then there would be no misunderstanding.

Susan remained standing and the other four appeared not too happy at my intrusion on their Sunday afternoon. Sandy O'Reilly lay on a lounge chair with her face to the sun. She opened her eyes looked up at me and said, "Mr. Pius, why are you here?"

Before I could answer she continued. "We're all dreadfully sorry about the woman who works for you. But, what happened to her just proves why you should stay out of this and let the police handle it."

"I never wanted '*in this*' in the first place, Sandy. I only got involved because Bill insisted I do him a favor." Bill started to interject and I cut him off. "Hang on, Junkie. You couldn't get the cops to make a move, so I got involved and a guy named Gavin gets killed and my best friend gets beat-up with a baseball bat—and the cops are very much involved—now!"

Peter O'Reilly scowled at me. "All the more reason for you to stay out of this, Mr. Pius." Before I could respond he added, "In addition, I understand from Bill you've been paid a generous amount of money for your trouble."

"Only if I cash the check, Peter." Everybody looked at me. "And I won't be cashing the check. And I don't work or report to any of you." Peter started to respond and I cut him off. "As soon as my friend is well enough to come home from the hospital I'm going over to Ireland and play golf for a week. And while I'm there I'm going to ask around about Tommy Gavin and what he did with the money your mother was giving him."

It was Junkie Bill's turn. "Harry I think we've gotten off the track," he said. "This is a tough time for us. We're convinced—and I think the cops are too—that Maggie was murdered and we're struggling with it. There's a lot we don't know and frankly we're afraid of what we may find out. It's obvious she was involved in something mysterious and we're all a little bit scared." His eyes took in the group and looked back at me. "Harry we don't want you to get in the way of the police," he stated. "Detective Brogger has assured us that adequate manpower has been allocated and the investigation is going to accelerate with…"

He didn't get a chance to finish. For the first time I got to hear Sean O'Reilly speak. It wasn't a whisper, but almost. His pale blue eyes were not quite open all the way and his mouth was fixed in what was most likely a permanent grimace. He looked as if he had a serious case of gastritis. He gave his wife a withering look and said, "Mr. Pius, everyone is being much too polite with you. We want you to stay out of our family affairs! Whether you cash Bill's check or not is immaterial—frankly, I wouldn't have paid you a nickel—you didn't do anything." He glanced at his wife and continued. "Oh, you're a very charming sort of man and I'm sure you have your ways of getting what you want." With another quick glance at his wife he went on. "But, Mr. Pius, we must insist that you sever your relationship with all the business of this family, immediately."

I looked at each family member and, except for Susan, they all nodded approvingly. She continued to have eyes only for me. I half expected her to come to my side and thumb her nose at the group. I confess I was perplexed. Were they scared or like me, simply confused? Or.... were they hiding something? In any case I was wasting my time and Sean had pissed me off. "Sean you don't know me or you would never talk about money around me and you sure as hell wouldn't make a crack about how charming I am. I didn't inherit a business, and the fortune that went with it, and I sure as hell don't have as much 'fuck you' money as you do. But," I said sternly, "I do have 'go shit in your hat' money and I suggest you all do precisely that."

I gave them my best "fuck you" smile, winked at Susan and left them to enjoy the rest of the day. As I made my way to the car I was struck by a thought. Where was Guille?

Thirty minutes later I was back at the hospital. Juanita was asleep. His brother had joined Manu and they were both slouched on separate couches in the visitors waiting area located down the hall from Juanita's room. They were watching a re-run of the Pearl Harbor attack on the History channel and glaring at the television. They were born and reared in Hawaii and their family had been around the island chain since coming from Samoa in the mid eighteen hundreds. The attack by the Japanese happened forty years before they were born but the family rage at the events of December seventh had been passed from generation to generation. Fortunately it was quiet and uncrowded on the ward because the two of them took up all the seating space in the waiting room.

I peeked in on Juanita and she was resting comfortably. The brothers had decided that Manu would stick close to me and Tua, along with their cousin Albert, would take turns watching out for Juanita.

On my way back to the hospital I had made a quick stop at one of my bank locations and hit the ATM machine for the maximum. Over his objections, I shoved ten fun tickets in Tua's shirt pocket to cover incidentals and an advance on Albert's fee. After some further instructions and sharing of schedules, Manu and I headed for the door.

An hour earlier as I had pulled out of the driveway leaving Junkie Bill's Hillsborough mansion, I noticed a black Chevy Suburban pull in behind me. I was curious to know whether it had found its way back to the parking lot at the south end of the hospital. Something in my convoluted thinking expected me to see a black SUV parked in the shade of an oak tree in the parking lot. I wasn't disappointed. There it was. My first inclination was to have Manu saunter over and throw the vehicle, occupants included, into the vacant field next to the parking lot. Caution and good sense dictated otherwise. I hit the unlock button on the key, we got into the car and headed for home.

24

Once on the freeway I made Manu aware of our tail. He smiled broadly. He probably hasn't busted anybody in the head for a couple of weeks and was looking forward to a workout, I thought.

He suddenly came alive. The lumbering giant had awakened. I cautioned him about turning and staring at our companions lurking three cars back, but I could sense the anticipation sweeping over him. Kind of like the look in a python's eyes just before the zookeeper throws a live rat in its enclosure. I still hadn't gotten a good look at the occupants of the SUV but I had a hunch they were the two guys from the bar at Dirty Sally's. Knowing one of them might have been the one with the baseball bat made it all the more tempting to unleash Manu.

Late afternoon fog was sweeping over the top of San Bruno Mountain and the warm Sunday afternoon was giving way to the usual early evening soup. The temperature had dropped twenty degrees in twenty minutes and the thought of a single malt scotch and dinner with Manu was inviting. Without thinking I suddenly flipped the turn signal up and weaving quickly through traffic exited the freeway at the Army Street off-ramp. I glanced in the rear view mirror in time to see the black SUV swerve abruptly to the right then dart in front of an eighteen-wheeler. Amid the blare of an air-horn their maneuver was successful and they closed the gap as we proceeded east on Army Street. What the hell I thought. Let's get this out in the open. Why deny Manu a ready-made treat?

There is a decades-old tradition that takes place Sunday afternoons at Crazy Mary's. The restaurant part of the joint is closed but if you go to the back entrance and make your way down a narrow flight of stairs you will enter another world. In the middle of a thirty by thirty foot walnut paneled room rests a hand carved rosewood pool table. Mother of pearl rail sights, leather pockets and a diamond honed slate base lend an air of total respectability to the scene. Wrong. Some of San Francisco's worst mingle with some of its best. I've watched our dapper former Mayor play nine-ball with the head of a west coast crime family. All connections and positions are checked at the door and everyone is always on their best behavior.

Whenever I've got a couple of hundred burning a hole in my pocket and a Sunday afternoon without anything going on I'll drop in and contribute to the welfare of one of the other players. It doesn't matter who I play…. I always lose. You would think a good putter on the golf course would be a decent pool player. I am the total exception to that concept. But, I enjoy the action…and the mix of people who wander in and out of the place is fascinating.

All eyes shifted from the action taking place at the pool table to Manu and me as we entered the room. As impressive as he is, Manu was not an oddity to the regulars—he's worked for most of them at one time or another. Instead, all eyes rested on me with the intensity usually reserved for the newest lap-dancer at Mitchell Brothers. Fresh meat and, best of all, the biggest pigeon in town was in the room.

Mary's husband Leo waved me over to the bar at the back of the room. He pushed a long neck Bud in Manu's direction and apologized to me, smiling slyly for the meager selection of single malts available on the top shelf. A quick glance and my estimate was about thirty different bottles. I didn't want a drink until I noticed a bottle of Dallas Dhu that had somehow found its way into Leo's inventory. I realized why Leo had been grinning from ear to ear. The Dallas Dhu distillery closed thirty-five years ago and a bottle is as rare as a first edition Raymond Chandler.

"Leo, give me about three fingers out of that black bottle up there on the right," I said. "And don't let me have more than one."

He poured a munificent amount in a crystal glass, shoved the cork back in the bottle and placed the treasure at the back of the row of scotches hidden from view. "I've been waiting for you to stop by Harry—I knew you'd appreciate my find—I've got two more bottles."

"My God Leo, where did you get them? No wait! Sell me one of the bottles."

"They're not for sale Harry. But, they're yours to drink whenever you come in," he assured me. "They came from an estate sale down in Carmel. Some old lady had three unopened bottles in a liquor cabinet. Mary's brother lives down there and he buys and sells stuff out of his store on Cannery Row. He gave me the bottles."

"Your brother-in-law must really like you," I said. "He gave you three grand worth of booze."

"He didn't know what he had," Leo smiled broadly. "He never would have done it if he thought they were worth much."

Manu finished his beer and looked at me, silently asking, "What next?"

I answered with a question for Leo. "Will you let us out the front door—there's a couple guys out back that have been tailing us and I'm gonna' let Manu engage them in a meaningful dialogue."

Leo's smile broadened again, "Sounds like fun—you need some help?"

We followed Leo through a door behind the bar. A narrow hallway led away from the front of Crazy Mary's and it became obvious we were entering the building next door. The hallway gave way to an enormous room dominated by steel shelving racked along all four walls. Each pallet rack was filled with cartons labeled with all makes and models of plasma television sets. All available floor space in the middle of the room was taken up by a grouping of metal desks. On the surface of each desk rested a computer, a telephone and an in-out basket.

"This is one of my other businesses," Leo announced.

The buildings at this end of Army Street are what I call Waterfront Dump. Most of them have been standing since the early nineteen hundreds and have all been used as warehouses at one time or another. The proximity to Pier 84 is the attraction and I could only wonder how often plasma television sets or other electronic items fell off the back of the boat and into Leo's "other business." Leo removed a metal brace from a door that faced the street, disengaged three different deadbolts and we stepped into a cold mist blowing off the bay. The street was deserted. If the two guys tailing us in the black SUV were still on duty they would be behind us between the buildings and the pier.

I was weighing several options about how to approach our friends when Leo said, "I'm gonna' walk around to the back entrance and I'll check out where they're parked—I'll be back in a minute."

He was back in less than a minute. "I've got good news and bad news." Before I could tell him which news I wanted first, he said, "The good news is they're still there—the bad news is they've got company."

"What do you mean they've got company?"

"Harry there's *two* black SUVs parked out there. They're parked side by side, facing in opposite directions, the way cops do when they want to sit and bullshit." Leo paused and looked at Manu. "It looks like there's two guys in one vehicle, but only one in the other."

"Not a problem, brudda." Manu responded.

The cold mist had turned to thick fog. The wind had died and several seagulls were scrapping over a dead fish at the end of the street. I couldn't see a way to get next to the two vehicles without being seen. We needed a diversion.

I was examining our options when Leo stuck a beefy finger in the air. "We need a diversion!" he exclaimed. No shit, I thought, as he proceeded to lay out his plan.

Ten minutes later the plan went out the door and all hell broke loose. What I first thought was a door slamming turned out to be a shotgun going off. When I heard the second shot and the screech of tires I knew we had a problem. As Leo, Manu and I ran around the corner of the building, two black SUVs roared by us and fishtailed west on Army Street. I admit I should have tried to get some license numbers but the sight of two bodies laying in the parking lot took all my attention.

Other bodies were running up out of the basement under Crazy Mary's. Some of them were carrying pool cues, rushing toward the scene of the shooting. Others were jumping into their cars and getting away from a situation that was bound to involve cops. What I didn't know was it already involved cops. The two guys on the ground with their kneecaps shattered were two of San Francisco's finest.

"Oh shit! Shit. Shit. Shit!" Leo exclaimed.

25

Two hours later Manu and I were seated at the table in my kitchen. We weren't alone. Her gray pants suit had given way to jeans and a sweatshirt, and Phyllis Bennett wasn't happy about giving up her Sunday evening. I was trying to brighten her mood with a bottle of Oban single malt and it was starting to work its magic. Bert Brogger was sitting across from her and his mood had brightened considerably when I produced a bottle of Level vodka. Manu had a beer and I was helping Detective Bennett with the Oban.

"Well Harry, you did it again."

I nodded in agreement at Bert Brogger's observation. Not ready to dig into the reason for the two detectives sitting in my kitchen on a cold Sunday night I said, "How do you like the vodka? A friend of mine says it's the best of the best."

"Vodka is vodka, Harry." Bert sipped, shuddered once and said, "Please, spare us the bullshit. We don't have time."

It was Detective Bennett's turn. "Yes Mr. Pius, why don't we get straight to the problem of this afternoon—you tell us what you think is going on."

I passed on making a Marvin Gaye joke. "Detective Bennett I'm not sure what exactly is going on, but I think we're dealing with some bad guys who have a problem with my involvement in Maggie O'Reilly's murder." I expected a reaction and got none. "You *do* accept that she was murdered, don't you?"

"Maybe." She spread her hands out on the table and tried to stare through me. "We don't know what to think at this point. The only thing we know for sure is you are becoming an increasingly huge pain in the ass!"

"I'm not exactly sure what it is I've done to make you think I'm a pain in the ass, Detective." I answered.

Bert finished his first vodka and poured himself about four fingers over fresh ice. I was struck by the thought of him thinking he was "off the clock." "Harry, I think you make an art form out of being a pain in the ass. But do you think the guys tailing you were waiting for an opportunity to jump you or just watching?"

"I think they were waiting for the right time to jump us. I don't know if they planned on shooting us—but I don't think they wanted to just shoot the breeze." I crossed the kitchen to the refrigerator and grabbed a beer for Manu and more ice for the hard drinkers. "You haven't told us what happened with the two off-duty cops—why did they walk up to the bad guys?"

They stared at me for a long time trying to decide whether I was a friend or foe.

"Look," Bert finally said, "Those two guys fucked up, big time. They had just enough to drink to make them dangerous and they decided to play 'tough guy' and it backfired."

"What do you mean 'tough guy'?"

Detective Bennett answered. "They're both on the narc squad and they thought there was a drug deal going down. Big black SUVs are the vehicle of choice these days for dealers. Parked side by side in a deserted parking lot on a Sunday afternoon was too good to pass up for a couple of off-duty cowboys."

"Any trace of the vehicles?" I asked.

"Yeah, we found both of them in a vacant lot near Candlestick Point—on the north side of the stadium."

My grandfather had an expression to describe the Phyllis Bennetts of the world. He would have said her face had more facial tics and twists than a "bullfrog in a rainstorm." She arched an eyebrow and continued. "The two vehicles were Avis rentals...rented with phony drivers licenses and bogus credit cards—and they were wiped clean. We haven't found a finger print anywhere."

"Nothing?"

"Zero—zip," she answered. "Usually a rental car that's driven for more than a couple of days will have a print or two on the gas cap, specially a gas guzzler. Both gas caps were clean. These guys are pros," she added.

The phone rang.

It was either Julie or Vanessa and I didn't want to talk to either one of them. A ringing phone halts conversations. When my three companions realized I was going to ignore the caller, Bert Brogger chimed in, "Harry, somebody out there has the connections and resources to bring in some 'muscle'—and we haven't got a clue what's goin' on."

"Well, you've got two people murdered, Juanita's in the hospital with a broken leg and there's two cops with missing kneecaps, courtesy of a sawed-off shotgun," I stated the obvious.

Detective Bennett arched an eyebrow, tugged at an earring, bit her lower lip and frowned. "Don't get the wrong idea, Harry. We've got some ideas to explore." She paused. "But for my enlightenment give me the short version of how you got involved. Please start from the beginning."

An hour later the Detectives were fully informed. Also Manu, who had been flying blind, but out of trust in me didn't care, was now in the loop. Detective Bennett had asked a couple of questions about Gerry Murphy, which prompted me to ask a couple of my own.

"Why are you looking into Gerry Murphy's involvement?"

Bert answered. "We've talked to a lot of people. Most of them don't know much of anything. Mrs. O'Reilly's family—they don't know squat—but Murphy's name keeps popping up. It seems he and the lady were involved in some charities nobody knew much about." He took a long draw on his vodka and poured himself another four fingers. "The guy's got a lot of money and he hangs out with some people who are definitely not part of the Social Register."

"You could say the same thing about me Bert," I said.

"True," he responded with a smile. "Don't get the wrong idea. We're not saying there's anything to it, but Murphy's name finds its way into every turn of the investigation."

Phyllis Bennett yawned and tugged at her ear. I was starting to keep track of her quirky mannerisms. "I'm beat," she said as she stood and stretched. "I've got an early briefing in the morning with the Chief—if I'm late he'll roast my ass."

"Would that be the hot shot Mr. Dean?" I asked.

"You know the son-of-a-bitch?" She spat out the words.

"Only by reputation," I said and looked at Bert. "I don't know much about the guy. I hear he's got a hot girlfriend."

Manu continued to sit impassively. I was afraid to look in his direction. Paranoia is uneasy in the presence of guilt. "I've never met him—I hear he'll be our mayor some day."

"I don't even want to think about it," she responded. "I'll find a job as a meter-maid in bum-fuck Idaho if he ever gets to be mayor."

Bert Brogger swallowed the last of his drink, looked at the half full bottle, decided against another four fingers and joined Detective Bennett as she headed for my front door. We said our good nights and Manu and I decided to call it a day. His girlfriend had shown up earlier with a suitcase containing enough clothes to last him awhile and he was now settled in the guest room on the first floor facing the street.

I sat on the edge of the bed in my room and realized I didn't have any idea what had gone on in the world for the last three days. I hadn't read a newspaper or seen a newscast since Friday morning. The United States could be at war with France or even better the Giants could have won two in a row over the Dodgers, I thought. I hit the button on the remote to turn on the television set located in the center of the bookcase in my bedroom. The eleven o'clock news with the talking bobble heads was starting. And speaking of the devil, there he was. Willie Dean, the Chief of Detectives, was front and center, along with the mayor and a crowd of City dignitaries, explaining the security precautions necessary for the upcoming arrival of the former Prime Minister of Great Britain Margaret Thatcher. The Ice Queen herself was making a brief stop to deliver a luncheon address at the Commonwealth Club.

I like Margaret Thatcher. She was smart enough to recognize the wisdom of Ronald Reagan's foreign policy strategy when it came to dealing with the Russians. The rest of Europe was scared shitless of the Russians, but not Thatcher. She and Reagan looked Gorbachev in the eye and he blinked. Once he blinked the weakness of his Socialist system was exposed and the Soviet bloc fell apart. History will be generous to Thatcher and Reagan. I made a mental note to reserve the date and coerce one of my upscale friends to invite me to the luncheon.

The phone rang. I didn't answer.

26

By ten o'clock the next morning I felt as if I had put in a full days work.

First there was a phone call from Dr. Jack Swift giving me good news about Juanita's progress. He put me in touch with a physical therapist whose office turned out to be in the neighborhood. She was within walking distance of the house and assured me that coming to the house twice a day to work with Juanita would not be a problem. Mrs. Mulhaupt stopped by to inquire about Juanita's condition and one thing led to another and I convinced her to accept a part time job as housekeeper/nurse. I knew she could use the extra money plus she was one of the few ladies in the neighborhood that Juanita liked.

Manu and I decided the first floor guest room was better suited for Juanita and he was busy converting the second floor guest suite into something he could live with. That meant buying a king-size bed and having it delivered immediately. I was leaving the selection to him.

The three stooges called and informed me they would stop and see their mother on the way out of town. They didn't ask about what arrangements were being made to care for her and I didn't volunteer any information. They had always been able to rely on my involvement in the welfare of their mother, which took them off the hook. It was their loss.

I had two calls left to make and I needed to think before I made them. I poured some coffee in my favorite mug and headed for the roof.

Between nine and eleven o'clock in the morning is the lazy time of day in any neighborhood, especially mine. The morning rush is over and the mid-day scramble to get ready for the evening is yet to come. It was quiet on the roof and I was trying to think of a way to extricate myself from the spell of two women who were more trouble than I could manage. Why was it so complicated? Why couldn't I ever have a girlfriend or a wife that didn't fill my life with drama?

Sweet, sweet Julie—a bright, beautiful, talented woman with the moral fiber of a goat.

Dynamic, deadly Vanessa—a brilliant, sexy, multi-faceted woman with the self-centered nature of a praying mantis. Maybe it's me, I wondered.

I decided to postpone the two phone calls that were covering me in confusion and concentrate on something simple in my life like murder. I called Junkie Bill.

"Hello Harry. I just hung up from Detective Brogger. Why don't you go on a vacation or something?"

"I may do that," I said.

"Well, we've got my dead wife, a dead Irishman and a couple of cops with their legs shot out from under them—swell!"

I agreed that it was "swell." A lot of the things he had said from the very beginning I agreed with, but Bill Morrison was starting to be a severe pain in the ass. "Bill I'm ready to step away from this mess. Yesterday I was intent on avenging the attack on Juanita. Today, I just want to take care of what I've got. I don't want to get shot and I don't want anybody I know to get hurt, either."

"Yeah and now the cops are swarming all over this because a couple of their own got shot. Plus, your buddy Gerry Murphy is having a shit hemorrhage because the cops are asking too many questions—he couldn't keep his mouth shut when you first got involved and now he's pissed because the cops are snoopin' into his business. Hell, they want to know what time I go to the can everyday. Ya know, you should have cashed the check Harry. I just wanted you…"

"I told you," I cut in. "I didn't earn the money. I'm sorry I ever got involved. But, one thing bothers me most of all—why are the bad guys coming after me? I don't have a dog in this fight."

"You happened to be..."

I interrupted again. "Bill, I'm curious—were you and Maggie ever in Northern Ireland?"

"Only in Belfast.... and just for a couple a days to visit a bombed out school. Why?"

"You started to say I 'happened to be in the wrong place' and it made me think of what a 'wrong place' Northern Ireland can be at times," I said.

"Maggie has a cousin who lives in Belfast and we stopped to see her about a year ago on our way to Dublin from Portrush. There's a Catholic girls school up on a hill in an area they call the Falls Road. Maggie gave them a few bucks. Her cousin's daughter teaches at the school and when she took the money she told Maggie it was just a spit in the wind because of the 'troubles'. But, it was important to Maggie, so I didn't say anything."

"Okay, but you never made it down to Newcastle?" I asked.

"You mean where that golf course is? You know—the one you like so much."

"Yeah, Royal County Down," I answered. "It's still my favorite and if Juanita keeps improving I think I'll go over there and play golf with my Irish buddy and just hang out for a week or so."

"Harry, I think that's a mistake. You'll get over there and start asking questions about Tommy Gavin and it'll just lead to trouble."

"I don't think the trouble is over there," I said. "I think there's something going on here that's causing all the shit to come down. I'm hoping the cops latch on to something soon—anything that's a clue about what all this stuff means."

"Well, I suggest you stay out of it and let the cops take it from here. I hear the doorbell.... I gotta' go." He hung up.

A phone call to Gerry Murphy proved to be even more frustrating. I didn't get to say anything for the first three minutes and his voice bellowing at me was at the level of a rock concert. Once his voice lowered to an acceptable level he made it clear that the cops intruding on his life was "not going to be tolerated" and it was my fault. Before I could respond he informed me that the "next time you want a golf game, get another pigeon" and told me not to call him. If he hadn't been on his cell phone I'm sure he would have slammed the receiver in my ear. As it was, I thought he might have thrown his cell phone at something as a signal the call was finished.

I was having trouble convincing people to stay on the line.

27

Over the next ten days nothing happened. Unless you count a Texas Hold'Em game in Alameda that put enough in the safety deposit box to cover the next six months' living expenses. I only played for about six hours. I split when Annie Duke showed up at about four a.m. Texas Hold'Em isn't my game of choice and competing against one of the best players in the world, male or female, is not my idea of fun. I introduced myself to Annie and she acted like she knew me—all the more reason to leave.

Manu and I got Juanita home from the hospital, an ordeal that proved to be something akin to a space shuttle launch. We had the first floor bedroom outfitted for Cleopatra with a broken leg; Juanita turned out to be the bitch from hell. And poor Mrs. Mulhaupt! We almost lost her after the first fifteen minutes. Juanita bitched at her about the flowers, the position of the bed, the lamp, the television, the color of the bedspread—you name it. Almost everything else she found wrong was my fault. But even poor Manu got caught in her opening tirade. It seems he had gone to her house and brought over some of her clothes and the realization that he had packed her underwear was outrageous to her. When she demanded that Manu explain how she would get her underpants on over her cast she reduced the three hundred fifty pound giant to a midget.

But, we survived her opening onslaught and settled into a daily routine of sponge baths, physical therapy and healthy food. Manu and Tua were our constant companions, with an occasional break supplied by their cousin Albert. Juanita even came to appreciate Mrs. Mulhaupt and looked forward to her meal preparation. I've never liked German food, but Juanita thrived on it. That didn't bode well for my future diet, I surmised.

Bert Brogger checked in once or twice with nothing to report and Detective Bennett dropped by the house with some pictures of bad guys for me to look at. I couldn't identify any of them as the two men I had seen in Dirty Sally's.

Susan O'Reilly called to invite me to lunch or "something." I told her politely "no thanks."

Junkie Bill called three times to ask if I was going to Ireland. Three times I said I wasn't sure. And each time he said he thought it was a bad idea. I was beginning to think Shakespeare was right about protesting too much.

Tim Flynn called on the tenth day, at noon his time in Newcastle, forgetting the nine-hour time difference. At three a.m. my time, I had the presence of mind to confirm that yes, I would be honored to be his partner in the annual Royal County Down member-guest golf tournament.

Julie called everyday, but didn't broach the subject of a repeat performance in my bed. Most of the time I was pleased she didn't bring up the subject. We chatted about Juanita's progress and let it go at that.

Vanessa was angry at me, but not for the expected reason. She wanted to come barging in the front door, naked under her Burberry coat, and attack me on the living room floor. When I told her that Manu and Juanita would get a kick out of watching, her enthusiasm waned. Her Willie had Margaret Thatcher and her impending visit to San Francisco on the brain and wasn't paying any attention to little ol' Ethel Mae. I wasn't sufficiently sympathetic to suit the situation she found herself in, and as she put it, "Harry, I'm really horny for you." Without enthusiasm on my part I told her I'd call back in a couple of days.

Comfortable under my roof we had all settled back into a semblance of our former routines and it was alarming to think we might be losing sight of the simple art of murder intruding in our lives.

28

At its scheduled time, Delta flight 35 from San Francisco to Dublin, with a stop in Atlanta, lifted off the north/south runway at SFO. The stretch 767 banked sharply to the right, keeping San Bruno Mountain in view off the left wing tip. As we gained altitude I could see the bright orange towers of the Golden Gate Bridge poking through the fog bank in the distance. The tips of the towers looked like the braces of a child's swing set stuck in blowing sand. It was difficult to imagine the steady stream of cars rushing across the span that crosses one of the most treacherous bodies of water in the world; hard to imagine since most drivers don't think of it as a bridge—it's just another traffic bottleneck in a city paralyzed by vehicles.

The Captain turned off the Fasten Seat Belt sign and announced his expectation of a smooth flight into Atlanta. Because of our on-time departure, coupled with a favorable jet stream pushing us along, we could expect to arrive approximately thirty-five minutes ahead of schedule. Seasoned travelers take "ahead of schedule" announcements with a skeptical outlook. It usually means sitting on the ground waiting for a gate to open once you land. I would rather spend the time in the air asleep than sit on the ground and fidget.

I didn't sleep on the flight to Atlanta. I put a blanket over my head several times and tried, but sleep wouldn't come. I didn't eat the lunch snack, either. There was a time when first class was really first class, but those days are over. I had a couple of Johnnie Walker Blacks and some crackers with the hope that dinner on the international flight would be palatable. My high school English teacher Barbara Brown—*Miss Brown to you*—was fond of saying, "We live in hope and die in despair." My hope for a decent dinner on the flight to Dublin was not realized. I avoided the temptation to load up on scotch and awoke an hour before landing to a cup of coffee and two boxes of Cheerios.

I felt better than I had in a month. Juanita was on the mend and mobile with the aid of crutches. I was proud of her. The intense physical therapy had been an ordeal for a woman her age. She took every difficult exercise the therapist handed her and made it a game. Manu had joined in the game and the two of them were competing to see who could get in the best shape. I smiled at the thought of Manu losing fifty pounds trying to keep up with a sixty-five-year-old woman.

I had been living like a monk for a month and enjoying it. Vanessa had decided to give me some time to come to my senses and Julie was intent on proving to me that she had changed. Of course, I had no idea what either one of them did when they weren't calling me on the phone and I didn't much care. At least that's what I kept telling myself.

I experienced a sudden rush of excitement when I glanced out the window of the plane as we circled over The Island on our approach into the Dublin Airport. The Island Golf Links is one of the golf courses in Ireland I don't tell anyone about—I don't want anyone to know of its existence. It's a treasure best kept as a secret.

The landing was uneventful as was my trip through Customs. I retrieved my suitcase and golf clubs and made my way to the Hertz Rental Car counter. When the lovely young redhead behind the counter looked at me with her piercing blue eyes and said, "Good mornin' Mr. Pius. How ya' keepin'?"—I was putty in her hands. She sold me on an upgrade to a Mercedes sedan and gave me a free cup of coffee to go with it. I drive a hard bargain.

Twenty minutes later I was motoring up the N1 expressway, which would take me through Drogheda and Newry before heading east toward the Irish Sea and the town of Newcastle.

I've never had any trouble adjusting to driving on the "wrong" side of the road—it takes me about ten minutes and I'm driving like a native son. It's going through a roundabout and shifting gears with my left hand that gives me trouble. Only in Ireland or Scotland do you routinely get a luxury sedan with a stick shift. Of course, I could rent a vehicle with an automatic transmission, but where's the challenge in that?

As I guided the Mercedes through the center of Newcastle I couldn't contain the adrenaline rush overwhelming me. This special place captivates me like no other. Heavy, dark clouds covered the sun and Dundrum Bay lay quiet in the shadow of the mountains of Mourne. There was a soft breeze blowing in from the sea carrying the occasional spit of rain. It couldn't be a better day to play golf, I thought.

The one-hundred-year-old Slieve Donard Hotel rose up before me as I pulled into the car park at the end of Downs Street. I am always in awe of its architectural elegance and precise location at the water's edge. The four story red brick hotel dominates the landscape with Victorian grandeur and is a timeless reminder of English refinement.

Tim Flynn was waiting for me in the lobby dressed for golf. "Harry, you've got thirty minutes to get settled and then we're on the tee."

"Hello to you too, you old renegade," I said. It had been six months since my last visit and Tim's reaction to my arrival was as if he had seen me only yesterday.

"Oh, we can get to the hellos and pleasantries later. The ladies have a competition this afternoon and the course will be closed to the men within the hour. We've got to hurry if we're going to get in a round today."

"Give me ten minutes to get my gear up to the room and change clothes," I responded. "I'll see you on the tee."

Royal County Down Golf Links is considered by everyone in the world of golf to be one of the ten best golf courses in the world. Yet, it doesn't have a practice facility. It doesn't have what we Americans call a driving range, much to the displeasure of the first time visitor. For me, a driving range would only detract from its charm and sense of history—I love it just the way it is. Another knock on the course is the number of blind shots you experience during the course of your round—blind shot in the sense that you cannot see your target when playing the actual shot. Of course, you can walk ahead of where your ball lays and select something to aim at in the hopes you guess correctly. My thought has always been along the lines of a blind curve in the road; it's only blind the first time you drive on the road. Many of the top ranked professional golfers on the American Tour don't understand or appreciate the beauty of a blind shot.

With just a couple of perfunctory practice swings Tim and I hit perfect drives on the par five opening hole. And with two young boys carrying our bags, we made our way down the first fairway bordering the edge of Dundrum Bay on our right. This began, what for me, is the closest thing to a "religious event" I can experience.

29

The two men walked along the beach where the first series of erosion barriers protected the shore from the onslaught of winter storms. The tide was out and the vast expanse of sand stretched a quarter of a mile on their right to the water's edge. They had entered the beach at the north end of Newcastle town center and passed to the right of the first tee of the golf course. They carried fishing poles and knap sacks strung across their shoulders. At first glance you would have thought it odd they were not wearing boots or shoes befitting fishermen. Even more odd, on closer inspection, would have been the absence of fishhooks or bait in their possession.

They walked as close to the first hole on the Royal County Down Golf Links as possible while still remaining hidden from view. The two golfers the men were watching made their way slowly away from the first green toward the second tee. It was only then they were close enough to confirm their identities. Flynn, the Irishman, was well known to the men. It was the Yank they were most interested in.

He was taller than they had been led to believe and appeared to be younger. He was wearing a white baseball cap of the type most favored by Americans and a dark brown cardigan sweater. The men had been told that the Yank was in his late forties, but his fluid golf swing and spring to his step suggested a man half that age. Also, his narrow waist and broad shoulders gave a hint of someone who might be in superb physical condition, which could present a problem.

The two men continued to stay hidden in the dunes and followed the two golfers until they finished playing the third hole.

The fourth tee is the highest point on the golf course and affords a majestic view of the mountains in the distance and the town of Newcastle below. The spire of the hotel is visible from this point and, for the first time player of the golf course, this location is always a "Kodak moment."

The American paused and seemed to be enjoying the view whereas the Irishman played his tee shot quickly and with rather poor results. The two men pretending to be fishermen had quickly determined that the Yank was the more accomplished golfer.

The two men were waiting at the bottom of the path as the golfers and their caddies made their way down from the tee. They ignored the Irishman and focused all their attention on the look and manner of the Yank. They later acknowledged that the description they had gotten from America did not do him justice. He had the look of someone not to be taken lightly.

"Good afternoon" greetings were passed easily between the men as the golfers crossed the path that angled diagonally across the Links. The two men with the fishing poles turned and walked slowly along the path back toward the bay.

The teenage boy caddying for the American wondered aloud as they walked toward the fourth green, "Those guys sure are dumb…nobody in their right mind goes fishing when the tide is all the way out."

30

I hated for the day to end. Michael Martin, my young caddy, was sprinting to my ball where it lay in the middle of the eighteenth fairway. I was only a par away from shooting a personal best on the toughest links in all of Ireland. Four more strokes would bring me in at a three under par score of sixty-nine; however, I was thinking ambitiously of making a birdie for sixty-eight. Michael was more excited at the prospect than I.

A perfect three wood second shot, followed by a crisp pitching wedge that settled ten feet from the hole and I had a score of sixty-eight in my grasp. It was not to be. The ten-footer broke away from the hole at the last moment and hung on the edge of the cup. I tapped the putt in the hole for my par and gave the ball to Michael. He excitedly informed me that he had never caddied for anyone at Royal County Down who had posted a score in the sixties and could he have the ball as a souvenir. I was happy to oblige.

Michael and I had become fast friends over the course of our four hours together and I realized early on that he was a young lad of good character. Without him saying it, I surmised the money he earned as a caddy when he wasn't in school was important to him and his mother. His father had died five years earlier when Michael was only eleven and his "mum" had turned their large house into a bed and breakfast. In the evening she served dinner, but could only accommodate eight patrons in her dining room. Michael did an excellent job of selling me on the fact that "mum is the best cook in Newcastle" and he could arrange for Tim and I to dine that evening if we arrived after eight o'clock. He knew she was booked full, but would take care of us after her regular guests had departed. We told Michael we'd be there and he reminded us to bring our own bottle.

A warm shower and clean clothes gave me renewed energy. Tim had thoughtfully provided me with a bottle of Glenmorangie single malt scotch and I was taking in the view of Dundrum Bay when I thought of Juanita. It was mid-morning in San Francisco; she would be finished with breakfast and her first of two physical therapy sessions would be out of the way. I reached for the phone, got an international connection and punched in the number I know best.

Manu picked up on the second ring. "Hey brudda, how's everythin' wit you?"

"Couldn't be better…. How's Juanita doing?"

"She doin' good…. Driving us crazy, tho. She getting a new cast in two days and want me and Tua to take her to Las Vegas."

"She can't go anywhere until the doctor says she's okay to travel…. tell her I said so."

"Man, I ain't tellin' her nothin'. Here you tell her."

Boom! I got an earful. She finally wound down when I told her the connection was bad and I needed to say goodbye. "I just wanted to say hello and see how you are feeling. I know you're bored, but hang in there."

"Harry, don't hang up on me. The connection is fine—I got something to tell you about that cop."

"Which cop?"

"The one who drinks too much—you know, his name is Bert something or other. You know I think he's smarter than he lets on. But, anyway, he wants you to call him as soon as you can."

"I'll call him as soon as we hang up," I said. "But, Juanita, listen to me. Don't be bugging Manu about taking you to Las Vegas. You're not going anywhere."

She started to shout at me again and I cut her off. "If you go to Vegas you might violate my Rule Number Two and we can't have that, can we?" Before she could bellow at me again I hung up and tried to reach Detective Brogger. I got his voice mail and left a message.

I poured myself three fingers of Glenmorangie in a traveler and headed for the lobby to meet up with Tim for our dinner date with Michael's mum. Almost as an afterthought, I turned back, retrieved the bottle and took it with me.

31

Wild salmon, fresh from the Irish Sea, must be broiled with the utmost care and dedication, and Katherine Martin gave it the attention it deserved. Michael was correct; his mother was not only the finest cook in all of Newcastle, but in my judgment maybe the best anywhere. I had finished the most exquisite meal that I could remember eating and was settled in the sitting room of her Moorings Bed and Breakfast enjoying an after-dinner scotch. Michael had bid us a "see you tomorrow" and his mother promised to join us when she and her helper were finished in the kitchen. Tim Flynn, drink in hand, was grinning at me with an air of smug superiority.

"You can forget it, Harry. Better men than you have tried, including me."

"Tried what?" I didn't need to ask.

"Come on Harry. We should have left an hour ago, but when the boy introduced you to Katherine you looked like you were struck by lightning—she does that to everybody. Hell there's dozens of yanks that come and stay here on a regular basis in the hopes she'll go on a date with them." Tim continued grinning. "You think you'll work that Harrison Pius magic on her and, trust me old friend, you haven't got a chance. When Eamon Martin died, young Michael took up all the room in her heart and there isn't a man in the world that will change that."

"He must have been quite a guy," I said.

"I only met him once, but I've heard the stories about when and how he died…. it was a shock."

"What happened?" I asked—thinking it probably had something to do with "the Troubles."

I was wrong and Tim's answer surprised me. "He worked the land and a more robust man you'd never meet, I've been told. They had a strip of land on the coast road toward Ardglass and he raised potatoes." Tim paused and I sensed a sadness come over him. "Eamon was a man of about your size and strong as an ox.... and he was a handsome bloke, as well. One afternoon about five years ago he came home early to this house and told Katherine he was tired and needed to lie down. She put him to bed and when she looked in on him—some thirty minutes later—he was dead of a heart attack. Forty years old and he was gone. She was thirty-six, a widow with a young son and, to her thinking, a major portion of her life was over. She sold the farm and now she and the lad have this bed and breakfast.... and they make a living."

I had finished my scotch and, as Tim finished his story, I reached for the bottle to pour a refill. At that moment Katherine Martin entered the room with an empty glass in her slender hand.

"Mr. Pius I'll have a wee dram," she said. "And Tim—how are you keepin' after all that food?"

"Couldn't be better, Katherine," he responded.

"And Mr. Pius. You as well?" Her piercing blue eyes went straight through me. "Did you enjoy your dinner?"

I poured her a "wee dram" and responded. "Dinner was wonderful.... Michael told me you were the best cook in Newcastle. He didn't do you justice. And Katherine, please call me Harry or Harrison."

She took a sip of her drink and cocked her head thoughtfully to the side saying, "I think I prefer *Harrison* instead of *Harry.*" Then she added, "You are Michael's new hero.... he was most impressed at your prowess this afternoon on the links."

I couldn't look at Tim because I knew he was grinning like a fool in anticipation of me making a move on our hostess. He couldn't have been more wrong. "Katherine, it was me that was impressed. You should be very proud of Michael...I think he is an outstanding young man. As we walked along today we spoke at length about his schoolwork. For such a young man, he has a wonderful attitude about where he wants to go with his life."

"It's a good thing you speak of, Harrison—and I know it well. The last few years have been hard on the boy. I just wish he didn't have to work so hard. He's a high honors student and a fair golfer you know, but he hasn't the time to play and it's become so terribly expensive, even for the locals."

"Tim and I are playing again tomorrow afternoon and I've arranged with Michael to caddy for me again. Maybe I'll have him play a few holes with us using my clubs."

The ever present smile on Katherine's face brightened. "He would be most pleased at the prospect of showing you his game—of that I'm certain," she replied. "You're aware he has school until one o'clock," she added.

Tim looked up and said, "I have some work issues that will occupy me until the afternoon and Harry has some people to see—we won't play until around one thirty or so."

"That will be perfect for Michael," she said.

"Perfect" came out as "parfect" and in my mind it was charming. Tim could only smile at her hold on my attention. We finished our drinks and stood—signaling an end to what had been a "parfect" evening.

"I will bid you gentlemen a very pleasant goodnight. If you wish to have dinner with us again, just let Michael know." She quickly added, "And if there is something special you would like me to prepare, give us a little notice and I can always try to accommodate a special request. I hear a farmer near Castledown has some nice spring lamb available."

Tim spoke for both of us and said, "That would be lovely indeed. We'll see you tomorrow evening at eight."

Tim and I had come in separate cars, which turned out to be a blessing. The overnight guests had taken all the available parking places in front of the Moorings and I had been forced to park across the lane adjacent to some wooden stairs leading to the beach below. The breeze had freshened, pushed by the incoming tide, and the moon was beginning to dance among the clouds, reminding me of a ghostly galleon described in a long forgotten poem. I fumbled for the key to the Mercedes and noticed Katherine waving at me from her front entrance. She held an almost empty bottle of scotch in her outstretched hand as she walked to the gate of her white picket fence.

Growing up on the farm in Salinas had its drawbacks, but the wisdom gleaned from living with Uncle Ambrose had served me well on many occasions. He insisted that my brother and I conduct ourselves like gentlemen at all times. That windy evening, across the lane from the Moorings, my gentlemanly behavior saved my life. Leaving the engine to idle I hopped out of the car and ran across the lane, not wanting Katherine to venture out in the cold evening air because I had forgotten my precious scotch. Later it was determined that I had only gone about thirty yards when the first blast propelled me to the ground. It wasn't like in the movies—not a big bang—it was more of a WHUMPFFFF. And I landed in the grass at the edge of the picket fence. The second blast was just like in the movies though, and the fireball from the exploding Mercedes lit up the sky. Then the wooden stairs caught fire, fueled by burning debris, and we had a hell of a mess.

By ten o'clock the next morning, fortified with two hours' sleep, I was back in the office of the Newcastle Garda answering the same questions I had been answering since the fire response units had arrived the evening before. Katherine was sitting next to me and her anger and frustration at both the Duty Officer and me was reaching the boiling point.

The look on her face said she wasn't going to respond favorably to my invitation for lunch. She had already informed Michael that he could try and pick up a caddy job after school, but he was to stay away from me. In her words, "Being around Mr. Pius is too dangerous."

First Duty Officer Malone narrowed his eyes at me and asked again. "Mr. Pius, why are you insisting that your visit to our quiet village is strictly for the pleasure of our golf links?" Before I could respond he added, "We've been in touch with Detective Brogger in San Francisco and he has suggested we arrest you, and throw away the key. Our bureaus have been cooperating with the Detective about this business involving the murder of Mr. Gavin and the American woman and we have provided him with a large measure of information. Our agency and his are in agreement that your involvement is most unwelcome."

His mention of the word *murder* brought an exasperated sigh from Katherine and I knew she was regretting she had ever laid eyes on Harrison Pius. I tried, once again, to explain my motive for coming to Ireland, but nobody was buying it. I wanted them to believe something I didn't really believe myself. And now someone had tried to kill me. I've had jealous boyfriends take a swing at me and sore losers threaten me, but a car bomb, with my name on it, was a different deal. I was severely pissed off—and, I was scared.

"Officer Malone, I admit I had every intention of looking into the background of Tommy Gavin once I arrived in Newcastle, but my first priority was to spend some time with my old friend Tim Flynn and play some golf." I paused and tried to look into Katherine's face. She avoided my eyes. "I assure you this kind of trouble does not follow me around."

We kept at it for another hour and got nowhere. I couldn't come up with names or reasons for someone blowing up my car. It obviously had something to do Gavin and Maggie O'Reilly, but *what* was anybody's guess. Katherine was anxious to get back home; she had guests leaving and new ones checking in and she was concerned about the look of a bombed out Mercedes parked across the lane from her bed and breakfast. Officer Malone assured her that the car would be gone by early afternoon—at least what was left of it—they were transporting it to Belfast for further tests. Earlier I had gotten a call from a not-too-happy Hertz district manager informing me that a replacement rental would be delivered by late afternoon. As we were leaving Officer Malone's office I was hoping Katherine's anger at me wouldn't prevent her giving me a lift back to the hotel.

"Get in Harrison. I won't have you walking back to the hotel." I caught the faint edge of a smile as we pulled away from the Garda headquarters.

32

I played golf in the afternoon with Tim Flynn, but my heart wasn't in it, and I played terrible. My caddy was an old gentleman who was half in the bag, and should have been sleeping it off someplace. I had looked forward to Michael Martin carrying my bag—I thought once more about what a fine young man he was. I would have surely played better had he been my caddy. The golf tournament was still three days away and I was in hopes his mother would have a change of heart and let him caddy for me then.

Tim played awful, as well, and we agreed to pass on getting together for dinner at the hotel. Katherine had politely declined my request for a dinner reservation at her establishment citing the unavailability of provisions for more than her overnight guests at the Inn. In other words—"get lost."

I was alone for the evening with no plans so why not snoop around. There was a new rental car in the car park delivered that afternoon by Hertz. Maybe this one would last more than two days.

By eight o'clock that evening I was seated at a corner table near the fireplace in The Whistling Oyster sipping an after dinner scotch. Dinner at the Slieve Donard had been a tough sirloin steak sliced too thin accompanied by a variety of potatoes presented in a half dozen different ways. At least the tossed salads were improving. Ten years ago a tossed salad in Ireland was as rare as Buddhist monk.

I recognized the caddy master from the golf course having a pint with a couple of his lads and invited them over.

One of the two lads spoke up. "Ah, Mr. Pius, it was a grand show your vehicle put on last night." He nodded in the direction of Ken the caddy master. "We haven't had fireworks such as that since the Provos blew up the front door of the Hotel last year."

"And it was a joke too," Ken added. "The cowards wanted to celebrate Bobby Sands death—it's been twenty years ya know—and the best they can come up with is a coke bottle full of petrol and some soap shavings." He snorted, "Some bomb!"

"The Iron Lady was right, ya know," he said. "Them buggars in the Maze didn't want to eat, they could fuckin' do without. They called it 'goin' on the blanket'. Well I say fuck 'um, and old lady Thatcher said the same thing." He raised a finger and pointed in my direction. "Ya know she's over in the states, right now."

I vaguely remembered Vanessa telling me about Margaret Thatcher's trip to The City. I asked, "You mean she's in San Francisco?"

"No, no," Ken answered. "She's traveling around the states—she and Bush are big buddies. I think she ends up in Frisco next week."

I winced at his use of the word "Frisco." We San Franciscans don't call it "Frisco." "I heard she couldn't travel…. something about a stroke."

"She's a tough old bird," he said. "Her husband died and she's had a couple of strokes. She spends most of her time in a wheelchair, but she'll still give a speech to two drunks leaning on a lamppost if they'll agree to spit on the IRA."

"She still is fighting that battle?" I asked. And a glimmer of an idea flashed behind my eyes and was quickly gone.

"Bloody hell, man!" the oldest of Ken's companions exclaimed. "The fuckin' Provos tried to kill her a half dozen times. They almost got her in Brighton twenty years ago and she's still pissed off. I think those Provo boys would like another shot at her, if they had the chance."

Signaling for another round of drinks I asked, "What happened to the peace accord? I thought all that shit was put on hold after 2002."

"For the most part it has quieted down," Ken said. "But, it'll never really be over…'The Troubles' go too deep. You've heard the old joke that 'the worst Irish are always Englishmen in disguise' haven't you?" He saw the confused look on my face. "A lot of the bad-ass Republicans are blokes that did time in Wormwood after getting kicked out of England."

By this time Ken and his lads were beginning to feel the effects of several pints and I realized a discussion of Ireland politics was a subject that usually resulted in a shouting match in an Irish pub. I changed the topic. "Did any of you boys know Tommy Gavin?"

"Ah, he was a bad one, that boy." The youngest of Ken's lads said, "He got what he had coming—we know for sure."

I could think of a number of things Tommy Gavin probably had coming, but I went back to my original question. "Did any of you know him or know how he came to have enough money to travel back and forth to the States?"

Ken pushed his chair back and stared into the glowing coals of the peat fire. "Tommy was full of grand ideas—he fancied himself as what you Yanks would call a 'mover and a shaker'." He picked his glass of beer off the table, started to take a drink, thought better of it and continued. "Tommy was a tough guy in a crowd with his mates—get him alone and he was a chicken shit little bastard. He came out of the Clonard area in Belfast and he got his start throwing rocks at the Protestants when they came down the Falls Road to Shankill. He was nothin' more than a Falls ghetto rat."

"But, did he cause trouble around the golf course?" I asked, taking a sip of my scotch and thinking about the problems Gavin had caused in the caddy yard at the Olympic Club in San Francisco. "If his sympathies were with the Catholics, he had to be in a minority among the other caddies and members."

"Oh, he caused problems all right," Ken declared. "Our members come from all walks of life and they don't take to politics and religion gettin' in the way of their golf…especially when the problem is the result of one of the caddies shootin' his mouth off."

I shifted in my chair so as to move closer to the fire. I decided to push the issue and see if I could get Ken or his lads to give me a better understanding of just who and what Tommy Gavin had been all about. Maggie O'Reilly had been killed because of money, I was certain of that. But, why kill Tommy Gavin? He and Maggie had to be connected, but how and where? Had she been to Newcastle? Junkie said he and Maggie had gone straight from Belfast to Dublin. A side trip to Newcastle would have taken them well out of the way.

I looked at Ken. "Do you ever remember Gavin caddying for an American woman—an older woman, but still attractive—would have looked to be about sixty."

"That was his specialty," Ken said. "Tommy liked the older ladies…. and he liked the older ladies from the States the best. Said they tipped the most—and, of course, he was always tryin' to put the moves on anything that walked." Ken smiled broadly and went on. "He patted the wrong lady on the ass the last day he caddied here at County Down. Her Aussie husband clocked old Tommy out on the fifteenth fairway—that's when we run him off for good."

"But do you remember an American woman by the name of O'Reilly? She would have been with a craggy old guy named Bill…. he would have looked about ten years older than her."

"Nah," he said, a little too loudly. The pints were starting to kick in. "We get too many Americans for me to keep track. They all start to look alike. They sure all act alike—too much money." He paused and sheepishly looked around. "Course I don't mean you, Mr. Pius. You're different than most Yanks."

I knew what he meant. I worked hard at not acting like the "ugly American." In particular, I made it a point to stay out of religion, politics and anything to do with the conditions that exist between Northern Ireland and The Republic. I once had a guy take a swing at me in a bar in Dublin. I innocently, I thought, made a comment about how much better the roads were once you crossed the border—all hell broke loose.

"I take that as a compliment, Ken." Staring into an empty glass I looked around for the barmaid. Ken's two companions stood to leave and after telling him they'd see him in the morning they weaved their way through the heavy oak front door of the pub. Ken remained seated and I ordered more drinks. Ken switched to brandy—unusual for an Irishman.

"Course, if it's all that important to ya' I could go in early tomorrow and check the sheets to see if the name O'Reilly is listed." Then he added, "I'd need to know how far back you want me to go."

"You mean the tee-time sheets?"

"Yeah, we keep the names of all the non-member guests that play the Club—and when they played—we only keep the sheets for two years, though."

How good was my memory, I wondered. Junkie Bill told me he and Maggie had gone to Belfast…but when were they there? The scotch hadn't dulled my memory—Bill said they stopped to see her cousin *"about a year ago."* I didn't need to know any more about Tommy Gavin, at least from Ken. But, I did need to know if Maggie and Junkie Bill had ever been to Newcastle.

"Ken, if you could start from six months ago and go back a year, that would be great. Of course, I'll pay you for your time."

"Forget it. If it's important to you Mr. Pius I'm happy to do it." He swallowed the rest of his brandy and shook my hand. "I'll give it a go in the morning. The Club Secretary will think I've taken leave of me senses, but that makes me no never mind…check in with me around nine." "O'Reilly" he muttered to himself and left me in front of the fire in the pub.

Maybe I've taken "leave of me senses" too, I thought.

33

I rarely dream. When I do, I don't remember the dreams. But, I often go to sleep bothered by something that I can't figure out. But then, often in the middle of the night I awaken and everything suddenly seems crystal clear.

After leaving the Whistling Oyster there was something bothering me. I was missing something and the nag was like a mosquito bite. If I left it alone it would no doubt go away, but I kept picking at it. I got nowhere. I turned on the ignition in the rental car and started driving to the hotel. The drive was a nervous ordeal even though I knew Officer Malone had assigned one his men to watch the car and me. I made it back to the hotel in one piece, informed my bodyguard that I was in for the night and fell into bed.

I checked the clock before I fell asleep. It was twelve-twenty one. I made a note of the time only because it reminded me of my birthday. At shortly after five I sat straight up in bed and told myself what I had said hundreds of times; "Harrison, you are one dumb shit."

A quick shower and I was in shape to meet the day. I took the stairs down two at a time and made my way to the basement kitchen where a grizzled old man in a chef's hat was frying bacon and watching television. The place was deserted. The TV displayed a snooker game on the BBC. He gave me two cups of coffee from his private pot and a couple of hot-buttered scones to go. The strong coffee jumpstarted my heart and I practically flew out the back door of the hotel.

It was still dark. The lack of wind made the waves seem to smash on the beach louder than usual. The gravel path leading to the pro shop and caddy yard wound along an enormous hedge of Italian

Cypress that shut out the morning light. I knew the way with my eyes closed.

There was a soft glow coming from the caddy master's office and Ken was bent over sheets of paper the size of a desk pad. The six pints of Guinness and two brandies he had consumed the previous evening didn't seem to have done any damage to his faculties. He was alert and wide-awake.

Each sheet in front of him had a block of four lines spaced evenly down both sides of the sheet. Beginning with the first line at the top of the page was a designated time. The first line read 7:00 A.M. with three lines under it. This allowed the starter to enter the names of four golfers and their starting time on the first tee at 7:00 A.M. Each sheet contained forty-three blocks of four lines, which covered a day's play from 7:00 A.M. until 2:00 P.M.

Ken was bent over a sheet using a plastic ruler for a guide as he looked at each line. I hoped he hadn't gotten very far because we were going to have to start over.

"Thanks for the coffee," he said. "I haven't found anybody named O'Reilly that's played here between April and May of last year…I figure they wouldn't have been here before then, the weather's too bad."

"Ken, I'm sorry," I said taking a scone from the bag and handing it to him. "I can't believe I didn't think of it last night, but we might be looking for the wrong name."

"You're shittin' me…. Sorry Mr. Pius I didn't mean…"

"No, it's all right," I said softly. "It's my fault. I should have thought of it last night. We should be looking for a different name—I keep thinking of her as Maggie O'Reilly, but her new last name is Morrison. We should be looking for William and Maggie Morrison."

And there it was—eighty-two starter sheets into our search—the longest day of the year; June twenty-first. I was born on the shortest day of the year and Junkie Bill and Maggie had played golf on the longest day of the year. June twenty-first of last year they had played golf at Royal County Down Golf Links in Newcastle, Northern Ireland at one-twenty in the afternoon. They had played by themselves—what the Irish call a two-ball—and penciled next to their name on the starter's sheet were the letters TG.

"The question is," I said. "Do those letters mean what I think they mean?"

"One of two things," he answered looking closely at the sheet. "Either Teddy Grainger caddied for them or Tommy Gavin did…. and I don't think it was Teddy."

"Why's that?"

"Teddy's seventy years old and he can only carry one bag…. it was probably Gavin."

The hot buttered scone felt like a bowling ball in my stomach. Some hotshot private eye, I muttered to myself.

34

Bert Brogger was sober. It was eleven p.m. in his world and his voice was clear and crisp. After leaving Ken at the caddy shack I had found a quiet place on a bench near the first tee of the golf course to make my call to the detective.

He answered on the first ring and came to the point quickly. "Harry, I'm glad you called. We've got a situation here that's thrown all of us for a loop." He paused and when I didn't respond he went on. "Bill Morrison has turned up missing...he's disappeared."

"What do you mean disappeared?" I asked. But something told me I shouldn't have been surprised.

"He's gone. No one has seen him for two days. The O'Reilly boys were supposed to meet him at their corporate attorney's office on Monday morning and he didn't show. As near as we can tell he hasn't been home since Sunday night."

"What about a car...did he leave in a car? Did he pack a bag? Is there any sign that somebody took him forcibly?"

"Harry, you're getting way ahead. Slow down and listen, for a change..." He didn't finish.

I said quickly, "Bert, I always listen to you. I don't always follow instructions to your satisfaction, but you must admit I'm a good listener. Go ahead."

He ignored my feeble attempt at humor. "Listen Harry. The O'Reilly clan is having a collective shit hemorrhage. They don't understand what the hell is goin' on. Morrison has come up missing but nothing else."

"What do you mean 'nothing else'?"

"I mean there isn't anything else that's missing. All the cars, his clothes, personal effects—all accounted for. Peter spoke with him on the phone Sunday afternoon and there's been no sign of him since then. Plus, there's another thing..."

I interrupted. "I've got other things, too. But keep going."

"We spent most of the day with Sean and Peter going through their mother's house and we came up empty. Except we did find Morrison's appointment book and there's something I want to ask you about."

Before I could ask "about what," he continued. "Like I said, he was supposed to meet the boys and the lawyer Monday morning and that appointment was logged in his book. But, we think he had another appointment scheduled for later in the day."

"With who?"

"All it said was *Murphy Grounds* and the number *2* next to it. But, we think...."

"So, you think he was supposed to meet somebody named *Murphy Grounds* at two o'clock Monday afternoon—that doesn't make sense." I interrupted again.

"Harry, you're not listening—let me finish. There was a slash mark between Murphy and Grounds. We think Murphy is the name of someone—some one we know about, but we haven't got a clue about Grounds."

"How about Gerry Murphy?" I asked. "You think it could be him? Have you tried..." Suddenly from around the corner of the first tee came the rumble of an approaching maintenance vehicle and, just as suddenly, I flashed on the meaning of the word *Grounds*. As the four-wheel cart sped in front of me I said, "Bert, one of my golfing buddies at Pacific Heights told me that the Board of Directors had appointed Gerry Murphy to head up the Grounds Committee. There might be a connection."

"We're ahead of you on that one—which reminds me."

There was a long pause on the other end. Bert had something to say, but it seemed like he was having a hard time getting it out. "What's the deal with your friend Murphy and his old lady?"

No one saw me shake my head and sigh, but I shook my head and sighed anyway. "It's a long story, but the short version is they have what might be called a marriage of convenience—mostly Gerry's convenience. He's got a thing for young college girls and his wife looks the other way."

"How can that old fart get…"

"Money, Bert. Money gets you anything. If a young, good-looking coed needs some help with her tuition, books or spending money…Gerry's her man." I quickly added, "It's an underground operation among girls that are willing to put out for financial help. It beats student loans and he gets more referrals than he can handle. Of course, all of his girlfriends would be the first to tell you that prostitution is disgusting. Why are you asking?"

"Like I said, we're ahead of you. But, we haven't talked to him yet and his wife hasn't been any help. She says she hasn't seen him since Monday morning and he didn't come home last night—she didn't seem to be bothered about it…. him not coming home."

The best nights of the week for Gerry's wife were the nights Gerry didn't come home I could have said, but I wanted to get back to the *Murphy/Grounds* notation in the appointment book. "Are you thinking that Gerry Murphy and Bill Morrison had a meeting scheduled for Monday afternoon?"

"Yeah, and we want to speak with Murphy and find out if Morrison kept the appointment."

I had the beginnings of a Rolaids moment. My early morning heartburn was zigzagging through my chest like a freight train on a dirt road. Maggie—dead, Gavin—dead, Juanita—busted up, Junkie Bill—missing and Gerry Murphy—who knows where. And the little matter of a Mercedes rental car sent to its great reward.

Detective Brogger interrupted my thoughts. "You got any ideas about a connection between those two?"

"I can't imagine a scenario where Gerry Murphy would have anything to do with Junkie Bill—he still thought of him as a drunken old caddy."

"Yeah, a 'drunken old caddy' with twenty million bucks," Bert said.

"That wouldn't mean anything to Gerry.... He thinks money is just something you play around with. He has big bucks and knows he's a shit, so he figures most people with money are shits, too. But, you know come to think of it, Gerry might have tried to get Bill involved in the construction project we've got scheduled for later this year up on the hill."

"The hill?"

"We've got some old buildings up on the hill that overlooks the fourteenth hole—it's the highest place on the property. The plan is to tear down the old buildings and put in a recycled water system." I added, "It's going to cost a lot of money. Maybe Gerry planned on hitting Bill up for a big donation—maybe a donation in Maggie's name."

"You think Morrison has access to that kind of money this soon?" Bert asked. "We know her will is still in probate and he hasn't got his inheritance finalized."

"He told me my budget was a million bucks to investigate Maggie's death, so he must have access to some of her money. She may have set up a trust account to tide him over until the will goes through probate." I said. Then I changed direction. "I told you I had a couple of things of my own to talk about."

"Make it fast. Don't forget, it's almost midnight here."

"There's something you should know," I said. "Bill Morrison lied to me." I waited for a reaction from Bert and got none. "He told me he and Maggie were in Ireland last year, but never got over here to Newcastle. I checked it out and I know for a fact they played golf here on June twenty-first and here's...."

"You're kidding," he shouted.

"Wait, let me finish, Bert," I said. "And here's the best part. Our old friend Tommy Gavin caddied for them the day they played—so much for Bill not having any knowledge about Gavin."

"Could Gavin have caddied for them and Bill didn't know who he was or make the connection when Gavin showed up floating in the Bay?"

"That's possible, but why lie to me about never being here with Maggie?"

"Harry, this thing gets more confusing all the time. When are you coming home?"

"I'm not sure. I planned on sticking around here and relaxing unless Juanita needed me. I'm not worried about her as long as Manu and Tua are living in my house, but I'm starting to have second thoughts…. I may come home early." The warm morning sun on my face prompted me to suddenly think of another thought I had awakened to. "Bert, can you do us both a favor?"

"I'm asleep on my feet, Harry. What now?"

"Call Florida Atlantic University in Boca Raton, Florida and, in your official capacity as a cop, request all the information they have on William Morrison, former English professor at their institution."

"I'm way ahead of you Harry. I called this afternoon. I made the call on my cell phone and the woman I spoke with wouldn't give me anything until she calls back to an official location. She's calling me at the Station house tomorrow at eight, my time." He paused for just a second. "That's why I need to get to bed—it's already tomorrow and I'm beat. Stay in touch and be careful, Harry."

At least he hung up the phone gently. I continued to sit in the morning sun trying not to think of the turmoil swirling around in my life. Someone had tried to kill me and I was surprisingly unafraid. Juanita was safe and would remain that way even if I had to put Manu and Tua on a permanent payroll. I didn't miss the companionship of anyone else in my life either…it was a good feeling. I realized I had been sitting quietly with my eyes closed and that alone was both surprising and alarming. I never sit with my eyes closed and relax in the sun. There's always someplace to go. I slowly opened my eyes and saw there were wisps of clouds circling the summit of Mourne Mountain and the glistening water of Dundrum Bay was quiet in its shadow. I could feel the quiet. I heard the solid sound of a golfer hitting a ball off the first tee and the voices of his companions shouting "good shot." I should be playing golf, I thought. And young Michael Martin should be caddying for me or, better yet, we should be playing golf together. After golf, we could take Katherine for a drive to Arglass and have a late lunch at Carburry Castle. The more I thought of Katherine the more I thought of the two of them. She was an extremely attractive woman, but whenever my thoughts drifted in her direction it was seeing Katherine and Michael together that warmed my heart.

Harrison, I thought—you always find a way to surprise me.

35

I don't remember how long I had been warming myself in the morning sun, but the rumble of the maintenance cart broke my reverie as it skidded on the gravel path and came to a stop in front of the hedge twenty-five yards to my right. At first I didn't notice the driver of the cart and I didn't see the orange ski mask pulled tightly over his head. Turning my head further to the right, I saw the man get out of the cart and reach for what at first appeared to be a hedge trimmer, but this hedge trimmer had a barrel.

The first burst of bullets ripped into the edge of the bench sending sharp splinters of wood into my face and neck. I didn't stop to think about what was happening and instinctively dove to the ground as the second barrage of bullets sprayed dirt and gravel around my feet. As I tried to crawl behind the bench I had a sudden urge to scratch the bee sting on my right calf. I scraped at the stinging sensation and my hand came away covered in blood, dirt and gravel. I looked up in time to see the gunman begin to walk toward me. He was moving slowly and trying to keep himself low to the ground while circling to my left seeking a better angle of attack. Abruptly he stopped and knelt on the gravel path aiming his weapon once again in my direction. I could hear shouts coming from the direction of the first tee—I could hear a dog barking excitedly from the direction of the maintenance vehicle—I could hear the slap of waves on the shore of Dundrum Bay. I wondered if these were the last sounds I'd ever hear.

Suddenly the gunman twisted his head for a moment toward the rush of footsteps running on the gravel path behind me. At that moment I heard the loud *CRACK* of a single gunshot from the direction of the beach. The gunman's ski mask seemed to explode and bits of orange wool, gray mush and bright red liquid sprayed the path and the bench in front of me.

I looked toward the beach and saw Officer Derrick Malone, with his gun hanging loose at his side, waving at a group of golfers to stay back as he advanced on the almost headless body of my attacker. The gunman's green windbreaker was covered in blood and his right leg was sticking out from under his body at an odd angle. It was then I noticed the dog. A brown Doberman was nervously pacing back and forth in front of the dead man.

I got a sudden chill as the shadow from a passing cloud drifted over me—then I threw up a hot-buttered scone, all over the cool green grass, and passed out at the feet of Officer Malone.

The crunch of shoes on gravel was the first sound I heard. I was comfortable on my back in the grass and the cotton blanket that someone had used to cover me felt warm under my chin. Very cozy, I thought. And then the reality of what had just happened swept over me and the nausea returned. Nobody writing books or making movies ever tells it right. What they don't tell us is that getting scared senseless will induce a severe case of the shakes, nausea and gut-busting diarrhea. I had already vomited all over the grass, now I had the shakes and I was holding on for dear life to keep from really embarrassing myself with a bout of diarrhea.

A medic in a starched white shirt was swabbing something cold on my leg and telling Officer Malone how lucky I was. I found out later they found forty-two spent casings scattered on the ground and only one of the bullets had hit me. I had a three-inch slice on the side of my leg and a bruised ego. I had thrown up, passed out and almost fouled the footpath out of fear.

"Mr. Pius, you all right?"

"I'm fine," I said.

We all come close to getting it right eventually. For some it's early and for others it comes thirty seconds before they check out and walk into the bright light of eternity. I was starting to see my own special light and it didn't involve the beacon on a speeding train coming straight at me. My eyes were open and it struck me that the young man holding my hand was the closest I had ever come to experiencing love at first sight. He had caddied for me one time—a total of four hours—it was as if I now had the son I'd never known I wanted.

"Why aren't you in school, Michael?"

"It's a bank holiday, sir. We've no school today."

I sat up and got a sharp rebuke from Officer Malone and the medic. But, fully conscious I felt foolish lying on my back with about thirty people staring at me. "Michael, help me up," I said. I put my free hand on Michael's shoulder, grasped his other hand tightly and was on my feet. "I promise I won't throw up anymore," and gave him a hug. He was hugging me back as his mother came running down the path shouting his name.

She had the frozen look I was beginning to understand. She watched the world with frosted eyes. The only time there was a thaw was when she looked at Michael.

"After I dropped Michael off I heard the sirens and saw people running—I should have known it was you." Her voice was about two octaves higher than normal. As she looked me over, she shook her head sadly. "Mr. Pius you've brought too much trouble into our little village—why don't you go back where you belong."

"Mr. Pius isn't going anywhere just yet," Officer Malone said. "He and I are going to have another 'heart to heart'. And isn't that a fact Mr. Pius?"

The two questions came at me from different directions and I nodded in the direction of Katherine Martin. "You could make a good case for me not belonging anywhere, Katherine. I would like to tell you about it sometime. Will you give me the chance?"

Before she could answer I addressed Officer Malone. "Yes, we need to have a 'heart to heart'. We can start here or go to your office, but before we go anywhere can you tell me who this guy...."

One of Officer Malone's assistants had covered the dead body with a black plastic sheet. Michael was tugging at my sleeve and pointing at the body. He said, "Mr. Pius I recognize his jacket. That's one of the fishermen we saw Sunday afternoon out on the fourth tee—remember they were the two dummies going fishing when the tide was out."

I had no wish to peek under the plastic sheet. I didn't recognize the jacket and decided to take Michael's word for it. I had no desire to view a man's face with the back of his head missing. I was thirsty, I smelled like puke, and I was very tired.

The police were dispersing what was left of the crowd and a white van with *GARDA* painted on the side had weaved its way through the hedgerows. One of the occupants of the van was unloading a gurney while the other one stared at the plastic sheet in obvious disbelief. Officer Malone was busy shouting directions and orders to his assembled minions stopping only to ask the medic if I was fit to travel to the police station.

As the medic was nodding his head approvingly I tried engaging Katherine in conversation but failed. However she spoke decisively to Michael. "Young man, you're coming home with me—no caddying for you today."

He started to protest but she wouldn't have it. "I don't care if it is a school holiday," she stated. "I want you to spend the rest of the day with me." She turned abruptly and walked up the path pulling Michael by the elbow.

The breeze had shifted. It was now coming from offshore. Dundrum Bay remained flat with small waves still splashing against the sandy beach. Normalcy had returned to the first tee area and golfers were once again pursuing the mastery of a game that has never been mastered. A man lay dead on the ground while twenty yards away other men were chasing a little white ball across an expanse of grass. I smiled to myself, remembering one of Gerry Murphy's favorite jokes. It tells the story of four gentlemen playing golf on a Saturday morning. They had played at the same golf course every Saturday for twenty years. When they were about to tee off on the sixth hole a funeral procession passed by on a road bordering the hole. As the hearse moved slowly into view one of the members in the group removed his hat and placed it over his heart. One of the other golfers, touched by this show of respect commented, "What a lovely gesture Phillip—removing your hat for a funeral procession." At which point Phillip solemnly replied, "Ah, it's the least I can do…. we were married for forty years."

My smile turned to a frown as I wondered if Gerry had turned up. Something told me to prepare for the worst.

36

If a man with an AK47 automatic weapon uses it trying to kill you, there's a pretty good chance he had a reason. If that man is now dead and you think he has a partner lurking in the vicinity, it might be a good idea to look for the partner. It might also be a good idea to find out the reason they wanted you dead in the first place. Officer Malone had a lead on the partner, but not the reason for wanting me dead. And neither did I.

"Mr. Pius, I think Mrs. Martin has the right idea—maybe its time you thought about going home to San Francisco."

Sewing a couple of stitches in my leg was the easy part. The tough part was the medic spending the better part of an hour getting the wood splinters out of my neck and the right side of my face. I looked like someone had scratched me with a lawn rake from my eyebrow to my chin. I haven't had a cigarette in twenty years, but getting lectured by an officious Irish cop while my face was itching like crazy was getting bothersome. For some strange reason I wanted a cigarette and wondered if they still sold Pall Malls.

"Officer Malone, I don't like calling you Officer Malone, so if you don't mind, I think I'll call you Derrick." I didn't wait for his approval. "Derrick, I love this place like no other, but I can't wait to head for home. I spoke with Tim Flynn a few minutes ago and we've decided to withdraw from the tournament, so there isn't anything keeping me here except my stubbornness. I want to know who tried to kill me this morning and why—also, who and where is his partner."

"We think we've pretty much solved the 'whom'." He couldn't resist the subtle correction of my faulty grammar. "But, we don't have a clear indication of the 'why'. The man who attacked you is a local lowlife and we're familiar with most of his mates—we're rounding them up now. They've all spent most of their lives 'doing the double'..."

He saw the confusion on my face.

"Doing the double is what you Yanks refer to as going on the dole. Or, they trade on the black-market side of things, buying and selling unwanted gifts. If you leave your golf clubs unattended and they come up missing, in their mind you have made them a gift of something you didn't want in the first place. I had a gentleman from Arkansas tell me that the Irish have 'outhouse logic' after he made a 'gift' of his golf clubs to a couple of local lads."

"Are you going to tell me the 'whom' anytime soon?" I asked.

"We think his name is Barry McLain and we suspect he was connected to the spray job at the Avenue Bar last month in Downpatrick."

"I think I can guess what a spray job is," I said. "But, why don't you tell me anyway."

"Well, Mr. Pius, it's similar to what happened to you this morning. Only, most often, a spray job occurs in a confined area, such as a bar, and there are a goodly number of casualties because of the weaponry employed. It's a cowardly act because so many innocent people die during a spray job."

"It would seem to me Mr. McLain wasn't very good at his job," I observed.

"Or you were just very lucky."

"I've been wondering how..."

"...How I happened to be in the neighborhood when you were under attack?" He smiled, enjoying the suspense. "I called the golf shop looking for you and I was told that you were sunning yourself on a bench behind the first tee—it's a five-minute walk from here. It was really quite simple and lucky for you, I should think."

I agreed with him about my good fortune and asked him for more information. "What about the other guy—the one he was with the day I played golf—the one young Michael Martin thinks he might recognize if he saw him again."

"It's a sad thing to say, Mr. Pius," he said. "But I would be saying that Michael will be of little help to us. His mum is put off by this business and will not be cooperating with us." He paused, shuffled some folders from one corner of his desk to the other and continued. "I'm not sure what you've done to get Katherine's knickers in such a bunch, but she's got a fire in her eye where you're concerned. I wouldn't want to say it, but she'll be yelling at both of us in the 'Irish' if we're not careful—we wouldn't want that on our heads."

"I think I get your drift, Derrick. Why, other than a concern for Michael's safety, do you think she has a 'fire in her eye' whenever I'm around?"

"It's not just you…. It's all of us Mr. Pius. All blokes, that is, but you seem to set her off more than usual. I think it's the look about you."

"The look about me—what's that mean?"

"It would be Eamon you have the look of, I'm sure," he said. "I think she's got a pisser in your direction because you remind her of her dead husband."

Before I could register total surprise, he spoke quickly, as if he might lose his nerve if he thought too long about his words. "I made my first Holy Communion kneeling by the side of Katherine O'Hara. I've known her my entire life. She's the most remarkable, headstrong person I've ever known. My own wife thinks that a part of me is still in love with Katherine, but that could be true of half the men in Antrim. Eamon was the only man in her life and she transferred all that love to her son. Your look is an unwelcome intrusion in the life she made to suit her needs."

"That sounds farfetched, Derrick."

"I don't take strong drink myself—only an occasional pint of Guinness—but I'll bet you the pub she is put off by the look of you…. you even have his manner."

"I don't know what to think of her or what you're saying because I don't know her. But, what I've seen of her son I like a lot. He is a very impressive young man and seems to have adjusted to the loss of his father quite well."

He stared at me for a long moment. I sensed a lecture coming on. "It's important you understand. She doesn't want any man to come between her and the memory of her dead husband and the same is true for Michael. If he's had any good words to say about you it would surely explain her way toward you. Still and all I can't be telling you what to do, but you might want to give the Martin family a wide place on the path."

Derrick Malone couldn't have known how bad I was when it came to taking advice so I let it pass and changed the subject. "You didn't answer my question. Have you got a line on the other guy?—You know, the guy with McLain."

"Yes. Katherine can sidetrack us all any time she wants," he said by way of answering. "But we surely believe the other man is Devon Clarke." He explained the relationship between McLain and Clarke and how the authorities in Belfast had explained their connection to the IRA. It seems they were considered to be mid-level soldiers in the Provisional arm of the movement. He went on to complain about the Provos, the R.U.C., U.V.F., the Unionist's and even his own government's Northern Ireland Office for Great Britain and their involvement in the Anglo-Irish Agreement. It was all too confusing for me and I needed to lie down and rest my aching leg.

Telling him I didn't need a ride I limped out of his office and headed for my hotel. After only two blocks I was exhausted and regretted my decision. As I opened the door to my room I glanced at the clock on the nightstand and realized it was only noon—I felt like it was the middle of the night. As I fell on the bed I made a mental note to call Bert Brogger by three my time. Hopefully the Director of Faculty Information at FAU in Florida would be willing to open the book on one William Morrison, PhD.

37

The call came at two-thirty. I was on the edge of awakening and answered without looking at the clock. I assumed it was a call from Detective Brogger and quickly realized it was too early for his call.

The voice was quick—too quick. A let's-get-it-all-out-in-one-sentence outburst with all the information delivered non-stop. "Harrison I want to apologize to you. Indeed, you put me to a challenge. It's Godsend that you don't have more trouble. And there you are because my only task is for Michael's safety. I know all of this trouble is not your fault, but I don't want to expose my son to the danger that seems to be following you around. He's sixteen years old and I can't keep him locked up. He's pestering me, no end, about how unfair I am and that you're really a swell bloke and I should let him caddy for you and you're a successful business man and he can learn a lot from you and maybe you could give him some advice about what he should study in college and why do I have to meddle so much in his life and…."

"Stop, Katherine! You're going to get blue in the face unless you take a breath. You have no reason to apologize to me, and I don't want to expose Michael to anything that might endanger him, either." I took a deep breath of my own. I wondered why she had called, but didn't want to be blunt by blurting out "Why?" "Can I help you with anything?"

"Yes." Now she was struggling for words. "I would like—that is, Michael and I would like to invite you over for dinner tonight. The two of you can eat together while I take care of my other guests—I only have four tonight—and I'll join you later. I want to speak with you about Michael, alone—if you don't mind?"

"I'll be there around seven, if that's okay?"

"That would be grand," she said, and hung up the phone. It was still too early to be calling anyone in California. I hit the remote on the thirteen-inch TV and, killing time, caught a BBC newscast in progress. The very proper newscaster was bringing his viewers up to date on Margaret Thatcher's arrival in Washington D.C. Her first stop on a four-city speaking tour was a visit with fellow Reaganite, President George Bush. The Iron Lady had been an unabashed admirer of Ronald Reagan and correctly viewed Bush as his heir apparent. Although still recovering from a stroke and the death of her husband, she was as strong willed as ever and supremely confident that she and Reagan had been correct in their view of the world. Like them or not, history will accurately portray that they forged a partnership which fueled a conservative movement and transformed the political face of the West.

The BBC talking head, in a dull monotone, was making a lot of the fact she was traveling on a commercial aircraft. A British Airways 747 was her choice of transportation and she insisted that, in the wake of the 9/11 attacks, British Airways was still the safest way to travel. The last stop on her tour, five days hence, was a speech to the Commonwealth Club in San Francisco. One second I thought I had it and then I couldn't hold it. I was left with a blurred image of William Crawford Dean as the solution to Margaret Thatcher's security when she arrived in the City.

I'm always surprised and a little amazed at how the mind works. A couple of pieces in the puzzle popped into my head. I didn't know where to put them, but I could see them. We knew Maggie O'Reilly was giving money to Tommy Gavin. Gavin was shuttling back and forth between the States and Northern Ireland. Gavin, after a few drinks, was quick to condemn the Brits and was violent in his hatred for Margaret Thatcher. Gavin and Maggie were both dead. If Maggie was the source for funds and Gavin was the courier—why kill them?

It didn't make sense.... and why try to kill me? And where were Junkie Bill and Gerry Murphy.... were they dead, too? Was any of this connected to Margaret Thatcher's visit to the City? The IRA tried to kill her when she was in office.... were they still out to get her? I didn't have any answers.... everything was coming up empty. I suddenly realized I hadn't given Vanessa, or Julie, a thought in days...had I finally emptied them out of my life? The buzz of the bedside phone interrupted my reverie.

"Harry, hang on to your hat and if you're standing up you better sit down." Bert Brogger wasn't mincing words. It was unmistakably clear in his voice.

"OK," I said. "I'm sitting down and I'm not wearing a hat. What's up?"

"Morrison and Murphy haven't turned up—we're treating them both as unaccounted for—and get this. The O'Reilly's just realized that they haven't seen the housekeeper around for a couple of days. We think she may be AWOL as well." Before I could say anything his voice went up an octave and he blurted out, "But it gets better!"

It didn't get better. It got worse. "Harry I just got off the phone with the Information Office at Florida Atlantic University and William Morrison didn't teach there in 1963.... the school didn't open for academic enrollment until 1964."

"Another lie from our boy Junkie Bill," I said.

"Yeah, what's true is William Morrison started there in late 1964 and there was a terrible boating accident a few years later. The bodies of his wife and son were never recovered."

"I know that much," I said. "He washed up on the beach. And they never..."

"Yeah Harry—he washed up on the beach all right. There's only one problem though!" he yelled into the phone. "When William Morrison washed up on the beach he was dead."

If I had been a cartoon character there would have been a *WHOOSH!* exploding from my mouth and a look of astonishment on my face. "Bert, you can bet I'm stunned, but something tells me I shouldn't be surprised that Junkie Bill isn't who he's supposed to be. Maybe he pulled the con job of all time on the entire O'Reilly family—and on me too. This whole thing stinks and I'm starting to feel like a bigger fool than ever for getting involved in the first place." He started to interrupt and I delivered the news that in turn stunned him. His reaction to the fact that someone had tried to gun me down was quick and to the point.

"Harry, get your ass home now!" he exclaimed.

"I'm coming home in a couple of days," I said. "I need to feel a little better first and I need to get my head on straight as well. I've never had anyone try to kill me and now it's happened two days in a row. I'm pissed off and, I admit, I'm scared."

"All the more reason for you to get outta' there," he said. "Take some advice for a change…. you know, if you had listened to me in the first place none of this shit would have happened to you."

"I know. I know," I said impatiently. "What's going on with the O'Reilly clan…. they gotta' be feeling they've been had. Remember the old axiom, 'follow the money'…"

"Yeah, they're pretty upset and they're like us—they're startin' to wonder if Morrison was implicated in their mother's murder or has he been set up as a target, too. And, just in case, they're checking and double checking all the financials."

"Yeah, but Bert—why did he set up the story about his past—why cook up the big lie?"

"Maybe the lie was just part of a con job…and maybe her murder and his disappearance aren't part of the con."

The television was still tuned to the BBC and Margaret Thatcher's image flashed on the screen again. It gave me the flicker of an idea. "Bert, listen to me. Check out the security arrangements for Thatcher's visit. Call…."

"What visit?…Who's Thatcher, Harry? What the hell are you talkin' about…ya' know you're all over the place. Did one of those bullets hit you in the head?"

"Just listen, will you?" I said. "Margaret Thatcher, the former Prime Minister of Great Britain is on a speaking tour of the States and she'll be in the City in a few days. Gavin hated her guts because of her stance on the IRA and was always talking about how somebody should take her out. She's old and she's had a stroke, but she still has a lot of clout in the world, especially with the Bush people. Maybe there's something goin' on."

"Hold on, man. You just took this thing to a whole other level. We don't have any reason to…."

"Bert, you hold on a minute. You've got two people dead and three that are missing. I would think you could poke your nose anywhere you want. You don't need any more reasons."

"You heard me say another level," he said. "Well, lemme' tell you, if politics gets in this mess the whole thing ratchets up the chain pretty quick. We'll be in a shitstorm so quick it'll take your breath away. In five minutes nobody will remember or give a crap about Maggie O'Reilly, Tommy Gavin or someone taking shots at you in bum-fuck village, Ireland. Anyway, you've made a big leap here. Why?"

"I'm starting to remember bits and pieces and some of it doesn't make sense, at least not yet." I answered. "Do yourself a favor and get a hold of your old buddy Willie Dean and see what's going on with their security arrangements for Thatcher's visit."

"Willie Dean!" he exclaimed. "You gotta be fuckin' kidding me! Why would I want to get involved with that asshole?"

Before I could respond he asked the magic question. The one I couldn't answer. "Why are you bringing up his name? He's a Chief of Detectives—what's he got to do with security for some old broad from England?"

"He's involved in the security task force assigned to her visit," I answered. "Who knows…. he and his team are probably working with the Secret Service. She's flying into SFO—I'm surprised you and your department aren't involved."

"Harry, that shit doesn't filter down to me—I'm too far down the ladder. And if it hasn't made its way to me," he said sarcastically. "How in the hell does one Harrison Pius, the 'Pope of San Francisco,' know about Willie Dean and what he might be doing?"

"I can't tell you," I said. "You've got to trust me on this one, Bert. Willie Dean and the SFPD have a task force assigned to Thatcher's visit—that's all I can tell you. Why don't you give Detective Bennett a call and see if she knows anything?"

"That's just fuckin' perfect. *'Give Phyllis a call,'* you say. And what do I tell her? That I've got a professional gambler who thinks there might be a plot involving a couple of dead people with no connection to anything we know—and Oh! By the way, my informant can't even tell me how he arrived at this dumb-ass conclusion. Trust you on this—gimme a break, Harry."

Usually I don't give a damn what other people think, but Bert Brogger was different. Beneath the surface there was a lot going on with this guy and I valued his opinion. And, for all his posturing with me, I had the feeling he trusted me and valued my opinion as well. I didn't want to let him down. "You're probably right. I guess your first priority is to find Junkie Bill and Gerry Murphy.... Guille too. Maybe this whole thing is just a shakedown. But, who's doing the shakin'?"

"We'll figure it out," he declared. "I've gotta go and Harry I'm gonna' tell you again.... get your sweet ass outta' there and come home!" He wasn't on his cell phone because this time the phone slammed down as he hung up.

I sat on the edge of the bed and thought about Vanessa confiding in me about what Willie Dean had been doing. I could only hope that his special assignment was common knowledge otherwise a different kind of excrement was going to hit the fan. I smiled, comforted by the thought of what Uncle Ambrose was fond of saying. "What the hell, you may as well relax because everything always comes out in the wash, anyway."

38

If you're dining in a restaurant in San Francisco you begin the meal with an appetizer. If you're having dinner in a small B&B in Newcastle, Northern Ireland, you begin with a "starter." Michael Martin and I were each finishing a starter of steamed mussels prepared in a broth of clam juice, carrots, celery, bay leaves and saffron. It was the saffron, I surmised, that set the dish apart from any mussels I had ever eaten.

Between bites Michael had been talking non-stop about his schoolwork and what it meant to him. I took a final bite of soda bread that I'd soaked in the saffron broth and said, "Michael, let's make a deal. I want to hear everything about what you want to study in college and where you want to go. But, please drop the 'sir' and the 'Mr. Pius'—from now on just call me Harry or Harrison. Got it?"

"Me mum won't like it."

"Don't worry I'll cover it with your mother."

"As you wish, Mr..... I mean Harry." And, away he went again.

With every passing minute I felt drawn ever closer to the young man. I didn't have any experience with teenagers and what I knew I got from newspapers and television. Michael didn't fit the notion I had in my mind of a typical teenager—he was a human being and not some monster from Mars. Every sentence out of his mouth didn't begin with the word "like" and what he said made perfect sense. He seemed to have a clear picture of what he wanted to accomplish, at least in the short term. He revealed rather quickly that staying in Newcastle beyond his preliminary schooling held no attraction for him. He was concerned about his mother and in particular her finances—her ability to finance a higher education for him was in doubt; thus his eagerness to caddy as much as possible and save his money. I had the germ of an idea, but it was too early to spring it on him. Plus, I didn't want to run the risk of raising his hopes and at the same time incurring his mother's wrath. I suspected he was all boy just from the way he looked at his mothers' helper Fiona. She appeared to be in her early twenties and was attractive in a red-faced, wind-blown sort of way. When she served our mussels the fabric on her blouse was stretched tight across her chest revealing the absence of any undergarment. Michael seemed to take particular pleasure in the sight and Fiona, smiling and winking at him, made no move to hide her endowment. Of course, I never notice things like that.

At my request Fiona served our salad with the entrée. Katherine had prepared a summer salad of dandelion greens, watercress and Swiss chard tossed in a dressing of tomato puree and sour cream. I found out later that the lamb cutlets entrée was baked in a casserole with green tomatoes, yellow onions, white wine and a thin strip of center-cut ham steak, and the recipe had been in the O'Hara family for years. We were offered walnut pudding for dessert and I had to pass. Much to his mother's dismay, Michael ate both his and mine.

Her dinner guests had departed or retired to their rooms and Michael was trying to make sense of *Ulysses* up in his room. During dinner I had told him not to worry—nobody, including most college professors, have a clue what the book is about. As we settled comfortably in front of the fireplace in her parlor, Katherine surprised me and produced an unopened bottle of Glenmorangie.

"When your car exploded I dropped your bottle of scotch—this is the least I could do," she said. "Although I must say you have expensive taste. I would put you up for two nights and give you change in place of this whiskey."

I sat comfortably in an old leather chair with my feet on an ottoman. I was as relaxed as I had been in a very long time. "Katherine you should raise your prices. The meal I just ate would cost a hundred dollars in San Francisco and you charge only nineteen Euros, which, by the way, you wouldn't let me pay."

"You were our guest, tonight.... my way of apology for being so put off. Michael says I'm getting worse in my old age."

I wanted to tell her she was strikingly beautiful and didn't look a day over thirty, but thought better of it. "He must think I'm a tottering old codger."

"Quite the opposite," she replied. "Would it be a wonder that you could be a superman in Michael's young eyes? That is all we hear—he has Fiona convinced that you are ready for sainthood. The first saint that is a scratch player on the links, I might add."

We discussed Michael for the next few minutes, and to my surprise she spoke freely about him "leaving the hearth." She recognized his need to explore the world outside of their little village and the possibility that he might want to get out of Ireland altogether. My germ of an idea moved closer to my lips, but I wisely held it in check. The peat fire was reduced to glowing coals and we were silently enjoying the warmth. Katherine moved to the sideboard, refilled my glass and came to the point.

"Harrison, there can be no doubt that my son has taken to you and I think you to him. A wonder it is, because of his memories."

"His memories?"

She took her first sip of the Glenmorangie, paused and continued. "Michael was only ten when his father died and he only remembers the giant of a man that was Eamon.... not in the physical sense, I mean, for he was not a giant in that way. But, his father was a manly man and the best example of splendid character a young boy could have. Michael loved him dearly and has become critical of all others."

"Others in his life or in your life?" I asked and instantly regretted the question.

A flare in her eyes shot in my direction and quickly died. "That is surely a question that comes naturally to you, Harrison. I shall not be offended by it. You assume that because I have been a widow for these six years there must be other men in my life. That is surely not to be." She studied me for a few moments. Her red hair shimmered in the firelight. She frowned, glanced at my empty glass, poured another dram and said, "Eamon was, and still is, the only man in my life. That will always be. But, for Michael you have become another matter."

"And what is that?"

"It is that you are the image of his father and it has not come to him yet. He feels drawn to you and he doesn't know why—you are a wonder to him and that is all he knows."

"Is it a problem for him…. or is the problem with his mother? And—how do you know it is a problem for him?"

"I know my son, Harrison," she replied abruptly. "In his eyes you occupy this grand place in the universe and it's a place he wants for himself, as well. But, in a matter of days you will return to your glorious world and he will be left with his ordinary life in a little village in Ireland."

"Suppose he had a window to my world, Katherine. What then?" There it was—out in the open. "Suppose—with your permission, of course—he could have the opportunity to realize his dream?"

"Very close-mouthed he is, my Michael. And how is it that you know his dreams? Of those he doesn't confide in me. Did he tell you as much?"

"He didn't tell me exactly, but aren't you aware he's thinking he might want to study medicine…be a Doctor."

"He wouldn't say," she replied. "He would know it would not be within our finances and he wouldn't want to trouble me with it."

"Let's suppose again. What if finances were not a problem? What if he could go to a major college in the states? Would you let him go and…"

She bristled. "He is not your son, Mr. Pius."

I bristled back. "No he is not my son, Mrs. Martin, but he is my friend." We were dangerously close to sliding back to our previous relationship. In the last hour we had come a long way and I didn't want to lose it. "Please Katherine don't misunderstand. I don't want to replace your husband in the eyes of your son, but if I can help him—I want to do it. Helping Michael would make me very happy.

If I can't spend my money on the things that make me happy, what's the point of having it?"

"You have that much money? Paying for a lad's education would not be a tremendous burden?" She shook her head back and forth, "Dear God, I can't believe I'm having this conversation. Mind you, this is not my way."

"This is not my way either," I said. "I'm not in the habit of pushing myself in the middle of other peoples' lives. It's just that you and Michael are a wonderful family and I envy what you have. If I can make it better in some way, I want to do it." She was still shaking her head. "Believe me, Katherine, the money means nothing. Helping Michael with his education will not alter my lifestyle in the slightest—I have more money than I can spend."

"It must be grand to live the way you do," she said.

"I don't know if I would call it grand or not. I know it's sometimes lonely. I know a lot of doors in my life are closed—doors that might lead to doing something really worthwhile. Maybe Michael is a door I can walk through. I know he admires me and I would like nothing better than for him to get to know me and have that admiration based on who I really am." I took a deep breath and said the other part...the part I was most afraid of saying. "And I'd like for you to get to know me, too."

Her eyes dropped and she stared at her hands. "In the name of God this is more than my bonnet can hold. You are a man of many things, Harrison Pius," she stated. "Which tells me—do you have to answer any silliness about your name?"

"All the time, Katherine," I smiled. "Some of my closest friends call me 'the Pope'."

"I will never call you as such." She stood and placed the fire cover on the grate. "For now I've run out of things to say and I've got a busy morning ahead—so, it's off to bed. Please don't speak with Michael about our talk. With his schoolwork, his caddying and helping me here at the Inn he has too much to worry about as it is."

"I won't say a word, but I would like to talk to you some more," I said.

She walked me to the door. I was pleased with the way the evening had unfolded and decided to press my luck. "I'm driving to Down-patrick tomorrow and you could do me a big favor by going with me."

"And why would that be?" she asked.

"I don't know the way and I don't want to get lost."

She laughed out loud and then broke into a broad smile. "This wouldn't be a date you're asking me on, would it?" Before I could mutter a response she grinned at me, "I don't date, but if Michael approves I'll accompany you and you can treat me to a proper lunch. I'll ring you at the hotel in the morning." And with that she gave me a very proper kiss on the cheek and pushed me out the door.

As I made my way to the rental car I noticed the scorched spot across the lane where the Mercedes had been parked. I hoped my luck was improving. I knew for certain that if Katherine asked Michael's permission to join me for lunch—he would approve.

When I walked into my room at the Slieve Donard the phone was ringing. My first thought was who would be calling me at midnight but then I realized it was only four in the afternoon at home.

Juanita said, "Harry where have you been? I've been trying to call you for two hours."

I was bone tired, but I knew better than to complain. So I lay back on the bed and listened. I listened to a litany of complaints. Mostly, I got advice about the future conduct of my life and how I should mind my own business. And speaking of business, Juanita was quick to point out that two of my biggest clients had been calling on a daily basis wanting to know when I was going to come home and get back to work. "Harry, I want you to get your butt home and go to work. Put all this private detective nonsense behind you. Besides, you need to take care of your business—we need the money!"

"We don't need the money…. relax."

She changed the subject and I got another ten minutes of "Juanita bashing" about Manu and Tua—she wanted them out. She and Mrs. Mulhaupt were getting along nicely and they didn't need two big bodyguards underfoot. I calmly and forcefully told her "no way"—Manu and Tua were going to stay under my roof until I knew we were all safe. Juanita finally ran out of steam, told me she still loved me and hung up the phone.

When I hung up I noticed the message light blinking. I had received a call while I was talking to Juanita. I hit 33 on the phone pad and Bert Brogger's voice greeted me. "Harry, not much new here. Still no sign of Morrison or Murphy…. we think the housekeeper may have skipped to Mexico. I've got Phyllis Bennett working the Thatcher angle and that's a can of worms. Willie Dean is ascending to the hierarchy of assholes, but that's another story. Call me."

I was too tired to talk to the detective—it could wait until tomorrow. First, a trip to Downpatrick to check out another idea and I'd be ready to talk. I reached to turn out the bedside light, saw my cell phone on the nightstand and checked for messages. I had five—one from Brogger, two from Julie and two from Vanessa. I flipped the cover of the cell phone closed and turned off the light.

39

Much to Katherine's dismay I went too far and blew past the correct approach at three separate round-abouts on our way to Downpatrick. At all three I had to go around in circles before being able to get back on the correct route. Risking her concluding that I couldn't drive at all, I had missed the turnoffs on purpose. Paranoia set in early on our trip and I was suspicious of any vehicle I thought might be following us. However, all three of the vehicles I was watching scooted on by and I breathed easier. Katherine didn't say anything beyond, "Harrison you're going the wrong way," but I caught her rolling her eyes twice.

She made me go over the story of my involvement in the murder of Maggie O'Reilly from the beginning. That was one of the conditions she set down when she called earlier that morning. "Harrison, I want you to tell me what this is all about—start from the beginning and don't leave anything out."

I'd picked her up at eleven-thirty and she surprised me dressed in jeans, a black turtleneck sweater and a tan oilcloth jacket. Carrack boots with three-inch heels brought her up to my height and she looked as if she had just stepped off the cover of Esquire magazine under the heading of "Women We Love." For the first time since we met I had the feeling she had dressed to get my attention. In turn, I had fished a Gore-Tex rain jacket from the bottom of my golf bag and with jeans of my own I had a bit of the grunge look going. It had been one of Snoopy's "dark and stormy nights" and we were both dressed appropriately, although she was much more the stylish one.

The rain began again as soon as we were underway and my first priority was keeping the rental car out of the hedgerows. But I did manage to tell the complete story starting with the phone call from Junkie Bill. I left nothing out, except my relationship with Vanessa and Julie's unexpected visit. I was certain she didn't think I lived the life of a hermit, but I didn't want her to think I was a playboy either. I was eager to tell her of the past months events because it gave me the opportunity to bring all the characters that populate my life into her vision of me. I told her about the house I live in with its five empty bedrooms. I told her about Juanita, our friendship and how important she is to me. I told her some of the crazy stories involving my golfing buddies, and described in detail my home away from home, the Pacific Heights Golf Club. We talked about my consulting business and how little I work at it. I gave her a few examples of recent consulting contracts and realized the most recent had been four months ago. I could sense her confusion about my chosen profession and she asked, "How is it you are so successful if you spend so little time…."

"Working?"

"Yes, you have this grand lifestyle, yet you don't work very much. Did a rich relative leave you a fortune?"

"The only relative I have is a brother and he's a farmer. Juanita is the only mother I've ever had and she didn't take over that chore until I was in my twenties. My father's brother raised us and when he died he left his farm to us. It wasn't a place I wanted to stay, but my brother loves the life and he's got six kids so it works for him."

"Oh, he must be a Catholic," she said.

I laughed. "No, but his wife is."

"And that would be the way it was with us," she said. "It was me the Catholic and Eamon not. His family disowned him—not that they owned anything to begin with—when he married me. It's not to be believed, but the grandparents have not seen Michael in his life. They didn't even come to their son's funeral. They're a sad lot, they are indeed."

We were approaching the town of Clough. Katherine cautioned me to be on the lookout for the A25 expressway heading east into Downpatrick. I saw it just in time and remembered the best advice I ever got about driving in Ireland, "look right—go left." We had another twenty minutes on our journey and I thought it would be about the right amount of time to tell the rest of the Harrison Pius story.

"Katherine there is another side of me I want you to know." She gave me an "Uh-Oh, here it comes" look and I quickly shook my head. "No, it's not bad—it's just.... different."

"Different?"

"Let me give you an example. I…"

"Harrison, I don't know if I should be curious or worried. Michael and I have no money, so you can't be thinking about holding me for ransom." She smiled broadly when she said it.

"It's nothing like that," I paused more for effect than anything. "Let me give you an example. Pick four numbers at random like.... Say 1-2-2-1 times four other numbers."

"Is this a game we will be playing?" She continued to smile and said, "OK, I'll play. What is 6621 times 4378, Mr. Smarty?"

It took me about five seconds, longer than normal because I was concentrating on my driving, before I answered, "Twenty eight million, nine hundred eighty six thousand, seven hundred and thirty eight."

"You would be making it up," she exclaimed. "How is it you would know how to do such a thing?"

"I don't know how to do it—I just do it."

She swiveled to face me and excitedly said, "Do it again."

"OK, try this." I had something to explain to her, but it wouldn't hurt to show off first. "There's a map of Ireland in the glove box. Unfold it and you'll see a distance chart with mileage listings for all the major cities in Ireland. Read, out loud, the distance between each city from top to bottom as quickly as you can."

She scanned the map and asked, "You mean the numbers on the graph between Athlone and Wicklow?"

Seeing me nod my head in approval she read off nineteen different numbers in rapid-fire succession. I immediately gave her the answer, 3551, and repeated back to her the nineteen numbers in the order she had given them to me.

"My goodness, Harrison, would you be a genius?"

"Katherine, I can't remember what I had for breakfast this morning, but I can repeat back to you, verbatim, six-way conversations I had a year ago in a client's office. It is a gift and a curse wrapped in the same package."

"The gift part must help you in your business," she said.

We were fast approaching the town limits of Downpatrick. I wanted to tell her how my gift helped me and I was desperate for her to understand and not be put off at the prospect of associating with a professional gambler. I had made up my mind that no matter where our relationship went I would level with her about who and what I was. It seemed she was committed to a life of memories and devotion to her dead husband and maybe the best I could hope for was a friendship, but there would be no secrets—at least from my direction. I pulled off to the side of the road and killed the engine. She sensed I had something to say and that it was important. She remained silent. Finally I said, "Katherine, I'm a card player—I gamble in high stakes card games—I play for a lot of money and I win more often than I lose."

I thought I was telling her something that would shock and surprise her. When she threw back her head and laughed it was her turn to surprise me. "How grand! Would you be willing to teach me and Michael the hold'em game we watch on the telly? It's all the rage, you know."

"Texas Hold'Em is not the game I'm most proficient in, but I can teach you and Michael how to play," I said. "I didn't think you would approve of someone who supplemented their income by gambling."

"Harrison, I'm not quite the prude you think I am. Which reminds me…. I want you to take the bottle of Glenmorangie scotch with you when we get back to the Inn. I fear I could become an admirer of the taste and I don't need the added expense." Her infectious smile was dazzling as the rain began again and beat on the roof of the car. "You Yanks are such hypocrites. You think wagering amongst individuals is either a sin or illegal, yet you approve of state run lotteries that milk the poor. If you make your fortune in games of chance against other men, such as yourself, I say all the better for it."

"It doesn't give you a bad opinion of me then."

"Don't be silly," she replied. "I would be gathering an opinion of you, but it wouldn't have anything to do with playing games of chance."

Feeling better for having explained how I make my fortune and wondering what her opinion of me would turn out to be, I re-started the car. I got back on the main road and began looking for the first turn on the left before the Town Limit signpost. It came on us suddenly—I almost missed it because of the rain. Turning left on Down Road we made our way to the end where a cattle guard separated the road from the entrance to Down Golf Links and Hunting Club. Officer Derrick Malone had briefed me earlier that morning about the location of Devon Clarke and Barry McLain's last place of employment. He had known from the beginning they were from the Downpatrick area, but had only recently discovered they were groundskeepers at the Hunting Club. There was still no information about the whereabouts of Clarke, but it was assumed he had somehow made his way to the States before the attempt on my life. Officer Malone thought it foolhardy of me to poke around in police business since he had previously conducted all the necessary interviews at Down Club. I didn't want to formally interview anyone—I wanted to see if I could get an idea of what Devon Clarke looked like. If I bumped into him in San Francisco I wanted to be ready.

The gravel parking lot was empty and, luckily, we were able to park the car only a few feet from the entrance to the main clubhouse. We were lucky because the rain and wind had gone from what the Irish call 'soft' to what I call a downpour. The front door led to a wide hallway that opened into a dining room with a bar at the far end. One wall of the hallway was covered with framed photographs of what looked to be winners of various events, both golf and hunting. Several brass plaques were scattered indiscriminately among the photographs depicting the winners of the more important events. It was dark in the hallway. We waited to enter the large room before shedding our jackets. The dining room was dominated by floor to ceiling windows that gave an unobstructed view of the eighteenth hole of the golf course and what looked to be a skeet range to the right and in the distance. There were two men seated at a table in front of the middle window engaged in a heated conversation about the merits of different brands of golf balls. I picked up just enough of the conversation to determine that neither one of them had a clue what they were talking about. The room smelled of bacon and beer. I gave a silent prayer for a fresh cup of coffee.

We took a table in the corner and hung our dripping jackets over a couple of empty chairs. I went to the bar and gave out a soft "Hello in there," which brought a "Be right with you" from somewhere in the back. Followed by, "Coffees?" I yelled out "Make it two," and went back to the table. I was ready to give up hope when she burst through a swinging door to the side of the bar with a cup of coffee in each hand. She had blond hair done up in a ponytail, a flannel shirt, cutoff khaki pants, black high top tennis shoes and as Katherine told me later, she had to be at least seventy-five years old. "You're too late for breakfast and too early for lunch, but I could be fixin' you a snack," she said.

Katherine spoke for both of us, "Coffee will be just fine. We won't be a trouble to you for you seem to be busy even if it has the look of a slow day."

"Ugh, I would still be cleaning up from last night—there was a party and it was a frightful mess. The night crew leaves me the worst part of it. Of course, they're nothin' but a bunch of assholes."

There's something about a seventy-five year old woman with a foul mouth that makes me smile. "You look as if you could take a break. Why don't you join us for a cup of coffee—I'd like some information. If you can help me out I'll make it worth your while." I put a twenty-pound note on the table.

She scooped the note off the table, tucked it in the front pocket of her shirt and said, "Gimme' five minutes," as she bustled back to the kitchen.

Katherine gave me her rolling eye look and said, "Harrison, are you forgetting your rates? You just gave that old woman the equal of thirty-five dollars. Another fifteen and you could stay in my bed and breakfast for a night and I would give you breakfast in the morning."

I didn't get my money's worth. She was back in less than five minutes announcing that she didn't drink coffee, but was going to use the occasion to enjoy her first pint of the day. She knew every member and all the employees and yes, she knew those two assholes Barry McLain and Devon Clarke. She knew McLain was dead ("Good riddance!") and she knew Clarke had disappeared (another "Good riddance!"). The local authorities with a policeman from Newcastle had been to see her and she told them all she knew. She said, "Those old boys were a pair of bad apples and no mistake they was probably a couple of Provies just lookin' to make trouble. They was discharged twice and let to come back...should never have let 'um come back. But, they was good with the guns."

"The guns...what do you mean the guns," I asked.

"The shotguns," she replied. "We are a skeet club as well as a golf club, and part of their duties were to take care of the members' guns. They was real good at it, too. That's why the manager kept takin' 'em back."

Her name was Maureen, and fortified by three pints of Bass Ale she gave us more than we needed to know about McLain and

Clarke—and just about every member in both clubs. We knew for certain there was "a lot of hankie-pankie goin' on" with some of the new members and their wives. Too much new money from Belfast, she surmised. Figuring I had gotten my twenty-pounds worth, she stood, and pushing her chair back announced that she knew who I was and thought Katherine might be the widow of that "lovely Mr. Martin." "He was a dear, dear man you know. He would give potatoes and vegetables to our house-bound senior citizens. A place I never hope to be.... of that I'm certain," she added.

The look on Katherine's face told me she had just learned something new about her husband and, as with everything about Eamon Martin, it made her spirits soar.

"One more thing, Maureen," I said. "Would you be able to describe Devon Clarke? I'd like to know what he looks like."

"Oh, I wouldn't be any good at that for sure. He's just an average bloke, maybe a little on the heavy side, has one of those scruffy little mustaches. I'm not any good at tellin' about blokes. It was nice visiting with you but I've got to get back to me work."

After she left, Katherine and I sat quietly for a long moment. She said, "Harrison, you owe me a lunch, but not here."

The rain had stopped and we grabbed our jackets without bothering to put them on. Sunlight was pouring through the large windows and the room was filling up with golfers hoping to grab a quick bite to eat and get in a fast eighteen holes. The aroma of fried bacon had been replaced by the smell of wet wool. The dark hallway off to our right was now bathed in light and shadow as we made our way to the front of the building.

Naturally I didn't see it. I can tell you instantly how old you would be if you were born on the fourth of July in any year you care to choose, but I often look at things right in front of me and then can't tell you what I've seen. I totally missed it. It was just lucky that Katherine had agreed to come along and keep me company. We were almost at the front door when she turned and stepped back. We almost collided and with my arm awkwardly around her shoulder I realized it was the first time I had ever touched her—I don't count shaking hands as touching. Out of a maze of old photographs and plaques lining the wall her eye had caught the right one.

"Harrison, didn't you tell me your missing friend in San Francisco is named Gerry Murphy?"

I looked at her finger pointing to a faded photograph in a black frame hanging on the wall. There were four men in the photo standing at attention, each with a golf club in his hand. They were most likely standing on the eighteenth green of the Down Links Golf Club because the clubs they were holding looked to be their putters. A white slip of paper about one inch wide by six inches long, behind the frame at the bottom of the photo, identified the event, the date and gave their names as members of the winning foursome. Without the name on the slip of paper I would have never recognized the face in the photo as my old friend Gerry Murphy. That is, until I looked closer. His wild unruly mane of hair was darker in 1960, but the fierce competitive spirit I had seen so many times on the golf course was ablaze in the eyes staring back at me. The two men on either side of Gerry were not really men. They looked to be not much more than teenagers and the slip of paper identified them as Barry McLain and Devon Clarke. It was the other face in the picture that made my knees buckle. I placed my hand against the wall, took a deep breath and muttered, "I'll be damned."

Without touching Katherine I sensed her stiffen. I said it again, "I'll be damned."

The other man stood slightly apart from Gerry and the other two. He was the only one of the group that wasn't looking into the camera. His gaze was directed elsewhere as if he was searching for something in the distance to the left of the camera. He had a complete look of detachment and disregard for his companions. The white slip of paper identified him as Billy Morris, but I knew him as Junkie Bill.

40

Her directions were simple and to the point. "Take the A24 to Dundrum. I know of a lovely place in the harbor, if you fancy seafood."

Katherine correctly sensed my need for time to think as we settled into the comfort of the car. I sat motionless and stared at the dark clouds shrouding the deserted links. I had an almost overwhelming urge to call Bert Brogger, but I knew it was too early. Also, I knew I had to get back to San Francisco, and soon.

When I was growing up on the farm in Salinas, Uncle Ambrose would constantly remind me that the most unpredictable animal was a human being because it was the only one that would surprise you. Nothing a horse, a cow, a dog or any other animal would do should be a surprise. He would laughingly say that animals were "predictably unpredictable." Now I knew my old friend Gerry Murphy and Junkie Bill went way, way back—at least forty-five years, and my surprise bucket was overflowing. Were they still friends? Why had they kept the past a secret? Why did Gerry speak with such disdain about that "bum Junkie Bill?" Gerry and Bill had been friends with a man who tried to kill me. Had they still been involved with him? And, what about Tommy Gavin?

We sat silently in the car outside the Down Links clubhouse for a long five minutes and it had started a hard, driving rain that was blowing sideways across the car park. I wanted to ask Maureen one more question. I navigated the twenty steps back to the Club House entrance as quickly as I could and still got soaked. I found Maureen in front of a flat grill flipping cheese and tomato toasties. She looked over at me as I entered her kitchen and informed me, "You can't be comin' in here."

I said sternly. "One more question Maureen. Did you ever know a man by the name of Tommy Gavin?"

"You only know assholes, do ya'?" she said. "Yeah, I knew him—he worked here—out on the golf course and caddied a bit, too. A real hothead, he was—hung around with them other two you was askin' about. Heard he got himself killed over in the States. Now get yourself going before me manager catches you where you don't belong."

When I got back to the car I was wet and confused and suddenly realized I was very hungry. It was then that Katherine told me again to take the A24 to Dundrum.

The restaurant at the edge of the harbor in Dundrum was as good as she remembered. We sat outside under an awning. The rain had stopped but the awning was snapping in tune to a stiff off shore wind. We were both wearing our rain jackets and the bracing air gave me an excuse to sit closer to Katherine than I would have ordinarily. She seemed so out of reach I was self-conscious about how close I sat to her in a restaurant. Go figure.

I downed two Ardbeg single malts before Katherine had taken two sips of her Australian pinot grigio. She said, "Keep that up and I'll be driving my first Mercedes."

"I'll be all right," I told her. "I'm hungry. I'm going to have the fish and chips and wash it all down with a pint of Bass ale. The two scotches are just to jump start my heart."

Her expression changed. I saw something in her smile that was warmer and more accessible. She nodded her head as if to acknowledge a newfound awareness. "Something tells me it doesn't take much to jump start your heart, Harrison."

"I might surprise you," I said. "I have a hunch you have an opinion of me that's not entirely accurate. I'm not the typical jerk that blows in and out of your B&B—the guy who wears his hat backwards, drinks too much and makes a pass at any woman under the age of eighty."

She thought it over, shaking her head. "You're not typical and you're certainly not a jerk—if you were, I wouldn't be sitting here. It's not something you would make much of, though."

"Much of what?" I asked.

"Me sitting here…With you, that is."

"I'm not sure what you mean."

"We're in a public place. There are other people present, but we're alone at this table. It's not something you would know. It's not something you would understand."

"I'm getting more confused by the minute, Katherine. What are you telling me?"

"I've never been alone with a man other than my husband."

A thin young man in a white apron came up to our table with his pencil poised over an order pad. We gave him our order and he muttered something about the haddock being fresh and we had made a good choice. His interruption had given me a chance to let Katherine's comment sink in. My first thought was I had never met a woman so utterly unassuming. Then I transitioned from my view of her to an image of who I wanted to become. In that instant I knew I wanted to be Katherine Martin's knight in shining armor. I wanted to be Harrison Ford and Brad Pitt rolled into one. I smiled inwardly as I thought, as long as I'm wishful thinking why not throw in some Tiger Woods and create something really special.

"We're not exactly alone," I said. "It's not like…. you know…. it's not like we're actually on a date or anything like that."

"I'm making a muddle of this, of that I'm sure," she said. Slowly and deliberately she brushed her hair away from her face. The breeze freshened and she pulled the collar of her rain jacket tight under her chin. "Harrison, I've never been on a date with a man except my Eamon and we were only on two dates, without a chaperon, before our wedding day."

"Do you think we're on a date now?" I asked.

"Let's speak of something else." She looked away, staring at the ocean. "I'm not sure—would it be that I'm confused or embarrassed? You are too much of the world for me—you should pay me no mind, Harrison. Please."

The thin man in the white apron served our fish and chips with an exuberance usually reserved for beef Wellington. At first glance it looked like he was correct—we had made a good choice. What his part of the world refers to as "chips," we Americans call "french fries." The chips were remarkably good.

"I'll make you a deal. How about…"

"Uh-Oh, a Yankee deal," she said, smiling as she reached out and brushed my hand, then quickly taking her hand back and grabbing at her napkin.

"No, I'm serious. The deal is this—you have touched me in a way that even I don't understand. And because I don't understand—I don't want to try and analyze it. I don't want to dissect it or talk it to death. I don't want to pick at it and I don't want to make you uncomfortable. I want you to get to know me. I want you to know the real Harrison Pius…. the one that no one has ever known. And there's no rush. I want to be Michael's friend and I would like nothing better than to help him realize his hopes and dreams—whatever they happen to be. He's a terrific young man and it would make me very happy to help him. I've got some ideas about how I can help him, but we can talk about that later. But right now, at this exact moment, I want nothing more than to enjoy the fresh air, the sounds and smell of the ocean and the absolute joy of having lunch with an incredibly beautiful woman." She started to respond and I continued. "Relax Katherine. Eat your fish and have another glass of wine."

The drive from Dundrum to Newcastle was quiet—we were both lost in our melancholy, tempered by wine and single malt scotch. Later that evening Katherine had a full house scheduled for dinner and didn't trust Fiona beyond salad preparation, so she was anxious to get back. Also, I had scheduled an early evening with my old friend Tim Flynn. In as much as we had dropped out of the golf tournament we decided that getting together for dinner might be the last time we would see each other for awhile. Before we left the restaurant Katherine paid a visit to the ladies room and I took the time to telephone Delta Airlines. They didn't have a seat available the next day, which meant an extra day in Ireland, but booked me in Business Class straight through to San Francisco on their Friday morning flight. Of course, they charged me a one hundred dollar fee to change the reservation. Why is it we have to pay the airline a fee when our plans change, yet they take no financial responsibility when they change their plans? Uncle Ambrose would say it's the same reason a big dog licks his balls—"because he can."

At dinner, Derrick Malone said, "We think McLain, Gavin and Clarke were all joined together in a renegade offshoot of the IRA."

Almost as an afterthought I had invited Officer Malone to join me and Tim at the Slieve Donard for dinner. As I had from the beginning—starting with my first conversation with Junkie Bill—I had a lot of questions. My problem was I wasn't certain I was asking the *right* questions. Malone was doing his best to satisfy my curiosity and yet, not answering the big questions. Maggie and Tommy Gavin had been killed because they were somehow involved with Terry McLain and Devon Clarke, but how were they involved…. and why? There had been two attempts on my life…. why? I didn't have a dog in this fight…. I didn't even know what the fight was about. Although, we were all starting to think the events of the past few weeks were somehow connected to the impending visit of Margaret Thatcher to San Francisco. We had a three-way call with Bert Brogger earlier, before dinner, and got the expected "you've got to be fuckin' kidding me" when I gave him the news about our old friend Junkie Bill who was known in Ireland as Billy Morris. It was easy for Officer Malone to run a trace on one Billy Morris—he was a minor celebrity when the IRA began to re-group in the early nineteen seventies. There were some who gave Billy Morris credit for re-writing the revolutionary manual, the Green Book which advises its members on everything from weaponry to torture survival. According to the Royal Ulster Constabulary, Billy Morris was an American who came to Ireland and promptly got himself thrown into Wormwood Scrubs prison for trying to blow of the front door of the Wellington Park Hotel in Belfast with a petrol bomb. He had gained the respect of his fellow inmates as a Yank willing to go "on the blanket" to protest the denial of Special Category Status—a status that allowed prisoners to wear their own clothes. He had served the bulk of his two-year term walking around naked under a blanket and by some accounts once went a year without taking a shower. Upon his release he joined an outlawed paramilitary group that operated out of the town of Dundrum. He had fallen off the authorities' radar screen in the mid-nineties and they had wrongly assumed he was dead. Probably killed, they thought, by the group he had been trying to help who didn't like it when an "out of control Yank" sent the wrong message to rich American supporters of the IRA. Americans had become hypersensitive to any group that fell under the heading of "terrorist" and were reluctant to loosen their purse strings for support. It seemed obvious that Junkie Bill had made Maggie O'Reilly a target from the very beginning of their relationship because of her purse strings but, why kill the goose that sat on such a large golden egg? Peter and Sean O'Reilly were going to have a difficult time accepting the fact they had been conned so easily.

Brogger was anxious to convey the latest news to them so they could get their Company auditors busy tracing any transfer of funds to other bank accounts that might be controlled by Junkie Bill. Of course, he pointed out that both the South City and San Francisco police departments were still looking for Bill *and* Gerry Murphy. They were all wondering why Gerry Murphy had come up missing—I was even more curious. The local newspapers had picked up the story and because of Gerry's prominence it had become front-page material. The possibility of an IRA connection was still under wraps, but Bert figured it was just a matter of time until some enterprising reporter would put two and two together. The problem was two and two kept coming up zero. Also, I had another problem. Bert and Detective Bennett had gone to Chief of Detectives Dean and laid out the possibility of everything being connected to Margaret Thatcher's visit and Dean had hit the roof. It seems his Security unit was a special assignment and a closely guarded secret. They were compelled to give him my name and Bert had made an interesting comment, "Harry, I think the asshole knows you." That would explain Vanessa trying to reach me on my cell phone. I made a mental note to listen to the messages she had left on my voicemail.

"Harry, are you feeling okay?" Tim asked.

"Yeah I'm all right. I just feel like I should get the hell out of here." I said. "There's some bad stuff going on back home and I'd feel a whole lot better if I was there. I'm still worried about Juanita. I spoke with her before I met up with you two and she's doing a lot better. She's got the two bodyguards I hired, but I'm still worried."

Derrick Malone took a last bite of salmon and pushed his plate away. He smiled and winked in Tim's direction. "Frankly, Mr. Pius, Tim and I are surprised you would be in such a hurry to leave our little town. After all you set a record this afternoon that just might be entered in the town books."

"Don't go there, Derrick. And Tim you can wipe that stupid grin off your face, as well," I replied good-naturedly.

Tim beamed back at me. "Oh, don't be so sensitive. You're the envy of us all and the talk of the town. Before you dropped Katherine off, word had already circulated that the two of you were seen having lunch at the Old Pelican in Dundrum this afternoon. Could it be there's a crack in the armor that surrounds the fair Mrs. Martin?"

I remembered the drive with the *fair Mrs. Martin* from the restaurant in Dundrum back to her Inn. Mostly I remembered the silence. I was beginning to see a different Katherine than the brittle, closed woman she presented to the world. She had reclined in the car with her head resting against the window and her eyes closed. I imagined her asleep and resisted the urge to reach out and stoke the strand of hair that had drifted across her eyes; the hair that was glowing a sunset red in the brilliance of the afternoon sun. From time to time she would sigh, open her eyes and glance in my direction. I got the feeling she was surprising herself and struggling with the idea that she could relax and feel safe when she was with me. On my part, I was determined not to give Katherine Martin any reason not to trust me.

"You two can get rid of any thoughts you might have about Katherine and me." I said. "She and I have a common interest and his name is Michael. I have developed a genuine fondness for the young man and I plan on helping him with his future plans—if his mother approves." I quickly added, "That's all there is to it—pure and simple." I didn't think they believed me, because *I* didn't believe me. My feelings for her might be pure, but they were definitely not simple.

They were both thinking it over when a waiter approached our table and asked if we wanted an "after-dinner libation." I had noticed an unopened bottle of twenty-six year old Laphroig stuck in a corner of the shelf behind the bar and decided it was an appropriate way to end the evening. At fifteen Euros a shot I understood why it had been relegated to the back shelf and was unopened. After the first sip, Tim and Officer Malone agreed it was worth the price. And since I was hosting our little dinner party they jointly decided that in order to give the malt a true evaluation it would require a second sample. I was happy to oblige.

Derrick Malone extended his hand in my direction as he prepared to leave—and he confessed. Katherine and I were not the talk of the town because we were seen having lunch together. He knew our movements because he still had one of his men following me around. I had been correct in my assumption that we had a tail on our tail when we drove to Dundrum. It would be nice to let Katherine know I wasn't the awful driver she thought I was. I would let her know when I saw her later in the evening.

I shook hands with Derrick Malone and thanked him for his help and concern for my safety. Tim and I exchanged shakes and hugs and I promised I would get back to Ireland as soon as possible. I didn't realize at the time how soon it would be.

41

When I got up to my room I called Katherine to let her know I was leaving the next morning. Delta had called earlier and told me they had secured a business class seat on a flight from Gatwick to San Francisco the following afternoon. My flight from Dublin to Gatwick was scheduled at ten a.m., which meant I had to leave the next morning no later than six-thirty to get to Dublin airport by eight-thirty. Katherine had made a fresh blackberry trifle and invited me to have a late dessert with her and Michael. I told her to expect me in fifteen minutes. I hesitated before going out the door and decided I couldn't postpone the inevitable. I grabbed my cell phone and punched the automatic dial for Vanessa. She answered on the first ring.

"Harry you are a first class son-of-a-bitch."

"I'm happy to hear your voice, too," I said with as much nonchalance as I could muster. "I'll be home tomorrow afternoon around six o'clock San Francisco time. Why don't we leave the name calling until then...maybe we can get together for a drink or something."

"A 'drink or something' my ass, Harry," she yelled. "You know how strong my feelings are for you—I don't deny it—but Willie Dean is my future and I'm in serious damage control with him right now. He isn't buying that you and me are just friends. That dumb shit cop Brogger and his dyke buddy Detective Bennett have covered their ass and left me swingin' in the wind. Somehow Brogger knows about us and he says they found out about Willie's special assignment from you—and the only way you could have known was from me. Willie's already talkin' about how he's gonna' mess with you."

I was expecting it. There it was—the threat. I paused and told Vanessa to hold on. I wanted to be calm and very collected when I said what I had to say. "Vanessa, you've known me long enough to know when I'm deadly serious. Now is one of those times." I paused again; knowing what I was going to say was going to leave a leaden taste in my mouth. Knowing I wouldn't like myself later when I thought about it, but knowing it had to be said. The Willie Deans of the world understand only one thing and it was time for me to mark my place in his jungle. "If your boy Willie comes after me and tries to mess with me, there is a man in Chinatown who will be very unhappy. This man has a name that Willie will instantly recognize and this man is deeply in my debt. I have developed a process whereby he escapes financial detection by the IRS and pays very little in taxes—it amounts to millions of dollars every year. He rewards me handsomely, as well. Also, he assures me that my enemy is his enemy—no questions asked."

"Oh come on, Harry. Who do you…"

"Listen to me Vanessa," I commanded. "If Willie mentions my name again, tell him the man from the Bamboo Garden will not take it lightly if anything should happen to me. My bet is, when you mention the man from the Bamboo Garden, William Crawford Dean will have a sudden urge to visit the men's room." She started to interrupt again. "Pay close attention, Vanessa. If I should have any kind of accident—if a car hits me, if I fall off a ladder, if there is the slightest hint that Willie has caused any harm to come to me, no one in his world will be safe. Not his mother, his father, brothers, sisters, cousins—no one. If he's got a dog, which I can't imagine, the dog will be on the menu in a restaurant in Chinatown."

"Harry you're scaring me. What is with you?"

"I'm in no mood to fuck with your future husband, so he better not fuck with me. Tell him to stay away from me and tell him I'll stay out of everything and everyone in his world." I wanted the last word and I got it. "And, Vanessa, that includes you." I snapped the cell phone shut. I stared for a moment at the phone in my hand and thought about what I had just done. I somehow felt lighter. I grabbed a jacket and headed for the door. Like sugar plums at Christmas, a vision of Katherine, Michael and blackberry trifle danced in my head.

It took me less than ten minutes to get to the Moorings from my hotel. I parked the Mercedes in the blackened area reserved for car bombers and said a silent prayer to a mythological saint. When I was in the third grade Sister Monica told us we should believe in Saint Christopher in the same way we believed in Santa Claus—it was the promise of trust that mattered. I hoped Saint Christopher had room in his heart for a Hertz rental car.

The rain was gone, the moon was getting tossed among the clouds and the front door of the Moorings swung open. Katherine stood in the soft glow of light from her hallway. She wore faded jeans and a white cotton shirt tied at the waist. Her hair was wet and tied in a ponytail and she shivered as she grasped my hand and pulled me out of the night air. Just as quickly she released my hand and gave me a crooked smile. But, tonight there was something in her smile that was different. It seemed like a smile not reserved for a stranger. It made me wonder if I was searching for a sign that would provide us with some awareness of each other, an awareness that could help us get past her barriers. Maybe she was discovering something about me that I had wanted her to know from the beginning. In her smile there seemed to be a change of attitude, a veiled acceptance.

"Harrison, I hope you saved room for a sweet," she said. "We were starting to worry over you—and Michael is pestering me about the trifle."

"You should have started without me." I followed her into the parlor and settled in front of the fireplace. Fiona came out of the kitchen followed closely by Michael. In the words of Uncle Ambrose, Fiona's pants were "so tight you could see what she had for breakfast." Michael's eyes never left her ass. I noticed the look on Katherine's face and it wasn't a look of approval.

"Well," she said. "How was your dinner at the hotel—would it be as good as mine, I doubt it." She pointed at the sideboard and nodded in Fiona's direction. "Fiona, be a dear and bring Mr. Pius his bottle of the single malt and then you can serve us our sweet."

Fiona did as asked and, between bites of blackberry trifle, Michael gave us a blow-by-blow account of his day at school. His enthusiasm was contagious and I found myself asking endless questions about his schoolwork. He was obviously intrigued by all of his studies that involved science and he had a keen interest in math. Katherine sat and observed us without saying anything. I wondered if she was watching me or Michael—or both of us—looking for some sign that would allow her to stretch her imagination to a place where the three of us could exist as one. I quickly dismissed the notion as too much, too soon.

"Michael, you have a long day tomorrow, so we'll be saying good-night to you." Katherine leaned forward in her chair allowing him access to the top of her head for a goodnight kiss. I stood and my hand was brushed aside and instead I got a rib crushing hug followed by a choked, "When are you coming back to see us, Harry?"

"I'll be back as soon as this mess I'm tangled up in gets settled, Michael. I promise. After all, I haven't had a chance to see if you're any good on the golf course and I want to hear some more about your future plans." They both gave me curious stares. "We didn't get to explore some of the ideas I've got about college."

They exchanged glances and Katherine silently shook her head at Michael. "Off to bed with you, young man." As he left the room she turned her attention back to me. "And what might your ideas about Michael and his college be?" she asked.

I went through it for her and I didn't give her a chance to inter-rupt. I told her about my affection for her son and I admitted to my conflicted feelings about getting involved in his future plans. I sipped my single malt and it got quiet in the room. A sudden squall threw spray at the shuttered windows and, for the briefest of moments, I thought I could smell the ocean. After an awkward interlude, I decided my best course of action was to get straight to the point. "Katherine, I can get Michael into the University of San Francisco as an undergraduate student—it's a Jesuit institution and I've got some connections with the administration. I'll pay all of his tuition and he can live with me—he will have the entire third floor of my house as his own. Juanita will be overjoyed to have another man in the house that she can boss around and she'll teach him how to eat Mexican food. He can caddy on the weekends at my golf club for his spending money and he can fly home to see you whenever his schedule permits." She started to say something; not in protest, more of a question. I held up my hand. "Let me finish, let me get it all out, then you can jump all over me. If he only caddies exclusively for me, he'll make a minimum of two hundred dollars a week. If he does well in school, and I know he will, he'll have his summers off and can come home to Ireland. And, I'll arrange for you to come to San Francisco for a visit whenever you can get away. You can have the first floor of my house all to yourself and stay as long as you wish."

"I don't understand why you would do this," she said. "You barely know him…. or us, I mean."

"You don't understand because you're making it too complicated—you think there's more to it than what I just told you. There isn't, believe me. What if Michael was awarded a scholarship to a university in the States, donated by some anonymous American—would you turn it down?" I saw the quizzical look on her face. "Of course not. You'd be crazy to deny your son the opportunity to chase his dream." I went on about medical school and commitment and a grab bag of challenges Michael would face in the next few years.

When I was finished she sat straight up in her chair and said, "I would never stand in Michael's way…for anything he would want to do with his life." She smiled and glanced in the direction of the kitchen. "Of course, I only wish his father was here so he could be talking to the young rascal about the way he's starting to look after Fiona. And you—you're just as bad I might add, Mr. Harrison Pius."

"Who…me?" I laughed.

"Yes, you! You're shameful...as bad as poor Michael. Only you should know better...he's just a lad. You've both got the devil on your shoulder." It was her turn to laugh. Her bright blue eyes softened and she continued, "But I'm confused about the devil that you carry with you."

"I don't think of myself as a devil and I don't understand why you're confused." She frowned and brushed a strand of hair away from her eyes. It was obvious she had something important to say and was struggling for the proper words. "Katherine, just say it. You don't have to tip-toe around me...you should know that by now."

She thought it over and gave a hint of a smile over the rim of her glass. "I told you I could learn to like your whisky Harrison."

"You're stalling."

"That I am." She stood and with her back to the fireplace she drained the last of her single malt. "Harrison I see how you watch me. That is, I see how you look at me and you're different than the others."

"What do you mean?"

"Other men look at me and I know what they're thinking. A lonely widow who'll give them a quick tumble and nobody's the wiser. I don't think you see me that way and that bothers me...I prefer when I know what to expect. I find myself drawn to you and I feel guilty." She saw the look of confusion on my face. "I know this won't make sense to you, but I'm still married to Eamon and will always be, I'm sure. I know I'm scattering around, but..."

"Go ahead and scatter, I'm listening."

She came back and pulled her chair closer. "You're a man of the world, Harrison. You've money and power—in that way you're like so many of the American golfers who come and stay in my Inn. Yet, there is a difference about you that is out of the ordinary. It's as if you have every reason to be a roundabout and you choose not to be, with me. You're a wonderful looking man, as well. I'm sure you have many lady friends—and they are poorer for it because of their broken hearts. I don't think I have anything to give to you and I'm at a crossroad—I mean I'm still myself, of that I'm sure. But, what is it you want? I have so little to give."

"This might surprise you Katherine, but I don't want much more than what I have this very minute. Yeah, you're right, I've had more than my share of pretty ladies down through the years. But, I wouldn't trade this minute…. this moment with you, sitting in front of a warm fire, listening to the roar of the ocean and the rush of the wind for anything or anyone. You're maybe thinking this is the time in our relationship I tell you I'm falling *in love* with you and you would be wrong. What I will tell you is this—I think the world of you and that's more important. For me it has more meaning and that is what you *give* to me. I've never told anyone *I think the world of you*, never said it because I've never felt it. Oh Hell, I wish I had a nickel for every time I've whispered the words *I love you* in some young ladies ear at midnight and by noon the next day I can't remember her name. But, I do think the world of you…. and Michael, too. Yes, he's as much a part of my new world as you've become."

"But, you wouldn't be…"

"Knowing you?" I asked. I liked the fact there was no instant rebuke. "I know all I need to know and that's why, for the first time in my life, I can tell someone I think the world of them. And Katherine…. I like it. I like the sound of it. I like the feel of it and there's something else I like. I like that you keep your husband in a special place in your heart—I hope you never lose that. I know your son fills your heart to overflowing, too. But, I think you have a very big heart and maybe someday you'll make room for someone who thinks the world of you."

She studied me, her expression a combination of acceptance and wariness. "If only…" Her voice fell to a whisper and I leaned in closer. "If only there could ever be a time for holding hands and walking along the beach with someone who thinks the world of me." She paused and stared intently at the glowing remnants of the peat fire. "I think not," she said reflectively.

"I will live with the hope," I replied.

42

My flight from Dublin to Gatwick was as smooth and uneventful as the drive from Newcastle to the Dublin Airport had been. I had given some thought to arriving in Dublin early and paying a visit to the Colussus Casino on Montague Street, but my heart wasn't in it. My Rule Number Three in life is "Never play cards with a guy named Doc," and an adjunct to that rule is, don't gamble when you're pressed for time or tired. Instead, I got to Dublin with very little time to spare and ended up sleeping for most of the flight into Gatwick International Airport.

I had slept fitfully the night before, filled with troubled thoughts of Katherine, Michael and what lay ahead of me at home. Katherine had given me a chaste peck on the cheek as I left the Moorings and I didn't get what I expected. I expected a "when will I see you again?" from her, and I got a "have a safe trip home," instead.

My bags and golf clubs were checked straight through from Dublin to SFO and I had time to kill at Gatwick. I found a small pub in the main concourse and decided an eye-opener would be appropriate. Normally I don't drink in the morning, but for some reason the idea of a gin Bloody Mary sounded pretty good. A skilled Indian with a diamond the size of a marble stuck in his left earlobe served me. He was as adept with the Worcestershire as he was with the onion salt. His Bloody Mary was so good that I drank the first one in two gulps and quickly ordered another. It was quiet at my corner of the bar, while I watched the rush of travelers struggling with luggage, yelling at their kids and trying hard to enjoy the experience of traveling.

Enduring the hassle of airport security in this post 9/11 world is right up there with bowling as something I try to avoid.

My peaceful reverie was shattered by two thirty-something Americans who broke the quiet as they scattered handfuls of pound notes on the surface of the bar. One of them said to no one in particular, "We can't take this funny money home, so we may as well drink it up."

His partner, in a matching Polo shirt with a Hitachi logo on the sleeve, shouted in the direction of the bartender, "Hey pardner, give us a couple of woodies and set up our friend down at the end."

I shook my head in a "no thanks" way and tried to ignore their behavior, the type of foolishness that gives me a royal pain in the ass. Loud Americans in a foreign country make me feel tired. Both were wearing baseball style caps with the requisite St. Andrews logo on the front and both had the bill of the cap turned to the back. It was likely they had been playing golf in Scotland and were on their way home—probably to someplace like Boca Raton, Florida or Long Island, New York. They would have been shocked to learn that their over-tipping, boorish behavior was scorned by caddies, bartenders, servers and just about everyone else they came in contact with. They are thought by the locals to be alternately laughable and incredibly dumb.

The bartender was confused by their order and I suddenly had a bell go off in my head. With an outward sigh I smiled at the two young men. "Friend, I don't think our server is familiar with what you mean by a 'woodie'," I said. "I'm not sure, but I think you're going to have to translate—he may be thinking it's something you carry around in your pants."

My comment brought a roar of laughter from the two young men and the inexplicable high-five exchange between them. What is it that requires most non-athletes to high-five one another for the most mundane of reasons? It too often seems the rising or setting of the sun is cause for them to celebrate. I've observed New Yorkers cross a busy street and exchange high-fives, applauding their success at navigating the traffic. Grown men playing golf with a towel tucked in their belt, black shoes with brown socks and wearing their hats backward are especially prone to seek out a high-five recipient upon the successful completion of a two-foot putt. Unfortunately the two studs at the bar had the look of golfers on holiday and they were definitely from the States. I hate it when a fellow golfer acts like an idiot—we all get painted with the same brush that shows the wrong color. The taller of the two waved a hand at the bottom of the shelf, stopped mid-way and pointed at a bottle. "There Mr. Bar-Keep,—yeah there," he said. "The bottle of Boords gin. Anything made with Boords is a 'woodie' and we'll take our 'woodies' on the rocks."

The bell in my head had just gone from a faint ping to a five-alarm siren. While sitting quietly in a pub at Gatwick Airport in England, I realized I knew only two individuals who drank woodies and they both lived in San Francisco—and no one knew where they had disappeared to. But, what took the alarm in my head to five bells was I remembered when Maggie O'Reilly was found murdered the only thing found in the car, other than her dead body, was an empty bottle of Boords gin.

I grabbed my carry-on, threw some pound notes on the bar and headed for my gate and the flight home.

43

I was on my way home. The Boeing 767 gained altitude quickly as we left Gatwick and the Captain informed us we could expect a smooth ride, at thirty-seven thousand feet, all the way to San Francisco. The flight attendant was thoughtful enough to provide me with a dinner menu and a gin Bloody Mary. My hope was to sleep through dinner, but there was too much going on in my head for sleep. My sense of order was in chaos and I needed to take inventory of events.

Why did Junkie Bill ask me to investigate the death of his wife? Was it a smoke screen? Is he just a con man or is he involved in something more sinister? Did he solicit my help with the knowledge he was hiring an amateur who wouldn't get anywhere? An amateur sleuth who would muddy the water and get law enforcement to look elsewhere?

Why kill Maggie O'Reilly? Did she know something…or did she discover something? Did the same person kill her and Tommy Gavin? And why bring in a couple of out-of-town thugs to attack Juanita?

Frightening. I had never been a target for assassination, either. Yet, in the space of three short days there had been two attempts on my life. Why me? Was I a diversion away from something much bigger?

And what about Gerry Murphy? Were he and Junkie Bill somehow linked together? We knew Junkie wasn't on the square, but was my old friend Gerry Murphy a bad guy? And where were they?

I must have dozed off. Fully reclined in my first class seat I struggled to sit upright. I was suddenly wide-awake and re-running my mental checklist—*"I had never been a target for assassination."* My subconscious had reached out for that word and in my slumber it had hit me between the eyes. Assassination.

They were going to try to kill Margaret Thatcher. But, who were 'they'?

44

"How and when?" I asked.

Bert Brogger smiled ruefully. "Once more, Harry, we're way ahead of you. We had enough assholes in a meeting this morning to start a new political party. We've got Secret Service, FBI, two law enforcement jurisdictions and Willie Dean's special task force all looking into the 'how and when.' But, the bigger issue is 'if.'"

"If? You mean you doubt there's a plot to kill Margaret Thatcher?"

"Yeah," he answered. "All we've got are a bunch of possibilities. There may be nothing to this except coincidence. Remember, the only connection to this Thatcher broad is Tommy Gavin shootin' his mouth off about how much he hated her. Bill Morrison may have killed his wife for her money and killed Gavin because he found out about it. None of this may have anything to do with some old retired politician from England. And, Harry what's this business about Boords gin?"

So I filled him in about woodies and the fact that both Junkie and Gerry Murphy drank Boords. Even though he had obviously forgotten the name on the bottle found in Maggie's car he seemed unimpressed and stifled a yawn. But, I noticed he scribbled some notes on a pad he kept in his jacket pocket. "Okay. But, why me?" I asked. "Why did Junkie get me involved? And what about Gerry Murphy? Where's his connection?"

"Well, we know Murphy knew that Morrison wasn't who he said he was—maybe Murphy was ready to blow the whistle on good old Junkie Bill. Plus—and this will probably surprise you—your pal Murphy is broke."

"Broke? You mean like…. no money?"

"Harry, I mean like NO money. Zero. The guy owes everybody and his poor wife is goin' crazy. Not only is her husband missing but also her comfortable sheltered life is crashing around her ears. She doesn't have a fuckin' clue what's goin' on."

"Look," I said quickly. "I've known Gerry for twenty years and he's one of the wealthiest guys I know."

Bert Brogger looked intent. "You don't know squat about this guy. He's got banks, loan sharks, the IRS—they're all after him. He doesn't have two nickels to his name. And everybody is looking for him. If the bad guys can't find him it's no wonder the FBI and the Secret Service can't find him. And don't forget—he knew our boy Junkie Bill as Billy Morris in Ireland over thirty years ago. Why didn't he ever tell anyone about the connection?"

I didn't have an answer. "So, what's the plan? What's the super-cop Willie Dean doing?" I asked.

He shook his head thoughtfully. "He's trying to tap dance through the raindrops. Acting important. He's got all these government agencies crowded around him, plus the Mayor is on his ass and Willie doesn't have a clue. At least the Feds have had two weeks of practice."

"Practice?"

"Oh, Hell yes," Brogger said, smiling. "Thatcher's been in five cities, so far, and the Feds have investigated over a hundred death threats. They know the drill—Willie Dean doesn't." He smiled again. "Harry, what's with you and Willie? Shortly after you left for Ireland he called me. Funny, he didn't want to talk about anything except you. I didn't give him jackshit, but he was sure curious. You ever cross paths?"

"Never met the man," I answered. Had Vanessa developed a conscience and confessed her affair with me to Willie? Or had Willie found out about us on his own? Or was my super paranoia in overdrive?

"Well he seems to know a lot about you, but he didn't get any of it from me. He's a sneaky bastard, Harry."

I didn't want to talk about Willie Dean. "Speaking of sneaky. What's going on with the O'Reilly boys? Have you shared all the information about Junkie Bill with them? Do they know how badly they were fooled?"

"They're in shock, but I forgot to tell you the other surprise." His smile broke into a muffled laugh. "Peter O'Reilly and his CFO have found some more money. At least it was available money until about a week ago."

Bert Brogger took a hard hit on his third vodka on the rocks. I had called him the minute my flight touched down at SFO and we agreed to meet at Bertolucci's for drinks. It was two in the morning in Ireland and my circadian rhythm was losing its battle with my overall fatigue. "Don't tell me there's more secret bank accounts."

"You got it. Up until about a week ago Bill Morrison and Maggie O'Reilly had a joint account in a bank in the Cayman Islands."

"How much?" I stumbled on the words and took a gulp of scotch. "A week ago…"

"Eight days ago—a Friday—he cleaned it out. A little over a million bucks."

45

In the early morning I woke up and thought of Katherine. It was Sunday morning and she was most likely at Church—probably at the eleven o'clock Mass. It was a little after three a.m. in San Francisco and I was wide-awake. I had only slept about four hours, but felt rested and ready to confront the day. Only I didn't have anything or anyone to confront. I had arrived shortly before eight o'clock the previous evening and was made to feel like Caesar coming home to Rome. Juanita was truly happy to see me. And Manu and Tua were ecstatic. Their bags were packed and they didn't even stick around for me to pay them. Manu said "catch us later" and they were out the door. I followed them to the street where Manu's lady friend was double-parked.

"That bad, huh?" I asked.

Manu looked up as he opened the passenger door to the bright red Hummer. "Worse," he replied.

Tua was crawling in the back seat and looking back over his shoulder he said, "Worse, brudda. Like that woman is crazy."

"Your roommates seemed happy to be leaving, Juanita. It couldn't be that you were unpleasant to them...could it?" Out of the corner of my eye I noticed Mrs. Mulhaupt grinning broadly. She was heating a couple of enchiladas for my dinner as Juanita hobbled around the kitchen on crutches, supervising the preparation.

Juanita sidled up to one of the barstools at the kitchen counter and perched one cheek of her broad butt on the edge. She looked like she had lost some weight—as a matter of fact, except for the cast stretching from ankle to mid-thigh, she looked better than I had seen her in years. She eyed me and said, "Ya know, Harry, those two are just overgrown little boys. They may be thugs to some people, but I think they're just a couple of harmless puppies."

"They might be puppies, but they're far from harmless," I replied. "That's why I didn't worry about you while I was in Ireland—I knew they were here."

"We got along just fine—we didn't need them. All those two did was eat and watch the television—and you know what they watch? Cartoons!" Juanita smiled at Mrs. Mulhaupt for approval and continued. "And Harry they eat enough for ten people. I've never seen anything like it and the stuff they eat—My God!—You know they eat raw fish and they mix it with rice and seaweed. Makes me sick."

The enchiladas were a welcome change of pace. The food being served these days in Ireland has improved dramatically over the last ten years, but I've yet to find a decent Mexican restaurant. There is one in Sligo Town that comes close, but succumbs to the Irish sin of overcooking rice and beans. As I devoured the food on my plate Juanita verbalized a long list of questions about everything that was going on. Plus, she still had a well-deserved curiosity about the attack that had left her with a badly damaged knee. So I went through everything for her. I downplayed the two attacks that had been made on my life, and she reacted with first anger and concern then exploded into a rage about me minding my own business. As always, she got all over me about the amount of cash that was going out and she "don't see nuthin' comin' in."

I reminded her. "You know, my darling, at the rate I'm spending money I'm going to be flat broke in twenty years."

She looked at me, tilted her head and smiled. "Harry, I'm really glad you're home. It's my role in life to worry and you take up way too much of my time."

Four a.m. I wasn't going to get any more sleep. I found myself preoccupied with a name. Devon Clarke—where did he fit in? I had my doubts about Junkie Bill; after all, he had stolen an identity and maybe stolen millions of Maggie O'Reilly's money. Were he and Clarke part of some grotesque plan to kill an old woman because she had been an enemy of the IRA? And my old golfing buddy Gerry Murphy. Had he gotten himself in over his head in some strange plot that had gotten out of hand? I figured if Gerry was somehow involved it must be about money—but Bert Brogger said he was broke.

I crawled out from under the covers and put both feet on the floor. It was cold in my room and I could hear the wind whistling through the eaves of the rooftop overhang. Resisting the urge to call Katherine, I took a quick shower and shave and decided what I needed most was an egg salad sandwich from the Happy Donut. Twenty minutes later I stepped out on the street and realized I was underdressed. There were about ten hardy souls at the corner of 24th and Church waiting for the J Streetcar. The way they were dressed you would have thought they were waiting for a ski lift in Aspen. I settled into a back booth at Happy Donut with my first cup of coffee of the day and while waiting for my sandwich I glanced at a discarded newspaper. It was the *Chronicle* and it was the previous days' edition. On the back page was Gerry Murphy's picture. The accompanying article gave little detail except for some biography that was misleading and an overblown depiction of his role in the affairs of Pacific Heights Golf Club. My mind was so clogged with confusion I had forgotten Gerry's involvement in the Capital Improvement Committee at the Club. When you're stuck; follow the money. Maybe it was time I had a talk with our Club manager Palmer Peters to see if Gerry had approached Junkie Bill about a contribution to the building fund.

The front page of the day-old newspaper had a picture of Margaret Thatcher and President Bush under a headline—**San Francisco Welcomes The Iron Lady.** I wondered what the welcome would be.

46

Devon Clarke was impatient. And he was cold. Let no one ever complain to me again about the weather in Ireland, he thought. He had awakened at four a.m. and driven to the rest area located across the freeway from the back entrance to Pacific Heights Golf Club. From his shabby motel room in San Mateo to the rest area was only a fifteen-minute ride, but his ease at locating the rendezvous spot did nothing to ease his anxiety.

Sometimes it seemed unsettling to him that he was living in this fog-shrouded city about to participate in the defining event of his life. The journey to this time and place had sustained him for almost five years. But, it was the eventuality that supported the hardship not the choice of location. It had been only six months since the agreement that San Francisco would provide the best opportunity for success. Now the time had come.

Clarke had never been an official member of the group. He didn't share the others' fanatic dedication to the cause. Sure he was pleased to do something as "payback for the miners"—his family had been in the mines for a hundred years and Thatcher had displaced them from hearth and home. A pit village wasn't much of a home, he thought, but it was all his parents had. Instead, he was comfortable coming in and out of the occasional assignment, always for the money. His first contact with his old friends had been in 1999 and since then he had participated in numerous other assignments but always kept this one as a priority. Those who knew that he was the best at what this project required had quickly agreed to his inflated fee. He was bothered, though, by how quickly his fee had been accepted. The bothersome thought vanished when he realized his exit strategy was flawless.

He was amused at the thought of his so-called expertise. Hell, anyone could fire the goddamn thing—all you had to do was aim and pull the trigger. It was acquiring one of the bloody birds that took talent—that and money. Someone told him the American CIA had a fifty million dollar war chest to try and buy back some of them from Bosnia and Afghanistan. No luck—they haven't been able to buy even one of them back. They're scattered from Sri Lanka to North Korea and all points between. The Russians got hundreds of them from the Afghan army. What the Russians didn't get went to Iran, except for the one across the freeway, stored in a crate in a deserted maintenance shed. Funny how a redheaded Irishman from Downpatrick could intercept a FIM-92A Stinger Missile headed from the Mujaheddin to Qatar.

That's why they were willing to pay him the big money. Now, the money was even better, because he didn't have to split the fee with that dumb little fucker Barry McLain. How goddamn stupid was it, he thought, to try taking out the American after we agreed it made no sense. McLain got his head blown off, he did. Course he always thought he was smarter than all the other lads.

Clarke checked his watch and gave out an exasperated sigh just as a hard rap on the passenger side window snapped him to attention. He straightened and stepped from the car. "I was beginning to think something had happened to you. You're never late—what's goin' on?"

"I got stuck in traffic around the airport. Come on, we've got to get up on the hill before the greenskeepers finish mowing the greens. We don't want anyone to see us once we get to the course."

The two men walked the fifty yards to the underpass that exited the freeway leading to the rest area. They crossed under the freeway and climbed a shallow grassy area to the edge of the pine trees that bordered the fourth fairway at Pacific Heights Golf Club. From there it was a short hike across number four fairway to the path that led up the side of the hill and the abandoned maintenance sheds.

When both men were satisfied they had not been seen they moved from the cover of the trees and picked their way carefully up the abandoned road. The morning sun sparkled on the dew in the trees and Devon *caught a brilliant flash of light off the tail section of a jumbo jet as it hur-tled down the runway at SFO in the distance. He smiled to himself and a surge of power rushed through his body. How many people in that plane? Where are they going, he wondered. If I had an extra bird I could practice on them. He shuddered as he realized how cold his heart had become toward his fellow man. Well, fuck 'em all, no cocksucker ever gave me an even break so why should Devon Clarke pay heed—even on this bright new morning.*

The brush was cleared from the door and the two men entered the room. There was no electricity so the morning light would have to suffice. Devon reached for the claw hammer wedged in the space between the crate and the sawhorse. "Oh, but doesn't it have a lovely look to it," he said as he rested his hand on the oil soaked wood. He nodded toward a wire bound manual lying on top of the crate. "We won't be needing this, but you can take a look if you've a mind."

The other man began to casually leaf through the pages of the manual. "How much does this thing weigh?" he asked.

"The missile or the launcher?"

"The whole damn thing, Devon," he said impatiently. "How much does it weigh when you've got it on your bloody shoulder and ready to fire?"

"I'm not sure—it's not a burden to be sure—maybe fifteen kilos."

Devon pried the lid off the crate and began to slowly remove the pack-ing material. He looked at the other man and shook his head. "I can do this myself, you know. It wouldn't be a two man job."

"I want to be here in case something goes wrong. That's why I want you to tell me how this thing works."

Devon turned away from his work. "And what the fuck could go wrong? This thing is nothin' more than a digital camera. Point and shoot. It'll even cover your mistakes."

"Mistakes?"

"Yeah, you can't fuck it up." He moved some packing material aside and caressed the blunt end of a five-foot long tube. "This end's got an infrared digital camera in it and if you got a target that's less than five

miles away and it's flying at an altitude of less than eleven thousand feet this little missy will fly right up its ass."

"How does it know?"

Devon Clarke grasped the tube in both hands and casually removed it from the crate. Seeing the look of apprehension from the other side of the dimly lighted room he quickly advised, *"Don't worry. This is a field weapon and it'll take all kinds of abuse."* Holding the tube in front of him he directed his attention to the narrow end. *"That's the launch engine here at this end. Working your way up the missile you've got your rocket engine, your guidance system and the infrared camera."*

"And all that stuff is in a skinny—what—five foot long tube."

"It sounds pretty simple and, up until the time you pull the trigger, everyman's baby sister could fire the fucker. But, then it gets complicated."

"Complicated? How?"

"Well, the whole thing is heat seeking, so once you've got the missile hooked into the launch system and pointed at the target you wait for the buzzer to go off in your ear. When you hear the buzz it means you're locked on to the target. Then you pull the trigger and the fun begins. The launch rocket shoots this missile I'm holding out of the launch tube, the rocket engine ignites and away it goes."

"Devon, bloody hell! That's all well and good, but what do you mean it gets complicated? I don't want complications."

"That's not what I mean, for Christ's sakes! It only gets complicated for the missile, and that's when the navigation system kicks in. This beauty thinks for itself. If the target changes direction or speeds up it makes navigational corrections at tenth of a second intervals. Once you pull the trigger the target is surely deader than an English cousin."

"We can't fail, Devon."

Devon Clarke had made it a point to always keep the percentages in his favor. Failure didn't enter into his plans. He regarded the other man with mild annoyance. *"Afghan soldiers with the brain power of a goat shot down over three hundred Soviet fighter jets with this weapon during their war. It succeeded eighty percent of the time. Our target is ten times* the size of a Soviet MIG and will be flying one third as fast. We can't miss."

"I don't know any other way to fight this war, Devon. The only way we can win is to inspire our own people. Whether you believe in our cause or not...she has this coming." He pulled a folding chair away from its resting place in the corner and sat. "You're right, we can't miss."

Devon finished his preparations efficiently and covered the assembled weapon with a tarpaulin. He and the other man quickly covered the door to the shed with brush and pine boughs after securing the lock. They made their way undetected down the hill to their waiting vehicles. The entire operation had taken less than two hours.

47

The Boxster roared to life. There's something about sitting with your spine pressed against 258 horses that gets your adrenaline flowing. It was a fine May morning and I was headed to the Club. I wasn't sure why, but I needed to feel useful. Maybe a conversation with the Club Manager would point me in a direction I hadn't thought of.

Palmer Peters had been our manager for over twenty-five years and his father had the position for thirty-five before that. It was Monday so the golf course and clubhouse were closed. That meant he could dress casually, so he wore slacks and a crisp, starched white shirt complemented by an old-school tie. In the world of Palmer Peters he was decadently casual. The kitchen staff was off so he prepared our coffee himself. Not surprising, he poured from a sterling silver pot into bone china cups.

"Mr. Pius, it goes without saying we, I mean the staff and I, are distraught over the events of the past week. To think that two of our members might be in peril is distressing indeed."

I realized that the very reserved Mr. Peters would be an unlikely source for information, but I had an idea I wanted to explore. "I'll get straight to the point Palmer. Do you know if Gerry Murphy was involved with Bill Morrison in any way?" I saw the perplexed look on his face and continued. "By involved I mean—were they working on the capital improvement project together or anything else that would have been Club connected?"

"Well, as you know, I was working very closely on the project with Mr. Murphy. It is a sizeable undertaking for the Club—I often thought it was becoming a burden for him, it seemed, because he wanted to do everything himself. In answer to your question, I don't think Mr. Murphy wanted any help from anyone."

"Did he talk to you about raising money from outside regular Club funds—could he have been looking to Bill Morrison for some kind of contribution?"

"If he was soliciting help from Mr. Morrison he didn't confide it in me." He paused and delicately sipped his coffee. "By the way, I should tell you the authorities have gone over all of this with me. A Detective Brogger has been quite persistent in his questions about their possible relationship."

We finished our coffee and I could feel his anxiety over wasting valuable time. Monday, without any members bothering him, was the opportunity for our Manager to catch up on paperwork. I thanked him for his time and made my way to the side entrance.

Walking to the parking lot I felt the vibration of my cell phone in my jacket pocket. "Harry, where are you?" the voice barked.

"Bert, I was just going to call you. I'm in the parking lot at the Club. What's up?"

"Stay there. I'm about ten minutes away. We need to talk."

Bert Brogger frowned at me. He was bouncing around on the balls of his feet like a boxer before the opening bell. He knew something was going to happen in the next two days and he was no longer in the loop. "Shit Harry. The Feds and the Willie Dean team have got the City locked tighter than a bull's ass running down hill."

I wondered if Bert had ever met my Uncle Ambrose—he had just used one of his favorite expressions. The Detective had come roaring into the parking lot and I was surprised he didn't have lights flashing. "If you're out of the investigation why are you in such a hurry?"

"This whole thing is headed in the wrong direction. They're not listening to anybody—certainly not me. They've got the Thatcher broad so surrounded she can't even move. I hear through the grapevine she's really pissed at all the security."

"You'd think she would be happy for the protection," I replied.

"Well, she's got the speech this afternoon and the dinner tonight with all the bigwigs, but she wanted to go sightseeing tomorrow and they're trying to talk her out of it. My bet is she'll go wherever the fuck she wants. I hear Willie's ass is so puckered he can't wait for her to get on the plane tomorrow afternoon."

"Have you met with him?"

"Oh yeah. I spent over three hours in a meeting with him and the Feds. What a fuckin' waste of time."

"Let me guess. They still don't think there's a connection."

"You got that right, but I'm sure there is. What few brain cells I've got left that aren't soaked in booze, tells me Murphy, Morrison, Gavin and the old gal O'Reilly are all connected—and the Thatcher broad is at the center of it. But nobody's listening to me. And ya' know, Harry, somebody went after your housekeeper and tried to get you—twice. What's that all about?" He paused and fumbled with an unopened stick of gum. "By the way I haven't had a drink in four days."

"Hey, good for you. What do they say—'one day at a time'? Make today your fifth day." We were sitting in a golf cart that had been left at the front entrance, probably left there by one of the maintenance crew. Palmer Peters pushed through the large oak doors and walked briskly toward us.

"Mr. Pius, I'm so pleased you're still here—and Detective, you as well. It may not be important, but seeing the two of you sitting in the cart reminded me of something I had completely forgotten about."

He had our attention. "I saw Mr. Morrison and Mr. Murphy in a cart together about two weeks ago."

"Were they playing golf?" I asked.

"No. No. That's why I thought it odd. They were going past the first tee—it was very late in the day—and I thought it strange they would be out in a golf cart without their clubs."

"Do you have any idea where they were headed?" Brogger asked.

"None whatsoever." Peters turned to leave and said, "Sorry about my lapse in memory. I hope I didn't leave out something important."

Brogger and I thanked him and he went back into the clubhouse. Brogger said, "I feel like I'm on one of those bungee cords—maybe I should just cut the fuckin' cord. If I called Detective Bennett and told her to tell Willie Dean we had someone who saw our two missing guys together—she'd probably say 'so what'." He pushed his hand through his unruly hair and shook his head slowly. "I got a missing sixteen-year-old girl I should be lookin' for and a caseload as thick as your wallet. I don't have time to mess with this anymore."

He walked me to the Boxster. His eyes wandered from the back of the car to the front and he tapped the left front tire with his foot. "I must be doing something wrong," he muttered as he walked away.

48

Back at the house I realized I needed a quiet place to think. Mrs. Mulhaupt fixed me a couple of grilled cheese toasties with sliced garlic pickles on the side and I headed for the basement and my cave. I grabbed an Anchor Steam on my way toward the stairs. As I opened the door the house phone was ringing. I reached for it quickly. I didn't want Juanita to awaken from her afternoon nap. She didn't really need the rest, but Mrs. Mulhaupt did.

Julie's voice was abruptly cold. "I haven't heard from you Harry. It must not have meant as much to you as it did to me."

Before I could respond she began what was obviously a well-rehearsed lecture. "Harry, you and I are a bad mix. Even when I extend myself you exhibit the cold nature that drove me away in the first place. I came to you in your hour of need and I feel like you used me."

It felt good to hear Julie's voice. For the first time in five years the sound of her voice had not ripped through me and tumbled my insides. It was a relief and I actually felt embarrassed for her. I cared about her in spite of her transparent frailty, yet I knew there was nothing for me in her mixed up world. I couldn't get angry with her anymore and it felt wonderful. She was finally out of my life. Instead, I felt an odd sense of detachment and I smiled at the realization that my primary concern was my sandwich getting cold.

Also, I was sure she had found someone new. There was a guy out there who had figured out the quickest way to get her in bed was to tell her how bright and beautiful she was. If he was really clever he would recognize that he could seal the deal if he convinced her they shared a common pain. He would tell her he was married to a woman who drank too much, verbally abused him and embarrassed him in public. Julie would demurely offer herself up like a sacrificial lamb, but she wouldn't be able to resist the urge to show him what a real woman could do for him sexually. In a few months she would be heartbroken at the realization he was only interested in sex and didn't care if she had a brain in her head. But, she would continue to see him and rationalize her behavior with the idea that their stolen moments were still something special. She would never admit, even to herself, that what drove her from bed to bed was the undeniable fact that she was, pure and simple, horny and was turned on by the thrill of forbidden sex. On my part, the proper approach would have been to challenge her logic about "who used whom." Instead, I decided to let her off the hook. "You're absolutely right, Julie. I think it's time we moved on. There's no future in me—and you deserve better. You're drop-dead gorgeous and the smartest woman I've ever known. You deserve the best." I said good-bye and replaced the phone in its cradle. I took a big bite of grilled cheese and smiled. Yes, dear Julie, you might be one of the smartest women I've ever known, but you are definitely the dumbest. One down and one to go.

I finished the sandwich, took a last swallow of beer and called Vanessa. I got her voice mail and left a message. I spent the rest of the day doing the mundane chores associated with hearth and home. Paying bills and re-submitting an invoice for twenty-five grand to a former client. I was expecting a partial payment, but didn't hold out much hope. I called my brother in Salinas for an update on his kids and listened to an analysis of the upcoming Little League season. It seemed my ten-year old nephew was the next Roger Clemens. I talked to Brogger twice and was not surprised to learn that Margaret Thatcher had delivered an impassioned luncheon speech to the Commonwealth Club about the war on terrorism. She had stressed the need for the United States to continue its role as a world leader in that war. Later, a very private dinner with the Mayor and our two U.S. Senate

Democrats was scheduled to take place in her suite at the Fairmont Hotel. I thought how enlightening it would be if I were a fly on the wall and could observe our two lightweight Senators trying to match wits with the Iron Lady. She was not scheduled to leave the hotel after the dinner, but had informed everyone concerned that she planned on sticking with her sightseeing plans the following morning before her scheduled departure in the afternoon.

I had my own quiet dinner with Juanita and Mrs. Mulhaupt—the conversation centering on my adventures in Ireland. I kept the description of the car bombing and attempt on my life as low-key as I could, but Juanita was too savvy and saw through my nonchalance. She asked too many questions, so I changed the subject to Michael Martin. At first, her eyes brightened at the idea we might have a teenage boy underfoot, then her eyes narrowed as I tried to casually describe Michael's mother and my non-relationship with her. Juanita's smirk was expected, "Harry, you're not fooling me."

I was up early the next morning and skimmed through the Sunday paper paying close attention to a rather long, unflattering article about Margaret Thatcher. What would you expect, I thought, from a newspaper whose most recent crusade was to correct the inequity associated with some city employees being referred to as "Receptionists." The *Chronicle* was demanding that individuals seated at a reception desk who attempt to direct you through the maze of bureaucracy be given the title—"Director of First Impressions." Political correctness is important in our City.

I had the phone in my hand trying to gather the courage to call Katherine and instead, decided to try Vanessa again.

"I was just picking up the phone to call you, Harry."

"Great minds…."

"No, I don't think it's anything like that. I know you're avoiding me and I think I understand." She got strangely quiet. Softly she continued. "Harry, I've got myself in a real jam. There's stuff you don't know about and I need to sit down with you and tell you about it."

"There isn't anything about your life that would surprise me. Plus, you're a survivor. What could be so bad?"

"This is when I get pissed and tell you what a naïve little boy you are, Harry, but I'm not going to do it this time. You need to trust me on this...and you definitely need to hear my story."

"Can you give me a hint? I'm hearing from a friend of mine, who's a police detective, that your boy Willie has taken a sudden interest in me. Did you tell him about us? Or did he find out on his own?"

"What I need to talk to you about has nothing to do with Willie and, yet, it could have everything to do with both of you."

"What are you..."

"I know, Harry. I know. Please, I don't want to talk about it over the phone."

I heard the clang of the bell on the J car as it crossed the intersection of Church Street. I couldn't help but think how pleasant it was to sit in my comfortable cave while the rat race pushed itself past my front door. I thought of Ireland and who was there. I took a sip of coffee and closed my eyes.

"Harry, if you're still there I'll tell this much." Her voice was quiet. "Remember the time we were sitting on the bench at the beach and your friend Gerry Murphy came walking by and saw us?"

My eyes popped open. "Of course I remember. What does that..."

"It was no accident that he saw us. I want to tell you about it...and I'm worried."

"Vanessa, do you know Gerry Murphy?"

She answered so softly I asked her to repeat it. "Yes. Yes."

"Where are you?" I shouted.

"I'm in my apartment."

"I'll pick you up out front in fifteen minutes." I dropped the phone and rushed to the Boxster.

We were seated in the back booth at the Fog Horn. Nick was at his usual spot behind the bar and Janice was in the kitchen. I had a Bloody Mary, untouched, in front of me and Vanessa was on her third Irish coffee. Her face was turned upside down and she was having trouble breathing. Finally, she blurted it out. "I've known Gerry Murphy for ten years, Harry."

The air in the room was heavy. Nick, behind the bar, seemed to move in slow motion. I could hear Janice banging her pots and pans in the kitchen, yet she seemed to be off in the distance. For some strange reason my brain, in milliseconds, flashed to a reality of this moment—I knew it would last a lifetime. Funny, too, that in that flashing moment I thought of Robert Frost—*"I shall be telling this with a sigh somewhere ages and ages hence."*

"Go on, but I have a hunch I know where this is headed."

"Yes, I was one of his girls. I would have never gotten through school if it wasn't for him and his friend."

"You wouldn't have gotten through school? Or you wouldn't have gotten through school living in a fancy apartment by yourself and driving a new BMW. Lots of young women—most young women—get through school without peddling their ass to rich old fuckers, Vanessa."

"Maybe I deserve that, Harry. But, you could never understand. Never in a million years would you know what it was like for me. I'm not proud of what I've done and I'm not proud that I've continued the relationship. I…"

I interrupted loudly. Nick's head jerked up at me from behind the bar. I lowered my voice. "Are you telling me you're still seeing him?"

"He's had me under his thumb for the last five years." She answered. "First, he threatened to tell Willie and lately he was going to tell both of you about my past if I didn't continue to…. well…. you know, take care of him. He didn't mind if you saw him the evening we were at the beach…he wanted *me* to see him…his way of letting me know he was still in control. And until about two weeks ago he was calling me constantly, always asking questions about you. Then, all of a sudden, he got really interested in Willie's special assignment and was asking me all kinds of questions about that. I'm worried."

"Worried?"

She reached across the table and laid her hand on mine. "Harry…. Do you think Gerry's involved in something weird?"

I was beginning to think he was involved in something more than just *weird.* "So…. He's known all along you and I were involved," I said. "Just curious—what do you mean 'continue to take care of him'?"

"He has unusual needs," she replied. "I've given him every weird, kinky experience a woman can give a man. His specialty is unusual places. He likes to do it in elevators, his office, and the back seat of his car—once in a taxi while the driver watched. He even had an old shack, with a mattress on the floor that he used to take me to. We partied there a few times with Dermot. Mostly Dermot's role was photographer—there's dozens and dozens of pictures of me in one of Gerry's scrapbooks. If those pictures ever…."

Her head collapsed to her chest. After a moment she lifted her chin and choked back a sob. There were tears forming in the corners of her eyes when suddenly a muffled giggle escaped. "But, Harry…I never let him kiss my feet."

I didn't smile. Nothing about her was amusing. For the second time that day I was embarrassed for someone who had been an important part of my life. And with Vanessa I was experiencing an overwhelming sadness. "So you had a reverse Oreo with Gerry and Dermot O'Reilly?" I asked. "Wait a minute." It was my turn to catch my breath. "Vanessa, where was this shack?"

"It was up on a hill. Hidden in some trees. Just an old maintenance shack that overlooks the place where you play golf."

I didn't take the time to pay the tab. I knew Nick would understand. I grabbed Vanessa by the hand and we rushed to the car.

49

The parking area reserved for British Air employees was closed. Bay Area Paving had finished their prep work and the hot oil resurfacing trucks were in place. British Airways Captain Paul Rivers was mildly annoyed. He had more important issues to worry about and tried not to let the necessity of walking an extra fifty yards add to his anxiety. The shuttle from the Marriott dropped him and the rest of his flight crew at the north end of the building housing Flight Operations for British Air. The first of three fully loaded trucks was beginning the methodical application of hot seal-coat on the parking area. The application of top based material commonly known as blacktop would come later. "Why today?" he thought. "Why not do it on Sunday afternoon?" He smiled to himself as he realized there was probably a union restriction that prevented work on Sunday. "Typical for the Yanks," he muttered to himself.

It was twelve forty-five, two hours and fifteen minutes before their scheduled departure for London, when Captain Rivers and his crew of fourteen left the foul smell of seal-coat behind them and entered the Flight Ops Center. His first stop was the incoming mail slot and his annoyance went up a notch when he noticed the thicker-than-usual batch of revisions he needed to insert in his Terminal Procedure Manual. Annoyance gave way to satisfaction when he saw the revision at the top of the pile. "It's about bloody time!" he exclaimed to no one in particular. "They're finally putting in Vasi lights. This is the foggiest airport we fly in to—worse than Heathrow—and we're finally getting visual glide slope. Strobe lights have only been around for thirty years—what took so long?" He continued thumbing through the Approach Plate Terps and placing them in his five-

inch black binder. Now and again he could be heard swearing silently to himself.

*Captain Rivers' First Officer and Engineer had been giving their skipper a wide berth since their acrimonious meeting earlier that morning with the Task Force from the San Francisco Police Department and the American Secret Service officials. They met in a conference room at the Marriott and the Engineer, with his eye for detail, had counted thirty-two people in the room, not including the British Airways crew. The first question asked had been the same one that was asked at every stop on Margaret Thatcher's journey; why was she flying on a commercial aircraft? The answer was always the same. It was her message to the people of Great Britain that it was safe to travel on British Airways and she would not accept special treatment not otherwise offered her fellow countrymen. Most security officials thought it pompous grandstanding and Captain Rivers was the most vocal. At one point, the meeting had gotten so heated the British Airways Director of Operations had called a recess and they had taken a fifteen minute break so Captain Rivers could calm himself. It was one thing for Flight 81 to load the passengers and push back from the gate with twelve U.S. Marshalls aboard; it was quite another to taxi to a holding area and board the former Prime Minister and her security crowd separately. Captain Rivers knew what a "pain in the arse" it was going to be. Especially when the Director told him that he would have to shut down the engines once they taxied to the holding area. This meant doing everything twice. All pre-flight procedures would have to be repeated. As everyone who had ever flown with the skipper knew, he did everything strictly by the book, even if he was doing it for the second time. And, he would do it in the proper sequence. He would even brief the Flight Attendant Supervisor twice. He and the First Officer would go over the thirty-question checklist again. He would insist on the First Officer reminding him, once more, of his time-honored memory list—**parking brake, brake pressure, gear lever**. It wouldn't do for him to re-start engine number three in the rotation and then start rolling.*

The meeting had fallen apart when the Chief of Detectives from San Francisco made light of the fact that Flight 81 would have to get taxi instructions a second time. That's when the Captain exploded. His voice took on the sound of a man bellowing into a fifty-five gallon drum. "No one—I repeat no one—gives a British Airways Captain 'instructions.' Ground control will provide 'clearance.' They will never give 'instructions'!"

Chief of Detectives Willie Dean shrugged. "I apologize, Captain Rivers. I'm not familiar with your protocol. But, we must have Mrs. Thatcher board after the other passengers have been seated. And, it must be done away from the terminal."

A Secret Service operative wearing a black windbreaker and an earplug in his ear had heard enough. With a dismissive wave of his hand in the direction of Willie Dean he said, "You must understand Captain, we can't protect her as well in a crowd as we can if we isolate her in a location of our choosing." He held up a finger for emphasis, "We won't decide where you're going to park until you hear Ground Control tell you 'Captain, clear to taxi.' You'll be on frequency two-eighteen with a clearance to runway twenty-eight right. The old adage that you 'taxi no faster than a grown man walks' will be your procedure and it's then—and only then—that we'll re-direct you to a holding area. You will park in the holding area and shut down your engines. Leave your anti-collision light on…remember—leave it on! Once Mrs. Thatcher and her entourage are safely on board, Ground Control will advise you that you are free to resume all the pre-flight procedures designated by FAA and British Airways. When you have completed all of your checklists you will call Air Traffic Control for clearance to London 'as filed.' Ground Control will come back to you and give you clearance to 'start your engines.' Once everything is back up and running again, and you have received taxi clearance once more—and this is most important—you must respond, 'This is Speedbird 81 to London.' If we don't hear you say 'Speedbird' all hell is going to break loose. Got it?"

The Captain had "got it" and now, three hours after the meeting at the Marriott, he had just about "had it." The Dispatcher had given him the flight plan with a minimum time track and now they were arguing about the alternate flight plan. After twenty-seven years in the first seat—the last eleven years flying 747s—Captain Paul Rivers wasn't about to sign a dispatch release without everything meeting his rigid guidelines, including an alternate flight plan based on worst-case weather. He knew the passenger load was going to be a little off, but the weather, flight plan and fuel load had to be right on the number or he wouldn't sign. And none of the Company policy about twenty minutes extra fuel would apply to a transcontinental flight under his command. It was one hour extra fuel in the tanks or he didn't go. The sound of his First Officer's voice interrupted the discussion.

"Captain, we've got one hour until we push back. The shuttle is here to take us to the terminal."

Captain Rivers slammed the dispatch release on top of the Dispatchers desk and said, "Get this to me with an alternate flight plan in the next thirty minutes or you're going to have the United States government on your arse like a bee in the Queen's bonnet."

He started out the front door and remembered the truck spraying hot oil on the surface of the parking lot. He turned and left through the back entrance.

50

At various times lately, I've thought about what happened that fine Sunday afternoon. I think of the danger and I think of what might have been. But, my thoughts always start with the ride to Pacific Heights Golf Club. Driving a five-speed, high-powered sports car is hard enough without trying to dial a cell phone and listen to your passenger scream all at the same time.

"For God's sake, Harry, slow down!"

I ignored Vanessa and hit the speed dial on my cell phone. He answered just as his message started to play. I had to wait while he hit the right button. Immediately I knew he had fallen off the wagon. His speech was blurred and sleepy. I yelled over the roar of the Boxster's engine. "I think I know where Murphy and Morrison are holed up. Meet me in the parking lot at Pacific Heights. Just do it! Trust me on this—don't ask questions." He tried to interrupt. "Bert, listen to me. I don't know what's going on, but I think I know where they are. I'm hanging up. Meet me. Ten minutes!"

Vanessa had her eyes closed and her shoulders pressed against the seat. Her face looked like an astronaut at liftoff. Putting the pedal to the metal in a Boxster S will do that to you.

From the almost empty Bayshore Freeway to the 380 off ramp took less than ten minutes. The usual morning fog had given way to mid-day sun and any other day I would have stopped and put the top down. Any other day I would not have seen my speedometer hit one-forty either. Although there was a valet on duty I sped into the parking lot at Pacific Heights and slipped into the first empty slot near the electric cart storage barn. There was a young man washing the floorboard on a cart parked at the front door of the barn. He recognized me and gave a perfunctory wave as Vanessa and I jumped in an empty cart. A husband and wife group was preparing to tee off on the first hole as we pulled off to the side and waited for Bert Brogger. One of the wives—the one wearing an ugly yellow visor—took a long, slow look in our direction. Vanessa wasn't wearing a collared shirt, her shorts were too short and her open-toed sandals fit none of the dress code requirements. Of course, the fact that she was a black woman in the company of that notorious womanizer, Harrison Pius, might have had something to do with it. By the time the woman in the yellow visor hit her tee shot and sat next to her husband in their golf cart I could see her jaw flapping up and down. I thought, poor guy's probably getting an earful about how the "Club is going to the dogs."

I was reaching for my cell phone to try Bert Brogger again when I looked up and saw him walking gingerly in our direction. I say gingerly because it was obvious he was in a lot of pain. He looked like he was trying to pick his way through a minefield. Every step mattered. He hadn't fallen off the wagon; he had done a belly flop.

"This better be good, Harry." He stared at Vanessa and leaned against the windshield of the golf cart. "What's she doing here? Is this Willie's squeeze?"

Vanessa didn't like being referred to as somebody's squeeze, but she let it pass. I made the proper introductions then attempted to bring Bert up to speed without giving him all the sordid details of Vanessa and Gerry Murphy's relationship. Vanessa quickly grew impatient. "Detective Brogger, Harry is being too nice and I don't have the energy or patience for niceties any more." She paused and exhaled, "I traded pussy for college room and board. Gerry Murphy put me and several of my girlfriends through school and all we had to do for it was put out. I've stayed in touch with him because he wouldn't let go—plus, he's got pictures."

Bert Brogger sighed all the way down to his toes. He steadied himself against the golf cart, looked at me and said, "I'm going to start calling you 'The Pope' from now on. You're just one fuckin' miracle after another."

Just then one of the Men's Locker Room stewards walked by us with an empty tray. I called him over. He gave us the once over and recognizing me he said, "Oh, it's you Mr. Pius. What can I do for you?"

"Bring us three large cups of coffee and a king size vodka Bloody Mary. Put the bloody in the biggest go cup you can find." As he hustled away to fill my order I shouted at his back, "And heavy on the vodka please."

Twenty minutes later Detective Brogger was back among the living. "Hair of the dog" works every time. For the first time since he arrived I felt like I had his attention. "What time is her plane scheduled to leave?" I asked.

Brogger glanced at his wrist and realized he wasn't wearing a watch. "What is it? A little after one right now?" I nodded an affirmative. "Her flight's supposed to leave at three, but they've got to load her entire group—there's about thirty of them—onto the plane last. I hear every flight she's been on has been late. It means if there's some plan to mess with her it's gonna' be in the next couple a' hours. Maybe there's something cookin' once she gets to the airport, but I doubt it. They'll load all the regular passengers and back away from the gate without her and her party being on the plane. Then they taxi to a holding area, park and wait for all the SUVs to arrive with her and her people. Willie's boys and the Feds will be on the ground and on the terminal rooftops, plus there'll be a helicopter or two circling overhead. I'm told she can't climb stairs so they'll deposit her and her staff on a lift platform that'll put them right at the door into the first class cabin."

An idea was beginning to grow on me. I was having a hard time with it. My back stiffened and my knees went weak all at the same time. But I didn't say anything.

"Okay, we're here. What do we do now? Preach to the choir?" Bert's eyes lost focus for a moment. "Hey, I got an idea…. We could call Willie Dean and tell him we're sittin' in the parking lot at a golf club drinkin' Bloody Marys and we've come up with the idea that somebody might be out to kill the old broad he's been babysitting the last couple a' days."

Vanessa cringed. She peered into her coffee. I could tell she was terrified at the prospect of Willie Dean connecting all the dots about her relationship, not only to me, but with a police detective from South San Francisco as well. Willie's explosive nature would never allow him to see beyond the obvious. The obvious, I thought, might be more than Margaret Thatcher safely seated on a plane. Maybe none of us could rest easy until the plane landed safely in London.

Vanessa said, "I don't think Willie will listen to anything we have to say. He won't even listen to the Secret Service—they've been at each others' throats from day one." She went on, "Harry you said you wanted me to see one of the old buildings out on the golf course. If it's the shack we partied in, we never got there from here. We always parked across the freeway and walked up a hill—I remember that much. It's been several years since Gerry took me to the shack—I think the walk got to be too much for him." As it turned out Vanessa underestimated Gerry Murphy's stamina.

We squeezed into the golf cart. I drove. Vanessa was wedged between us and I could see that Bert was having difficulty concentrating with her long brown leg pressed against him. He raised his eyes and said, "Harry, look.... I don't know what this is going to get us."

"Bert, there's too many loose ends to all this. We've got less than two hours before her flight, so let's try and tie up one of the loose ends. Humor me, OK?"

51

Clyde Billings was hot, but he couldn't park his hot-oil rig in the shade because there wasn't any shade at the entrance to the British Airways parking lot. It would be another hour before the foreman on the job would wave him into position. He was still third in line and his diesel engine would keep the oil-based seal coat at the required one hundred and eighty degrees while he waited. Not unlike all the drivers who worked for Bay Area Paving, Clyde was pissed off most of the time. Today was no exception. Dispatch had sent him too early and now he had to wait. He spent most of his time on the job waiting. He hated to wait. At least he had a clear view of the airport runway and he could watch as the planes roared down the runway straight toward him. He had been uneasy at first, as the jets seemed to get airborne at the last minute before passing over him. Once he realized they weren't going to plow into him he relaxed and welcomed the distraction they provided. The other distraction he was dealing with was his bladder. Soon he would have to find a place to pee. Maybe if he went over to the fence at the edge of the runway no one would notice.

Staying on the paved cart path it took us less than ten minutes to get to the bottom of the hill that bordered the fourth fairway. The road to the top of the hill being abandoned made it easy to miss, unless you knew it was there. You could smell the citrus fragrance, courtesy of the Myoprium bushes growing out of control and hiding the road. I stopped the golf cart and got out. I didn't want to alarm Vanessa, but I had no choice. "Bert, do you have a gun?"

"Harry, I'm a cop. Even though I'm not on the clock I've got my gun—it's the rules. You don't think we're going to find anything up here do you?"

I didn't know, but I had a hunch. I directed my attention to Vanessa. "Is this the road to the place Gerry and Dermot took you?"

"Harry, I don't know. I was usually strung out on booze and coke—it made the going easier. I'm not sure."

A Delta 767 with engines whining glided over our heads, drowning out any conversation. My sense of dread heightened. I had a feeling that the top of the hill held the answer. I hand signaled them back in the cart and eased my way toward the abandoned road.

At the top of the hill the scattered pine trees were twisting in the wind. It was quiet and empty.

We moved past the first building. The windows were intact, but painted with a dull gray paint. There was an area where wild Kikuyu grass had gained a foothold and was threatening the foundation. One edge of the roof was crushed where a piece of equipment had bumped the corner at a wrong angle. A large mound of sand and decomposed granite had been dumped under the damaged corner. A truck had obviously gotten too close to the building and crushed the overhang when it dumped its load. There were weeds and grass growing in the sand. Someone had been digging. A shovel was firmly stuck in the ground, while the sand around it had a wet, freshly turned, look.

There was a second, smaller building at the edge of a steep embankment facing east. It had a clear view of the airport in the distance. A path had been cleared through the overgrown brush to the door. The door was open.

Captain Rivers couldn't hide his frustration, but he knew it would be unprofessional to take it out on his crew. He and the First Officer had made their way to the flight deck of their Boeing 747 and were adjusting their seats. In a calm voice he turned to his First Officer and said, "Let's do the checklist."

Thirty questions later the checklist was complete. He was one of the old guard who demanded the cockpit door be closed during pre-flight to avoid unnecessary distractions. Pre-flight complete, he summoned the First Flight Attendant and gave her the anticipated time in route and their projected cruising altitude.

The First Officer flipped the anti-collision switch to the on position as Captain Rivers requested clearance from Air Traffic Control to proceed to London "as filed."

Why was the door open, I wondered. I had the sudden urge to tell Detective Brogger to get his gun ready, but quickly dismissed the idea as over-reacting. Yet, I instinctively knew my early warning system was on full alert.

Too late, much too late.

Gerry Murphy stepped around the corner of the building and pushed aside the overgrown brush. He cradled a twelve-gauge shotgun against his hip. "Well, Harrison, it's come to this—and you've got our girlfriend with you. Too bad."

Captain Rivers heard the crisp voice of Ground Control in his headset. "Captain, clear to start engine." At that instant he raised the start lever to the 'on' position and his First Officer went to the 'start rotation' beginning with the number three engine. Watching the temperature as number three reached forty percent RPMs, Captain Rivers flipped number three to the 'off' position and turned on number four. They went through the three, four, two, one engine startup on their Boeing 747 without incident. The First Officer then proceeded to the after-start checklist.

Once more Captain Rivers acknowledged the crisp voice of Ground Control in his ear. "Captain, clear to taxi—see you next trip." British Airways Flight 81 began its pushback from the gate.

I was caught in a wide-awake nightmare. A bad dream that was unfolding in front of me, but it couldn't be about me. This had to be a dream about someone else. One of my oldest friends was pointing a shotgun at me and he had a look about him I had never seen before. I knew I was looking at Gerry Murphy, but I didn't recognize him. It was the eyes. Gone was the gleam that saw through all the bullshit in the world so he could get to the real bullshit. Gone was the laughter that had turned his eyes into a reflection of a once jolly soul. His clothes were rumpled and his tousled hair looked like it hadn't seen a brush in days. He had always had a disheveled look, but it had been disarray with a certain polished elegance. The man standing in front of us was neither polished nor elegant; rather he had a certain sickness about him. A man I didn't know. Suddenly I was keenly aware of Bert and Vanessa standing next to me. Vanessa had begun to sway gently from side to side and she was beginning to gasp for breath. Detective Brogger, on the other hand, was motionless, but I could sense that his eyes were riveted on Gerry and the shotgun.

Gerry wasn't alone. Even as I foolishly thought the three of us might have a chance against one man and a shotgun I glimpsed a figure in shadow at the open door. He stepped into the sunlight and I had a vague recollection of a fisherman on the beach in Newcastle. He displayed a look of anger and frustration that was in sharp contrast to the relaxed attitude exhibited by Gerry Murphy. Gerry addressed the other man without diverting his attention from us. "Relax Devon, get back to work. This doesn't change a thing. We have plenty of time. Your only concern is the weapon. I'll take care of these three."

The words "I'll take care of" had an immediate effect on Vanessa. The clearing in front of the deserted shack swirled in a moving scene of sunlight and shadow, and the only sounds were the whisper of wind through the pine trees coupled with her muffled groan.

Gerry stepped closer. "Vanessa, my darling, you must relax. I am not going to kill one of my oldest friends. The Pope is incredibly naive and a hopeless romantic, but he doesn't deserve to die. As for you, my darling, why would I destroy an endangered species? I remember a movie where a woman was described as the 'fuck of the century'. My dear, sweet Vanessa; that is a perfect description of you.

I won't be the one to deny countless other men the pleasure of your talent in the future. But, you must not try and stop us."

He waved the shotgun back and forth between us. I sensed a tension between Gerry and Devon Clarke that signaled a possible difference of opinion about our fate. I tried to look into Devon's eyes but he avoided my gaze. "But, Gerry, I suspect you are about to kill four hundred innocent people and create an international incident. Why would you concern yourself with the three of us? What are three more dead bodies?" Looking at my old friend I had a chilling revelation. "After all, you've tried to kill me twice…and…. you went after poor Juanita with a baseball bat."

"None of that was my doing, Harry. That was that dumb shit Billy Morris…he was always too smart for his own good. First he kills his wife because he thinks she's gotten wise to him. Then he thinks that if he hires you there's no way the authorities will circle back to him. He underestimated you Harry. And you, as well, Detective Brogger." For the first time since confronting us with a shotgun Gerry Murphy smiled. "Yes, he most certainly wasn't up to the task at hand. He killed Tommy Gavin when all Tommy wanted was to go back home and stay out of the final part of the plan. And his biggest blunder was to hire a couple of thugs who thought it was smart to go after an old woman with a baseball bat and then, to top it off, they shoot a couple of off-duty cops. How fuckin' stupid can you get?"

Gerry Murphy seemed to want to talk. I was willing to listen and stall for time although I wasn't entirely sure how much time we had left.

"Why, Gerry—why are you doing this? What could possibly be wrong in your life that would justify doing something like this?"

"Pope, everything is wrong in my life," he shouted. "I've got a PSA count in the hundreds—I've got, maybe, six months—but I'm not gonna' check out drooling in my soup in some fuckin' hospice. It's payback time for me and I've got one last chance."

"Payback for what?" I exclaimed.

"Pope there are things you could never know. Have you ever had a British soldier spit in your face?" His glance shifted away from me and quickly returned. "Or watch your parents wither and die because a fuckin' politician decides to close a mine and kill a town. That god-damn Thatcher is a curse on the good people of Ireland. I hope she rots in hell. Billy and I watched our parents almost starve to death because of politics."

"I thought he was from Oklahoma."

"Hah! He grew up there, lived with an uncle after his parents died. The guy you knew as Junkie Bill was born in Northern Ireland." He moved the shotgun cautiously back and forth. "He was a genius, ya' know. But, his whole life was a fuck-up. Everything would have worked perfect, but he got stupid and killed Maggie when she asked a couple of simple questions about where the money was goin'. She thought it was going to some schools in Belfast and Billy wasn't clever enough to keep her in the dark. So he panicked and killed her. Dumb."

Vanessa was slumped against the back fender of the golf cart and Bert Brogger had gradually worked his way to the back of the cart and had one foot hooked on the ledge where the golf bags usually rest. The top half of the split windshield on the golf cart was lowered giving Bert some protection from the line of fire, however Vanessa and I were sitting ducks. Most of my attention was focused on his partner Devon Clarke. Devon was working in shadow on the other side of the open door and from time to time Gerry would shift his attention from the three of us and glance nervously over his shoulder in his direction. He continued to wave the shotgun back and forth in front of us while barking commands at Devon Clarke, "Devon get your ass in gear! You're taking too much time. We've got about ten minutes. You've got to be ready and in the proper place in the clearing." Gerry's eyes darted to my left and focused on Bert Brogger.

I glanced at the Detective as he slumped nervously against the back of the golf cart. I thought he was going to faint. Where was the tough cop? He seemed to be numb with fear. I realized I had been expecting some kind of miracle. A fast draw. Anything. There was nothing.

Gerry Murphy's eyes were bouncing all over the place. From over his shoulder at Devon Clarke and back again to the three of us, but the shotgun never wavered from its intended target. I reached out to steady Brogger as Devon Clarke stepped from the open door with the deadliest weapon I had ever seen outside of the movies. I had never seen a Stinger rocket launcher before, but I instinctively knew what it was. Most important, I realized my hunch had been correct. My suspicion that a jumbo jet with four hundred passengers, including the former Prime Minister of England, was going to be blown out of the sky seemed inevitable. A collective gasp involuntarily escaped from Vanessa and me. Brogger continued to slump against the back of the cart, one hand hanging limp at his side. He began to rub his leg and moan.

"Pope, I think your cop buddy is getting ready to pee his pants." Gerry chuckled as he said it and then watched as Devon Clarke braced himself against the trunk of a pine tree at the edge of the clearing. The rocket launcher was resting on his shoulder.

I saw Bert's hand swing across his leg. Gerry saw the same movement and raised the shotgun. It was quick.

Captain Paul Rivers could see the convoy of black SUVs approaching his British Airways 747 where it was parked in the holding area adjacent to runway 28R. There were six of the vehicles containing an additional thirty-six passengers including the old dame herself. The hydraulic lift vehicle was in place beneath the aft cabin door and everything on the plane had been shut down except air re-circulation and the anti-collision beacon. The First Officer began the thirty-point checklist for the second time in the last hour. With a heavy sigh Captain Rivers began with his memory list.

"Parking brake."

"Check."

"Brake pressure."

"Check."

"Gear lever."

"Check."

The hydraulic platform ascended to the open cabin door and the first of the security contingent stepped into the plane.

Brogger's hand was a blur as in one flowing motion he snatched his gun from the ankle holster on his left leg and fired. The bullet caught Murphy in the right shoulder and as he spun to the side the shotgun exploded. Vanessa screamed and I felt a thousand bees stinging my left side. Murphy dropped in slow motion and was in a sitting position in front of the cart trying to lift the shotgun to a shoulder that was a mass of shredded flesh. Brogger had spun to the side and taken Vanessa with him. She was crawling frantically toward the corner of the shed away from Murphy. I was trying to keep the golf cart between Devon Clarke and myself because he had produced a handgun and was trying to balance the rocket on his shoulder while peppering the cart with slugs. I could see a large circle of blood forming on Brogger's thigh as he rolled to the sparse cover of the underbrush that had been used to conceal the door to the shed. Murphy transferred the shotgun to his left side and was sliding his hand toward the trigger when Brogger fired again. The bullet caught Gerry in the chest with an explosion that knocked him on his back in the dirt. The shotgun lay at his feet in front of me. Devon Clarke continued to fire his weapon from the cover of the pine trees.

Clyde Billings couldn't wait any longer. He had to pee…and he had to pee, now! He was still thirty minutes away from his turn to spread oil in the parking lot. He reset the gauge over the dashboard to maintain a constant one hundred eighty degree oil temperature and the diesel burners reacted instantly. He pulled the hand brake to the hold position, jumped from the cab and made his way to the edge of the fence that bordered the west end of the runway. In the distance he could see the shape of a jumbo jet parked to the side of the runway. He wondered why they were loading passengers from platforms so far away from the terminal building.

Clyde laughed to himself as he unzipped his pants. I wonder, he thought, if they can see me. He would have been amazed to know that not only could they see him, but Special Agent Mary Barnes, from her perch on the terminal roof, had her binoculars focused and was watching him with the intensity that highly trained Secret Service Agents are expected to exhibit. Her professionalism couldn't hide the faint trace of a smile on her face.

From the corner of my eye I saw Vanessa crawl behind some manzanita bushes, stand, and then begin to run down the hill. I could hear a faint gurgling sound coming from Gerry's direction. His right foot was bare and I could see it twitching rhythmically in time with his heaving chest. Brogger was trying to crawl closer to the concealment offered by the pine trees on our right. I realized I was caught between him and Devon Clarke. Devon was firing the occasional shot in our direction to let us know we were trapped. I focused my eyes back on the shotgun lying at the feet of Gerry Murphy. Brogger had found his way to the base of a large pine and was also focused intently on the shotgun. He motioned me in the direction of the gun and at once began firing his weapon in the direction of Devon Clarke. I reacted quickly and jumped for the shotgun. It was then I noticed, for the first time since the shooting started, that the bee stings I felt were bleeding. The first blast Gerry fired had missed me except for a few pellets in the left shoulder. It didn't stop me. I crawled back to the shelter of the golf cart with the shotgun pressed to my chest as Brogger continued his rapid fire at Clarke.

Human beings are strange creatures, I thought to myself. For the first and only time in my life I had someone shooting a gun at me and I was smiling. At the utmost moments of stress we can be amused by strange memories. I was smiling at the notion that I hadn't fired a shotgun since Uncle Ambrose took me rabbit hunting on the farm when I was ten years old. I could only hope that thirty-eight years hadn't destroyed my ability to fire the damn thing. I was relieved to know the gun was an automatic and I had four shells left.

The cabin door for British Airways flight 28 closed and six SUVs and two food platform loaders backed away from the giant 747. Captain Paul Rivers and his First Officer began, once more, the methodical pre-flight ground clearance.

"Skipper, we're still on frequency two-eighteen."

The Captain didn't usually respond to the casual use of the word "Skipper," but the day had had enough aggravation. He let it pass. "Get taxi clearance, again."

Through both headsets a gruff voice barked. "Captain clear to taxi."

An equally soft voice spoke in his ear. It was the Flight Attendant Supervisor. "Captain Rivers, the Prime Minister has decided to sit on the upper deck in seat sixteen A. She says she likes it up there and pointed out she's not afraid of heights."

While not amused by her lighthearted humor, Captain Rivers remembered his orders. He switched back to frequency two-eighteen and announced to Ground Control, "This is Speedbird eighty-one to London."

A voice crackled in his ear. "Speedbird eighty-one you're clear on runway twenty-eight. Have a safe trip."

Devon Clarke had maneuvered himself behind the largest of the pine trees that bordered the clearing. It was quiet again. I could see Brogger prone on the ground under the cover of the underbrush. Brogger was holding up two fingers and pointing at his gun. I took it to mean he had two shots left. That gave us six between us. Time was getting short. The sound of another gunshot exploded from behind the pine tree in front of me. Brogger screamed and grabbed for his foot. In the distance the sound of sirens pierced the silence. I had to get closer.

Bert Brogger was sitting up clawing at his shoe and trying to motion me forward at the same time. I began to move toward the edge of the shed. Clarke saw me and extended his arm, but was restricted by the rocket launcher on his shoulder. Brogger fired a slug into the edge of the pine tree sending bark and splinters flying. I heard a cry of pain and surprise from Devon Clarke. I sprinted for the safety of the shed.

Flight 81, designated "Speedbird," was first in line for takeoff and proceeding to twenty-eight right at the east end of the runway. "We'll go through the gap at an attitude of twelve degrees," Captain Rivers announced to his First Officer and Flight Engineer. "Through the gap" would take the jumbo jet over the Pacific Heights Golf Club at an altitude of twelve hundred feet and they would reach the headlands and be over the coastline thirteen minutes after liftoff. The Captain had already decided to increase the designated airspeed at liftoff by ten knots over the data card requirement. 747 Captains all agreed that V1 airspeed was too slow. He had a full load and wanted maximum take-off thrust.

Captain Rivers and his First Officer completed the take-off checklist and he announced, "Flight Attendants secure the cabin for takeoff."

Former Prime Minister Margaret Thatcher closed her eyes, silently hoping she could sleep. It had been an exhausting two weeks and she was ready to go home. She felt the British Airways jumbo jet start to move slowly as the Captain advanced the throttles to take-off thrust.

I could see the tip of a silver tube extending past the edge of a pine tree on my left. I didn't know it at the time, but the winglets at the end of the tube were the stabilizers on the launch engine of a Stinger Missile system. It was horizontal to the ground and low enough to suggest that Clarke was on his knees with his back to me. Just when I thought it might be safe to advance further he turned and fired another shot from his handgun into the right front tire of the golf cart. He didn't know I had moved to his right and I was in the comparative safety of the maintenance shed. He was still trying to keep me pinned behind the cart. I was twenty yards to his left and he didn't know it. For the first time I had a glimmer of hope that we might prevent him from accomplishing his deadly mission. In the distance I noticed a jumbo jet was beginning to hurtle down the East/ West runway.

Clyde Billings leaned against the perimeter fence and finished relieving himself as the 747 rushed toward him. Fifty yards away his tanker oil-truck idled at the edge of the parking lot. Clyde was anxious to begin the seal-coat process, but thought he would hang out at the fence rather than wait in the hot confines of his cab.

"Devon Clarke," I yelled his name loudly. "I've got four shells left. You're going to have to stand up to fire that thing and when you do I'm going to blast your ass into a million pieces."

Clarke's high-pitched laugh broke the silence. I could smell cigar smoke…the son-of-a-bitch had fired up a cigar. Was he having a final smoke? He yelled back at me. "Oh Mr. Pius it's a lovely day for dying. It surely is. I would be knowing for sure that you have me—you surely do. But, it's been over for me for a long time now. Yeah, you'll blast my ass into the great reward, but it'll be a grand show before you do."

There was an audible sigh and then a grunt as I detected movement from the direction of Clarke's concealment. Turning and looking to my right I could see Brogger lying flat on his stomach at the edge of the thick undergrowth with his weapon grasped in both hands in front of him. He and I had a clear shot at Devon Clarke if he stepped from behind the tree. The length of the launcher across his shoulder would require him to step away from the tree if his target was the airport in the distance. We still had a chance.

Captain Rivers concentrated on the voice in his ear.
"V1, Captain. Approaching eighty knots." The voice of the First Officer was crisp in the headset. He continued, "Approaching VR—at the count rotate." The nose of the 747 began to lift toward initial attitude.

It all happened quickly. I saw Clarke step away from the tree with the rocket launcher on his shoulder. I heard Brogger's gun explode from behind me. Before I could react I saw Clarke's knees buckle, tipping the launch tube down a fraction of an inch as the distinctive click of the Stinger missile's launch mechanism signaled target engagement. Simultaneously, I saw my rapid shotgun blasts turn Clarke's upper body to a gelatinous mess, but not before a solid rocket engine ignited, propelling a Stinger missile at Mach 2 speed toward its target.

On a direct line, three miles in the distance, Clyde Billings turned and looked up as the Boeing 747 thundered over his head. From the corner of his eye he thought he saw a puff of smoke from a hillside in the distance. He turned back to the fence and zipped his pants. He thought to himself that no one had watched him take a leak, but he didn't want anyone from the nearby building to catch him. Having his back to the hot-oil tanker idling at the far end of the parking area saved his eyesight and maybe his life. The explosion was deafening. Five thousand gallons of hot oil ignited in a blaze that was seen as far away as Oakland across the bay. The British Airways Flight Operations building was awash in flames and the twenty-two people on duty were scrambling out the back entrance. Covered in hot oil, Clyde Billings was rolling in the dirt at the edge of the fence when the crew from the other tanker truck began spraying him with fire retardant foam. The next day at Saint Mary's hospital, his wife and five grown children all teased him, with obvious relief, about not dying with his dick in his hand.

I stood at the edge of the clearing and watched the building burn in the distance. I thought of Brogger and rushed to his side. He had torn his t-shirt in two pieces and had tied one piece tightly around his ankle and the other around his thigh. At least he wouldn't bleed to death, I thought, but I knew he wasn't going to be running races with his little boy any time soon. A British Airways jet banked to the right above our heads and in a matter of seconds disappeared in the fog that was rolling across the foothills that stood like sentinels along the coastline.

Brogger and I were alone with the bodies of Devon Clarke and Gerry Murphy. From the front of the golf cart Gerry's hand moved and I heard the gurgling sound of my name, "Pope, Pope."

Speedbird 81, non-stop to London, achieved a positive rate of climb and retracted the landing gear. At twelve hundred feet the flaps were retracted on schedule, as well. Captain Paul Rivers flipped the intercom switch to the 'on' position. "Good evening ladies and gentlemen. This is Captain Paul Rivers and I would like to extend our welcome from the flight deck. We anticipate a smooth flight into Heathrow this evening and we expect an on-time arrival. I would like to apologize for the later than scheduled departure. However, I'm sure you will agree it was worth it, because we are privileged to have on board with us a very special person..."

52

I was holding Gerry Murphy's hand, watching him die. I had never watched someone die. The hole in his chest had stopped gushing blood and the color of his face had turned to a soft shade of blue. He tried to sit upright and fell back with a thump. His eyes kept switching back and forth from my face to the pile of sand at the entrance to the clearing. I asked him, "Gerry is there something in the sand pile?" He responded by squeezing my hand tightly. Within a matter of minutes one of the Club maintenance workers, who had responded to the gunshots, unearthed a foot clad in a Gucci loafer. It had been a long journey for Junkie Bill. From the squalor of Northern Ireland to the plains of Oklahoma only to end up buried in a sand pile on a golf course. At the last Gerry tried to say he was sorry for his life, but he was talking to the wrong guy. When someone has done something terribly wrong and they say they're sorry, they almost always want you to say it's okay. I'm not any good at saying "Hey, don't worry about it, it's okay." Most of the time it's not okay. This was one of those times. In his moment of death Gerry was completely alone—as we all will be. He just didn't have anyone there to tell him that everything would be all right and he would be missed. There is no easy way to check out, but I suspect there is a right way. Gerry Murphy went out the wrong way.

As it turned out Vanessa had run down the hill and onto the golf course. She had a hard time convincing the foursome on the third green that there was an emergency up on the top of the hill, but she eventually got her point across. We had six South City cop cars, two ambulances and a helicopter contending for the space in the clearing.

Brogger and I went to the hospital in one ambulance and what was left of Clarke and Gerry went in the other. I had a hunch Bert Brogger and I had a lot of explaining to do and I was right. It took the Secret Service and some other law enforcement agencies over a week to put it together. But, while Bert and I were being prepped for our ambulance ride, an unmarked San Francisco police car pulled into the clearing. Vanessa was hustled into the back seat and the vehicle quickly left the scene. She didn't say good-bye. As the two ambulance attendants were lifting Bert into the back of the van he looked up at me and asked a question, not expecting an answer. "Pope, you think she knows we're okay?"

"Bert, at this moment—believe me—Vanessa is not thinking about you and me."

We had plenty of professional care on our way to the hospital. For the first time in the last hour the enormity of the situation had begun to overwhelm me. Suddenly I felt cold. One of the attendants put a wool blanket around my shoulders and I put my head back and closed my eyes, lost in thought. I wondered then, as I do now, why Junkie Bill let himself get trapped in such a diabolical arrangement. He could have lived out his life with a woman who loved him and had more money than the two of them could ever spend. Instead a dying man he thought was a friend caught him up in an age-old plot that was nothing more than a get-even scheme. His old friend ended up killing him the same way Junkie had killed his wife. Junkie always was a sucker for a woodie. And I guess I never really knew Gerry Murphy—no one did. Certainly not his wife. She didn't even know he had terminal cancer. And all of it came to nothing; except for a rocket up the ass-end of a hot oil tanker that lit up the sky.

Epilogue

Juanita took the stairs slowly. She was making progress but she knew it would never be the same. Her dislocated hip had healed nicely, but her shattered knee was slow to mend. She was drawn and weak and wanted to sleep when she knew it was time to get up and face the day. Harry had wanted her to continue staying under his roof but she needed her time alone—and Harry needed his time away from her. So she'd gone home.

He had given her everything he had to give and his remorse had become a burden between them. There was no reason for regret because it had not been an act of negligence or indifference that caused the attack. It was simply bad luck.

She reached the back door to Harry's house, paused and leaned against the railing. In the distance she could see the morning fog settled like a pool of milk beneath the second deck of the Bay Bridge. It was still early and quiet in the neighborhood. She wanted to save this view and all the other views she had too long taken for granted. With a long sigh she slumped against the railing, finally admitting she wanted to give in to her need to allow someone to take care of her for a change. She had spent a lifetime taking care of everyone else and she had a dead husband and three worthless sons to show for it. And there was Harry. Juanita smiled at the thought. Harry was the only man in her life who had never wanted anything other than to be her friend. She remembered many of the times she bitched and complained to him about who he was and what he was doing with his life and those remembrances troubled her. They were troubling because she loved him more than her own sons and she was immensely proud of him. Why had it been so difficult for her to accept his love? She wondered if she could let him be the son to her she knew he wanted to be.

Juanita pushed through the back door and entered the quiet kitchen of Harry's home. She could see the message light on the phone blinking. The counter on the console showed sixteen messages received since the day before…she knew who they were from. As she stood in the silence of the deserted house she knew she had grown weary of so much turmoil in their lives. There had been too much violence, too much uncertainty, too much of everything that was disruptive. Standing at the sink Juanita poured spring water from a bottle into a metal teapot and dropped a teabag into her favorite cup. She was happy with her thoughts and she knew this moment was important. She resolved that when Harry returned he would be pleased with her. It was time for something good to happen to Harrison Pius and Juanita wanted to be part of it.

The phone rang. Juanita didn't pick it up. She sat on the bench in front of the window and let the morning sun warm her back. The phone rang again. It had been ringing constantly since she arrived. Finally, she had had enough.

"Hello—this is Mr. Pius' residence."

"Don't act so formal with me, Juanita. Put Harry on the line."

Gathering a newfound patience that surprised her, Juanita replied, "Ms. Johnson, I'm very sorry but Mr. Pius is not available at this time."

Vanessa could barely conceal her contempt. "Listen you old bag. I know you don't tell Harry when I call. I think he's changed his cell phone number—I can't reach him. You tell that son-of-a-bitch he had better talk to me and now."

"I repeat, Mr. Pius is not available," Juanita said politely. "Besides, he's gone to Ireland."

"What! He just got back from Ireland! He's probably got himself some two-bit barmaid over there that he's chasing."

Juanita laughed. "No, I don't think Harry has gone back to Ireland to chase a two-bit anything." She continued to chuckle. "I think his days of getting involved with cheap bimbos are over."

This brought an outpouring of invective from Vanessa. Juanita held the receiver away from her ear and waited for an opening. "Ms. Johnson, it's really very simple. Harry got a invitation to go for a walk on a beach. He decided it was something he had always wanted to do, so he left." Juanita gently hung up the phone.

Five minutes later the phone rang again. Juanita rubbed her knee. She smiled and took another sip of tea.

The phone rang.

THE END

Special Thanks

Thanks go out to P. T. Reavis for his invaluable technical assistance.

I would also like to thank my critics—Alice, Harry, Margaret, Pete, Sue, Randall, Pam, Bill, Fred and R.H. Clark—for their encouragement and support.

And, of course, thanks to Margo for everything else.

One last thing…. Thanks to Chuck (the original Pope) for the inspiration.

978-0-595-39386-2
0-595-39386-1

Printed in the United States
63069LVS00001B/1-39